AMONG
Gods AND *Monsters*

Praise for FALLEN GODS:

Beneath the fantasy and horror, a simmering love story brews. One that left me uneasy and completely unsure how to feel. Not because Ms. Simper failed, but because she succeeded so very, very well.
-Evie Drae, author of Beauregard and the Beast

Simper has created a brilliant combination of gruesomely dark fantasy and scorching romance. The protagonists are both so flawed, you are at once drawn to and repelled by them. Simper takes the idea of grey morality and writes it to perfection.
-The Lesbian Review

Simper has created a complex, immersive world for the series and that's not even touching on the well-developed characters or the complicated, fucked up relationship you can't help but ship anyway.
-Manic Femme Reviews

Praise for SEA AND STARS:

"If you like your fantasy with an extra dark twist, exceptional world building and deeply complex characters then reel this book in fast. You'll be hooked."
-The Lesbian Review

"The Fate of Stars, the first book in the Sea and Stars trilogy, is delightfully dark and sexy, full of lush imagery, vibrant characterization, and enough adrenaline to keep me up way past my bedtime."
-Anna Burke, award winning author of THORN and COMPASS ROSE

Praise for Carmilla and Laura:

A beautiful retelling . . . perfect for anyone who likes darker-themed romance, horror stories, or plain ol' lesbian vampires.
-The Lesbian 52

Other books by S D Simper:

The Sting of Victory (Fallen Gods 1)
Among Gods and Monsters (Fallen Gods 2)
Blood of the Moon (Fallen Gods 3)
Tear the World Apart (Fallen Gods 4)

Carmilla and Laura

The Fate of Stars (Sea and Stars 1)
Heart of Silver Flame (Sea and Stars 2)
Death's Abyss (Sea and Stars 3)

Forthcoming books:

Eve of Endless Night (Fallen Gods 5) – *2021*
Chaos Rising (Fallen Gods 6) – *TBA*
Fallen Gods (Series 2) - TBA
Fallen Gods (Series 3) - TBA

Among Gods and Monsters

S D Simper

For Parker

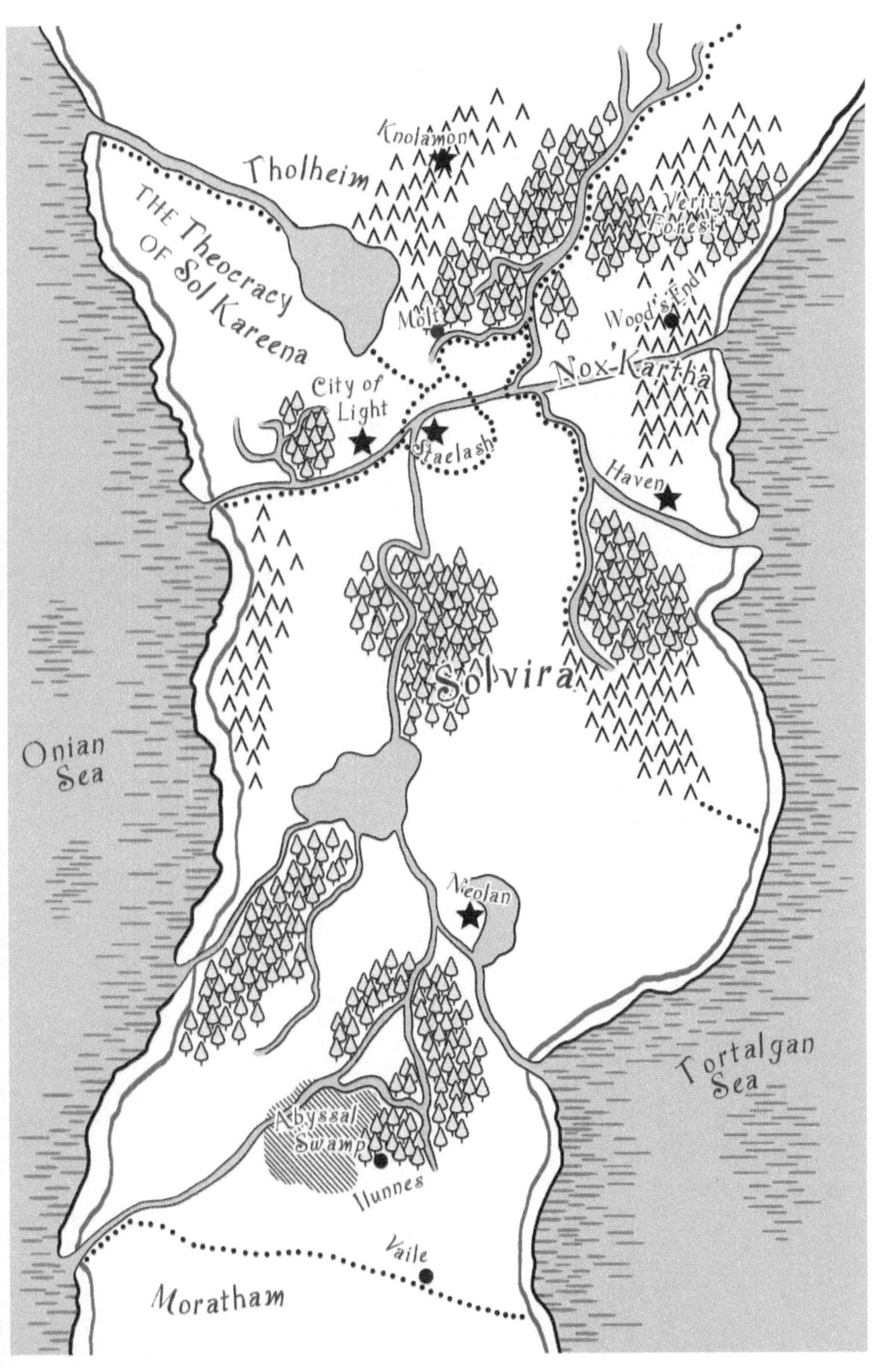

Tholheim
Knolamon
Verity Forest
THE Theocracy OF Sol Kareena
Molt
Wood's End
Nox'Kartha
City of Light
Staelash
Haven
Solvira
Onian Sea
Neolan
Tortalgan Sea
Abyssal Swamp
Ilunnes
Vaile
Moratham

Names

THE ROYAL COUNCIL OF STAELASH

Marielle Vors – Mair-ee-el Vohrs

Etolié – Eh-toh-lee-ey

Thalmus – Thah-muhs

Flowridia – Floh-rid-ee-uh

Sora Fireborn – Sohr-ruh Fire-bohrn

FOREIGN DIGNITARIES

Xoran – Zoh-ran

Lunestra – Loon-es-truh

Ayla Darkleaf – Ai-luh Dahrk-leef

Zorlaeus – Zor-ley-uhs

Casvir – Kas-**veer**

Murishani – Mer-eh-shah-nee

Alauriel Solviraes – Ah-law-ree-ehl Sohl-veer-es

OTHER PLAYERS

Khastra – Kas-truh

Odessa – Oh-**des**-uh

Soliel – Suh-**lil**

Demitri – Dih-**mee**-tree

Tazel – **Taa**-zuhl

Kah'Sheen – Kuh-**sheen**

Mereen – Mer-**een**

VARIOUS GODS, ANGELIC AND DEMONIC

Sol Kareena – Sohl Kuh-**ree**-nuh

Eionei – **Eye**-uhn-eye

Alystra – Ah-**lees**-truh

Staella – **Stey**-luh

Neoma – Ney-**oh**-muh

Ilune – Eye-**loon**

Izthuni – Iz-**thoo**-nee

Ku'Shya – Koo-**shy**-uh

Onias – Uhn-**eye**-uhs

A door of dark wood and gold plating stood between Flowridia and freedom.

Her spirit lingers, or so claimed the demon from the woods. Ayla was gone, and Flowridia had been given all her beloved had left behind. For courage, she gripped the ear around her neck, now with all three earrings shattered and cracked. Swallowing tears, she pushed open the heavy door.

Seated at a desk was Imperator Casvir. Enormous and armored, his sweeping horns only increased his stature but the sheet of his white hair, pulled into a tail, added a subtle aura of civility to his otherwise monstrous form. Whatever hints of skin she might have imagined beneath his armor spoke of uncontested strength.

No reaction. Flowridia stepped inside and shut the door, too drained to be intimidated by the vast figure. She watched quietly as his hand wrote whatever notes a particularly demonic De'Sindai might need with his quill and ink.

His hand stopped scribbling, and he finally spoke. "Hungry?"

Flowridia shook her head before realizing he couldn't see her. "No," she whispered. She watched him nod and return his attention to the quill in his taloned fingers. Scratching on parchment again met her ears.

The conversation would be over if she did not push for more. She took a step forward, and then another, her feet utterly silent upon the stone floor. Flowridia kept her stare strong as she stood across the polished wooden desk. Even seated, he was barely shorter than she. "You're the one who gave Demitri to me," she dared to say.

"Yes."

His voice reminded Flowridia of some ancient underground thing—dark and ominous, a harbinger of cataclysm.

Could a volcano speak?

Flowridia studied his focused demeanor before casting her eyes down onto his document. Even upside down, she saw immaculate script, void of any flourishes or flare, but as perfect as writing could be.

Flowridia's fingers turned white as her hands gripped each other. To provide an acolyte with a familiar bespoke power nigh unparalleled. "Then, are you a god?"

"Not yet."

Somehow, the response chilled her, the implications leaving a thousand questions unanswered. "Am I a prisoner?" Speaking was still difficult, but Flowridia willed her voice to steady.

"No," he said, and finally he set his quill down. When he looked at her with his blazing, red eyes, the stoicism of his countenance would have put any gambler to shame. "I have a proposition, Lady Flowridia, Grand Diplomat of Staelash. Will you hear me out?"

Flowridia nodded.

"I seek a magical artifact, one I felt resonate at the exact moment you cried out upon Ayla's passing. I do not believe in coincidence, and I believe you are the key to helping me find it."

Nervous, Flowridia asked, "What is this artifact?"

"I do not know."

She desired only one thing in all the world. "Bring Ayla back," she said, hating how her words quivered, how she groveled before him. "You've done it before."

He held her stare, and she swore every facet of her being lay under scrutiny. "I have already written up a separate agreement for Lady Ayla's return. She is not a part of this negotiation."

"What do you mean?"

Imperator Casvir, with his enormous clawed hands, delicately withdrew a single page of parchment. He slid it toward her; Flowridia dared to accept and read.

For the return of Ayla Darkleaf—

The paper shook. Flowridia realized it was her own hands.

For the return of Ayla Darkleaf, Lady Flowridia, Daughter of Odessa and Grand Diplomat of Staelash, will pledge her loyalty to Nox'Kartha and her services to Imperator Casvir, First and Last of His Name, until his death or hers, and beyond should she choose a path of undeath—

It continued on, detailing potential duties—*diplomat, gardener, magister of magic, etc*—along with addressing any loopholes one smarter than she could have foreseen.

And then, too, a damning clause—that Ayla Darkleaf would be pledged to his service, until his death or hers.

At the bottom waited a dotted line. The imperator's signature had already been written—beside it lay an empty spot for her.

"Why?" she asked, realizing her head grew light for lack of breath. Coldness seeped through her core, unnatural and sickening.

"I know the potential you hold."

He would say nothing more, she knew. He offered the hope of her love's return, but despite Flowridia's heartbreak, despite the crippling loneliness threatening to consume her, Ayla had hated this man. Ayla had given her life for the chance to escape him. Flowridia set the contract down and said, "Let me think on this."

"Of course."

"But what of your artifact?"

Casvir's expression never changed. "Consider what Nox'Kartha can give you." He returned his attention to the parchment.

The words held an air of finality; Flowridia knew he would speak no more. She offered a respectful nod, unsure if it were proper to bow, and trembled as she approached the door.

But as she gripped the knob, a thought, insane yet redeeming, prickled in her mind. She had held her own artifact of depthless power not hours before. "Imperator Casvir," she began, subdued in her newfound confidence, "I know you know my kingdom seeks orbs. Help me to find one, and I will join you on your quest for the artifact."

When Casvir looked up at her, she swore she saw a subtle flicker of intrigue in his countenance. "This is your bargain?"

"I will help you however I can to find your . . . your item. And you will help me find an orb."

"I will write out a contract dictating the terms of our arrangement. Once it is signed, you will be returned to Staelash."

Flowridia frowned. "I will?"

"An ambassador of Nox'Kartha was responsible for the death of your general. I have no wish for conflict between our kingdoms, thus I will be financing the funeral as a gesture of goodwill. Ayla acted on her own accord, but Nox'Kartha must take responsibility. You and I shall attend—and then, we leave."

Flowridia gave a slow, tentative nod. "What of Ayla's body?"

"Her body and belongings will be kept safe until your final return to Staelash." His expression remained the same, yet his next words chilled her blood. "Or until you sign the agreement for Ayla's life."

Flowridia forced a smile before leaving Casvir alone.

Chapter 1

For all her connections with death, Flowridia had never attended a funeral. She had always imagined rain, the sky weeping in response to whatever tragedy had stolen the loved one prematurely from life.

Instead, the sun beamed down upon the scene, the sky content to shine hope and beauty upon them. Perhaps that was best. When Khastra had smiled, it radiated a joy unconstrained by her age. And Meira never smiled, but her devotion to her Goddess had led to as spectacular an end as any acolyte could wish for.

Beside her, a Celestial wept, Etolié's tear-streaked face providing the rain the sky denied them. Khastra, her body still fresh from death, lay clad in her armor, her hammer still in the Theocracy where she had fallen—a final jest, and one the half-demon would have approved of, that no one could lift her weapon after her passing.

From her garden, Flowridia had provided a crown of lilies to grace the half-demon's head, a softer accessory than she ever would have worn in life, as well as for Meira, who lay in a coffin beside her, serene in both life and death.

Queen Marielle spoke, but Flowridia barely heard. Nearly half of Staelash had come to give their final farewells, soldiers and commoners alike, the general a well-known and beloved pillar of their kingdom.

Of the three founders of Staelash, only Etolié remained. Marielle stood in the shoes of her deceased father, but inexperience still clouded her judgement and decisions. Whoever would be named to fill Khastra's place would need guidance. Etolié stood at the head, shaking under her silent tears and the weight placed upon her shoulders.

Imperator Casvir stood like a volcanic shadow, the threat of a far-off doom pervading his silent aura. His armor must have been sweltering in the sunlight, yet Flowridia saw no sweat upon his blue-tinged brow, nor at his stark-white hairline. But his eyes shone red, missing nothing as he surveyed the funeral onlookers, his curved horns the only crown he needed.

Flowridia watched as Marielle concluded her remarks, her eyes leaking tears though her voice remained strong. She stepped aside and gestured for the bodies to be lowered into the ground.

A new voice spoke. "Etolié—"

From the corner of her eye, Flowridia saw Etolié turn away from the name, her soft tears replaced by a gasping sob. Someone approached, the woman who had called for her, but Etolié looked ready to crumble, her hands gripping her silver hair. The Celestial spared a glance for the open graves, then pushed her way through the crowd, urgency in her steps.

Instead, Empress Alauriel Solviraes of their patron kingdom, Solvira, stepped in to fill Etolié's vacancy. Her silver eyes were rimmed with red, her gentle smile bespeaking her sorrow. Forcibly still, she held her breath and swallowed back tears, then said, "Etolié told me of your bargain with Imperator Casvir. You're doing a great service to your kingdom and my empire. I won't forget this." Her voice lowered, barely a whisper, unheard by anyone but she. "And my deepest condolences, for your own heartbreak. I cannot fathom the burden you bear."

Her words were gentle. Flowridia shattered.

She didn't fight when Alauriel—or Lara, as she was known among friends—pulled her into an embrace. With her hands gripping the velvet fabric covering the empress' waist, the first of her sobs shook her body.

She hadn't cried an audible tear since returning from Nox'Kartha, but here in Lara's embrace, oh, she crumbled; she fell. A hitched breath, and then came a flood. Fear washed over her like an ocean wave, thoughts of demonic tyrants filling her with dread, but Lara's soft hands parted the seas, a rock amongst turbulent water. Flowridia let her eyes fall shut, her grip growing tight. Lara whispered, *"Shh . . ."* and steadied her cries. Tender strokes soothed along her thin back.

Something sweet lay mingled in the scent of Lara's hair; something clean; something that bespoke the magic coursing through the woman's veins. Descended from the Moon Goddess herself, Lara's bloodline held magic unparalleled. It touched upon Flowridia's senses, settling into her memory as they clung to the other, and she felt no need to part. "There is no shame in mourning someone you loved," Lara whispered, "even if the world wouldn't understand."

"Thank you–"

A sudden rumble shook the earth. An ear-splitting *screech* destroyed the sorrowful peace. Flowridia and Lara both brought their hands to cover their ears, even as the screech lowered both in volume and tone.

A voice she did not know boomed through the air, but it bespoke a familiar cadence—the language of Sha'Demoni, the tongue of demons.

The sky darkened. Shadows rose, but one formed a ghastly, enormous figure towering above even the manor in height. First a formless mass, but it slowly warped with every word from its tongue, not solid, no, but sharp. Flowridia saw a gigantic, multi-armed monstrosity and swore that four glowing, black pits stared out among the mourners.

The crowd gasped and cowered. Flowridia watched as a mace materialized in Casvir's hand, his face twitching as he visibly calculated this potential opponent. Lara grabbed her, placing her own small body between them, when the very ground shook.

The shadow stood tall as if to speak, unfathomably large as it blotted out the sun itself, but then a glowing light from behind rose to face the behemoth.

The crowd parted for Etolié—but not Etolié, for she shifted and grew, first her eyes glowing and then the very pores of her skin as she allowed the deity she claimed to possess her. Eionei, the God of Drinking and Freedom and grandfather to Etolié, cast his fractal wings wide and lifted his rapier aloft. *"There is no place for demons here, Ku'Shya."*

Flowridia knew the name, horror settling at the realization of this demon's identity—the Goddess of War herself had come to bid her eldest child farewell. The booming voice seethed, this time speaking their kindred tongue. *"I had to see for myself if my daughter's death was true."*

"If you're here to make a heartfelt speech and perhaps join us afterward for a drink and some cards, we're more than happy to accommodate. Otherwise, we'll have to ask you to leave."

"I am to be banned from my Khastra's funeral?" Flowridia swore heat radiated from the monstrous figure. *"Disgraceful. I shall hear no more words from hateful demi-gods."*

Flowridia's blood chilled, yet a part of her soul softened at the words. Ku'Shya was as terrifying a goddess to ever manifest on this plane, but even demons loved their children.

Ku'Shya looked past Eionei, the black pits of her eyes settling onto the closed coffin. When the shadow came closer, Eionei stepped forward to meet her, stealing her attention. *"Do not interfere with my mourning, you pathetic little man."*

"Me? Pathetic?" The Drinking God had the audacity to laugh. *"And here I thought we were friends. Now, kindly step away from the crowd of squishy innocents."*

"No more words from you. But in deference to my Khastra's loyalties, I will speak to the Daughter of Stars."

Eionei froze a moment, then said, the voice having definitely changed, "Speaking."

This time, the shadow's voice came subdued; Flowridia heard not a terrifying goddess, but a parent mourning her child. *"Tell me, truly, Daughter of Stars—this is my daughter's body? No tricks?"*

"No tricks, ma'am," Etolié said, and though it was Eionei's face, it was her own voice and tears. "I swear upon my mother's name. I saw it all myself. She died a hero's death–" Etolié's voice caught. Flowridia had no doubt she would have burst into tears without Eionei's restraint.

The possessed Celestial approached the casket, trembling as she undid the latches and lifted the ornate lid. Ku'Shya merely stared.

The taut silence grew tense with every passing second. Flowridia swore the shadow stole a breath to speak—

And *roared.*

The whole crowd cowered, hands flying to cover their ears. Flowridia joined them, head aching at the furious cry. It held agony and anguish yet anger unparalleled. This was a cry for vengeance.

And then it faded. Dissipated into the void. There stood no shadow, nor any sign of her presence—save the lingering aura of dread. Etolié's light faded. She fell on her bottom, content to hide her face in her hands.

Ears ringing, Flowridia knelt beside her. Lara quickly followed. "Eionei whispered that he would take this up with Sol Kareena herself," Etolié said, trembling from either tears or exhaustion. Either was viable. "Ku'Shya is not a deity to trifle with."

A shadow fell upon them. Flowridia cowered as she turned, expecting the return of the demon goddess, or perhaps Casvir, who haunted her every step—and was surprised to find Thalmus instead. "Flowra, are you all right?" the half-giant said, fear etched into his scarred face.

"I'm fine."

"Will you come with me? I have something for you, if you'll accept it."

When he offered a hand, she clutched it in both her own. A childish gesture for one whose childhood had abandoned her long ago, but she longed to hide behind Thalmus' quiet strength. Beside them, the crowd radiated panic, threatening to blow into a frenzy. She watched Lara rise to calm them, every bit the monarch as she pulled their focus away from the scene and to her.

Except for familiar, glowing red eyes. Casvir stood readied for battle, but his attention remained on her.

She looked away.

She knew Thalmus' path, for his workshop came into view. Away from the mourners he stole her, though fear had risen to mask the sorrow.

Whatever Ku'Shya's intentions, Flowridia knew she would be a fool to not fear.

Thalmus, too, it seemed. "If Ku'Shya's wrath has been sparked by Khastra's death, we may all be in grave danger. There's little she can do without a host, but even as a shadowed manifestation, some say demon gods can affect the mortal plane in certain parts of the world."

"Not the most comforting thought . . ." But her words faded when she glanced up at Thalmus' face. For all her startled composure, she saw palpable fear on his normally reserved face. "What's wrong?"

"You leaving is abominable."

Flowridia shook her head. "I already agreed to it, and should we succeed, we'll have an orb and a way to stop Soliel."

The God of Order had not been seen since his calamitous battle at the Theocracy of Sol Kareena—the same terrible night that had stolen Khastra, Meira, and Ayla.

"And if you fail, we won't have you."

She squeezed his hand as they walked past her treasured garden entrance.

Thalmus stopped, studying the floral path. "I promise to care for it while you're gone," Thalmus said, his voice a comfort to her agitated soul. "I can't match your skill, but I will do what I can."

She stopped beside him, sparing a glance for her beloved sanctuary. The garden flourished, but without her care, its majesty would wane, she knew. The magic needed maintenance, something Thalmus couldn't give. But she trusted his words, and for him to even offer pulled a genuine smile to her face.

He kept walking; she followed behind. "Please know you have a home here and a family that loves you."

Flowridia looked into his scarred face, realizing his eyes glistened in the sunlight. If he knew of her crimes, would he still hold that sentiment? Behind Thalmus' gentle heart was a core of iron, incorruptible and immovable. Flowridia knew her soul was as soft and malleable as her physical form.

She saw it immediately, placed lovingly on a table within his workshop—a spear as tall as she, carved from light wood and glazed and polished until it shined. The design brought fresh tears to her eyes; embossed into the wood were the familiar plants at the entrance of her garden, the same collection of leaves and flowers Thalmus would see should he look up from his workspace and find her.

The spearhead reflected the sunlight, a clear and sturdy glass, rougher than what she'd seen him create in the past, but still bearing beauty. The edges held a waved design—not purposeful, no, she thought, recalling his methods. Broken from a larger piece and carefully cracked to form the proper shape.

"I wanted to have it completed before you left. I pray you never have to use it, but it looks like you may need all the protection you can get."

Lighter than Demitri, the spear was buoyant and perfectly balanced. Flowridia held it tight in her hands, the simple remark of, "Thank you," as much as her lips could summon.

She wrapped her arms around him, grateful when he returned the gesture. Flowridia lingered in that hug, putting his touch to memory, his smoky scent, how his skin seemed more granite than not, as well as the safety she felt in his embrace. She'd never known her father, and Thalmus had filled a void she'd never realized she'd had.

"Remember who you are, my little flower girl," Thalmus whispered, his voice reverberating against her ear.

"First I have to find out who I am," Flowridia said. "But I promise to come home."

She thought of Casvir's bargain and prayed she spoke the truth.

The faint prickling of her treasured familiar bespoke his presence in Etolié's library. Flowridia, with her spear in hand, entered the arcane masterpiece, weaving through the maze of shelves until she reached the center, lit by a skylight. Directly beneath the patch of sun lay a large pile of scarves, upon which snoozed Demitri. The wolf's steady breathing rose and fell, his dark grey fur absorbing the sun's light, a patch of warmth within the plush pile.

Beside him sat Etolié, her hand lazily caught in his fur. In her other hand, she nursed a flask, her posture more teetering than usual. She glanced up at Flowridia's entrance and said, "Nice spear." She took a long sip, and Flowridia saw evidence of recent tears on her swollen face.

"It's a gift from Thalmus." Flowridia knelt beside the scarves and offered the spear forward, but Etolié gave it no mind, instead taking a gasping breath before having another drink of ale.

"Lara's dealing with the aftermath of our godly interloper, reassuring the masses and all. Insisted I disappear and drink. A goddamn saint, that little moonbeam. I raised her well."

Scattered outside the sea of plush comforts, just within Etolié's reach, Flowridia noticed a familiar array of trinkets—polished gems, the maldectine knuckles, an impressive collection of jewelry, and more. She glanced at the shelves where they typically rested and saw they had been emptied.

Flowridia had never asked, but she'd always quietly suspected the truth—Khastra was the one to lavish her dear friend with handmade gifts.

Khastra had cared for Etolié when Etolié could not care for herself, and now, with the half-demon's loss, Flowridia feared she would waste away. The Celestial's proclivity toward self-destruction was difficult to watch even when she was well.

Demitri stirred beneath Etolié's hand. Bright golden eyes met Flowridia's own, and she smiled at her young familiar as he rolled over, his stomach absorbing the sun's light.

When are you leaving?

"We leave tonight, Demitri," Flowridia replied, kneeling as she pulled the wolf into her arms. A heavy weight; the young wolf stood taller than her knee now.

You leave tonight. I'm staying with Etolié.

Flowridia frowned, her lip trembling as her protective hold tightened. "Dearest Demitri, the last thing I need today is your belligerence. I'm not leaving you behind."

Not belligerent. Honest.

"Demitri–"

But Flowridia stopped when Etolié held up a hand. The Celestial, with a permissive glance to Flowridia, stole the wolf from her arms and cradled him in her own. "Flowridia needs you," Etolié said softly, exhaustion in her words. "Be her protector. Give her hell—she deserves it—but she's gonna be all alone soon."

From the air, Etolié withdrew a small hand-held mirror engraved with silver leaves. Flowridia recognized it, having seen the Celestial use it numerous times to contact Lara.

"Lara and I agree you need this more than she does," Etolié explained, still holding it out. Flowridia accepted it, letting her fingers brush against the ornate carvings, palpable magic tickling her senses. "In case there's any danger of demon gods. Or if you're lonely. Or if Imperator First and Last ever tries to hurt you." Etolié shook, her breathing unsteady, and Flowridia watched her eyes rim with red. "I'll come get you, Flowers, Casvir and his bargains be damned."

Etolié's words did nothing to part the clouded guilt in Flowridia's heart. She sucked in a choking breath, forcing her emotions away, and simply said, "Thank you."

Still cradling the wolf, Etolié stole her flask once more and took a final drink. It disappeared with a slight glimmer as she tossed it aside.

"Etolié, I'm worried," Flowridia whispered, placing her hand on her friend's shoulder.

"You fucking should be," Etolié replied. "Going off on a road trip with the resident Tyrant Asshole was scary enough, but now there's the mother from hell–"

"That's not what I meant. Will you be all right while I'm gone?"

Etolié's jaw trembled. Fresh tears brimmed in her lavender eyes. "Everything hurts," she whimpered. "I'm sorry. Your blood-sucker is gone, and I shouldn't lean on you."

Flowridia's fist clenched against Etolié's spine, not expecting the sudden bombardment of emotion at the words. "Yes, Ayla is gone," she said, forcing her voice to steady. She had thought it before, yet to say it caused her tongue to tremble. "But my hurt doesn't mean you're hurting any less."

Etolié only sobbed in response. Her breath hiccupped, drunk and brokenhearted. Flowridia released her fist and instead ran soothing lines along the Celestial's back.

In her bedroom, Flowridia gathered what little she would need for her journey. Wrapped in one of her changes of clothing was a green bracelet, a maldectine token from the late half-demon, as well as Etolié's gifted mirror, reminders of home. Demitri suddenly perked up, not moments before a knock pulled her from her task.

It smells like Sora.

Clutching her gifted spear, Flowridia twisted the knob. There stood Sora Fireborn, as Demitri had said. White and gold in shades to rival her long, rope-like hair colored her tunic and tabard, bearing the sigil of the Goddess—a spear and the sun. Upon Meira's death, she had been proclaimed her successor. But true to her character, she wore breeches and boots beneath it, and a knife at her hip.

There, too, was the little bird at her shoulder. Sol Kareena herself had granted Sora a familiar.

They hadn't spoken since Flowridia had made a wish to Ayla for her murder. The half-elf lived only because of Sol Kareena's will.

Tension settled between them, Sora's silent gaze unreadable, her lips nearly white in their purposeful line. She broke their stare, sparing a glance for Demitri on the bed. "You were innocent," she said to the wolf. "I'm sorry." Flowridia's grip on her spear tightened as Sora looked back at her. "They all think the world of you here. I won't disillusion them of that."

Despite the insult, the statement settled Flowridia's nerves. Sora knew enough to have her hung in the town square. It evoked a question. "Why?"

"Because left alone, you're a fool, but you're a harmless fool. Ayla Darkleaf charmed you. She would have damned your soul to hell, but now she's gone. For me to tell Etolié what you did would destroy your life." Sora's words stopped, and for a faint, unmistakable moment, her demeanor cracked, and Flowridia saw not anger or hatred . . . but pain.

"I don't want to ruin you," she continued, her voice scarcely a whisper. "I want to forgive you, because Sol Kareena would do the same. I'm still working on that." Her gaze hardened, her stare narrowing. "But don't mistake this for mercy. This is a warning. I won't hesitate to slip the knife next time."

Flowridia said nothing, her skin prickling at the threat. Sora took a step back, holding her gaze as she disappeared down the hallway.

Flowridia shut the door, knowing she deserved every hateful word from the half-elf's mouth. Sora had met a hellish fate.

It seemed they would be at odds for all their lives—one sworn to slay Ayla Darkleaf, and one sworn to love.

Within minutes, Flowridia finished packing her things. With Demitri at her feet, she quickly ascended the stairs to the council chambers, centered at the third floor of the manor.

She came upon a familiar room filled with a circle of thrones. An uncomfortable mood pervaded the space—Queen Marielle, quiet as she twiddled her thumbs, Zorlaeus, utterly stiff as he stood beside her, and Imperator Casvir, silent as well.

The tension shattered at her entrance. Marielle perked up immediately and ran to greet her.

As Marielle embraced her, she said, "You'll be back for my wedding, right?" Were her plan to murder Flowridia by suffocation, she would certainly succeed if she didn't release her soon.

"I hope so," Flowridia said, voice muffled by Marielle's dress and cleavage. Within six months, Marielle would be wed to the unassuming De'Sindai gentleman beside her.

When she pulled away, she realized Marielle's plastered rouge was ruined, smudged by the monarch's own tears.

Zorlaeus, his maroon, fluffy hair curling around his ram-like horns, offered a hand, unable to quite tear his gaze away from Casvir. "Best of luck," he said simply, his handshake limp and damp from sweat.

Then, vertigo; the world shifted upside down and sideways as Casvir ripped his claws into the air. A tear in space, one that opened into a portal. Casvir gave a nod to Marielle, his offered, "Farewell," polite and sufficient.

Flowridia released a breath, taking one final look around the room, then stepped into the portal.

For a moment, the world shifted into a thousand stars, the tear revealing a world between worlds. Flowridia marveled as she floated, weightless for a mere blink of the eye, until carpet cushioned her bare feet. The stone walls of Nox'Kartha appeared around her, well-lit by crystal sconces on the wall. Black sand stood in shifting pillars every twenty feet or so, and Flowridia sensed something dark radiating from the odd magical structures.

Demitri stumbled through the portal, falling at her feet as a soft whine escaped his throat.

Then, Casvir himself appeared, unhindered by the gut-twisting portal. It sealed behind him, leaving no trace of the potent magical energy. "We leave in the morning." He gestured toward a door Flowridia recognized—Ayla's room—and then his steps bespoke his exit, metal upon carpet.

Demitri's whispered words startled her. *He smells wrong.*

She offered no comment beyond a frown.

Encumbered by her gear, Flowridia went inside and carefully set Thalmus' gift on the couch.

She spared a glance for her fallen love's room, mesmerized at what she saw. A bedroom with no bed; Ayla had not slept. Odd trinkets triggered beloved memories: a fork from dinner; a flower she had healed; a tea cup; the shoes she'd left in her garden—all of it memorialized in glass.

A memory of gold—the white queen from her chess set at home, a stark reminder of her and Ayla's disastrous first meeting. Yet, it had meant enough for her love to preserve and seal it in a glowing globe.

It wounded her, to be surrounded by cherished memories, the pictures on the wall hand-drawn by her fallen love. Flowridia's bag fell from her shoulder as she blinked away tears.

A faint growl emanated from the young wolf as she unloaded her bag. *I don't like him. I don't trust him.*

"Demitri!" she snapped. "He has been nothing but cordial since–"

Since he stole you?

Flowridia bit her lip and released a stiff sigh. "My dearest Demitri, there is much you don't know yet." She set her bag down and knelt beside him, staring down into his sneering gaze. "He stole me, yes, but I'm surprised you don't know him. He gave you to me."

Demitri tilted his head at that. *Are you saying he's my superior?*

"It's because of him that I have you, so show some respect." Tentatively, Demitri began sniffing around the room as Flowridia continued her unpacking. "I don't know if I trust him either, but I don't think he'll harm us. So, if we uphold our bargain–"

Your bargain. The grumble in his tone was palpable. *You dragged me here.*

Arguing with her belligerent companion would only lead to anger, so instead Flowridia stripped out of her funeral dress in silence. Demitri continued sniffing around the room, content to investigate Ayla's closet, while Flowridia changed into her nightgown.

Once she had smoothed her gown across her figure, she went to Ayla's armoire, carved from wood and plated here and there with gold. The door swung open at her touch, and as she stole a hanger to hang her dress, a faint smile pulled at her lips for the odd predictability of Ayla's wardrobe—mostly black, all skintight, and each with their own unique, plunging neckline. As she dug, a bit of variety drew her eyes, at least among the fancier gowns. An icy blue one made with the softest silk she had ever felt; a deep green corset with a bustle; a rich maroon-

She recognized that one. Gingerly, Flowridia lifted it from the closet and hugged it close to her figure, familiar scents of earth and hints of blood welling tears in her eyes. Worn by herself to the unveiling of the Nox'Karthan Embassy, she recalled how self-conscious she had been with the plunging neckline but how beautiful it had felt to be adored by Ayla's gaze.

If she closed her eyes, she could still see the glittering lights, hear the blissful music. Ayla's touch had led her in sync with the flowing rhythm. Nothing could taint the memory of that perfect, final night.

Upon the table sat an unfinished sketch, memorializing the event in ink. Ayla's radiant joy remained unparalleled in her drawn form.

Flowridia realized, surveying her surroundings, that a blanket and pillow had been placed at the end of the plush couch, making for what she suspected would be a restful sleep.

Demitri merely glared as he sniffed about the room. *Why did Ayla steal your things?*

"What do you mean?" Flowridia said, genuine confusion bleeding into her tone. She kept the dress in her arms and approached the vanity next.

All these globes—these were yours. Did you give them to her?

"She took them, yes, but she didn't steal them. It's different."

Did she have your permission?

"I never said–" She frowned at him. "They're memories, Demitri. I don't care that she took them." The aged vanity held a mirror and a layer of dust. She pulled open the center drawer, her frantic heart steadying to see her quarry—before she had left for Staelash, she had stashed the cursed ear among a collection of knives.

Knives tucked away in a vanity drawer was so endearingly, predictably Ayla. It drew a sorrowful smile to her face.

But she did take them.

Something lay missing. Her heart stopped. Within her hand, she held the ear.

But the body had gone. She had placed it on the couch before she left.

Mom?

Gasping, Flowridia burst from the room. "Imperator—!"

There was no sign of Casvir. Only the brightly lit hallway and odd black sand flowing in ominous lines.

Flowridia's words threatened to choke her, but still she held them in her throat. She could not staunch her sudden tears. Instead, she fell against the wall, trembling as she fought the urge to sob.

"My dear, are you all right?"

Flowridia turned at the words, gasping as she brought her sleeve up to wipe the moisture clouding her vision. A gentleman approached her, one draped in luxurious fabrics and bearing opulent signs of wealth. His blonde hair fell in perfect waves past his shoulders, his features sharp and inviting, his smile as kind and sincere as she had ever seen.

Flowridia had never given much thought toward the supposed appeal of men, but even she could see he was exceptionally handsome. Beautiful, even.

Still, she froze despite his soothing voice. "Are you lost?" the man asked, quickly approaching her.

Flowridia shook her head, ashamed at the display of weakness in Casvir's home.

"Lady Flowridia? You are Lady Flowridia of Staelash, yes?"

She managed a nod, cowering as he stood before her. She wrapped her arms around herself, tears flowing freely. Demitri's nose against her leg did nothing to soothe her.

"Tell me what's wrong," the man pressed, and from the air he withdrew a handkerchief and offered it forward. Flowridia accepted the gift, a pungent perfume suddenly wafting from the gentleman's aura—almost floral, but sweet enough to upset her stomach. Flowridia crumpled the gifted cloth in her hand as she trembled. "Whatever it is, I can help."

Flowridia's hiccup masked a sob. "A-Ayla's body–"

When the sound of heavy armor met her ears, she shut her mouth and squeezed her eyes shut, determined to staunch the flow of tears.

Imperator Casvir rounded the corner, sparing only a glance toward the man before his glowing eyes settled back on her. "Lady Flowridia?" his voice rumbled.

Demitri tensed beside her, but Casvir made no move to step forward. Flowridia forced herself to stand tall. No use in lying. "Where is Ayla's body?"

"In the catacombs of my palace, safe from any who would steal it."

What a pitiful sight she must be, face swollen with tears, clad in only her nightclothes, unquestionably indecent as she stood before this monster of a man. Utterly embarrassed—both at her appearance and her implied accusation—she brought her arms up to cover her shame and protect herself when he inevitably tore her to shreds with his claws. She managed to nod. "Thank you," she whispered, staring at the floor.

The man beside her stepped forward. "Casvir, the lady is in crisis. Your boorish words–"

"Leave."

The man bowed in a dramatic fashion, arms spread wide. He took a step back, out of Flowridia's line of sight.

A blush blossomed across her cheeks, then she heard Casvir say, "Do you want it?"

She shook her head. "Yes, but not yet. Safer there, as you said."

Metal shifted. Flowridia dared to glance up. "I will not think less of you for mourning," he said, and he left her alone.

Flowridia laid herself down to sleep, the couch cozier than even her bed at home and wide enough to accommodate another two or three of her. The ear rested at its place above her heart, the weight a comfort. She clutched the maroon dress, stolen from the wardrobe. The scent both soothed and haunted her broken self, and when Demitri curled beside her, she wished that he would speak to distract her.

In the stark silence, her thoughts became unbearably loud. When she finally teetered on the cusp of sleep, she swore she heard a pained scream, one that shrieked at the cusp of familiarity somewhere far away.

Before she could contemplate it more, darkness fell upon her.

She recalled visions of Ayla, her voice and her touch.

Sensuous words caressed her ear. "I love you, Flowridia."

Within the darkness, she caught flashes of skin, of brilliant cyan eyes refracting the light. Cold hands skimmed her body, desperately groped her form, yet felt as nothing at all, the touch as elusive as shadow.

But once within her, sensation burst, ice freezing her to her very soul. She swore they were one, that Ayla moved inside her. And by every god, she *ached,* but when she tried to clutch the ghost, she was as smoke.

"Please, never leave me," the voice pled, and Flowridia felt tears upon her face.

She whispered, "Never—"

She awoke freezing, despite her blankets. Demitri's wet tongue licked her face. *Mom?*

Flowridia stared into Demitri's golden eyes, piercing even in the dark.

You were talking in your sleep.

Flowridia slowly sat up, pulling Demitri into her arms, recalling visions that were as clear as the ornaments decorating the room.

"Her spirit lingers." But what did that mean?

A knock caused her to stiffen. "Lady Flowridia?"

Not a voice she recognized.

"Imperator Casvir requests you ready yourself. You leave in an hour."

"Thank you," she muttered, as loud as she could summon.

Flowridia wore simple clothing for travel. With a bag on her hip, her maldectine bracelet on her wrist—though it brought her sadness to think of its maker—and a silver mirror in her pocket, she grasped the gifted spear, admiring the intricate carvings when another knock pulled her focus.

She quickly tucked Ayla's ear into her bodice, hiding it from view. She answered, surprised to see that Imperator Casvir had come to collect her himself. He stood back enough to not block her exit, but still she withered beneath his gaze. "Ready?"

Flowridia nodded.

"Our carriage awaits." His relentless stare left her face a moment, glancing down at her hands. "Allow me," he said, extending his arm.

For a brief, alarming moment, she thought he meant to take her hand. Demitri stiffened beside her, fur bristling as he sensed her fear. But she recalled the spear she held, one that looked far heavier than its craftsman had designed it to be, and cautiously allowed Casvir to take it.

His claws wrapped carefully around it, but still he stared at her expectantly. When she froze a moment too long, his deep voice rumbled, "Your bag."

She nearly dropped it as she fumbled to get it off her shoulder.

The demonic tyrant began trekking down the hall. Did he ever relax his stance? He held no weapon at his hip or back, yet he strode through his own home like a battlefield.

But as they walked, an alarming thought welled in her gut, the realization that she would be travelling alone with this strange and terrifying man, one who had been watching her since near her infancy, who had admitted to wanting to keep her here. At her hip, she kept Etolié's mirror, her hand reflexively reaching down to caress the magic-infused object, but careful not to summon attention.

He would never know she had it, Flowridia decided. It would be her one escape if Demitri's fears about his character were confirmed.

The hallways of Nox'Kartha twisted and turned, and by the time Flowridia thought to pay attention they appeared outside. The sun steadily rose, morning still new, and Flowridia's gaze fell to two enormous, armored horses hitched to a carriage emblazoned with the Nox'Karthan seal on the door—that of a skull embedded into a gold coin. Drawn to the animals, Flowridia stepped forward, Demitri close behind, and smiled. "What beautiful creatures you are."

They smell wrong. Demitri's voice chilled her blood.

Flowridia tilted her head as she studied their glazed expressions, the clouded white of their eyes. Between the plates of their armor, she noticed rotting flesh clinging to the white bones and exposed musculature. The horses were not pained as far as she could see, but the realization came with a curiosity that startled her. Undeath pervaded this nation, or so they said. Of course the horses would be among them.

With appropriate caution, she offered her hand, watching closely for any sign of aggression. It barely reacted when she placed a hand on its armored nose. With the same amount of care, she placed a hand on the opposite horse, surprised when it turned to face her.

That metallic echo, louder now against the stone road, drew her attention. Casvir watched, and she drew her hands back, hating how she flinched.

He all but ignored her, instead making his way to the carriage door. It opened at his touch, and he watched her expectantly as he offered a taloned hand.

Unease filled her, but she approached and placed her small hand into his own. Her breath hitched at the unnaturally cold touch, but she allowed him to help her inside, his claws offering a gentle cage around her skin.

Some illusion spell must have surrounded the carriage, for it appeared much larger within than without. Two carpeted benches, sized to comfortably seat someone of Casvir's substantial bulk, sat on opposite ends, vibrant red to juxtapose the black walls. A table sat between them, and Flowridia secured herself into the far corner as Demitri leapt inside. He sat himself upon her lap, the bottom half of him spilling out onto the seat, and growled when Casvir himself entered, whose horns narrowly avoided scraping the ceiling.

As he sat, he seemed to notice for the first time the intricacy of Flowridia's weapon. He inspected it with care, his eyes scanning the images lovingly carved into the shaft. With her spear in hand, Casvir leaned forward, mouth open to speak, but Demitri's sudden growl stopped him. Casvir, though, kept steady eye contact with Demitri as he placed the spear on the table between them.

"Your devotion to your mistress should be commended," he said, his eyes narrowing. Flowridia placed a hand on Demitri's back when the growling didn't cease. Casvir placed her bag beside it. "I understand—a man travelling alone with a young woman is cause for concern. But I assure you, it is misplaced." His stare turned ever so briefly to Flowridia herself before he focused instead on a chest situated beneath his seat. Flowridia watched as he withdrew the trunk and placed it at his side, methodically withdrawing documents and a quill. His eyes scanned the papers, placing some on the table, and Flowridia finally felt Demitri relax under her touch.

I don't like him.

She let her fingers run lovingly down his fur in response.

The carriage lurched. Flowridia took back her bag and spear, placing the latter beneath her when Casvir said, "Your weapon is impressive."

Flowridia nodded, bringing her knees to her chest. "You might say it's *breathtaking—*"

Horror struck her when she realized what she'd said. Here in the presence of Imperator Casvir, First and Last of His Name, Tyrant of Nox'Kartha and Marshall of the Deathless Army, she had made a joke so facetious, even Demitri looked at her with absolute bafflement.

Casvir stared, first at Flowridia, then to the spear on the floor. The wry smile came with a short, scoffing sort of chuckle that vanished as quickly as it appeared.

He returned his attention to his paperwork, but Flowridia looked out the window, unsure if it were idiotic or not to relax.

The grand city spread out before them, the morning light reflecting off the spiraling, white marbled castle they left behind. They descended a slope, the towers of the castle sweeping behind in smooth, effortless strokes, built into a great mountain that served as a wall around a portion of the city. Enraptured at the sight, Flowridia put the vision to memory, knowing it was as grand a building as she had ever stepped into. Though considerably younger than the Theocracy of Sol Kareena, Nox'Kartha held a richness and grandeur that betrayed its age.

They crossed a seemingly depthless moat, one Flowridia could barely see through the small window. The streets unraveled in every direction, spreading wide around the magnificent palace in the mountain. The white stone buildings and paved streets made it appear rich, and Flowridia wondered how anyone could look upon the city and think it evil.

De'Sindai made up most of the populace, and she didn't miss how they shied away and bowed at the sight of the carriage pulling through the streets. It was a busy scene, with shopkeepers and patrons, respectably dressed though with necklines far lower than Flowridia would have felt comfortable with. She realized that Ayla's outlandish taste in dresses was entirely typical in this foreign land.

But something odd caught her eye, something that juxtaposed problematically with the rich populace and clean streets. Flowridia narrowed her vision from behind the window of the carriage as she watched a street sweeper aimlessly clearing the sidewalk of rubbish. Aimless, because it meandered, teetering on unsteady feet—feet that had all but rotted away.

Its entire form seemed in various stages of decomposition. The ghoul held its broom with unsteady hands, and Flowridia fought back revulsion. Nox'Kartha, she had heard, employed the undead for menial tasks. Dead horses pulling carriages were a very different matter than a being once sentient and intelligent in life. Was this the price of citizenship? For Nox'Kartha to dare and play with dark magic, to utilize it into everyday life bespoke complete indifference to the wrath of Sol Kareena, the most powerful of the angelic gods.

Were the undead set into other menial jobs? Did they toil the fields and scrub the lavatories too? She glanced at Casvir, engrossed in his paperwork, and felt her voice shy away.

Instead, she returned her attention to the city, absorbing the grand atmosphere. Nox'Kartha wore its dark secrets on its sleeve.

That, or its dark secrets were so much worse.

Beyond the grand gates was an expansive, lush meadow, spotted with houses in the far distance for those who would dwell within the borders but not the city itself. Parallel to the road, a great river headed west, one that if Flowridia followed she knew would eventually lead back home.

She found it odd that they travelled with no guard, especially in so ostentatious a carriage. But she dared not question the imperator, looming like a volcano, though dormant with his quill and parchment.

Demitri snoozed on her lap, his deep breathing soothing to her mind. When he was young and new, she would count his sweet breaths in the night, a finger at his side to feel the precious rise and fall of his chest. So very tiny he had been, before they'd been found by Etolié in the woods, only days after the demon—after Casvir—had brought him to her.

De'Sindai, she corrected herself. No true demon could exist in this world without a host.

Casvir had, presumably, given Aura to her as well . . . and she had been a mere toddler stepping a bit too far out into the woods when the giant wolf had appeared to her.

She glanced up and watched Casvir, still focused on paperwork. Exhaustion pulled at her eyelids, having not slept properly for days, but her nerves had yet to settle.

She rested her head against the window, trying to decipher what use a demon might have for a toddler when, as her eyelids grew ever heavier, Casvir asked, "Will you be able to sleep in the carriage?"

Startled, she sat up. She realized he watched her, his eyes faintly glowing in the shelter of the carriage. Eventually, she managed a nod.

"We can stop to camp tonight, if necessary."

Shaking her head, she took a deep breath and dared to whisper, "What about you?"

"I do not sleep."

Of course he didn't. And though her mind buzzed at the new information, within minutes she succumbed to exhaustion.

Flowridia awoke to darkness, to a sky littered with stars and a half moon stretched into a coy smirk. With bumps on her flesh from a cold she knew not the source of, she shied away, else be reminded of gentle whispers in her dreams and tender caressing on her skin.

She realized, then, a soft baritone voice hummed through the carriage. Flowridia dared to glance over, realizing Casvir hummed to himself, still reading over documents while his opposite hand tapped a steady rhythm into the air. But his face surprised her the most—focused as ever, but relaxed. Content.

She found the sound soothing, something for her anxious mind to grasp beyond the troubling memories in her dreams. But it faded, and when Flowridia's eyes fluttered open again, she realized Casvir's red eyes stared straight at her, glowing under the reflected moonlight.

"You talk in your sleep," he said, no judgement in his tone. He spoke clinically, as though commenting on the sky or the color of the trees.

Still, she curled around Demitri's sleeping form. "If you tell me whatever it is you heard, I might die of embarrassment."

"You might."

The statement drew a blush to her cheeks. "I'm sorry. I didn't mean to bother you."

"Lady Flowridia, I am not bothered." Her title sounded so formal on his tongue, as did everything he said. Such an odd juxtaposition, his civility to his inherent menace. "Merely curious. Do you often have nightmares?"

The most she could summon the bravery for was a nod.

Casvir returned his attention to his paperwork. The only sound became the faint cacophony of night creatures from without and the gentle scraping of rocks against the carriage wheels. Peaceful to some, Flowridia was certain, but not to her, as the silver moon mocked her from outside the window. The stars accompanying it could be mistaken for fangs, evoking a longing Flowridia dared to not entertain.

"Imperator Casvir," she whispered, and she didn't have to face him to know she had his attention, "may I ask something?"

"You may."

With her head lying on the bench, she gathered courage enough to ask, "You said something before, on the night of Ayla's death—*'Her spirit lingers.'* What does that mean?"

"Precisely what I said. Her spirit cannot move on, and so it remains among mortals."

Casvir was a necromancer. She knew this from Ayla herself and from Etolié's drunken ramblings. "If you were to will it, could I–" Flowridia cut herself off, too shy to speak. "Never mind."

She shut her eyes, content to simply feign sleep, but Casvir said, "Ask."

As though iron clasped around her chest, Flowridia struggled to breathe, much less speak. She managed a nigh inaudible mumble. "Could I speak to her?"

"No."

Gods, her stomach ached. Casvir's stare, even behind her closed eyelids, bore a hole through her courage—it seeped out in droves.

"Were she a mere ghost," he continued, though not unkindly, "it would be trivial, assuming we held whatever object anchored her spirit to this world—in her case, her body. But she is something different, risen by The Lurker himself and so unique. It would take someone with more finesse than I to grasp her soul."

"But you could feel her?"

"I feel her now."

The words pulled a gasp from Flowridia's throat. She dared open her eyes, realized he stared not at her but at Demitri, asleep in the curve of her bent knees.

"It is faint, but her presence was always unmistakable. Did you keep the ear with you?"

Too shocked to speak, Flowridia managed to nod. Head swimming, she pulled the chained ear from her bodice, letting it dangle just above her face.

"A future with Ayla is still within your grasp. You know what you must do to enlist my aid."

He returned his attention to the work before him. Flowridia slipped the ear back into her bodice and let it settle against her heart.

Ayla was not gone. But did she hold awareness? Flowridia shut her eyes and thought of Ayla, of her visage and smile, clearing her mind of all else. If Casvir, as renowned a necromancer to currently walk the realm, could not touch her, she held no hope. Yet, the thought was enough to staunch her tears, even if memories of Ayla came with brutal screams as she watched the Goddess' spear penetrate her undead body, infusing her with holy light.

Again, that quiet baritone filled the carriage. No words, but Flowridia clung to the unknown tune, allowing it to distract her troubled heart.

When unconsciousness finally did steal her away, she awoke at sunrise to the memory of an airy alto voice and Demitri pawing at her thigh. *I need to go out.*

Flowridia ran a hand across the soft fur of his head. She sat up, suppressing a giggle at the desperation in his young voice. "Can we stop for a minute, please? Demitri needs to relieve himself."

Casvir nodded. The carriage pulled to a smooth stop. He stood and opened the door, stepping aside when Demitri darted out.

A stunning scene surrounded them. The smooth dirt road met her feet as Casvir helped her out, but the luscious grass caressed her once she stepped away. She smiled, invigorated by the cool breeze blowing through her hair. In the far distance, a mountain range divided the sky and the land. Casvir inspected the horses, and Flowridia noticed, for the first time, a hooded figure driving the carriage.

She scanned the meadow, thrilled when she noticed patches of violet pansies dotting the scene. She knelt before a particularly vibrant series of flowers, plucking the prettiest from the root and weaving the stem into her hair. Though no magic imbued the bit of life strung through the thick locks, feeling the lingering energy in the bud drew a sincere smile to her face.

In the distance, she could see Demitri running back toward them. Tongue hanging out, he fell at Flowridia's feet and rubbed himself against the grass. *We should never go inside again.*

"I agree," Flowridia said, her smile widening at Demitri's childish statement. "But the carriage is much faster than walking." Despite the risk of grass stains on her knees, Flowridia knelt and rubbed the soft fur of his stomach.

"Are you hungry?" Casvir's voice felt out of place in the bright sun.

She nodded, noting the hollow in her stomach. In the numbness of her sorrow, she realized she had not eaten since Ayla's passing.

Casvir went to the carriage and returned holding a chest, one that fit well enough in both his hands. Angelic runes—coordinates, for a place Flowridia could not guess—were inscribed into the polished wood. He placed it at her feet. "I understand you have a special diet. I hope I have accommodated you well enough."

When he returned to the carriage, Flowridia lifted the lid. The contents—fruits, bread, and vegetables, some of which she hadn't seen before—were fresh and moist, and Flowridia realized this was the most practical and innocuous use of an extra-dimensional space she had ever seen.

When Casvir emerged with a second chest, similarly inscribed with runes, he sat a few feet away. Flowridia dared to ask the question dancing on her tongue. "How did you know?"

From the second chest, Casvir withdrew some sort of raw meat. He tossed it at Demitri, who pouted as only the little wolf could. But he took a small bite and glared as he swallowed.

"Ayla spoke of your diet in passing, once," Casvir said. "There had been speculation of inviting your ruling council to visit Nox'Kartha, and she insisted I accommodate for you, specifically."

A quiet smile tugged at Flowridia's lips. She imagined how her first glimpse of the beautiful city might have been entirely different, how Ayla herself might have given her a tour, bashfully shown off her room and all its glowing, stolen trinkets. Absently, she touched her bodice, where Ayla's ear rested beneath. "She was always thoughtful."

"Thorough, perhaps. She was never thoughtful without an underlying motive."

The words stung. Flowridia hid her hurt behind a slice of fresh bread.

But perhaps it showed. "I apologize," Casvir said, the words startling Flowridia from her distracted state. "It is improper of me to speak ill of someone you care for."

Flowridia swallowed her bite, uncomfortable meeting his eyes. "You and she had a tumultuous relationship."

"We often fought, yes."

"I don't need you to lie for my comfort," she said softly, hoping the words weren't rude. But another question tugged at her mind, and she pulled a pink apple from the chest. Its shined surface turned nearly blinding in the sun. "Why did you keep Ayla around?"

Casvir, large and imposing with his fierce armor, so out of place sitting serenely in a green meadow, said, "Ayla's skill set was unique. Her usefulness outweighed her capacity for tantrums."

Ayla's skill set . . . Flowridia wondered if she needed to feign oblivious. She knew the truth, that Ayla's talent for charming foreigners held naught a candle to her skills with a knife. "She was a diplomat," Flowridia said, wondering if he would correct her. "Those are replaceable."

When he said nothing, Flowridia faced him directly, realizing he studied her with scrutiny. "I cannot tell if you are being purposefully opaque or simply a poor liar."

"A poor liar." Flowridia's blush burned hotter than the sun on her cheeks.

The disappointment in Casvir's normal stoicism quickly faded to indifference. "Ayla was a ravenous wolf kept on a very short leash. A diplomat, yes, and unquestionably brilliant at maintaining facades. All that paled to her talent for stealth. While I do not mourn her death, I do begrudge the loss of her talents."

Flowridia took a bite of her apple, unsure of what to say, but to her surprise, Casvir continued speaking. "Her efforts to subdue me became an annoyance, and when I finally reprimanded her, she began making attempts on my life. At first, she aimed for subtlety, but when she continued to be thwarted, she turned to shock and awe." His armor clinked as he brought his hand to his chest, just below his neck. "She once ripped a tree out by the roots and smashed it into my collar bone." With his hand, he followed the line of his chest and shoulder, then down his arm. "The force broke it in two. The rest of my arm was shattered." He nodded, his mind clearly elsewhere. "An impressive blow."

"That's blatant treason," Flowridia replied, distracted at the thought of Ayla heaving a tree large enough to break Casvir; a comical image, truthfully, given that Ayla was considerably smaller than even she. "How big was the tree?"

For the first time, she saw genuine confusion on Casvir's face. She prayed she lived to regret her next comment. "Large," he replied, the words slow on his tongue.

"High *tree*-son, then."

The confusion faded into a blank stare.

". . . with heavy infan-*tree*?"

Casvir quirked an eyebrow. Flowridia thought she might wilt into the ground when he said, "Congratulations."

Flowridia, still wary, said, "For what?"

"Typically I revel in the challenge of wordplay, but you have me *stumped*. I shall *leaf* you to your victory."

Flowridia bit her apple to curb her beaming smile. He said nothing else, and when she finally swallowed, she asked, "But, really, why would you keep her around?"

"Because I still won that fight."

Casvir, she realized, thought more highly of himself than any man she had ever met. Yet, unlike most others, Flowridia suspected he had earned every ounce of greatness he held to.

So how long are you kidnapped for?

Flowridia rolled her eyes, and outside the carriage rolled along. "We aren't kidnapped, Demitri," she said aloud, uncaring if Casvir heard.

He stole you. You're kidnapped. But I'm bored; when do we go home?

Flowridia sat up, the book in her hand all that entertained her on the long journey. The prospect of speaking to Etolié had become a temptation as the days dragged on, both for boredom and for worry for her Celestial friend, but her resolve stood firm. Best to let Casvir think she had no contact with her kingdom. "Imperator, Demitri would like to know how long we can expect to travel."

Casvir didn't look up, his focus kept on whatever scroll his red eyes poured over. "I do not know."

She looked to Demitri. "He said–"

I know what he said.

She returned to her reading, and Demitri to his pouting.

"Can you not feel it?"

Surprised at the inquiry, Flowridia glanced up from her book and to Casvir's scrutinizing countenance. "Feel what?"

"The artifact. The draw grows stronger as we move forward, but you feel nothing?"

Flowridia shook her head.

"Try."

A memory tugged at Flowridia's mind, that of a young girl compelled to wander far away with no identifiable aim. She never had forgotten how her soul had yearned and drawn her toward the horror she had been searching for. If she dug into her core, she could still feel that pull to her mother, to the swamp. Perhaps this was something similar.

"What does it feel like?" she asked, setting her tome aside. "You said you feel it resonate with me. What does it feel like?"

"Following the initial burst of energy, the power has waned but never weakened. It's a dark thing. An absence."

An absence . . . The memory of Ayla's death was something she refused to entertain, yet the emotional rupture had been unparalleled. Flowridia remembered her fear, her rage, anguish . . .

But before there was pain, there came grey, a void of feeling. Before Flowridia cried out, the world had grown silent, static.

Now, seated safely within the carriage, Flowridia forced her eyes shut. With the memory came a rising swamp of feeling, the anguish she forcibly fought down. She understood, however, what Casvir meant.

It took a few steadying breaths, but her emotions settled, and with a final sigh, she let them fade away. Eyes shut, she lingered in that moment of weightlessness, that void of feeling, and from within her core she felt a presence—something far away—beckoning her to come closer.

Flowridia opened her eyes. "I can feel it."

"Good."

He said no more. They lapsed into silence.

Every night, she focused on Ayla's memory, mellowing her senses to center on her immediate surroundings. She daren't ask for help, lest Casvir think her foolish. But she searched for Ayla—

Instead, she would fall asleep to tender dreams. At least somewhere there was peace—and when there was not, she mellowed her thoughts, grasping onto the void of feeling, as Casvir had taught, marveling at the call she felt radiating from far away.

Days passed. A morning came when the carriage rolled to a stop. When Casvir moved to open the door, she followed, curious, and accepted when he offered a hand to help her step out.

The road had ended days ago, the sturdy wheels of the carriage more than capable of crossing rougher terrain, but now the trees thickened. An ancient forest spread before them.

Casvir moved to unhitch the horses. "Do you ride?"

Flowridia was remiss to shake her head. "I've never learned."

"Then you will learn now."

Flowridia stared up at the massive skeletal mounts. They seemed docile, yet substantially larger than they had ever looked before.

Casvir brought a saddle, and Flowridia watched helplessly as he latched the various leather straps. Feeling lost, and thus rather foolish, she asked, "Should I unload the carriage?"

"It would be useful."

She grabbed her bag, her spear, her chest with food, and set them carefully onto the grassy terrain. When Casvir came to join her, she watched him strap their belongings to the skeletal creatures. At times, she caught sight of their legs beneath the armor—pure white bone, the skin clinging to it in rotted shambles.

Flowridia stepped forward and extended a hand. It gave no recognition, no response when she gently rubbed her hand against its armored nose.

Dizziness struck. Flowridia stumbled forward, nearly falling against the skeletal beast as a rip in space appeared beside Casvir. The carriage rolled through, along with the hooded figure seated atop. The portal sealed shut behind it.

Faced with a saddled horse, Flowridia swore the beast grew larger with every moment she studied it. She lifted her arms, hesitant as she reached for the saddle, then brought them back down, unable to quite fathom how in Onias' Hell she was supposed to scale this gargantuan creature. It might as well have been a cliff face, and as she nonchalantly went to the other side—perhaps it would be shorter there?—she heard a familiar rumbling ask, "Do you need help?"

She couldn't help her sheepish grin. "I . . . do."

Casvir showed her where to place her hands, how to slip her foot into the stirrup, and when she struggled to pull herself up, with permission held her waist and helped her rise. Even with his aid, her muscles strained, but it was far less humiliating than she'd anticipated.

Demitri stared from far below. *And what will I do? Walk?*

"I can hold you, if you want to join me."

But he snarled when Casvir faced him, bristling his fur as he poised himself for attack.

Flowridia glowered, unimpressed at his antics. "Demitri, stop being so dramatic."

Demitri relaxed his stance, but his growl remained until Casvir set him upon Flowridia's lap. *If he does that again, I will bite him.*

"I suspect he'll bite you back."

A shadow covered them. With his sweeping horns and clawed hands at the reins, Casvir cast an ominous presence, the very vision of terror atop his skeletal, armored mount. "Your horse will follow; all you need to do is hang on." His horse stepped away, Casvir perfectly serene.

Flowridia's horse trotted along, and she tightened her hold on both the reins and Demitri. He grumbled against her chest. *I don't like this.*

"You're complaining an awful lot."

Wolves weren't meant for this.

"Well, if you get any bigger, I'll simply ride you."

Demitri's fur stood on end, but Flowridia planted a kiss on the back of his head.

Shadows caressed her skin as they disappeared behind the tree line. Though daylight shone high above, the thick cover of trees cast them into darkness.

Demitri began sniffing the air. *Something lives here.*

"What do you mean?" Hints of daylight flickered about, but the cacophony of sound reminded her of night. Insects screeched. Birds cawed eerily in the distance.

I wish I knew. But it's infectious. The land is sick, like a plague.

Flowridia increased her grip on the horse's reins. "Imperator Casvir? Demitri senses something." Casvir's horse came to a stop, allowing them to ride up beside him. "He's not sure what it is," Flowridia continued, glancing about the shadowed woods. "But it's something . . . something dark."

"Animals sense what we often cannot." Casvir slowly let his eyes scope the terrain. "There is a strange feeling in the air."

"Is it the artifact?"

"No. Our prize lies elsewhere. Keep your wits about you."

The dense forest grew darker, though evidence of sunlight splattered onto the leaves. Flowridia's hold on Demitri remained tight. The pervasive feeling of eyes watching behind the trees lingered, drawing a chill to her spine.

Something lived here. She prayed simply that Casvir's own ominous presence was enough to drive it away.

In the evening, when the rare spots of sun began fading, Casvir proclaimed they would set up camp.

The weight of Casvir's clawed feet on the forest floor snapped twigs and crushed the littered pinecones. Yet, he moved with a smoothness he should not have possessed, not a man of his stature and bulk. Though armor covered the majority of his sickly-blue skin, Flowridia saw hints of bulk underneath, the thin skin stretching to encompass his musculature.

Demitri jumped down before Casvir could touch him, but Flowridia accepted the offered aid and allowed him to lift her off the great beast.

Sharp twigs snagged at her skirt. The dense trees stood as sentinels around them, though the feeling of dread had yet to dissipate. "Why here?"

"This forest is massive, according to my maps," Casvir replied. He returned to his horse and began unloading various bundles and crates, most of which Flowridia realized she hadn't seen before. "I would prefer to set up camp while there is still light."

Flowridia moved to unload what few items burdened her own horse, until Casvir handed her a large, rolled up bundle. "This will keep you warm," he said. On the ground, he placed what appeared to be a large crystal. It illuminated, flickering in various shades of yellow and orange, and the heat it generated was a pleasant thing in the chill evening air. He turned his attention back to her. "Will you be comfortable sleeping outdoors?"

"Very much so," she replied softly, and a faint smile pulled at her lips as she untied the knot keeping her bedroll intact. It unraveled all at once, and she spread it smoothly across the unkempt forest floor.

Casvir rolled out his own but simply sat upon it, at the opposite side of the warming crystal. Flowridia found it amusing how different camping was among different members of the ruling class. Etolié shrunk her tent and treated it as an extension of her own bedroom, whereas Casvir seemed content to embrace the outdoors.

Speaking of Etolié . . . Flowridia stood up and smoothed her skirts. "Imperator Casvir, I'll be right back."

She gave no explanation, content to let Casvir think she needed to relieve herself or do some other private, lady thing and stepped away from camp.

Her feet snapped twigs, and Flowridia kept her hands out, her fingers brushing past ancient, thick trees as she stepped alone into the forest. The smell of damp wood settled into her mind, nearly intoxicating, and the cacophonous night creatures grew louder the farther she stepped from Casvir's camp.

When the flickering crystal became only a small speck in her vision, Flowridia dared to withdraw the mirror sequestered in her pouch. She tapped the glass, unsurprised when it began shining. It lit her face, casting her shadow across the trees, and within moments she saw Etolié's familiar, relieved face. The Celestial's bloodshot eyes suggested sobriety. "Flowers, it's been over a week—!"

Flowridia placed a finger on her lip. "I've hardly had a moment alone since leaving Staelash," she whispered. "I don't have much time, but I'm safe. We're still traveling."

"Where are you going?"

"I'm not quite sure, but neither is he." Flowridia shivered in the cool night air, but the joy of seeing Etolié's face—even so irate and worried—was unquestionably surreal. "How are things at home? How are you?"

"Things are fine. I'm coping. Lara says her council is debating whether it's worth finding a replacement for a certain general who won't be named, and in the meantime, they want Marielle and I to appoint a new third for our oligarchy. She's pushing for Zorlaeus. Terrible idea."

"He is about to be her husband," Flowridia offered, but Etolié shook her head, visibly irate. While sober, the Celestial adopted a far different persona than the wise-cracker Flowridia had come to love.

"He bears the stench of foreign leadership. Nox'Kartha owns ten percent of the gold that goes through the embassy, and I refuse to give them any more of us."

"Then, who else?"

"Between Thalmus and Sora?" Defeated, Etolié blew out a breath. "Neither of them want it. Thalmus refused outright. I told Sora she never had to show up to meetings and that she could just second everything I say. That's what—" Etolié cut herself off, smiling curtly. "That's what someone else did, and the arrangement worked well."

Flowridia saw anguish in Etolié's bloodshot eyes, and while the journey with Casvir had been unexpectedly delightful thus far, she longed to stand by the Celestial's side and comfort her.

"But what about you? Casvir isn't holding you for ransom?"

"No, Etolié. He's a perfect gentleman." Odd to say, but technically true. "I should go back, otherwise he'll suspect something. But give my love to everyone."

"I will. Stay safe, Flowers. Call again when you can."

The mirror dimmed. Darkness swamped her vision, her eyes having adjusted to the bright light of the mirror. A strange coldness enveloped her, a sudden chill from the woods. In the distance, she could faintly see the flickering crystal, and she made careful steps towards it, acutely aware of every snag on her skirt and caress of the leaves against her hair.

Something softer touched her cheek. Flowridia gasped, met with the sight of only faint shadows and stars fighting to peek through the cover of branches.

"Lady Flowridia?"

The warming crystal disappeared, covered by the silhouette of Casvir as he approached her.

Heart pounding, Flowridia stepped toward him, but flinched when she accidentally brushed against the cold metal of his armored chest. "I thought I felt–" She cut herself off, berating her own foolishness. "It's nothing. I'm fine."

Demitri, she realized, had followed, and he nudged her before standing on his hind legs to lick the bottom of her chin. She lifted him into her arms, startled by his weight. Her familiar had grown, but she managed to keep him snug in her arms. She followed Casvir back to camp.

"Next time, bring Demitri with you," Casvir said, his soft voice rumbling. "We are not the only residents of these woods, and I am contracted to keep you safe."

Flowridia nodded, the wording of his request less than benevolent, but the promise of safety still of some comfort to her racing heart.

At the camp, Flowridia sat on her bedroll and withdrew an apple from the chest of food. "I presume you'll be keeping watch tonight?"

"I will."

Demitri's nose nuzzled her hand. *So will I.*

"Demitri, Imperator Casvir is perfectly suited to keep watch. You should sleep."

He'll just read all night. I'll keep watch.

"I don't think reading a book dampens his senses. Our safety is guaranteed in our contract, remember?"

Your safety. Not my safety. I'm keeping watch for me, not you.

From the corner of her eyes, Flowridia saw Casvir glance up from, as Demitri predicted, yet another large book, the title of which was obscured by his enormous hand. "You may assure Demitri that his safety is linked to yours. Were he to die, your connection to the magical world would sever, and then you would be of no use to me."

The statement unnerved her, the reminder that his care was hardly altruistic. But, feeling shy, she didn't dare to comment.

I don't like him.

"You've mentioned," she whispered.

He can read my thoughts. And yours.

"I think he's just particularly good at reading people, Demitri."

"One who can predict his opponent will never lose a fight." In rapid sync, Flowridia and Demitri turned toward Casvir's voice. The man kept his attention on his book.

Flowridia's smile flickered in tandem with the crystal. "See?"

This is supposed to reassure me?

Flowridia simply kissed him in response. Exhausted from riding, she settled into her sleeping bag, and though her thoughts drifted to Ayla and the ear around her neck, she passed out within minutes.

But she just as quickly awoke from tender and erotic dreams, Ayla's touch lingering at her lips.

The flickering light of the crystal was all that met her eyes. High above, if she focused, Flowridia could see a star or two daring to reach through the recesses of trees. Her grip on the blanket tightened, her body chilled despite the crystal's warmth.

When Demitri's steady breathing met her ears, she curled herself around his soothing fur. She realized, then, that Imperator Casvir watched from opposite the crystal. But he just as quickly looked away, his quiet voice mixing with the sounds of night. "My apologies. Your sleep has been fitful for some time. I had debated waking you."

Flowridia shut her eyes. "I'm sorry for bothering you."

"I am not bothered."

Still, shame settled hot on her face. Flowridia pulled the blanket over her head and prayed that sleep stole her quickly.

"There is no shame in sorrow." Casvir's voice only caused her to tense.

Tears stung her eyes, and she let a shaky sigh escape from her lips. No, no. Not here. Not now. Not under the cold night sky with nothing but a De'Sindai and a sleeping familiar for company. Ayla was dead, but she was not gone. Crying was foolish.

Instead, she forced her breathing to steady, clearing her mind of cold fingers and predatory smiles. That emotionless void settled. Within her came the awareness in her soul of an artifact far away, resonating against something powerful within her.

Yet, with meditation came a welling of something hollow expanding inside of her. She forced her mind to clear and felt that same energy from beyond crackling within— stronger than she had ever felt before. It fluttered like a butterfly in her stomach, weightless and light. When she sighed, the pressure abated.

"Lady Flowridia, open your eyes."

Flowridia obeyed. Swirling around her was a purple mist, caressing her fingers, seeping from the very pores of her skin. It teased of something dark, and when she gasped, it escaped with her breath. Flowridia sat up, the mist dissipating.

Demitri awoke. Across from her, Casvir stared, the intrigue in his gaze as piercing as his red eyes. Flowridia's breathing grew hurried, and she stared at her hands, waiting to see if anything came.

Nothing. But then Casvir spoke. "Did you do that on purpose?"

Flowridia shook her head. "No, I–" She shut her eyes, releasing a steadying sigh. "I was trying to clear my head. I felt the artifact, just as before."

"But you went deeper into that energy."

Flowridia nodded, her hands trembling as she said, "What happened?"

"The most powerful branch of magic is born of pain, Lady Flowridia. Or, rather, to set aside that pain." He did not smile, not quite, but something in his eyes spoke of interest. "Do it again, but take care to not touch your familiar. The living do not take well to this."

Demitri inched back, visibly wary. Flowridia shut her eyes. After a few deep, steadying breaths, she felt her racing heart quell. The world grew silent around her; she focused on the energy waiting within.

When the same hollow expanded in her stomach, she opened her eyes. In her hands, that same mist appeared. She gasped. It vanished.

"Necromancy is called from an absence of feeling. For you to summon this energy by accident bespeaks ... potential."

Awareness struck her, a realization of what she had done. Flowridia remembered Thalmus' mantra from long ago and repeated it to herself. "Necromancy is one of the great evils of the world," she whispered.

"And who decided that?"

Surprised at the rebuttal, Flowridia brought her hands back to her body, pulling the blankets around herself as a fortress. She faced Casvir and said, "The gods. Sol Kareena, I suppose."

"Gods are finite, and while I respect their power, I have no need for them. Sol Kareena teaches that the dead should remain dead, but only adopted that principle in the last thousand years—after the Solviran Civil War and the fall of the God of Death. One deity's evil intentions do not bespeak them all. Before Sol Kareena's time, they say that Chaos herself held a talent for necromancy and dictated the affairs of the dead."

Chaos, the same Old God who caused the Convergence and destroyed herself in the process.

Casvir continued. "Sol Kareena teaches that it is evil, but once she had no stance. Her morals are not eternal. You are pledged to no god. What do you believe?"

In that moment, Flowridia realized she didn't know. She remembered the blinding visage of the Goddess, one who issued a warning, who had stolen the love of her life with a single blast of holy light.

A love who, Flowridia knew, was an aberration in Sol Kareena's eyes.

"Consider the economy of Nox'Kartha," Casvir said, and the glowing red of his eyes reflected the emanating crystal. "Mine is a land of opportunity. Any one of my citizens can be whatever he or she wishes. Menial labor is done by the undead, giving the chance for living citizens—citizens who had spent generations on the same farmland merely surviving—the chance to be something greater."

"I think that's a benevolent use of it," Flowridia said, sheepish in her posture.

"Consider something else: suppose I stop. The dead, useless sacks of meat otherwise, suddenly drop to the ground. My people—hundreds of thousands—starve within months. It is a fragile balance I maintain to support my citizens, and this balance would be upset were I to eliminate that which makes my economy even possible. There is no lower class, no peasants to toil the fields and be spat upon by high society. So, what is the greater evil? To relinquish the dead and live a so-called 'respectable' life or allow innocents to die?"

Flowridia frowned, even when Demitri came to sit in her lap. "I've been told my whole life that there are evil magics. But I think it's what you do with those magics that makes it good or evil."

Casvir nodded, his expression content. "But who dictates what is good and what is evil?"

"The god you pledge to," she repeated, this time feeling uncertain in her answer.

"Finite Gods dictate finite morality. So-called 'evil' has been accomplished in channeling this magic. But that can be said of all things. The Theocracy of Sol Kareena has accomplished far worse with honorable magics," he said, and Flowridia wondered if she imagined the chill in his tone. "As you said, it is how you wield it. I have yet to meet an altruistic necromancer, but I have met many a corrupt priest."

Flowridia nodded, her mind steadily processing his philosophy.

"We have a long way to travel. I will tutor you, if you wish to learn. You would do well."

Her racing heart sped up again. Blood pounded in her ears. "I'll think on it."

"Consider your potential. A witch can be a fearsome thing."

Flowridia knew that very well, thoughts of Mother invading her head. She recalled images of corpses shambling outside the door, half-eaten by fungal life. The dead in Mother's garden had remained barely alive, sustained and thus slowed in decay by necromancy, and of course when she had stolen the life from Aura, causing her to shrivel and die.

"I will consider it," she echoed, and she slid back into her bedroll.

Demitri's cold nose invaded her space. *You don't have to do anything you don't want to.*

"I don't know what I want," she whispered.

Whatever you choose, I'll help you.

"I'm surprised you approve of this."

I don't. Not if Casvir is involved. But since Ayla died, you haven't wanted to do anything at all.

He wasn't wrong, she realized. She had lived in a fog ever since. Too many distractions held her captive, sorrow having stolen her motivation.

If this is what it takes, I'll support you.

Her lips brushed against his cold nose. "Thank you."

Flowridia awoke with sore thighs. Apparently, riding horses took more effort than she might have anticipated. But she saw no use in complaining, and once they'd packed their camp, she let Casvir help her onto her horse.

Demitri elected to walk.

They went on their way. In the early morning, the forest could almost be mistaken for peaceful, with birds whistling high in the trees and a gentle, rustling breeze, one the leaves sang to accompany.

For hours they rode in silence, and Flowridia clung to every pleasant noise and smell. She felt at home, in a way, though the lingering chill of something dark prickled at her senses. But the trees were large, the smell of pine needles and damp earth intoxicating, and the clean air invigorated her in ways the manor never could.

Aimlessly, Flowridia realized she had begun to hum along to the harmonious forest. Nothing with a tune, simply notes that sang along with the quiet breeze and birds, and it brought a smile to her face.

Another tone met her ears, and Flowridia realized that Casvir had begun humming along with her simple tune. Blushing bright, Flowridia stopped. Ahead, her duet partner ceased as well.

Silence ensued as she focused on the road, legs sore from the jostling saddle. The birds continued, as did the wind.

Though self-conscious at the attention, Flowridia centered herself before humming again, her breathy voice tangling with the breeze. Again, the pleasant baritone met her ears, and she smiled.

Still, an odd feeling lingered in the air. Flowridia gripped the reigns of the horse, as though that would protect her against whatever malevolent force might be watching. She recalled Ku'Shya, the great weight in the air before her shadow manifested, but found it was not the same.

Near evening, a new sound met her ears—running water. Flowridia glanced at the sky and deemed it dark enough to speak. "Imperator Casvir? There's a river nearby. Could we camp there for the night?"

In response, Casvir adjusted their path in the direction of the running water. "We can."

"Thank you. I haven't washed my travel clothes since..." Rather than embarrass herself further with a response, she buried it behind a grimace.

"If I cared to smell you, I doubt I would be offended."

Flowridia found his words amusing, though she knew he wouldn't have meant for them to be so. She followed, and the trees barely seemed to disperse at the water's edge.

Casvir easily stepped down from his horse and went to help Flowridia before she could slip off herself. She let him steady her, accepting his outstretched claw. "Thank you," she said, thick brush cushioning her steps.

"I will give you privacy," he said as she stole her small bag from her horse. "But keep Demitri at your side." Then, he led the horses away, presumably to set up camp.

Once he had stepped out of sight, Flowridia pulled her dirty change of clothes from her bag. Her keen eyes quickly scanned the opposite shore, as well as her immediate surroundings, her demure heart shy of the prospect of leering eyes.

I promise I'll keep watch. Demitri had joined in searching the river bank. *If Casvir comes back, I'll tear his eyes out.*

"I'm not worried about Casvir. I trust him at his word."

But she had spent her courtship watched by a dark shadow and was acutely aware that haunted woods hid all sorts of nasty things.

She stripped from her clothes, holding the dirtied mass in her hands as she stepped into the river. The water drew immediate chills to her skin as it swirled around her ankles. But it was clean and clear, dirtying only when she scrubbed with her nails along her dusty arms and legs. She knelt, the water up to her knees, and let the rushing stream pull at the grime in her clothing.

Demitri watched from the shore, glancing between her and the scenery beyond. "How are you feeling?" she asked. "Tired from walking?"

Staying awake for watch might be more difficult.

"But you won't trust Casvir with it?"

No.

Stubborn child. She scowled at his attitude.

A slight breeze stung her skin, bumps rising along her flesh. After briefly debating whether or not to wash her lengthy hair—to which the answer was a definitive *no*—she stood, wet clothing in hand. With a mild groan at the realization she had forgotten a change of clothing, she returned to shore, the thick calluses on her feet protecting her from any bramble that might try and stab her as she trekked toward camp, awkward as she covered her exposed self from the watchful eyes of birds and insects.

The light flickering from Casvir's crystal met her eyes in the dark evening, and she hung the damp clothing from branches high above, content to let the night air dry them. She approached with care, stopping when she could just see Casvir. Sequestered behind a tree, she said, "Demitri, could you fetch my nightgown?"

Demitri ran toward camp, and Flowridia couldn't help but giggle when she saw him try to drag the thin chemise from their camp. Silhouetted against the light, she saw Casvir stand and snatch it, fold it, and then hand it back into Demitri's powerful jaws.

Grateful, Flowridia accepted the gown—the only clean article of clothing she had left. Dried enough from the autumn breeze, she shivered in the thin fabric, grateful to see her bedspread was already set, as was her chest of food. Flowridia sat on the thick blankets and wrapped the topmost around her shivering form.

With one hand holding the fabric secure, the other snaked out and grabbed a piece of fresh bread. Casvir sat quietly, absorbed in *A Treatise on the Evils of Divinity*.

Thoughtful, Flowridia asked, "Imperator Casvir? Do you control *all* the dead in Nox'Kartha?"

"I do."

"But there are hundreds."

"Thousands." Casvir set his book aside, casting his gaze up to her instead. "I do not micromanage their actions; I give a command and the less intelligent will obey until told otherwise."

Demitri sat close and Flowridia, grateful for the warmth, leaned into his touch. "What about the more intelligent dead? Ayla tried to kill you. There must be others who try and resist you."

"I never attempted to control Ayla, but direct her. I wanted an intelligent, focused servant, and forcing my will on undead leaves them disoriented. The more powerful dead do not naturally fall to my power, no."

Chattering insects in the distance stole her attention. Flowridia finished her last bite of bread and shut her eyes, letting her mind clear. Purple mist filled her hands, growing even lighter as she cupped it together. It formed a dense ball, one she swore she could float away with if she clutched it.

"Throw it."

Casvir's voice nearly cut through her concentration. Curious, she managed to hold the energy between her thumb and forefinger, nearly visible as it radiated inward.

A small tree, several feet away, became her target. She flicked it. The tree blackened. Flowridia gasped as it crumbled into ash.

"Harnessing these energies can be dangerous," Casvir said. "But your capacity for greatness would be a crime to let go to waste."

Dread filled her stomach, yet it came with an intrigue that sickened her far more. Against her better judgement, she shut her eyes and breathed, searching for that void within . . . then searching for a void without, focusing on the vision of Ayla.

Pain struck her head. She groaned, opening her eyes to see lingering traces of smoke dissipating.

She wasn't ready. Perhaps she might never be.

Demitri set his head upon her thigh, and she finally remembered to breathe. "I haven't made any decision yet."

"And yet you practice on your own accord." When she didn't respond, he said, "Sleep for now. You are exhausted. And your lips have turned blue."

A slight blush blossomed across her cheeks as she let herself fall into the bedspread. Covered by her bedding, she became a bird in a nest, hidden from sight and the chilled breeze. Then, she hesitated, her next words breaching a familiarity she hadn't dared to touch.

She whispered, "Goodnight."

Demitri settled in beside her, digging his way into her bundle of blankets. Across the warming crystal, a deep baritone replied. "Sleep well."

Amidst the quiet cacophony of dreams, a knock resonated against Flowridia's head.

"Danger," a tremulous voice whispered, and Flowridia knew it, knew it like her soul. That single word echoed, softer with each repetition.

Flowridia expanded her mind to grasp it, hearing only stilted words.

"Dawn . . . approaching."

Early morning light burned her eyes. Flowridia's head swam, sharp pain pounding with each pump of blood.

She sat up, groaning lightly, realizing that sunrise would be soon. The distant sky, or what she could see of it, sang of its eminence. Her forehead dropped into her hands, too heavy to balance.

By every god—she was *freezing*.

"Lady Flowridia?" Casvir's voice broke through her pained fog. "Are you unwell?"

"My head hurts," she mumbled.

"Your sleep was more fitful than usual. We can stay here a while longer, if you need rest."

"I don't think that would help. But could I have some water?"

She heard rustling pine needles and snapping branches. When she looked up, Casvir knelt beside her, a water satchel in his hand. As she drank from the leather pouch, he studied her pallid countenance, then lifted a hand to her forehead. "May I?"

Judging his intentions, she gave a quick nod once she'd lowered the water from her mouth. He pressed the back of his hand to her forehead, the chill touch nearly warm against her flushed skin. "You do not have a fever," he continued, thin lips drawn into a frown. The corpse blue of his skin contrasted oddly with hers—a stormy sky and the earth, never meant to touch. "But I will be providing more blankets for you tonight."

When he pulled away, Flowridia dragged the blanket over her shoulders. "Thank you."

Casvir stood and glanced toward the dense forest. "Are your clothes by the shore?" When Flowridia nodded, he continued. "I will fetch them for you."

Flowridia's head slumped, her cheeks burned, but her mind dwelled on the oddness of her dreams. *Danger*, Ayla's voice had said. Upon her chest, the ear hung, innocent and damning, evoking suspicions she could not silence.

Her spirit lingers . . .

All the while, Demitri snoozed on her bedspread, oblivious to Flowridia's frantic thoughts.

"Flowridia?"

A whisper, haunting in its familiarity, caused her to pause. She glanced about erratically, sure she had imagined it.

"Flowridia, my love..." And from the shadows, dressed only in sheer black lace, came Ayla Darkleaf.

Stunned, Flowridia stood from her cocoon of blankets, stumbling as her feet grazed the warming crystal. A laugh met her ears—Ayla's laugh, though more melodious than her memory would have given her.

Ayla kept one hand on the tree as she brought her other up to shush her. "Quiet, my love, or he will hear us."

"Ayla–" But no words formed in her throat.

Ayla stood so coy and small before her, each slight curve of her body visible within the sheer gown. Her cheeks held all the sharpness of Flowridia's memory, her skin as pale as the fading moon. "There is no trick," Ayla said, and the smile she offered was so gentle, so genuine. Her eyes watered with tears. "I'm here."

A warning prickled in Flowridia's mind. Ayla was dead. The body waited in Nox'Kartha. "How is this possible?"

"Do you truly think death could keep me?"

Flowridia let lithe, warm fingers intertwine with her own. Ayla held her gaze so perfectly, those blue eyes blinding, piercing. A strange dizziness caused Flowridia's aching head to spin. "Come with me, Flowridia," she whispered. She stood on her toes, gaze darting between her eyes and lips. "I have something to show you."

Flowridia leaned forward, hesitating before their lips could press together. Her other hand reached up to cup Ayla's face, so warm and flush under her sensitive fingers.

The truth was simple. But the lie was so easy to simply accept. She let her thumb stroke against the imitation, so alive and warm, inviting. Tears welled in her eyes and she hesitated, trembling as she touched their lips together, savoring this beautiful trickery.

A spell passed between them. Ayla went limp in her arms, fast asleep.

Flowridia carefully set her down on the forest floor before crying out. "Casvir! Casvir, come quickly!"

Footsteps. Demitri stirred only a few feet away. Flowridia turned around—

Only to feel a stab in her side. The world turned black.

Flowridia's head pounded, stirring her into consciousness. The world had flipped—rather, she was upside down. Utterly immobile, she realized she was tied by some sort of silken rope, one that wrapped around her entire form.

As her vision steadied, a familiar face approached, unmistakable with her severe cheekbones and icy blue gaze. Ayla smiled, but it was soft, not a hint of predator behind it. "She's awake," the interloper said, and Flowridia struggled against her bonds, wondering at the earthen walls, the musty smell. Torches illuminated the underground room, casting her lover's visage in eerie shadows.

"You're not Ayla," she said, her breath half-constricted by her bonds.

Ayla laughed, melodious and light. The wrongness of it bruised Flowridia's wounded heart. "No, but for a face as pretty as yours, I can be anything you want."

She noticed, then, the rest—the circle of women, all of them bearing arachnid companions, some with large spiders, others with scorpions. All were beautiful in their way, yet fire shone in their unnatural eyes, intrigue in their gazes. Flowridia recognized them as kin, fellow witches with their familiars and palpable magical auras. But to what god, she did not know. The doppelganger Ayla stepped back to her place in the circle.

Flowridia didn't recognize the foreign words they began chanting, only that they bore the stain of demonic tongue. Shadows rose. Sickness welled in her stomach, the raw feeling of helplessness the most frightening of all.

But was she? Flowridia fought to steady her breath, willing her fear to abate into nothingness.

The chanting stopped. Pressure against Flowridia's back caused her will to wither. All the witches fell to one knee. "Child of Odessa, you are beloved of Izthuni Spawn?" a new voice said, the accent dark and unmistakably demonic. Reminiscent of Khastra, but more pronounced, without the years of practicing Solviran Common.

But it was not Ku'Shya either, whose voice had caused the earth to tremble. This tone held a high pitch, girlish in its curiosity. Flowridia fought to twist around but only shook within her cocoon of silken bonds. "Who are you?" She stared at Ayla, yet addressed this new figure, whatever being of power the witches worshipped.

The pressure stroked along Flowridia's side, revealing first an impossibly thin hand, then another, and two more. The woman who faced her bore four arms and skin as blue as the evening sky. She was utterly nude, her lithe figure bearing almost no curves, childlike in its frailty, yet her lower half held a spider-like abdomen, four spindly legs supporting it.

Four glowing eyes scrutinized Flowridia's every movement, but otherwise the demon's face appeared elven, from her high cheekbones to her pointed ears. Black hair spilled behind her back, barely contained in its braid. "No mortal is knowing my name," she said, lips pulling into a smile. "Ku'Shya sends regards."

At the mention of the demon goddess' name, Flowridia realized she had fallen into something dangerous.

"Strange witch you are," the demonic entity said, "to bear a wolf familiar."

Panic coursed through Flowridia. "What have you done to Demitri?"

"I am leaving him. No use for him. But I am watching you long enough to know." It seemed her strange cadence was not for show; perhaps the Demoni tongue didn't translate well to Solviran. The demon spared a glance for the Ayla doppelganger. "And knowing you enough to lure you away."

A clawed hand reached up to grasp Flowridia's cheeks, her gaze narrowing. She bore no pupils, merely luminous pits of sickly yellow, enthralling and depthless. Flowridia managed to ask, "What do you want?"

"There is war in Sha'Demoni. Khastra's death is insulting Ku'Shya's honor, and she marches her forces through Izthuni's land. But though he and Endless Night are to blame, you are complicit. Demoni law states Endless Night must be slain at Ku'Shya's hands for balance, but Sol Kareena is stealing the honor. As beloved, you must take her place.

"But Ku'Shya would waste your death as a demonstration," the demon continued. "I am thinking something better." Flowridia dared to meet her eye, though the claws had pierced her skin. Blood ran from the cuts in her cheeks, threatening to stain her hair. "You are seeing for yourself the God of Order's power, his own part in Bringer of War's death. Demons fight for honor, but the world will still end. He is greater evil than even you, beloved of Endless Night.

"None can channel Ku'Shya, The Great Spider, and live. Only Bringer of War held that power, and she is now dead. But Ku'Shya is having the power to save this world from the God of Order. Will you give your life to save mortal friends? To allow Great Spider to wield you as a hero?"

At the surface, it seemed an honorable thing, to give her life for Soliel's death. Yet, to save the world from Order, only to deliver it into the hands of the fearsome Goddess of War, who ate those sacrificed in her name, arguably sounded like a worse fate. "There are other ways to save the world," Flowridia dared to say. The demon bore no eyebrows but still managed to look unimpressed. "My kingdom seeks orbs–"

"Your kingdom wastes valuable time. But if you will not willingly give your life for the cause, there are ways to force it."

The words shot a chill down her spine. The eight-limbed demon gestured to their surroundings, then twisted Flowridia's silken cage to gaze upon it. "We have been preparing for some time," she said, and Flowridia saw evidence of a stage, a pedestal, and below them runes drawn into the earth. "Ku'Shya shall burst from beneath the earth to show the world its true savior."

The demon turned to the ensemble of women, beckoning with her many hands for them to rise. Flowridia struggled within her bonds, forcing her panicked breaths to steady.

"Sing, Witches of Ku'Shya. Sing for her greatness; bid her to come."

Demonic chants filled the air in discordant tunes, some semblance of a melody within the cacophonous sounds. The ground beneath her rumbled, the etchings of sigils beginning to glow—demonic markings, surely devoted to The Goddess of War.

Flowridia breathed out and in, summoning a void within her, letting the familiar gaseous weightlessness billow from her skin.

The demon scoffed, mocking as she said, "Oh, very scary. Tiny death cloud. Necromancy will not save you–"

From the ground, skeletal hands burst through the dirt. The dead rose, swarming the witches in a storm of bone and rotting skin. The glowing ceased, and Flowridia fell against the ground.

Her head slammed the earth. Her vision spun. But at the release of her bonds, the ones around her body unraveled. Flowridia pulled the sticky, rope-like substance from her skin, realizing Demitri was beside her, having severed the silken prison.

Behind, came the Imperator of Nox'Kartha.

Casvir moved like a battering ram, a juggernaut of size and strength, yet each movement of his summoned mace—one that swirled with that same dark magic she sought to control—held flawless precision, his shield crashing through his enemies like a tidal wave. Each step came in perfect sync, yet he moved with a speed he should not have possessed at his size, ripping through the crowd with ease. When the dead fell, more rose at his feet.

Purple smoke clouded Flowridia's vision, unhindered by her scattered concentration. "Demitri–"

When a witch came with a knife, Demitri tackled her, his jaw quickly stained by her blood.

The demon moved with the grace of a dancer, her movements reminiscent of Ayla herself. In her four hands, she wielded summoned knives, similar to the imperator's, and dove toward him—

Only to be bashed by his shield. Casvir swung his mace at her fallen form, but the demon rolled aside, into a shadow—

And vanished.

From her peripheral, Flowridia saw the flash of a knife.

Pain crippled her will. Blood spurted from a wound at her throat. With the desperation of the dying, she shot out her hand, swirling with dark magic, and grabbed her attacker—the one bearing Ayla's face. "Flowridia—!"

Ayla screamed; she shriveled and blackened. The very life within her flowed into Flowridia, intoxicating and invigorating, filling her with strength unparalleled. Her wound sealed; the knife clattered to the ground. Her veins pulsed with power, yet the world grew silent to all else. Beneath the damning pleasure, she felt Ayla die in her hands.

A corpse fell to the ground. Flowridia's own screams filled the void.

She didn't remember when Casvir lifted her, kicking and sobbing. But suddenly he cradled her tight, despite her protests, against his armored chest. Her strength failed; she brought her hands to her eyes, tears mingling with dirt and her own blood. She saw, amidst her tear-stained vision, a cave filled with corpses, blood staining the walls.

The darkness dissipated. Outside, the wind stung her face. But her mind stayed blank aside from the image of Ayla's shriveled corpse.

Flowridia heard water. Casvir knelt and gently set her on the ground at the bank of a river. "Are you hurt?"

She finally removed her hands, though they trembled and cramped. Sunlight burned her eyes. Casvir's armor and hair were stained with gore; in carrying her, it had coated her too. She managed to shake her head.

"You will clean yourself," he continued. "I will send Demitri with your clean clothes. These ones will be burned. And then, we will talk." Casvir stood tall, his stare firm but not unkind, and disappeared behind the trees.

Demitri's touch broke her focus on Casvir. He rubbed his face against her hair. *Do what he says. You're a mess.*

Flowridia leaned in and faced the water, the reflection distorting the blood-streaked horror of her face. She immediately dunked her head in the icy water and pulled out, gasping. Her hands, still stained red, ripped at her clothes, desperate to free herself of their touch and memory.

She let the river carry them away. Naked, she stepped into the water and scrubbed, rubbing her skin until it burned and chafed.

She shivered as she stood. One hand wrapped around her chest and gripped her shoulder. "Can you bring me my clothing, please?"

Demitri rushed away, returning in moments, and Flowridia, more vulnerable inside than out, let fresh tears fall down her wet face.

Dry and dressed, though her hair dripped like rain, Flowridia let Demitri lead. Imperator Casvir, armor cleaned, his hair well-kempt, waited in a clearing alongside their horses. The undergrowth had been cut away, perhaps by Casvir himself, who sat patiently on a fallen tree. "Tell me what you saw," he said, gesturing to the space beside him on the log. Flowridia sat. Demitri settled beside her.

Through her tears, she relayed her tale—of Ayla in the woods, of the demon, the witches, the cave, Ku'Shya, the song they sang . . .

"I don't know what any of it means," she finally finished, the birds high above mocking her fear and sorrow.

"I had heard nothing of a war in Sha'Demoni. But I have heard little of any kingdoms' affairs since the beginning of our journey."

"She said my death would stop it." Flowridia asked as she wiped her face on her long sleeve. "She said Ku'Shya could defeat the God of Order."

"The Goddess of War is known for hubris. Perhaps she could have, but you will not be sacrificed for that cause. Demons cannot possess an unwilling vessel—not without powerful intervention."

Flowridia managed to nod, but still she felt residual terror, saw the vision of Ayla behind her eyelids, withered and dying—

She gasped to hide her sob, wrapping her arms around herself.

"But that is not what scared you," Casvir said. No question laced his tone.

Flowridia shrunk, her chest caving in. "It's because of me there's a war. Ayla wouldn't have killed Khastra if it weren't for me. She wouldn't have died if it weren't–"

Shame filled her cheeks as she cut off her damning words. She shut her eyes, tears falling silently down her face. "Nothing good came of us. Not for the world. And not for her."

Casvir's words were soft. "You are very young, Flowridia. Forgive my assumption, but Ayla was the first woman you ever loved."

Flowridia managed a nod.

"And you blame yourself for her death."

Flowridia's breath hitched as she nodded yet again. Demitri's tongue flicked out to lick the top of her foot. She tensed at the touch, though she knew he meant it to soothe her.

The eerie silence in the clearing stood in stark contrast to the dissonance of days past. No creatures met her ears as Casvir collected his thoughts. "Ayla was known for flaunting her conquests, but she kept close guard over what she deemed truly hers. I knew of her flirtation with you from Zorlaeus and from her own mouth when questioned, but her silence on the matter spoke volumes of her feelings toward you. She spoke of you freely one time. Only once—when she proposed a visit from your ruling council. Murishani jested with her when she mentioned your aversion to meat, teased that she would change her ways for you." He stared at Flowridia directly now; behind the shade of her hair, she could feel it. "All she said, quite sincerely, was, 'perhaps I shall.'"

He paused, and Flowridia, confused by the anecdote, finally faced him.

"The dead do not change. They are forever stunted, even the intelligent dead, physically and emotionally. Perhaps they learn, but they do not grow, doomed to stay fixed in time for eternity. It is why ghosts will linger for centuries at the place of their deaths, why vampires never tire of toying with mortals. Intelligent dead never change. So you must understand what an unprecedented, remarkable occurrence it was when Ayla Darkleaf fell in love. Something so contrary to her nature, to care for another person, but Ayla loved you."

Those words broke something inside her, some invisible barrier she hadn't dared to touch. As he spoke, quiet sobs shook her body.

"Her love for you was the only redeeming trait I ever knew in her. You tamed a monster. And her sacrifice, in service of you, was as kind and poetic an end as she could have deserved."

Sitting on that tree, tears streaming down her face, Flowridia felt a shadow pass across her heart, some coldness seeping into her chest. Yet the pressure within her ribs, the pain she felt upon Ayla's memory, began to wane. Flowridia released a gasping breath. For the first time since Ayla's passing, she felt she had drawn air.

She wiped her swollen eyes on her sleeve, and though her heart ached, a pained heart still beat. Pain meant she lived.

"You have been through a harrowing ordeal," Casvir said. "We can rest today, if you would prefer."

"I would rather ride," Flowridia managed, though her voice quivered. "I don't want to stay here longer than we have to."

"Of course." Casvir stood and went to her horse. From out of the chest, he pulled out an apple, which he offered to her. "Eat as we ride." And when she stood, he lifted her onto the horse, then placed Demitri on her lap.

Flowridia hugged her familiar close. "You didn't growl at him."

I don't like him. But he raged the entire time you were missing. Not at you; at himself. Demitri curled into her embrace, heavy in her lap. *He used my connection to you to find you again.*

"You worked together?" Flowridia said, a faint smile tugging at her lip. "This is a true testament of your love for me, dearest Demitri."

Don't go getting yourself kidnapped by witches anymore. I can't promise I'll do it again.

Her tears slowly dried as they rode through the forest.

The lush forest remained vibrant and green, but the darkness pervading the scene had waned. Flowridia felt that with the death of the witches, the forest might flourish as a peaceful haven once again.

The demon remained. The thought chilled her blood. Surely she would be targeted again. And she recalled her dream, the screaming warning in her head, and knew not what it meant. Instead, she clutched at the ear, the fabric of her shirt shielding her from the cold accessory, haunted by the ghost that was perhaps more real than she had realized.

But Flowridia did not voice those thoughts. Instead, in the evening when Casvir sat across from her, she heard him say, "You performed a remarkable feat."

Flowridia glanced up and saw intrigue in his stare. "What do you mean?"

"You stole the life from the witch, then used that same energy to immediately fuel your healing and save your own life. While not unheard of, the ability to wield dark and light energies on so fine a ledge speaks well of your finesse."

Behind the pain had been an exhilarating pleasure in draining the life from the woman . . .

"Casvir? Will necromancy only kill?"

"Like all magic, it has many differing facets," Casvir said. "Most of it is directed in death, but some will cause only pain. And, of course, there is the matter of raising the dead."

"Killing the witch with it. . ." she admitted, shy to reveal much more. "It felt . . . I felt like I was . . ." She shuddered, recalling Mother, the memory of her odd appetites causing revulsion to rise in her stomach. ". . . eating her life."

"In a way, you were. Had you managed to sustain the magic, her energy would have been absorbed into your body. A word of warning, however," Casvir continued. "Addiction to consuming life can hold dangerous consequences."

The word 'addiction' caused any pleasurable memories to wither and dry like the life she had drained. "Would raising the dead have similar consequences?" she asked, hoping her change of subject wouldn't raise any eyebrows.

"No. Instead, it drains energy, though once your subject is raised, it requires little effort, unless someone else seeks to inflict their influence over what is yours."

So a more powerful necromancer could steal from a weaker one. Flowridia resolved to be careful with any undead in Casvir's presence. "I'm not sure what I would do with that sort of power."

"Some creativity is often necessary. I use them as an army, but also as servants."

"Are they . . ." Her brow furrowed as she considered how to finish her question. ". . . lucid?"

"Only if I want them to be. If I want merely their strength, they are but shambling husks, compliant to my will. But were you to die, your intelligence is something I would seek to preserve, and hopefully your mind would be strong enough to survive such a process. Your soul would be forced back into your corpse."

Flowridia's fingers lovingly stroked through Demitri's fur, a dangerous inquiry fighting to escape. "What about . . ." She bit her tongue and shook her head. "Never mind."

Casvir's gaze darkened. "Ask."

"It's a lost cause-"

"You are a poor liar," he said. "Disappointing, really, given your other talents. You wish to ask about Ayla."

Flowridia recalled words from long ago, spoken by the aforementioned woman. "You restored Ayla's life with a blood ritual."

"I did. A blood ritual is not true necromancy, given that anyone with the knowledge and a dead body can attempt it. But it can restore a corpse of any age to pristine form, with the proper blood." She swore his gaze grew piercing, and she shuddered beneath his intrigue. "I will seek to restore her life once more, when you sign the contract."

The words chilled her blood, causing bumps to rise along her arms. "You will 'seek' to restore her life?" she asked, refusing to give any definitive answer. Somehow, her soul revolted at the thought, despite her tentative trust in Casvir.

"Countless rituals were performed," he said, the flickering of the crystal highlighting every line upon his face. "For years, any prisoner meant for execution had their throat slit above her casket, but for nothing."

Flowridia felt her breath fade. "Years?"

"There was no precedence on a ritual to revive her. Ayla is a unique creature—not a true vampire, yet holding the ability to create them. Surely you know she was the first of Izthuni's?"

Flowridia nodded.

"I even sought guidance from The Lurker himself. There is a temple in my kingdom wherein he may manifest, but he would not appear before me. I began executing those of a higher caliber, of powerful and noble blood, but the end result surprises me, even now."

Flowridia shut her eyes, Ayla's words fluttering through her head, of the memory of being awoken in a warm bath of blood. "May I ask who it was?"

She swore she saw the shadow of a smirk upon the tyrant's countenance. "She was the last remaining priestess of Neoma, the fallen Moon Goddess. She had been granted a familiar a millennium ago and lived across the sea within the shadow of the great valley bearing Neoma's name."

Flowridia asked, "She was set for execution?"

Casvir's face remained the same. "By my decree, yes."

Nausea welled in Flowridia's stomach. She let her gaze drift to the crystal, remembering that Casvir held a reputation for justice toward his own and brutality toward the world.

She would be a fool to forget that.

"I will pour all my resources into restoring Ayla's life, upon your signature," Casvir said, finality in the words. "But it may take time."

Casvir withdrew a book from the chest by his side, and Flowridia disengaged, exhausted physically and emotionally from the day's events. She shut her eyes and imagined Ayla's face, yet struggled between the witch she had murdered and the woman haunting her dreams.

She dreamt of romance; no strange warnings in the night.

One week, and they finally reached the edge of the cursed forest.

Casvir gave assistance with practical applications of necromancy but nothing truly awe-inspiring. More of the same—learning to summon the dark energy and hold it in her palms.

Not quite euphoric, the feeling of holding power so visibly in her hands, but therapeutic, in a way. Thinking about absolutely nothing at all gave her spots of peace amidst her turbulent thoughts.

The forest ended abruptly at the thick slope of a mountain. Lush greenery surrounded them, the meadow and flowers scaling the side of the mountain colorful and full of vibrant life. When they stopped to walk, Flowridia gathered a bunch, marveling at their size and lively energy as she wove one into her hair.

By nightfall, the summit still seemed miles away. Flowridia joined Casvir in setting up the camp, but she saw no purpose in her bedroll; the grass was plush, and all living creatures scattered in the presence of Casvir, including insects.

And so it was for three days. As they scaled the mountain trail, the scenery grew sparse. Gone were the vivid plants; all life faded as they ascended the mountain. The elevation could be to blame, yes, but the absent tugging in Flowridia's heart spoke of something else. Casvir's prize grew closer each day.

The grass became rough and yellow under Demitri's paws. None of the trees quite reached above Casvir, stunted by the height of the mountain and a force Flowridia did not have a name for.

The sun beat down, though the breeze blew cold, and amidst the bramble and dying foliage, Flowridia spotted an emaciated figure. She stopped her horse, peering at the small, four-legged canine cowering in the shade of a tree.

Animal life fled from Casvir's presence, and Flowridia had no doubt this small creature—a fox, she realized—would do the same if it were capable. Sliding down with practiced grace, Flowridia's feet landed safely on the ground, and she silently stepped toward the frightened creature. "There's nothing to fear, little friend. I won't hurt you."

The fox, though it was scarcely out of infancy, trembled at her presence but yelped when a shadow suddenly loomed over Flowridia. Casvir stood behind her. "What is this?"

"There's something wrong with it." With no thought to regard his station, she added, "I need you to step away, please. You're scaring it."

To her surprise, she was not struck down for insolence. Casvir obeyed and stood beside Demitri and the horse.

Flowridia reached out a hand, the kit much braver now that Casvir had retreated. The baby fox took a shaky step forward, and she whispered, "I can help you."

The fox stumbled into her outstretched arms. Flowridia cradled it—her, she realized—and held the little creature tight to her chest. Maternal instinct took hold, and Flowridia stroked the soft baby fur, yet she frowned as her senses sought for something tangible to heal and hold. There was no injury in this creature, no disease. Yet, the kit was dying.

It isn't hurt. Demitri's words had never been so unhelpful. *I don't think there's anything we can do.*

"No. I have to help." Flowridia's eyes met the enormous, black eyes of the fox. "I can't leave her alone."

There are probably thousands of others just like it.

"Perhaps. But this one is mine." She stood, careful not to jostle the fox. The creature attempted to burrow into her arms when Casvir helped her mount her horse, but she soothed the dying fox with her words and tender gestures. "I promise to protect you."

Each step forward only seemed to weaken the kit. The land around them matched her failing health. Where there was once sparse grass grew only dried weeds.

"How are your feet, Demitri?"

I'm fine.

It couldn't be comfortable stepping on dried husks. But soon the ground turned charred and black, a scar upon the mountain. No birdsong met her ears, only desolate wind upon the dirt.

Then, creaking. Rattling. Flowridia looked up from her sickly fox only to match the gaze of a skeletal beast. Not quite pure white, some skin still clung in macabre sheets, but any blood had long ago dried. It held a canine shape, standing much larger than the little creature in her arms. A wolf, perhaps, but older than Demitri, and Flowridia watched as it stumbled toward them.

Casvir took little note. With a mere wave of his wand, it crumbled to the ground.

The undead beast lay utterly still, but Flowridia shied away as her horse stepped past. "Did you raise it?"

"No, but I did dismiss it."

"Are there more?"

"Not anymore."

Though her heart raced, Flowridia managed to focus instead on the struggling creature in her arms. She breathed with her, the baby breaths reminding her of a much younger Demitri.

When night fell, Flowridia assembled a nest of cloth upon her bedroll. The small kit curled within, reminding her of Etolié sleeping in her own pile of scarves and blankets in the midday sun. A smile spread across her face, one that widened when Demitri curled around the sleepy kit. "Look at you, Demitri—a natural mother," she teased.

If I have to be a mom, I'm going to be the best mom.

The fox's health had not improved, but it had not waned, her body warmed by Flowridia's embrace and now the makeshift bed. The fox snuggled against Demitri's fur, content despite her ill health. Watching them together, the little kit and her familiar, showed starkly how much Demitri had grown—he practically engulfed the small creature.

He was growing so quickly; it filled her with both pride and dismay.

She thought not of Ayla. Instead, Flowridia struggled to sleep, reaching over periodically to feel if the little kit still breathed.

When morning came, a fog had settled, one that blotted out the rising sun. She was slowly becoming accustomed to the bone-deep cold of morning, assuaged only by walking. The sky blackened as they continued forward. Flowridia could see Casvir riding ahead of her on his steed, but the landscape became murky and shadowed.

A chill descended. Evening fell when they reached the summit, but they saw no stars. Jutting from the craggy rocks stood an ominous cave, and within, Flowridia felt that void swell unbidden in her core. The artifact was close.

But overshadowing any victory was the horrid awareness of the final breath escaping her tiny fox's lungs.

Flowridia gasped as the weight went limp in her arms. "No, no," she said, and forced a healing spell to leave her fingers. It touched nothing but dead flesh; nothing to repair because nothing lived.

Her feet touched the ground, but her legs trembled as fiercely as her lip. Casvir would think her a fool for crying over this, but tears filled her eyes nonetheless. This fox had been her charge. She had sworn to protect this little one, to save her. Now, that promise lay as dead as the corpse in her arms.

Flowridia sniffled, turning away when she felt Casvir's presence looming beside her. "Raise it."

Through her misted gaze, Flowridia stared up and shook her head. "I can't."

"Yes, you can," he replied, his tone harsher than she'd ever heard him use. "You waste time crying when this is well within your capabilities."

With care, she knelt onto the black dirt, giving no mind to how it stained her skirt. Her hands shook as she placed the still-warm body on the ground. Demitri joined her. *Don't listen to him. Only do this if you want this.*

Did she want this?

Flowridia's hands grazed the kit's soft fur. "How?" she whispered.

"Close your eyes, and clear your mind."

She did so, pushing aside her heartbreak, sensing that now familiar hollow in her stomach.

"Summon the vision of its spirit."

A vague command, but magic often delved into grey areas of thought. Flowridia recalled the little kit, envisioned the darling thing who sensed sincerity and safety and fell into her embrace.

"Now grasp it."

When Flowridia clutched her hands, she swore she felt an invisible weight within them. She opened her eyes and saw purple smoke swirling in her hands, bearing substance now.

Instinct took over, and she blew the smoke toward the body of the fox.

It twitched.

Flowridia gasped. The small creature writhed and pulsed as the mist ate its flesh, revealing blood and muscle and sinew. In seconds, only clean, white bones remained—bones that stumbled to stand on their own.

A small skeleton stood before her. Flowridia's eyes widened as the tiny undead fox pranced around.

"Your first undead servant," Casvir said, amused. "Unintimidating, perhaps, but yours."

Flowridia held out a hand, and the fox placed what used to be a muzzle into her palm. "How long will it last?"

"Forever, if you want. Or, until someone more powerful steals control."

A smiled tugged at Flowridia's lip as the creature rubbed her skull affectionately against her palm.

"You managed to keep the soul intact," Casvir mused. "Impressive."

"I think she may be the cutest skeleton I've ever seen."

Demitri leaned forward and sniffed the fox cautiously. *Most casters don't consider aberrations of nature quite so cute.*

"Demitri, that's the rudest thing I've ever heard you say."

I don't like her. She smells like Casvir.

Flowridia flicked him on the nose.

Casvir's voice interrupted their spat. "Our prize is almost certainly in that cave."

Flowridia pulled her attention away from the fox and stared into the consuming darkness before them. The cave exhaled cool air, chilling her body and soul. "We should go before nightfall. I don't think I could sleep with that looming before me."

"Darkness is nothing to fear. Fear what waits within it."

Appalled that Casvir might consider those words a comfort, Flowridia merely stared, incredulous, before replying with, "Imperator, with due respect, I'm well acquainted with the most feared monster in the dark."

"Perhaps true, but upon her death, what rose to become the next?"

She suspected, somewhere in her heart, that behind the stoic line of his lip, Casvir teased.

"Take only what you need," he continued. "The horses will stay outside."

When Flowridia stood, the tiny fox followed closely at her feet. The clattering creature hid in her shadow when she turned, and she giggled, heart swelling in adoration.

From the horse, she stole the maldectine bracelet and her spear.

Casvir waited by the cave entrance, his stoicism turning to a slight frown when he looked down at her feet. "I cannot account for its safety if it follows."

Flowridia looked down at her tiny pet. "I'm not sure how to tell her to stop."

"It understands you. Command it to stay."

Flowridia knelt beside the skeletal fox. "Will you stay here? The horses will keep you company." The fox tilted her skull. From the empty sockets, Flowridia could almost see the doe eyes begging to follow. "Casvir, she *wants* to come."

"I believe you are imagining things."

Demitri bumped into her side. *It'll get crushed by Casvir's giant claw feet. Leave it.*

Pouting, Flowridia half-heartedly said, "Stay," and when she went to follow Casvir, the fox sat perfectly still.

The cave stood ominous and dark, but Casvir trudged forward with no sign of apprehension. Flowridia followed, the metallic clanging of his armor oddly comforting as the light dimmed. She gripped the spear tight, catching the occasional glimpse of the carved floral scene on the shaft. Her garden felt so long ago, the joy it brought muted beneath the descending darkness ahead.

Here in the cold, black atmosphere, pleasantries such as gardens and flowers didn't matter. Flowridia kept a hand on the rock wall, letting it and the sound of Casvir's footsteps lead her forward.

A few more steps, and the light faded entirely. Flowridia's hand touched rough stone, but she stumbled as her feet met unstable ground. She slipped.

Catching her fall, her hands split open against the ground. Stinging pain pulled a gasp from her throat. She sat back on her knees with a pitiful groan.

"Flowridia?" Casvir's voice came from above. "Are you hurt?"

"I'll be fine." Rocks threatened to tear the taut skin of her knees. A healing spell passed through to her hands, and she prayed no rocks settled underneath the patched skin. That would be unpleasant to fix later.

But the bit of light the spell gave seemed to illuminate the cave for miles, reflecting a moment off the stone walls and the shined blood dripping from her palm. Casvir's eyes flashed red, refracting the light just a moment before it faded completely. Again, she was drenched in darkness.

Casvir's clawed hand gripped her own and helped her to stand. "I see better in the dark than you do. I should have taken that into consideration."

"I'll be fine–"

As she spoke, a flash of white light appeared in Casvir's hand. A small crystal, one that gave no heat but shone like a star, rested in his hand. "You have a greater connection to the artifact than I do. Lead the way."

Cold seeped from the stone floor and through Flowridia's thin clothing. But the cave stayed wide and open, for which she was grateful. The mere thought of crawling on her hands and knees in the dark caused her to shudder.

Soon, not even the wind blew through the craggy rocks. All was silent, aside from the shuffling dirt beneath their feet.

Ahead, the cave widened. Something radiated from within, and when Flowridia stood to block the light, her silhouette revealed the faintest flickering of purple within the void of black.

Two steps forward, and the light shone once again. The enormous inlet stood hundreds of feet high, the shadows deep from Casvir's crystal. At the center, a black orb emanated a purple, gaseous substance. It sat at the center of an altar, one crudely constructed from thick, ancient bones.

Casvir strode forward, but at the first crunching of dirt under his feet, the ground shook. The altar rose, dust and rocks sifting as the bones shifted. The earth upturned as more bone appeared from beneath, revealing the altar as something far more ominous—first a skeletal claw, larger than Casvir, and then gargantuan bones. A creature of fabled stories appeared, long thought extinct, but unmistakable once the skull came unearthed: a gargantuan dragon made of bone, whose eye sockets suddenly glowed that same deep purple. It stared straight at Casvir, the orb secured in its claw.

A wicked chuckle echoed across the length of the room, and Flowridia saw lust glinting in Casvir's eyes as they wandered the length of the monster. He handed her the glowing crystal. "I weaken it," he said, daring to match the dragon's stare. "Then, I claim it."

"How can I help?"

In his hand appeared the familiar summoned mace, knitted together from dark energy. "Stay out of the way."

The dragon roared, and the dirt floor, as black as the scenery outside, rumbled. Skeletal hands burst from the earth, clawing their way from the ground. Flowridia shrunk back into the wall, clutching the spear as clattering bones threatened to deafen her. They rose, erratic in their motions, some wielding rusted weapons and others simply claws.

When the dragon roared, they rushed to Casvir, a great army of the dead. But the Tyrant of Nox'Kartha merely smiled. He raised a hand; they stopped, some invisible force holding them enthralled, suspended in limbo. Whatever compulsion drove them shattered. They broke formation and waged their attack on the dragon instead.

It seemed Casvir was the more powerful necromancer.

Weapons struck the dragon, rusted swords and nails clawing at the monstrous bones. But none struck as brutally as Casvir. Amidst the sea of dead, he rushed, and with a single blow of his mace, a bone in the dragon's foot split.

The monster roared. Crackling, purple lightning suddenly danced across the contours of its form, illuminating the room in near blinding, magical light. The lightning radiated across white curves and sharp turns. Shielded, it swiped, and Casvir narrowly leapt aside, managing to backhand the claw as he dodged.

Flowridia stood useless at the corner, realizing that the moment the dragon took an interest in her, she would surely be killed. Demitri, too, cowered beside her, fur bristled as he emitted a faint growl.

The dragon leered high above, and from its mouth it spewed flame. It shone the same color as the orb, and in Casvir's other hand, a shield appeared, congealed together by that same dark matter composing his mace. She saw him falter at contact, and though the dead climbed the mountain of bones and tried to pierce the monstrous form, she feared for his life.

One man and an army of death—but against an ancient dragon? Flowridia took a step toward the cave, but then the dragon barraged straight through the crowd, wings of bone suspending him in the air through magic she could not fathom—

And dove toward her.

It the moment before its claw swiped to steal her, Flowridia recalled a memory she cringed to consider, the damning mistake of utilizing healing magic on Ayla Darkleaf a lifetime ago. She remembered holding the white orb, sensing no malevolence.

She summoned that power all the same. She called forth the familiar spells to heal the living, let the warmth seep through her skin, watched her very pores glow as a shield of divinity covered her skin. Paper-thin, yet she shone like an angelic host. When the dragon touched her, she toppled—but it flinched.

On the ground, she looked up in time to hear the dragon roar. She covered her ears. A death of purple flame billowed toward her.

A bracelet of maldectine waited at her wrist. She focused her energy; a shield expanded around her—

But the fire never hit.

Casvir stood between them, his shield held aloft to divert the flame. When it dissipated, he charged.

Casvir leapt up and shattered the ribs of the dragon. The monster reeled, an agonized roar tearing from its throat. As Casvir landed, the mace bludgeoned the bones of its foot.

Lightning disappeared. Favoring its shattered foot, the dragon tried in vain to swipe Casvir with its tail. The great imperator dodged and shattered the small bones at the tip.

Then, Casvir dropped his summoned weapon and shield, letting them dissipate into the void. He raised his arms, audacious and proud as he stared down the dragon.

The echo of a roar reverberated against the walls, but the dragon itself grew silent. It held eye contact. Crouched on the ground, Flowridia watched their standoff with fear. Nothing moved; not the dragon, not Casvir, not even the undead surrounding them.

The glow in the dragon's eyes flashed. Slowly, bones creaking, it bowed its head before the Tyrant of Nox'Kartha. Casvir let his clawed hand touch the skeletal nose. "Come forward, Lady Flowridia. Meet my new pet."

Flowridia used the spear to stand. "It's tamed?"

"As docile as your little fox," he said, his wide grin unfamiliar and eerie.

The dragon offered a hand. Between its claws was a black orb.

A pit formed in Flowridia's stomach. Instead of providing light, it seemed to absorb what little the crystal in her hand gave off. True darkness; a perfect antithesis to the white orb held by the Theocracy.

When Casvir's hand touched the orb, a deep purple cloud emanated, engulfing him in a black hole of energy. The force beckoned to her, but Flowridia clung to the ground, unwilling to be ripped apart by the energy the orb craved. Was that all necromancy did? Consume the living?

A malevolent aura radiated from Casvir's form. The energy pulsed, bursting into the crowd of undead, bubbling only around her and Demitri. Everything it touched disintegrated. Bones shattered and clattered to the ground; their weapons turned to dust. Nothing but ashes remained.

The cloud dissipated. Casvir stood tall and thoughtful, the orb held at arm's length. "These are what the Old God seeks?" He brought the orb closer, the threat of a smile once again pulling at his thin lips.

But he tucked it away, the orb disappearing into his armor. Casvir offered Flowridia a hand. "Your services have been invaluable," he said as he helped her to stand. His grip was gentle, mindful of the scrapes on her hands and arms. "Thank you for your aid in finding this artifact."

"Well, we did have an agreement," she said, careful in her choice of words. So this was the artifact, one of the very orbs she sought. It was as lost to her kingdom as the ones the Old God held himself.

By every god—how would she explain this to Etolié?

"An agreement I will happily keep. The power in this orb should make it trivial to find another." Casvir's gaze drifted to the colossal bone behemoth. "This will take some creativity to transport home. In the meantime, I will return you to Nox'Kartha."

Casvir brandished his claws and ripped the air; a wave of vertigo struck Flowridia. Her stomach lurched, Demitri stumbled, but what began as a tearing in space split into a hole, one that shone black and ominous.

Flowridia stepped through the portal.

Chapter 5

Nox'Kartha came into view, and Flowridia nearly collapsed onto the desk.

She recognized Casvir's office, as sparse as when they had left it. Seeing Demitri stand beside the desk jarred Flowridia's unsteady soul back into her body. She gripped the wood, willing her legs to balance as she glanced between the rich design and Demitri's powerful frame. With wide eyes, she said, "Demitri, you've grown."

When they'd left, the young wolf had barely reached her thigh. Now, he stood well above her waist, able to lick her shoulder with ease if he tilted his head, with a frame that had bulked out to match. Demitri was not a child; she knew that in his ever-lengthening limbs and surly attitude. But among the trees and foliage, he had shot up like a weed.

Demitri, however, merely tilted his head. *Not at all. You've just shrunk.*

Casvir appeared behind them, the portal disappearing as he stepped through. Reticence settled on his face as he studied the walls of his office, and Flowridia wondered how he'd ever been convinced to settle into a castle. "Casvir," she asked, "how long were we gone?"

"A few weeks," he replied, his gaze falling to the orb in his hand. It no longer crackled but waited, docile and ominous.

Flowridia looked back at Demitri. "You've grown at least a foot."

More than that, I think.

She patted his nose, an impish grin dominating her features. "Your voice is the same."

He growled; she giggled.

"Your supplies have been taken to Ayla's bedroom," Casvir said, cutting off their exchange, "including your new servant."

Relieved, Flowridia thanked him, and moved to leave the room when he continued. "There is still the matter of your demonic capturer. We must assume you are still in danger."

Flowridia hadn't forgotten it. "Am I in danger, even here?"

"Because of Ayla's talents for stepping between worlds, my castle has no protections against those who can walk in shadows. It will take time to remedy. Stay in public areas and Ayla's room; the black sand will protect you. Bring Demitri with you wherever you go. Your safety is dictated in our contract and thus paramount." Casvir held up the orb, intrigue flashing in his brilliant red eyes. "It may take time to unravel the extent of this orb's power, but we will find one for your kingdom."

She thanked him and excused herself, then shut the door behind her once all her familiar's bulk had joined her in the hallway. "If you continue at this pace, you'll be too big for the hallways in Staelash."

Then make them bigger.

"Do I get to ride you instead of my horse?"

No.

"No?"

No.

"You'd barely feel me. Ana could ride too."

Were Demitri capable of raising an eyebrow, Flowridia knew now would be the time. *And who is Ana?*

"My fox."

Your undead servant has a name?

"She does, yes. I just thought of it."

Are you going to be this attached to all your precious aberrations of nature?

"Very likely."

The plush carpet felt unnatural beneath her dirty feet. She cringed at the flakes of mud trailing behind her, longing for a bath.

At Ayla's room, she paused, mentally bracing herself as she turned the doorknob. The room felt colder than the hallway, colder than the woods. Exhaustion hit her as she shut the door, and she couldn't say if it came from spending months in the woods or from the bludgeoning of memories.

Each glass globe brought tender feelings, cherished memories she clung to.

But Flowridia swallowed her emotions; instead, upon the desk was her bag, her spear, and her new undead servant sitting on top, wagging her little tail.

Her darling Ana, who did not yet know her name. A slight smile graced Flowridia's lips. "Ana?" The fox turned, perhaps distracted by the noise. A rattling of hollow bones met her ears as Ana jumped down from her perch and onto the floor. She wandered over and sat at Flowridia's feet, her skeletal tail wagging from side to side.

Flowridia knelt and let her fingers stroke against the smooth cheekbone of the small creature. When Ana pushed into the touch, she smiled and lifted the fox into her arms.

Demitri watched from the corner. *Why Ana?*

"Because it's a darling name, Demitri."

Does she actually have thoughts in her head?

"She must know something," Flowridia said, cradling the bony creature in her arms. "Otherwise, why would she be so affectionate?"

Perhaps she only responds to stimuli, like a plant.

"Then I'll care for Ana just as I care for my plants. I love them too."

Let's hope your love isn't wasted on something that can't appreciate it.

His tone sat unwell with her. She stepped closer before sitting against his warm fur. "Well, I certainly appreciate you, my dearest Demitri. If you get bigger, I won't need a bed." He grumbled; she giggled and placed a kiss on his ear. "I won't need a horse soon either." She couldn't help but smirk at his indignation. "You really won't let me ride you?"

You might stunt my growth.

She swatted him lightly with her wrist. "And when did I raise such a rude little boy?"

At least we know I wasn't raised by wolves.

"Funny, because I was."

Sleep stole them soon, exhaustion from weeks of travel settling in.

Flowridia savored the silent lingering between wakefulness and sleep. Demitri's deep breathing soothed her tired bones. Ana lay in her lap, utterly frozen like the dead creature she truly was. The chain trapping Ayla's ear tangled about her fingers, and in the stillness, she withdrew the small, familiar mirror from her pocket and tapped the glass, deeming herself truly and safely alone.

The mirror glowed a moment, and then Etolié's bloodshot eyes appeared, her face sallow and pale. "Kind of you, to grace me with your presence."

Surprised at her visage, Flowridia ignored the slight. "Etolié, when is the last time you've eaten solid food?"

"Literal weeks. Now back to you." The ire in her expression faded, worry seeping into Etolié's countenance. "Is everything all right?"

"Casvir and I are back in Nox'Kartha for the time being. We found his–" She cut herself off, wondering how in Onias' Hell she could explain to Etolié that she'd all but hand-delivered an orb to Imperator Casvir. ". . . his artifact." A question for another time. "We'll be leaving soon to find an orb."

"Good," Etolié said, and Flowridia noticed how the mirror kept swaying away from her face. "Flowers, while I am capable of tact, I pride myself on being honest with you. How has Casvir been treating you?"

Surprised at the inquiry, Flowridia frowned and said, "Perfectly well."

"So I've heard. Well enough for you to be incubating a parasite, if rumor serves."

It took a moment, but then Flowridia realized the implication behind Etolié's statement. "I beg your pardon?"

"Look, I know Ayla's barely dead, but I've heard a few too many whispers about you riding Nox'Kartha's throne–"

"Etolié, please–" Finishing the statement seemed too daunting a thing. Her skin crawled at the insinuation. "Casvir and I are friendly enough, but he's never— And I would never— He's a perfect gentleman, Etolié–"

"All right, all right. Flowers, I believe you."

Flowridia touched her face, realizing it burned. "Is that what people are saying?"

From opposite the mirror, Etolié nodded. "Thalmus has threatened more than once to march his way to Nox'Kartha and take you back."

Oh, Thalmus. Flowridia's homesick heart swelled. "Send him my love and reassurance that I'm fine."

"Well, while you're off gallivanting, the quest to trade for the Theocracy's orb continues with absolutely zero success. Despite certain Nox'Karthan deaths, Archbishop Xoran fears the next assassin will succeed and has politely refused to reopen the negotiation. Without it, searching for the rest is all but impossible. Orbs lead to orbs. I only hope that you and Casvir find one sooner than not. Then, we have a hope of stopping Soliel."

"Have you heard anything of him?"

"Not since he appeared in the Theocracy. Believe me—we're trying. But he's a slippery bastard, and we have little to go off." She smiled curtly, far too wide. "So if you hear of any magic explosions or world-ending type things, do let me know. It'll be more than we've heard."

"How's the empress dealing with all of this?" Flowridia asked, but she immediately regretted the question when Etolié grimaced. "Sorry–"

"No, no. Nothing wrong with asking. Understand, Flowers, my baby Lara has only been in power a few months, and the pressures of ruling are getting to her head. That, and she's barely had a moment to mourn her father, much less a half-demon who shall not be named. She's not coping well. Kind of you to ask, though. She thinks very highly of you."

Flowridia smiled at the thought, confused but amused that the neighboring empress thought of her at all.

"How are you, Flowers?" Etolié continued, the smile at her lips much too wide. "Ayla's gone."

Flowridia presumed to not imagine the insincerity of her concern. She tensed at the words. "She's gone, yes."

"And how are you dealing with–"

"I'm not." Flowridia clasped her hands together. "I'm still processing everything."

Etolié held some semblance of tact, it seemed— Flowridia was grateful the Celestial didn't push. "Good for you, Flowers."

"Etolié, do you know anything about a war in Sha'Demoni?"

Etolié shook her head, frowning as she did.

"When Casvir and I were in the woods, I was kidnapped by a demonic acolyte of Ku'Shya. She said Khastra's death was an insult to Ku'Shya's pride and that she'd started a war."

Etolié's frown appeared permanently etched on her features, forcibly stoic at the mention of her dead friend's name. "Makes sense. The Goddess of War is known for being a prideful, vengeful bitch. You were kidnapped?"

Flowridia withheld the detail of Ayla's doppelganger, shy at any mention of her deceased love, but told the rest—of waking encased in what she was now fairly confident was spider silk, the witches, the demon—

At which point, Etolié interrupted her. "She couldn't have been a full demon if she manifested in our world. Four arms, you said?"

Flowridia nodded.

"Kinda spider-y?"

"Very much so."

"Sounds like a Ku'Shya wannabe. Tell me more."

Flowridia spoke of the threat of her own death, of the ritual, and of her rescue. "Should I have done it, Etolié?"

"Absolutely not. Like you said—delivering the world into Ku'Shya's hands would be the literal opposite of a good thing. With the hammer missing from the Theocracy, we're already properly fucked–"

"The hammer?"

"The 'name we don't mention's' sworn duty on our world was to prevent her mother from stealing back her weapon—that over-polished crystal monstrosity."

Etolié smiled, but Flowridia saw hurt behind it. "Ku'Shya stole it?"

"It's missing from the Theocracy. If she's allowed a host, she might be able to fight Soliel—but what would stop her from causing her own apocalypse when she wields the orbs next? She can't take them to Sha'Demoni, but no one said she can't use them when she's here. She'd have everything to gain by wrecking half the world's populace— queen bitch of Sha'Demoni gains power through bloodshed." Etolié looked away, off in the distance of her library. "If a demonic entity came once, it'll come again. Be careful, Flowers."

Flowridia's blood chilled at the thought of the strange demon who had disappeared into shadow. "I think I'm as safe here in the castle as I could be." Etolié's smile highlighted her sallow cheeks. "Etolié, are you all right?"

"Breathing hurts." Etolié kept her smile, but Flowridia saw her jaw clench, watched the Celestial swallow back whatever else threatened to spill out with her words. "You don't know how much you need something until it's brutally murdered by your ward's lady-friend."

The words were said in jest, Flowridia knew, but they crawled beneath her skin and stung. "Will you eat something? For me?"

"Why ya gotta phrase it like that, Flowers-"

"Because you won't take care of yourself for you."

For the first time since leaving, Flowridia felt impatient to go home.

Etolié said nothing, merely stared off beyond the mirror, lavender eyes glistening. "For you," she whispered. She swallowed again, this time with audible sound—and pain. "Oh look, a visitor. Gotta go, Flowers."

"Etolié-" The Celestial's face disappeared, replaced with her own visage.

There was nothing she could do for Etolié except find the orb as quickly as possible. She wondered, idly, if offering a prayer to Eionei might do something; Etolié had once said Nox'Kartha held temples to every god—demons and angels alike.

She would be wary of Ku'Shya's domain.

Flowridia's body craved movement, her mind fully awake. Demitri's breathing remained steady as she stood. Ana jumped from her arms and followed closely at her feet, tiny bones pitter-pattering on the floor wherever she stepped.

Draped lovingly on the soft couch in the corner, several dresses caught Flowridia's eye, ones she knew hadn't been there the last time she'd visited. Upon the pile was a note, written in gorgeous script, gaudy flourishes in each stroke:

These were found among Ayla's projects. I could only presume they were meant for you. I hope they bring comfort to your broken heart.

It wasn't signed.

She went to investigate the apparent gift. Five total, she realized, each uniquely designed. A deep green drew her eye, and she lifted the fine silk into her arms, admiring the beaded bodice and train, though the revealing neckline brought a blush to her cheeks.

Another held all the majesty of the night sky, deep blue with silver stars, and one reminded her of a pale, yellow rose with speckles of green. But the one she chose had cream-colored lace, and each embroidered floral masterpiece upon the bodice held detail unparalleled.

Holding the extravagant garment reminded Flowridia that she hadn't had a proper bath since leaving Staelash.

Did vampires—or creatures like them, her mind habitually corrected—have to bathe? Perhaps only for aesthetic reasons.

There was no washroom connected to the bedroom. With care to keep the beautiful dress away from her dirty skirts, she left the room, Ana stumbling around her feet.

In the hallway, she sought a servant, anyone to help her find a path. But as she walked, she passed by one of the many ominous pillars of black sand. Before, she had felt something dark radiating, but now she swore she saw each individual grain and knew it was not truly sand but pure, radiant energy, condescend and weaponized. She herself could conjure dark matter into a ball, but this was a thousand times condensed. She gazed into the abyss, knowing if she were to thrust her hand in, she'd withdraw a stump.

It was docile to her. Any intruders would be met with a hellish fate.

"Lady Flowridia?"

Flowridia turned, happy to see one of the very hooded servants she sought.

"Casvir inquires to your well-being."

"Tell him I'm well," she replied. "How long did I sleep?"

"Half a day. The sun has set and risen."

Travel took a toll. This explained the rumbling in her stomach. "Could you help me find a place to bathe?"

It gestured for her to follow with its draped sleeve. "Lady Ayla travelled in shadows and had no need for her washroom to be connected to her bedroom."

The servant led her to what appeared to be a blank stone wall. It knelt, or bent rather, or did whatever sentient cloth did to move about, and brushed its sleeve across the wall from floor to the ceiling. Where it touched began glowing, revealing a perfect line, and once he'd reached the top, it parted, showing the clouded entrance to a room.

"She also had no need for a door," the servant explained, "and preferred her privacy." It gestured forward. "When you are ready to leave, simply trace a line up from the other side of the wall. It will part."

Flowridia nodded and lifted Ana into her arms before stepping through the wall.

As she did, the clouds grew sharp with detail. The wall sealed behind her, but Flowridia hardly noticed, too enthralled by the scene—a small room with ornate stonework carved into the walls and a washbasin in the center. Thorns and roses surrounded the tub, carved from stone yet lifelike enough to be their own entity. Upon the wall, it seemed an artist had thrown crystals in perfect, random order, glowing in blues and purples.

Flowridia set Ana on the floor and the dress upon a stone shelf at the corner beside a floor-length mirror. At the tub, a faucet caught her eye, and soon water gushed into the large bath. As it filled, she stripped herself of her rough travel dress and realized how much dirt clung to her skin. She removed the ear from around her neck and placed it on top of the clean dress, but not without a lingering caress to its shriveled curves. She wondered what Ayla would say, what she thought—what her awareness even was.

Enough to scream a warning in the night. Perhaps to comfort her in dreams. Flowridia was an insane woman by appearances, cradling the ear of her dead lover, but she could accept that—witches were known for far madder things.

The water did not need warming. Flowridia stepped into the bath, releasing a sigh as tension from her exhausted muscles seeped into the water. How often had Ayla sat here and soothed herself in the calming water? A blush colored her cheeks.

It seemed a lifetime ago, their encounter in Flowridia's tub. Yet, it had been scarcely two weeks before Ayla's passing, and in those days so much had shifted, both in Flowridia's heart and Ayla's. To remember those imploring words, the ones that burned bright and painful in her dreams: *"I love you, Flowridia. Please, never leave me."*

Tears welled in Flowridia's eyes, mixing in with the warm bathwater as she scrubbed her body.

In another life, they had run—far from duty, from contracts and gods. Ayla longed for fine things, but Flowridia would have given all to live alone in the woods, Demitri in tow, and care for her, hold her, teach her all that nature could offer. An odd family they would have made, but a family nonetheless.

Flowridia rinsed the soap from her hair, the fantastic impossibility of her dream evoking a quiet smile from her quivering lip.

It quickly faded. Casvir would own them both, should she sign her name upon the dotted line.

Flowridia wiped away her tears, though they still flowed as she stepped out of Ayla's bath. Rows of towels hung on a rod, and Flowridia let a comforting embrace dry her. She brought it to her nose, wounded when it smelled merely clean and not of Ayla's touch.

Thus began the arduous process of drying her hair. Her skin had darkened beneath the sun's light, more like unto the earth she tilled, but her hair remained a lighter shade, the color of amber at sunset. Her reflection stared back eerily in the dim light, too reminiscent of Mother. Perhaps she had begun the final lapse into adulthood, with her formidable cheekbones and ever-lengthening limbs.

Still, it chilled her. Flowridia looked away, instead changing into the beautiful gown. A hint of the plain, metal chain peeked around her neck, but the ear itself settled between her breasts, hidden behind the lacy fabric.

When she returned to her room, she was met with a rather grumpy looking wolf. *I need food.*

"We can find food, Demitri."

Demitri poked her with his nose. *You need food. I've grown, and you've shrunk.*

"Travelling will do that."

Flowridia set her dirtied clothing in a neat pile beside the couch, then the three of them went to the hall—she, Demitri, and tiny Ana, whose nails kept catching in the thick carpet.

Flowridia laughed as she lifted the little skeletal creature into her arms and headed towards Casvir's office, the only path she knew.

When she found it empty, Flowridia clutched Ana tight to her chest, realizing she was absolutely lost. Accepting the risk of treading down unfamiliar paths, Flowridia traversed a different hall and came across a staircase.

She headed downward. The hallway she appeared in looked indistinguishable from the previous floor, complete with plush carpet and black sand. Flowridia stayed at the center, wondering to which god she would have to pledge to stumble upon a kitchen.

But there were signs of life here, at least. Various servants—living De'Sindai, instead of the oft-seen hooded figures—chatted within rooms as they dusted and cleaned, and whose gossip Flowridia didn't care to listen to.

"Did you know the Viceroy has been planning the wedding since the proposal? Oh, I hope I'm invited to Staelash—"

And another room. This time, she lingered.

"Imperator Casvir is back, they say. The girl is still with him."

"Who is she?"

"The Grand Diplomat of Staelash, but they're saying she has higher titles in mind."

"You mean—"

"With Imperator Casvir?"

"He's never shown interest in—"

The trio of servant women stopped, suddenly aware of the wide-eyed girl standing in the doorway. Flowridia smiled, hoping it served to hide how awkward she felt at the attention. "Speaking of whom," she said stiffly, "do you know where Casvir is?"

One De'Sindai girl. with fiery magenta skin and hair braided down to her knees, nodded and pointed in the same direction Flowridia had been traveling. "Try the throne room."

She nodded and resolved to never speak a word of what she'd overheard to Casvir.

Flowridia continued forward, when Demitri's voice settled into her head. *So, you and Casvir?*

"Don't even joke, Demitri."

I'll bite his face off. That'll settle any—

"Demitri, please," she spat, but she kept her annoyance soft. "I only want to know how a rumor like that was started."

Even Staelash had heard the vile conspiracy.

Flowridia reached a massive set of double doors, ones that swung open at her touch. Within, her steps echoed across high ceilings and polished stone. Upon the walls were banners bearing the emblem of Nox'Kartha—rich arrays of red and black, upon which a gold coin embossed within a skull sat centered—along with all manner of trophies and weapons. Opulent and beautiful, yes, yet it radiated the slightest aura of menace. Marielle's throne room had displayed velvet and trinkets; Casvir's throne room matched the ruthless tyrant in grandeur.

Centered upon a pedestal of stairs was a lone throne, crafted from iron and plain cloth, bereft of finery. Beside it sat the very dragon she and Casvir had fought and subdued, utterly still though its eyes glowed an ominous purple. Its skeletal mass easily fit within the expansive room, docile as it loomed before the small crowd.

Standing tall was Casvir himself, surrounded by a gaggle of skittish De'Sindai and a lone speaker Flowridia recognized.

". . . really is in need of an upgrade. Imagine the spectacle! Any audience would see you, Casvir, seated upon a throne of bone–"

When Casvir turned at her entrance, so did the rest, including the handsome man Flowridia had met that first night, the one who had caught her crying in the hallway. Casvir's expression remained stoic as his red eyes bore into her, but the other man beamed, pure sunshine in every gesture. "Lady Flowridia! Your presence truly does brighten up this droll place." He gasped, utter delight in the gesture. "And I see you found your gift! The dress suits you perfectly, you lovely thing."

Startled at the attention, Flowridia dared to take a step forward, squeezing Ana tight to her chest. "Forgive me," she said softly as the man approached, wary of the eyes of the servants upon her. "But I don't know who you are."

The man's hand flew to his mouth. "No, no—forgive *me*," he replied, stepping forward quickly now. "I hadn't realized I'd been so rude." He stretched his arms wide and bowed. All of his actions seemed soaked in dramatics. "I am Viceroy Murishani."

So this was the man planning Marielle's wedding. When he offered a hand, Flowridia accepted, noting the saccharine fruitiness of his scent and the firmness of his grip. Unsurprising, really, given that he was the second most powerful man in this castle. "A delight to meet you, Viceroy–"

He waved off her words. "What are titles among friends?" He placed a hand on her back and escorted her forward, gesturing toward the skeletal dragon. "I was just telling Casvir what a grand display it would be if we were to craft a throne of bones—dragon bones specifically. Imagine, should any attackers approach, their fear when the very seat upon which Casvir rests turns into a *dragon.*" He smiled, his perfectly white teeth catching the light and gleaming. "What do you think, Flowridia? You seem to be a woman of fine tastes."

Casvir said absolutely nothing, looking unimpressed at best, and Flowridia fought the innate urge to stutter, unsure of how to answer. "I think it could be . . . something."

Murishani withdrew his hand from the small of her back, clapping in palpable delight. "She suits this place, Casvir, just as she suits you."

"I beg your pardon?" Flowridia whispered, ignoring the nervous rise of bile in her stomach.

"And here I thought our resident bachelor king would remain alone forever," Murishani said, a hand upon his heart. "But look at you—as beautiful as the sunrise. Of course he'd succumb–"

"Enough," Casvir said darkly, and Murishani promptly shut his mouth. Flowridia watched Casvir survey the room, the onlookers looking nothing less than shocked at the blatant insinuation. "Lady Flowridia is my ward and nothing more."

Murishani's hand rose to cover his mouth, yet Flowridia swore it only hid mischievous glee. "Was I mistaken, Cassie? Well, silly me."

Flowridia wondered what sort of death wish one had to have to refer to Imperator Casvir as 'Cassie,' but behind her, she heard the faintest beginnings of boisterous conversation from the hall.

"A pity," the viceroy said, with all the cares of a man who hadn't sassed the resident tyrant. "I was already naming your children; what lovely things they'd be, with her doe eyes and your enormous–"

"Viceroy Murishani," Casvir replied, and Flowridia shrunk at the palpable undercurrent of menace. "You and I will be addressing this in private–"

The doors slammed open, metal banging against stone. What Flowridia saw caused her to nearly teeter and fall. Ana jumped from her arms as they went slack; Demitri pushed against her back, keeping Flowridia upright.

Her presence filled the throne room, power in every hooved step. Flowridia swore that time slowed, the half-demon's entrance causing her heart to stop. Blue-skinned and tattooed in brilliant silver, Khastra was unmistakable, even with the brutal gash across her mouth—evidence of The Endless Night's onslaught. She wore no armor, and Flowridia swore it made the gargantuan woman stand even larger, every massive muscle beneath her thin shirt shifting as she walked. With sweeping horns to rival Casvir's—she stood a head taller at least, even without them—and a tail gently following behind her powerful steps, she spoke to the men flanking her on either side as her glowing eyes scanned the room. ". . . nothing to defend the citizens beyond the walls. The defenses of this city are adequate at best, but that is no excuse for–"

Her eyes settled onto Casvir and then the skeletal mass seated obediently beside them. "Imperator, I wanted to discuss the dragon."

Her accent held the familiar lilt, guttural yet charming, and Flowridia could only stare as Casvir nodded.

"The presence of a dragon would do well for protecting the villages beyond your city walls."

Faced with Khastra's back, Flowridia saw odd protrusions through the shirt—strangely flat and certainly not muscle.

Casvir said, "Tell me."

Khastra launched into an explanation filled with jargon Flowridia couldn't hope to understand, knowing full well she knew little of military tactics. But the woman spoke with an assurance and bravado Flowridia hadn't seen in Staelash. Well, bravado, yes, but only outside of official business. Many times, Flowridia had stumbled across Khastra and Etolié sharing some laugh in the recesses of the underground library, but otherwise, Flowridia knew the former Solviran General as . . . bored.

Flowridia understood, watching the supposed dead woman speak, why she was renowned. She also wondered, with all seriousness, if she'd fallen asleep in the bathtub—she couldn't say what was more outlandish: Khastra's apparent reappearance or Murishani's audacity in using the pet name 'Cassie.'

"Demitri," she whispered, all eyes in the room on the imposing woman, "is that really . . ?

She smells like death.

Flowridia's head grew light, disengaged until she heard a familiar voice say, "Tiny one?"

She looked up and met Khastra's eye, unsure if she were relieved to see that jovial smile or not, even as it steadily faded into surprise.

"General, I will consider your words," Flowridia heard Casvir say. "In the meantime, it seems you and Lady Flowridia have reason to speak."

With a respectful nod to Casvir, Khastra beckoned for Flowridia to follow her from the throne room.

Once the door had shut, Khastra stopped in the doorway. Unable to contain her surprise any longer, Flowridia said, "Khastra, how did this–"

"What are you doing here?" Khastra interrupted, her glowing eyes narrowing. A frown tugged at her elegant face. As she spoke, she crossed her arms, and Flowridia wondered if her biceps would burst through the shirt.

Flowridia had been on the receiving end of Khastra's scrutiny before, but an unfamiliar coldness permeated the former general's aura that froze her to the core. Steeling her courage, she rebounded with, "I could ask you the same."

"A story for a story, then," Khastra said, stance relaxing. When her gaze settled onto Demitri, the hint of a smile tugged on her lip. "He has grown." Then, she knelt on the ground and offered a hand to the skeletal fox. "A strange pet you have."

"She's my undead minion, as Casvir put it," Flowridia said, nervous at the admittance. Khastra was a piece of her life in Staelash, and she wondered how this new development would be received by the rest. "Khastra, why–"

"Of all the people to have a talent for necromancy, I would not have guessed you." Khastra seemed unbothered, and instead looked amused when Ana pressed her little skull against her finger. She returned to her feet—hooves, rather— and said, "You look half-starved, tiny one."

Perturbed at the remark, Flowridia was prepared to object to food for sheer spite. Perhaps, with Etolié's absence, Khastra felt the need to berate others for their eating habits instead.

Thoughts of the Celestial sobered her irritation. "I don't actually know where the kitchen is." Khastra beckoned for her to follow. "Are you truly dead?"

"I am. Casvir considered my death a waste."

Perfection, this half-demon woman in undeath, with the laughter lines around her eyes and the hint of a smile gracing her lips, even with the scar marring the corner. Yet, there must have been a catch. Something to miss. Flowridia glanced back down and saw the protrusions from her shirt.

Khastra's spine had been all but severed. What held her together now?

Still, leave it to Khastra to be all but indifferent about undeath. She didn't appear to be suffering much, neither in body or spirit. Casvir, it seemed, wanted her preserved for both her physique and her mind.

Yet . . .

Despite herself, Flowridia took Khastra's hand, noting its rough texture and its warmth. Before the former general could comment, she pressed a finger to the woman's wrist and frowned at what she felt—a pulse. "You aren't dead."

"I am dead enough, tiny one," Khastra said, stealing back the appendage. She stared a moment at her hand, flexing her fingers as she breathed out a sigh.

Khastra *breathed*.

"I am dead," Khastra repeated, as though this were some momentous truth to accept. She let her hand fall to her side. Her strides slowed, but still they walked. "A strange new adventure, but anything new is a rarity at my age. Necromancy keeps my soul and mind in my body. But my body itself, as was explained to me, is a new sort of experiment, something Imperator Casvir has never tried before. I am useful because of my age and knowledge. I will be announced as the General of the Deathless Army in due time, but my mother's blood grants me abilities beyond what I could achieve on my own. You have seen it."

Flowridia had. As Bringer of War, her birthright as a Daughter of Ku'Shya, Khastra held potent powers—such as the ability to turn into a monster and slaughter the God of Order.

Or, attempt to, rather, given that The Endless Night had intervened.

Flowridia shoved the raw memories aside. She simply gave a nod.

"They are working to preserve my power, which means my body must produce blood. My heart must beat. My body must continue biological function, despite remaining in stasis."

"Given that you're up and walking, I presume they've succeeded?"

Khastra remained silent a moment, lips pursed when she finally said, "I do hope so."

Decadent smells wafted against Flowridia's senses, and when Khastra held open the door, Flowridia stepped into a busy kitchen swarming with servants bickering left and right. "I need food for the tiny one," Khastra called out, every bit the military leader. The array of servants spared her only a glance before nodding their assent. "No meat. No mushrooms."

Flowridia couldn't help but feel touched that she remembered.

As the food was prepared, Khastra leaned against the wall, arms crossed as she asked, "Why are you here?"

Khastra knew absolutely nothing, Flowridia realized, and so she launched into her tale, finding it wonderful to speak of. She started at the beginning, of her deal with Casvir, detailing his words, withholding only the offer of Ayla's return.

Khastra might have been understandably bitter towards Flowridia's deceased love.

Her story was interrupted by the appearance of food. Soon, Flowridia sat in the room next door, seated at a small table with a plate of steaming vegetables and some sort of foreign legume. Demitri lounged on the floor, content with his meal of freshly killed ox, while Ana pranced around him, apparently amused by the sounds of him consuming his meal. Fortunately, she made no attempt to steal any, lest she be next.

Khastra moved to the doorway. "Are you settled, tiny one?"

Flowridia nodded, her mouth full of decadent flavor.

"Then I will leave you."

Khastra twisted the doorknob, but Flowridia forced her half-chewed food down her throat and cried, "Wait!"

The half-demon glanced back at her. "Yes?"

"Does anyone else know?"

Khastra's hand paled against the doorframe, so tight was her grip. Her face remained ambivalent, but Flowridia knew she had crossed an unspoken line. "No, they do not."

"Why?" Flowridia dared to press. "Has Casvir forbidden it?"

"Imperator Casvir has said little on the matter, only that we will wait to announce my position in his court until my body is stable."

"But what of Staelash?"

Sudden snapping of wood caused Flowridia's words to shrivel and die in her throat. The doorframe beneath Khastra's grip bore a lengthy crack.

The half-demon released it, the tension in her body relaxing as her lips twisted into a frown. "The best way to move forward is to cast everything aside and forget the past. I will do as much for Staelash."

Khastra left Flowridia and the broken doorframe behind. But Flowridia, shocked at the harsh words, followed. "Khastra, they will find out you're here."

"They will," Khastra said, though she did not stop walking. "I would prefer it not be by your tongue, but I cannot stop you."

Flowridia ran to catch up. When she stopped in front of the half-demon, the line of Khastra's mouth turned severe. But though she radiated a daunting aura, Flowridia had cried for her, had mourned for her. Her sorrow manifested as barely contained fury. "You gave your life for Staelash! How can you forget them?"

Khastra merely looked unimpressed. "You will recall I died in the Theocracy—not Staelash."

When Khastra stepped forward, Flowridia stepped back, keeping herself in front of her. Foolish, yes, but she remembered a tear-stained Celestial who wept for her broken heart. "Were you truly so miserable that you would abandon everyone who cared about you?"

"Yes."

Not the response she expected. "What?"

"In the time of extended peace, Emperor Malakh forgot what I am, and all of Solvira with him. I am Ku'Shya's eldest and greatest. I served Solvira for over two thousand years, and because of me, Solvira rose to become the greatest kingdom in the world. I have led armies of hundreds of thousands, so when the emperor asked me to serve as a *bodyguard* to the rulers of Staelash, it was an insult. I told him no." Behind her set jaw, Khastra breathed, and Flowridia imagined smoke escaping her nostrils. "Imperator Casvir respects my talents and my heritage. I will be serving in a position worthy of my time, and I revel in the prospect of shedding blood in his name. Nox'Kartha will rise to topple Solvira, and good riddance."

The words sent a chill through Flowridia's body. "But your friends–"

"When Staelash finds out of my presence in Nox'Kartha, bloodshed may be inevitable, knowing the brashness of their council. Empress Alauriel is wise and will do what she can to rein them back, but Marielle is a fool, and

Etolié . . ." Khastra's expression turned to steel, yet Flowridia saw the chink in the half-demon's armor, the slight twitch of her lip. "For all her façade of tact, she is impulsive."

"She's heartbroken," Flowridia whispered, and when Khastra didn't interrupt, she pulled the mirror from her pocket and added, "I spoke to her, not an hour ago. She's wasting away, and perhaps if you would talk to her–"

"She is not my responsibility anymore," Khastra said, finality in the harsh words. Flowridia flinched when Khastra stepped around her, not daring to tell her to stop.

The betrayal of Khastra's character stung, but then the woman stopped, and at her sudden gasp, Flowridia feared she was crying.

Khastra clutched at her chest, falling forward but catching herself on the carpeted floor. "Damn it," Flowridia heard her mutter, and then she rammed her fist against her chest, her bicep expanding from the force.

"Khastra, what's wrong?"

Between the thumps against her chest, Khastra stammered, "My heart is failing." On her hands and knees, she lurched, coughing as she gasped for breath.

Panicked, Flowridia said, "I'll find Casvir–"

But a hand against her ankle gripped her tight; even with Khastra's subdued strength, Flowridia had no hope to escape.

But then the grip grew entirely slack. Flowridia knelt beside her, fear in Khastra's gaze as their eyes met. "What can I do?"

"Burn my body so I can be at peace?" Khastra released a pained chuckle, and in her eyes welled tears. Her fist clenched around her chest, the one arm supporting her trembling as she hyperventilated.

Flowridia could not heal her, no—healing magic harmed the dead. Her hands shook as she ran her fingers through Khastra's hair, desperate to convey what comfort she could. "Has this happened before?"

Khastra managed to nod. Her face paled.

"What happens when–"

The unmistakable sound of metallic steps approached, as well as muted footsteps beside it. Flowridia kept her gaze on Khastra, stroked her anguished face with her gentle fingers. In her peripheral, she saw sweeping robes, heard frantic jabbering she barely understood, and then the unequivocal sound of Casvir's voice. "Disappointing," he rumbled, and then Khastra's head fell slack into Flowridia's arms.

The rest of her body remained tense, however, her fists tight and losing color. Her breathing stopped, but still she moved. Flowridia's breath caught as she listened to the commotion around her.

"The probes *should* have worked," said the unfamiliar voice beside her. Flowridia looked up to see a rather frazzled De'Sindai man staring at the half-demon corpse. "We will, of course, remedy this immediately."

"The cost quickly outweighs her use," Casvir said, the undercurrent of ire unlike what Flowridia had ever heard him use before. "Fix it."

More people joined, all swarming the fallen general. A cold, clawed hand on Flowridia's arm helped her to stand—Casvir pulled her back and away, protective as he loomed over the scene. "What's going on?" Flowridia asked, trembling against his side.

Amidst the flurry, she saw Murishani watching, his gaze drifting casually between Khastra and herself.

"Nothing you will want to see," Casvir said softly, the deep, underground echo of his voice soothing amidst the panic.

The De'Sindai present worked to lift the hefty woman to her hooved feet, whose eyes had glazed and stumbling steps swayed. With four servants, two clutching her forearms and two at her waist, they led her out. Khastra said nothing, merely held the resignation of the damned.

Casvir moved to follow, releasing his grip on Flowridia's shoulder. But she grabbed his hand, preventing his exit. He turned to meet her eye. "Casvir, will she be all right?"

"As well as she can. I will deliver news when I have it."

She released his hand, and Casvir disappeared down the hallway.

The crowd cleared; only Murishani remained. When Demitri began licking Flowridia's hand, he smiled and said, "A touching display." He stepped forward, curiosity in his gaze. "In all my years of knowing Casvir, I have never known him to be so . . . *gentle* towards another person. I say this out of all the kindness of my heart—be wary, Flowridia." Sincerity shone in his mesmerizing eyes. "Your love for him is innocent. I only hope his is the same."

The words unsettled her, ice seeping into her veins. "I-I don't think–"

"Such a tragedy, what has befallen your friend," Murishani said, stepping forward. He offered an arm, one she hesitated to take. "Let me assure you, she has gone through as much before and survived. Would you like to see?"

Casvir had warned her away, yet she saw earnest kindness in Murishani's offer. Something in her stomach clenched, but fear for Khastra caused her to nod.

With her arm around Murishani's, Flowridia was escorted down the hallway. Demitri followed, as did Ana, trotting along, oblivious to the tension in the air.

"Nox'Kartha leads the world in biological science, did you know?"

Flowridia shook her head.

"Casvir believes in wasting nothing—including citizens. Once they've shed their mortal coil, their bodies are donated to experimentation. Only their bodies; their souls move on to whatever afterlife awaits a loyal servant of Casvir. Lawbreakers, however, are often met with a different sort of fate. Many criminals lost their lives in the endeavor to keep your dear friend alive."

Flowridia frowned, unnerved at the remark. "Khastra?"

"Casvir won't risk damaging useful goods. It's why the continued failure of her physique is so frustrating to him. And it's such a pity; Lady Ayla might've had the intellect to save her on the first trial." Murishani smiled brightly, slowing his pace. "Such a genius woman, that one. May she rest in peace."

"What do you mean, she might've saved her?"

Murishani stopped entirely. "Didn't you know? Your Ayla was quite the scientist of her own field. Some of her technology has been employed in Casvir's experimentations on Khastra. A tragedy, her passing."

Somehow, his glowing words did nothing to soothe her. "She was very intelligent, yes," Flowridia said simply, sorrow filling her—because she hadn't known, and there was so much of her love she might never know now.

With a kind smile, Murishani released her arm and instead placed both of his hands on her shoulders. "And how are you faring, in light of Ayla's passing?"

Flowridia shook her head. "I try not to think about it."

"You're awfully young. Was she your first heartbreak?"

She nodded, breath hitching.

"You're so very brave, Flowridia," Murishani said, giving her shoulders a squeeze. "To face this tragedy with such dignity, to go off on a quest to serve your kingdom when you should be mourning your great loss—inspiring, truly. And with such a brutish man; Casvir is hardly civil company. You must miss your home greatly."

Sorrow mounted onto Flowridia's already waning resolve. She managed a nod, forced a smile, and said, "But it isn't forever."

"You courageous little girl," he said, and with a reassuring squeeze, he released her shoulders. Then, he placed a hand at the small of her back and gently led her forward. "Are you certain you're brave enough to see what fate befalls your friend?"

His beguiling words rang some alarm in the back of her mind, of the warning from Casvir, but Flowridia nodded nonetheless.

Murishani smiled, charm in the gesture, and led her onward. Everything about him, from his fine robes to the exquisite rings on his fingers, spoke of luxury and beauty. His hair fell in graceful waves, and he watched the world around him with fervent, bright eyes. All of it stood in stark contrast to Casvir, whose very aura radiated menace and, oddly, utilitarianism.

Perhaps it was why Casvir kept Murishani, yet while she could not deny his charisma and goodwill, she wondered at his teasing, his pet names. Never would she have imagined Casvir standing for any degree of disrespect.

Yet Murishani was second of his kingdom. There must've been something more to him.

They wound down a hall, up and down stairs, and when no light came from the windows—only the sconces on the walls—Murishani placed a finger on his lip. "He mustn't know you're here," he said, and then he placed a hand on the doorknob.

Whatever spell the door held, it broke the moment it swung open. Screaming filled the hallway. Flowridia gasped, brought her hands to her face, and when Murishani beckoned her forward, she ran inside, Demitri close behind.

They stood upon a railing, high above whatever atrocity awaited below. The richness of the castle vanished, leaving only stark metal and stone. An iron balcony supported them, a banister there to block the feebleminded from toppling down. The floor clung to the walls, wrapping around two entire laps before it reached the bottom.

Bright lights illuminated the scene below, leaving Flowridia and Demitri in shadow. De'Sindai rushed about, some wielding tools Flowridia had never seen—some burning, some crackling with energy. Casvir loomed beside them, watching with his arms held behind his back. Flowridia smelled fire; she smelled blood and chemicals too vile to name.

Centered, lay Khastra.

Flowridia heard her gasping, though she knew not how, for she held little of her chest cavity. She knew the color of torn skin from within, recognized the colorless mass of organs, and saw them place, from where she could not say, a heart into her chest-

And then an explosion. A scream. A De'Sindai touched two of the crackling instruments to her exposed heart, the sparks from which were blinding.

A sob escaped Flowridia's throat, but she nearly shrieked when a hand touched her shoulder. "Ghastly, isn't it," Murishani said, shaking his head. "This is the fourth heart that's failed her. They keep her lucid so they know it's taken. Once the blood begins pumping, she's stitched back together."

Gasping, Flowridia could not tear her gaze away. Her knuckles turned white on the railing as she watched Khastra's muscles tense against their bonds.

"Oh, this one does appear promising," Murishani cooed, palpably intrigued. "What I mean is, perhaps this will be the last of her pain. I cannot begin to imagine her agony."

Flowridia felt herself crumble, her knees suddenly weak. Khastra's screams shifted from agony to something barbaric, and Flowridia watched as her body transform to match her screams—expanding and shifting, her bonds stretching to match. When she had last seen Khastra's monstrous form, it had been in triumph, the Bringer of War coming to stand against the God of Order.

Here, her tattoos glowed, her musculature expanded, threatening to split her skin, veins popping, but it bespoke nothing of majesty—only survival. She saw Casvir withdraw the black orb from his armor, and when he glowed in ghastly shades of purple and black, he touched the transformed monster's forehead, and somehow her screams grew *louder*.

Flowridia ran from the room.

Demitri and Ana followed. As soon as the door shut behind Murishani, the screaming stopped. The ensuing silence rang loudly in her head, her own sobs all that filled the hall.

A presence knelt beside her. Murishani's hand landed lightly on her shoulder. "What is this place?" Flowridia asked between sobs.

"A city of death, Flowridia," Murishani said gravely. "At least Khastra's pain might have an end. Some of our criminals live out eternity in much worse states. Casvir is a man of brutality unparalleled."

Flowridia shuddered, forcing her breathing to steady. When she moved to stand, Murishani offered a hand, one she accepted. "Will you take me back to Ayla's room?"

Murishani offered his assent and led her through the halls.

Chapter 6

When they reached her room, Murishani placed his hand upon his mouth, his gaze lingering at each and every drawing and glass globe, flittering about excitedly as though they were something new and wondrous to behold. "What a spectacular display! Truly, this is remarkable. Ayla's talent for art was always unparalleled, but this is absolutely darling. Innocent, even." He raised an eyebrow at a nude piece, though Ayla had tactfully chosen to cover Flowridia's breasts with a blanket in the recreation, even if scandalous details hinted beneath the sheet. "In a manner of speaking."

Flowridia ignored her rising blush. "Have you not seen this before? I thought you delivered the dresses."

He waved off the words. "I have servants for that. No, I hadn't the pleasure. Ayla was very secretive when it came to you." Murishani placed a hand on his heart, his excitement fading. "And how are you, my dear? It was a ghastly display. Are you all right?"

Truthfully, Flowridia's felt prepared to sob anew, but she forced a smile, though her eyes bore evidence of tears. "I'll be fine."

From the pocket of his lavish tunic, he withdrew a small pink bottle, emblazoned with gold. "I feel terrible on your behalf. Your tender heart has already gone through so much. Take this; perhaps it will help you relax."

Flowridia plucked the offering from Murishani's hand, realizing it held liquid. "What is this?"

"Nothing fancy. Merely a bit of lavender for your bath, to help soothe your body and soul. It is the least I can do."

Guilt filled her at the suspicious weight in her gut; Flowridia let a bit of energy flow from her hands and felt, as sure as she felt her own breath, that Murishani spoke true—there was nothing magical here to be found.

"Ayla Darkleaf had a truly impressive washroom."

"I've seen it," Flowridia whispered, and the viceroy smiled.

"Did she take you there? Oh, of course she did; she did as much for all her conquests. Though you may be the only one who left alive." Murishani's wink brought the return of the weighted pit in her stomach.

"N-No," Flowridia said, her head suddenly light. "It was earlier today. One of the hooded figures escorted me. I–" She steeled her jaw. "I wasn't aware there were others. Or that–" She swallowed the rise of emotion, feeling suddenly sick. "What?"

Murishani's hand flew to cover his mouth. "Lady Flowridia, I am so sorry. I assumed you knew."

"Knew what?" she whispered, already dreading the truths she might learn.

"No, it is better that I say nothing. Look at all this beauty around you," he said, sweeping his arms out. "Best it not be spoiled with . . . *inconveniences.*"

"I want to know the truth."

Murishani pursed his lips and shook his head, his long, luxurious hair sweeping around his shoulders. "Absolutely not. This is a crime I cannot be complicit in." He tossed his golden locks aside, then placed a hand on his hip as he released a sigh. "But if you insist on seeking out the truth for yourself, I will not patronize you by standing in your way. Go and take a bath. If you know the path, you can find the truth."

Flowridia frowned, and when Murishani moved to leave, she said, "What does that mean?"

He held up a hand. "Complicit, remember? But you're a clever girl."

Murishani left her alone and baffled.

Flowridia looked down at the bottle in her hand. "Demitri, stay with Ana."

You're going to investigate?

Flowridia's hand turned white, so tight she squeezed the bottle. "I have to know," she whispered. Her jaw stiffened. "My heart may break, but I have to know the truth."

She left him behind. Alone, she let her feet take her to the blank wall hiding Ayla's bath. Line drawn, the wall parted, and Flowridia stepped through.

All remained the same. She pocketed the small bottle of lavender. Murishani had said if she knew the path here, she could find what she sought. Flowridia recalled the false wall, the portal she stepped through.

She shut her eyes, let her senses expand, and felt, near her, the false wall with its radiant magic and also . . . opposite it.

Another one.

Flowridia stepped toward the decorated wall and dared to touch the cold stone. Energy tingled at her senses. She knelt and drew a line upon the seam of magic, unsurprised to watch it glow. When it stood as tall as she, it widened and opened up into a door.

Not a portal this time, no. It seemed built into the wall, framed by intricate designs, and Flowridia peered through. A dark staircase descended. She stepped forward, flinching at the cold, dusty stone under her bare feet.

Twenty steps, and her feet touched the ground. A dark hallway, lit from some ambient, unknown source, extended in either direction.

Murishani had said her answers waited here. But what, exactly, was 'here?' Flowridia kept her right hand on the wall and made her way forward.

Absolute silence met her. Not even her quiet feet disturbed the ominous peace. The path turned, and Flowridia followed, keeping her hand on the wall as she slowly stepped forward.

In the distance, a shadow seemed to consume the path, but as she stepped forward, it moved back. The darkness was never more than a few steps ahead, yet she never reached it.

She stopped and stole a deep breath, skin prickling from nerves. Magic drenched the walls, but it was not evil—something dreadful lingered here, a wickedness that stemmed not from magic, no, yet it sickened her stomach. To fill the silence, she began humming a familiar tune, the very same Ayla had whispered to coax her to sleep.

The sound echoed faintly across the stone walls and floors. It bolstered her courage, though her skin still crawled as her bare feet brushed against the stone.

Murishani wouldn't have led her into danger . . . right?

She continued forward, until a split in her path met her view. With her hand on the wall, she turned to the right.

Cobwebs hung from the ceilings in sheets, threatening to cling to her hair.

Something flaked against her fingers. Flowridia flinched, then gasped when she saw what she'd touched. A smear of copper-hued grime matched the trail her hand followed, continuing until it suddenly veered into the ground.

Flowridia stepped closer to investigate the stain. Years of servitude to a mother with a penchant for cannibalism made her well acquainted with dried blood . . . but where had it come from?

She stepped to the middle of the path, keeping her hands to herself now. Several times, the pathways split. Flowridia kept to the right, unwilling to lose her sense of direction. She had seen nothing and so chose to believe it was abandoned.

Then, light. Relief filled her at the hope of an exit. She increased her pace, shading her eyes as the light grew blinding, the sun's rays bursting through—

A crystal emanated a light at the dead end, a mockery of celestial light. On the floor were chipped fingernails and evidence of blood on the walls.

Flowridia stumbled back, breathing labored, and kept her left hand on the wall as she backtracked. Whatever she had been meant to find could wait; her nerves were frayed from the ghastly torture. Every whisper upon the wall caused bumps to rise on her skin. Oh, she missed Demitri's warm fur. She could come back again, his amusing belligerence enough to lighten the atmosphere.

The pathway didn't turn left. It turned right. "No, no," she muttered. "That isn't correct." She touched the seam of the wall, expecting it to open, or perhaps to detect some magic spell. The entire labyrinth radiated energy, enough to prickle against her skin when she sought to feel it.

The crippling reality that she was lost settled, but she refused to panic yet.

Though her gut screamed the stop, Flowridia took the path to the right. Stagnant air sickened her stomach. She summoned her voice to sing again, though she knew not the words to the tune. Another crossroads, and again she turned left, forcing her breath to steady—

And jumped back. Smashed into the wall were fractured bones and the remains of a corpse. Splattered blood smeared every side, dried and caked along the wall.

Her breath left her. Heart racing, Flowridia ran. Left, right—what did it matter? Desperate to escape the ghastly vision, Flowridia raced down the forsaken path.

A distant howling met her ears. Metallic banging bespoke life. Flowridia's breathing grew erratic as she turned.

A dead end. Evidence of dried blood and gore caked the walls, along with the remains of hair and a corpse torn apart.

Flowridia ran. Gasping, panicked, she moved as fast as her lithe legs would take her. The stone walls were untouched, but bits of hair and bones littered the corners.

A light shone ahead. Tears welled, spurned by relief, and adrenaline pushed her to run faster.

The light radiated from a room, one that held no door, but an archway bearing the painted words: *The light shall burn away all your fears.*

She stepped into a nightmare.

A magnificent room with sweeping stone ceilings and a putrid smell bespoke grandeur and terror. It held the architecture of the Theocracy's cathedral yet stood in stark mockery of divinity. Flowridia's feet ran across rich carpet, but she froze, gasping at the monster before her.

A masterpiece of macabre beauty, Sol Kareena stood still upon her pedestal, serene in death, lifelike in a way that nearly caused Flowridia's stomach to upheave. She bore the intricacy of finely crafted leather, gems attached to the face to serve as metaphorical tears, her robes nearly transparent as they draped across her body. Her blackened hands were held out in welcome, and her chest bore an open wound, blood and organs preserved and eternally spilling, a spear puncturing the exposed heart.

Every piece of her sewn corpse had once been alive, and Flowridia whirled around—

Only to find the exit had been shut.

All around, her overloaded senses absorbed the ghoulish artistry, cast in shades of sickly red and brown, the results of a mind unhinged. At the windows, instead of painted glass were quilted patches of leather, depicting scenes of demon gods and their pantheons; in the pews of polished wood and velvet, richly carved, were patrons set in ghastly poses, some sewn into unnatural states. Flowridia's eyes landed on one in particular whose garb pulled memories from a lifetime ago, of a man who dared insult the pride of a monster he would not sleep within a hundred miles of.

When she looked at his face, gaunt and lifeless, it was one and the same.

Statues of bone and dried sinew stood stationed in corners and upon shelves, of animal forms and aberrations, of screaming skulls spliced together to form horror unmasked, of gangrenous rot sealing tight stitches.

Behind the bastardized Godly mockery, Flowridia saw a door slightly ajar and ran.

Her eyes veered away from the statue of flesh, instead glancing past the altar before her gaze, where stained in blood was the elven word for *burn.*

Through the door, the wailing grew deafening.

Inside, all semblance of civility, abominable as it was, disappeared. A laboratory of sorts, with metal tables and blood-stained walls. A gruesome figure shrieked in the corner, two torsos sewn into one form, half-rotted yet still full of malevolent undeath. Metals bars banged as it fought to escape. Flowridia jumped back, recognizing hate in its tortured cries. Her arms landed on something soft and warm.

Blood.

The figure strapped to the table could hardly be called that—carved and exposed on every plane, the entire front seemed peeled away. Ribs were cracked, pinned open, exposing each red-rimmed bone; lungs breathed; the heart beat. A network of veins—the entire cardiovascular system— lay exposed. Meticulously pinned aside, each section lovingly preserved and labeled, some were held up with small hooks, creating an elaborate, visceral mockery of the human form.

The face was carved to pieces, hair shaved. Flowridia glanced at the figure's eyes; intelligent, human, they held her gaze.

She sobbed, screaming as she stumbled backwards. Along the wall were diagrams, notes, drawings, well-lit and pristine. A bookshelf, a line of knives lovingly arranged on the table, bloodied hooks hanging from the ceiling, dark leather on the walls—all of it embedded into her memory. She began hyperventilating, until bashing metal pulled her attention. The monstrosity threw itself at the door with all its might, shrieking erratically.

Flowridia stumbled back, falling against what she prayed was cloth. It ripped at her step. She collapsed to the ground, tangled in embroidered fabric and weeping in terror.

Heavy steps in the distance flickered in her mind. Flowridia continued bawling, desperate to block out the ghoul, the smell of blood, the burning lights.

Cracking wood bespoke the shattered door. Casvir rushed at the caged creature, summoned mace in hand. It broke through the bars and the undead monster, smashing it to pieces. The howling stopped.

Flowridia's cries were all that echoed now. A gentle rumble of a voice, only a few feet away, reached her ears. "You are safe, Flowridia."

Vision obscured by tears and translucent cloth, Flowridia dared to peek up. Casvir knelt before her, purposefully blocking the view of the figure on the table. Anger raged behind those red eyes, and Flowridia shrunk back, shying away from the hand he offered.

Casvir pulled away. "Demitri sensed your distress and sent me to find you." He glanced down at his hand, and Flowridia saw teeth marks emblazoned in the sickly blue color. "Demanded, rather. But it is good he did."

Flowridia fought to free herself of tangled fabric, quivering as she whispered, "I'm so sorry."

"No. She should be sorry. Not you. You were never meant to see this. And for you to stumble upon it accidentally . . ." He trailed off, his expression fierce.

She did not correct him. "What is this place?" she whimpered instead.

"Her hobby. A place for her to fuel her chaotic streak away from my populace and keep her quiet."

"This really was hers?"

Casvir nodded. "She spent all her free time here, until she met you."

Horrified, Flowridia choked on her sob, coughing painfully. The last of the fabric fell beside her, but though free, she clung to it, bunching it into her fists. "Why, though? Why did she do this?"

"Any answer I could give would only break your heart."

"It's already shattered." Flowridia's voice broke on the last words.

In the ensuing silence, she looked down at the cloth in her hands, realizing dust from the floor had stained the white, translucent material. It bore an embroidery of flowers, a rainbow of colors with the softest of green to connect them.

Casvir's reserved words startled her. "In my research on Ayla Darkleaf, everything I found spoke of a highly intelligent and sadistic monster who charmed and brutalized her way into legend. Her curiosity is insatiable. She allowed me, once, to read some of her research, perhaps hoping to scare me. What I learned is she is thorough and gleeful in her torture."

Strange, the numbness that filled her at those words. Ayla had been thorough and gleeful in all things—her meticulous work in the kitchen, her merciless slaughter of the dwarves and the Skalmites, even the perfect placement of candles in Flowridia's room. Patient, no. But thorough.

"I know nothing of her history with the Theocracy, only that the display was a project she took pride in. She would bring her victims there, for what purpose, I do not know.

"To ask 'why' is to cry into an abyss. I do not doubt she once held the intention to hang you from the walls." He gestured to one such victim, dried and vivisected, organs displayed, head and limbs nowhere in sight. "But you evoked something new in her."

He looked down at the cloth in Flowridia's hands, the only spot of beauty amidst the ruthless scene.

She let the cloth drop. With her arms limp at her side, she stared at the remains of the cage. Purple mist swirled where the bars had been severed.

Again, Casvir offered a hand, and this time Flowridia accepted. Standing, she slipped her hand out of his and slowly stepped toward the table, eyes darting about at all the diagrams and models pinned to the wall.

Casvir's voice broke through her muted thoughts. "Flowridia, you will not like–"

"I know," she said, sharper than she intended. "But I need to see it."

She grabbed a scalpel from the desk and looked down at Ayla's victim, strapped to the table. It held no eyelids to hide behind. When their gazes met, Flowridia mouthed, "I'm sorry," before slitting the knife across the exposed throat.

Eyes glazed over; the heart stopped pumping. Flowridia noticed, then, the oddity, that stitched in gorgeous script, visible among the visceral layers of split flesh, was a name. It penetrated only the delicate top layer of tissue: *Flowra.*

And there, beside it on the table, Flowridia stiffened at the drawing. Gorgeously detailed in ink, her entire muscular system was labeled, her name written in perfect script above.

Flowridia's eyes narrowed, shivering at the thought of Ayla's hands caressing her back. She brushed the paper aside. Underneath, just as thoroughly detailed, was her own cardiovascular system, with some question marks here and there. Revulsion rose, and she set that aside as well.

Below, another diagram, with skin on, thankfully. Spread and entirely technical, her naked form lay labeled and detailed. Little notes—*"kiss here," "bite here," "slow down,"*—were scribbled throughout, and hearts danced around her name.

Flowridia crumpled it with her fist. Fighting tears, she swallowed her nausea and looked up to see other procedural diagrams pinned to the wall—a De'Sindai, a Celestial, a half-elf with a knife stabbed violently through the parchment, and more. Hand-drawn patterns decorated the far end of the wall, and as Flowridia stepped closer, she saw dress pieces, shoes, and more. There, next to them, a drawing of a child, the patterned pieces of shoes sketched into its back.

On the far end of the table lay a half-sewn book, but the dress form standing on the floor beside it stole her attention. Curious, she paled when she saw how the shoulders and neck were sewn together. It was garbed in the beginnings of a translucent gown, one that matched the embroidered veil she had discarded. But the lithe human torso, perfectly preserved, was too long to be meant for Ayla—

Oh.

Flinching, Flowridia stepped back, her hand landing on the book at the table. Embossed in fine script, the leather cover bore two words: *Flowridia Darkleaf.*

Hesitant, Flowridia trembled as she lifted the handmade book, noticing immediately the incomplete binding. But the soft leather brought reminders of the tanned leather on the walls, the dress form, of the patterns calling for the skin of a child—

She set the book down. "I've seen enough."

Casvir drew a line at the far wall beside the cage, and Flowridia wrapped her arms around herself as the wall parted, revealing a set of stairs. He beckoned.

Flowridia spared a glance for the laboratory, for the doorway leading to the cathedral hell, and realized she'd hardly skimmed the surface of the macabre display, of Ayla's mad mind. She tore her gaze away, eyes swollen from tears, and went up the stairs.

At the top of the staircase, Ayla's bathroom awaited. Flowridia left Casvir and the bathroom behind, hiding her tear-stained face from any servants she passed as she hurried down the hallway.

Ayla's doorknob was ice in her shaking hand.

Demitri nearly trampled her the moment the door clicked. He curled around her body, collapsing to the floor. Trapped, and too shocked to speak, Flowridia's arms wrapped around him.

I felt your fear. Where were you?

"Underneath Ayla's bathroom," Flowridia whispered. "I can't say anything more. Please."

Then don't try yet. Just know that you're safe.

Tears welled in her eyes as she buried her face in his fur. "You went to find Casvir."

I love you much more than I hate him. I thought that was obvious. Her fingers tightened in his fur.

He stood, and she clung to him, finding he could support her quite easily. The dim recesses of Ayla's room soothed her tired mind, but the glass spheres held no joy. The bar of soap, the teacup, each perfectly preserved flower . . .

All these trinkets; a shrine for love. Yet her heart wondered now if Ayla would have made a trinket of her as well. She had done as much for others.

Yet, Casvir himself had said she was Ayla's redeeming trait, that Ayla's love for her had been pure. Flowridia looked about the room, away from the stolen articles and to the pictures on the wall. So many of her sleeping, one with roses on the windowsill. Another of she and Demitri in the garden, beside a patch of tulips.

And some that weren't memories—depictions of them together, of Ayla kissing her by the light of a fireplace, of a cottage in the woods, secluded in trees.

Tears welled in Flowridia's eyes, recalling the shattered dream to run away. She couldn't be here.

Flowridia opened the door, unsurprised to find that Casvir had followed and quickly approached. "Casvir, I can't stay in here." Too many memories, too much pain, too much time to sit and contemplate . . .

He gave a curt nod. "Wait here."

Within the hour, she laid herself upon a fresh, nondescript bed, a guest wing meant for foreign politicians. Realistically, where she would have stayed were she anyone but Ayla's beloved.

It came with the promise of something new in the future. *"Accommodations more suited to your taste,"* Casvir had called it, but Flowridia had no energy to care. With Demitri wrapped in her arms, darkness descended upon her fatigued body. Sleep was not her enemy.

Her enemy waited in her dreams.

"You were never meant for that life."

Even in the dark void, Flowridia felt a pounding in her head, claws clutching her hips and back. Nothing amorous in the touch; merely desperation.

Weeping filled her ears. "I love you, Flowridia," the broken voice pled. "Please, never leave me."

Cold hands caressed her cheeks; a weight on her chest trembled and shook, threatening to suffocate her—

Flowridia awoke to a burning headache and exhaustion unparalleled. Demitri snoozed beneath her. Even Ana curled silently against her.

By every god, she was *freezing.*

She sat up, taking care to not jostle Demitri, then lifted her skirt. Upon her skin, at the crux of her hipbones, were vicious red lines, as though Demitri had scratched his nails—not breaking skin, but leaving a lingering, stinging mark. From her bodice, she withdrew the ear, the voice in her dreams filling her with fury and guilt.

She watched the severed ear dangling at the end of its chain, silently daring it to speak instead of listen. To ask why was to cry into a void, Casvir had said. But she would try. She shut her eyes, summoning an absence of energy within her core. She felt Ana beside her, acutely aware of her undead presence. In her hand, the ear pinged as some vestige of dark energy, but she felt no presence, no awareness. Nothing to grasp and harness.

Nothing to plead to for answers. Perhaps another tactic instead.

She stuffed the ear back down her dress, then gently jostled Demitri awake. "Demitri, will you come with me?"

The large wolf opened his eyes. *Where?*

"I don't know. Somewhere to find out more about Ayla. I have to understand."

Demitri, bless his heart, didn't ask. As he stood, Ana stirred, immediately hopping to her feet and bumping against Flowridia's leg.

A helpful hooded figure told her to try the third floor. That was where Casvir did his sparring.

It appeared similar to her second-floor living accommodations, with carpeted halls and stone walls, but Flowridia saw a pair of skeletal guards positioned at a large doorway. With trepidation, she approached, but though they stared, they did not appear hostile. "I was told Casvir was up here."

"Stay out of bounds," came an echoing voice, but the guard pushed the door opened and gestured for her to follow.

Within, Flowridia saw a spacious room with walls of stone climbing hundreds of feet into the air. Two figures clashed in a titanic battle, and the terrain shifted to match. Stone floors, where Flowridia waited, melded into dirt and grass. Imperator Casvir, fully armored and wielding his summoned mace, stood centered, surrounded by countless undead horrors. He moved with all the expertise they did not, their movements clumsy and awkward, but their sheer numbers setting them up as a formidable force.

They attempted to swarm a monster, one who batted them aside with graceful sweeps of her hammer, though she herself had transformed, the Bringer of War standing with claws and teeth. Her tattoos and eyes glowed, and though the dead rose once more when she cleaved through them in bulk, not once did she seem overpowered.

Until, she suddenly tensed, then allowed a few to get close for the opportunity to heave her hammer forward with all her might—

Directly at Casvir.

With the onslaught of dead in the path, he hadn't a hope to dodge—the hammer bludgeoned him in the chest as it continued to fly, landing on top of him when it finally fell.

Flowridia gasped and ran onto the battlefield, beckoning for Demitri and Ana to stay. "Casvir!" she cried, and as she approached, she saw Khastra tearing the dead apart with claws and teeth, all semblance of civility disappearing.

She turned her gaze on Flowridia directly, her monstrous smile twisting and dripping with black ichor.

Flowridia reached Casvir in time to watch him heave the great hammer from his body. Not lift it, no, but push it away, silent even as it further dented the armor through his flesh. "How can I help?" she asked.

"This is training."

When she looked up, she realized Khastra tore through the undead to reach them. "As I said, how can I help?"

Casvir stood back onto his clawed feet, the mace reappearing in his hand. "Get off the battlefield."

He charged forward.

Though slighted by the words, Flowridia obeyed and returned to the sidelines where Demitri awaited. *If things continue, Khastra will tear his face off for me.*

"I certainly hope not," she whispered.

The hammer suddenly flew back, though this time the great tyrant fell to the ground to avoid it. It returned to Khastra's hands, and she suddenly leapt from the fray, impossibly high, and landed between Casvir and Flowridia. She threw her hammer toward the prone Casvir, who clumsily rolled over to dodge. The undead shrieked as they skittered to swarm her anew, but Khastra turned her vicious countenance to Flowridia.

The berserker charged. Claws swiped Flowridia before she could scream. Nails threatened to pierce her torso, driving the air from her body.

Khastra held Flowridia aloft, high above the air. She spoke demonic words, her body growing brighter even as the shadows rose and lights flickered. Flowridia understood none of it, only the quick use of the name, *"Casvir!"*

The imperator in question approached, weapon wielded, undead rushing behind. A crushing grip clamped around Flowridia's face, smelling of blood and dirt. Panicked, she screamed, muffled as it was, and beat upon the hands that held her in vain.

"I yield. Release her."

The Bringer of War did so, gently placing Flowridia onto the ground, in tandem with a wicked laugh from her throat. Flowridia gasped for breath, then ran to Demitri who growled from his position by the wall. She didn't dare look at anyone, much less Casvir who would surely be furious.

The next words she heard were Casvir's once again. "You cheated."

"I did not cheat," came Khastra's voice—her true voice, the one that reminded Flowridia of nights in an underground library. "She stepped onto the battlefield."

Flowridia peeked up, and saw that Khastra, though disheveled, had returned to her natural form—if that's the one this was. "The true victory," Khastra continued, "is ours both. My heart has not failed." She held her arms out, a sardonic grin on her face. The hammer flew back into her grasp, and she gave a slight nod before she stepped through the door.

Flowridia ran to Casvir. "I'm sorry."

"You did not know," he replied, steps staggered as he made his way from the battlefield. The moment he stepped onto the stone sides, Flowridia watched and heard the terrain shift and settle. Like an earthquake, the ground split, and the undead in the arena were swallowed by the earth. The floor became flat stone.

"This place," Casvir continued, "is a training ground. And while winning is never a guarantee, I rarely lose. Khastra is as formidable an opponent as I had hoped."

"I'm sorry I ruined it for you."

"Do not do it again." He lumbered forward, no grace to his movements. As though summoned, an envoy of hooded figures filtered in from the outside, doting, for lack of a better word, upon him as the they unlatched the straps of his armor—rather, as the armor unlatched itself, given that they had no hands. "As you can see, your friend is well."

Flowridia looked to the door where Khastra had left. "I wouldn't call us 'friends,'" she muttered, slighted at Khastra's cruel streak. Yet, she could not be angry—Khastra was in pain, more than Flowridia could fathom. She remembered the half-demon's screams from the slab, saw Ayla's victim on her own—

Casvir had condoned it all.

"Did you rest well?"

Flowridia looked up at Casvir's words. "Well enough," she whispered, then added, "and I suppose I'm rife for abuse because..." She shut her eyes, swallowing the rise of emotion, shoving aside what horrors waited behind her eyelids. "I need to know more. I have to understand her. Where can I go to find the truth?"

"The library in the palace is where I learned what I know of her; perhaps you might discover something more." Casvir looked to one of the hooded servants. "Escort Lady Flowridia to the library."

The servant lowered its floating self as if to bow, then moved out. Flowridia followed, Demitri and Ana in tow. She was amused to find that her little fox had apparently learned the proper way to walk on carpet; in dainty measures, she lifted her sharp little claws with care, the carpet no longer a nuisance.

Nonetheless, when they reached the stairs, she held the fox in her arms.

The figure took her to the bottom floor and then farther below. The walls remained lit only by sconces. Flowridia realized they delved deeper and deeper underground. With a smile, she recalled Etolié's underground bastion of knowledge, lit by the skylight. "Is the library large?"

"The castle library harbors limitless knowledge and infinitely expands to accommodate it."

"You'll have to explain what that means."

"Knowledge is power," the figure continued, stopping before a large set of double doors. "Power is difficult to keep contained."

The doors opened as it raised its empty sleeve. Flowridia stepped forward, watching as a gargantuan room spread out before them. Books lined every wall and shelf, ones that reached well above the bounds of where the ceiling should have ended. Stairs to the side led up. Before her, they went down, opening up to a circular masterpiece of architecture.

They were not alone; patrons skimmed the shelves, academics sat at desks and tables. It was not busy, no, but hardly abandoned. Flowridia's heart skipped a beat when she saw some monstrous thing walking idly between the shelves—a humanoid figure, but double her height and composed entirely of books. She watched as it scooped up a pile of abandoned books from a desk and added them to its very makeup, then insert another onto a separate shelf.

"You need not fear the golems," the figure said. "They both maintain and protect the premises."

Were they ghosts or mindless beings? Flowridia watched the golem as it disappeared behind a series of shelves.

"With special permission from universities or from the imperator, researchers from every part of Nox'Kartha are welcome here. As are foreigners, but for a daily fee. By Casvir's decree, as an honorary citizen, you may come and go as you choose."

Flowridia nodded, smiling as the horrors in her memory muted beneath the peace of this place. It smelled of home, of books and ancient scrolls, evoking a longing for her days in Etolié's underground sanctuary. "Thank you," she said, turning back, and with a bow, the figure left her alone.

Her hand caressed Demitri's fur as she stepped forward, her other arm still supporting Ana, who wriggled in her grasp. "Stay beside me," she cooed to the little creature, and when she placed Ana on the ground, she did not deviate more than a step or two away.

Flowridia continued soaking in the magnificent array of books and knowledge, wondering if Etolié would be absolutely furious to know such a place existed without her to occupy it, curious to know if Ayla had ever spent her days here—

Her fists clenched. Thoughts of Ayla stung.

Flowridia spared a glance at the nearest shelf, hoping to have a hint of where to begin and realized, as she skimmed the array of books, that they were all treatises on Nox'Karthan history.

It stood to reason that Casvir would place evidence of his kingdom's own greatness up front.

Any time she swore she found an end, the shelves turned, more space appeared, and endless books met her view. Yet she held no fear of getting lost; any time she turned around, there the exit stood, up the stairs and well within sight.

The mechanics of the spacious room befuddled her, but magic had done stranger things.

Quiet muttering met her ear as she walked. A hooded figure spoke in hushed tones to a De'Sindai girl, not much older than Flowridia by appearances. She heard the girl ask for books on tide pools.

"Three shelves down, turn left and then right. Do not deviate, and you shall find it."

As the girl stepped away, Flowridia approached the figure. "I need information on..." She steeled herself, for now there was no going back. "...Ayla Darkleaf?"

The figure pointed with its sleeve. "When you reach the wall, go up the stairs. Three paces right, and then what you seek shall appear. Do not deviate from the path."

Flowridia thanked the being and did as directed, only stopping to scoop Ana into her arms when a passing golem threatened to trample her.

The gilded banister was pristine and polished, and Flowridia dared not touch it, for fear of smudging the wood and metal. She traversed up the steps with care, Demitri close behind, and came upon a smaller hall, the walls made of dark stone.

Three paces right, and then a door appeared, shimmering from the very air. Assuming this to be her quarry, Flowridia entered.

She came upon a spacious room, lined and filled with shelves and saw, upon the nearest one, *Engineers in Aerospace: The Mechanics of Zauleen.*

Zauleen meant elven literature. Flowridia set about skimming the shelves.

She saw, between the shelves, evidence of a golem passing one row beyond, but when Flowridia reached the end of the shelf—all of them specializing in engineering—she came across an elven man, who met her eye and put a finger to his lips.

He was dressed in the manner of a traveler, with boots and breeches, a vest over his brown tunic, and a rapier at his hip. His blonde hair, nearly as white as the moon, though not from age, had been sheared short—roughly so, as if by a knife—and what she saw of his skin lay riddled with scars. Knicks in his ear, his chin, and his hands were rough and discolored from flecks of black—frostbite? His skin had once been tanned, but he seemed sickly, somehow, as though he had not seen the sun in years.

What surprised her most was the tiny bird perched upon his shoulder.

Flowridia heard the golem; the man darted away, gone in an instant, in ways a common mortal could not mimic.

As the book golem approached, Flowridia widened her eyes, gasping as she pointed at the door from where she'd come. "He went that way," she said, casting fear into her voice.

The golem turned, picking up speed as it lumbered toward the door.

When it had shut, Flowridia heard a soft, masculine voice. "Thank you," said the elven man, suddenly behind her. He stood a full head taller, but his green eyes were kind as he smiled. "They shake me down anytime they find me, trying to empty my pockets. It's quite uncomfortable." He offered a scarred hand. "Tazel."

Amused, Flowridia accepted, noting his firm grip. "Flowridia. And that's Demitri. And Ana." She took her hand back, watching as Tazel cast a wary look upon both the undead cradled by her arm and the wolf at her side.

"And you all talk to each other?"

"Only Demitri and I. He's my familiar."

Tazel nodded, then looked to the bird on his shoulder. "This is Ferseph. She's mine."

For an elf to have a familiar was utterly unheard of as far as Flowridia knew, but she opted not to ask, fearing rudeness. Instead, she spared a glance toward the door. "May I ask why they try and empty your pockets?"

"You might say I've overstayed my welcome. Technically, however, I shouldn't have to pay until I leave." He smiled, friendly enough, but holding the slightest twitch. When he lingered, Flowridia suspected he didn't often get the chance to speak. "As a thank you for sparing me from the golem, I'll happily share my meal with you."

Flowridia looked to Demitri. *I'll bite his face off if he's creepy.*

She smiled back at Tazel. "That would be delightful, thank you," she replied, realizing she had barely eaten.

"Follow me," Tazel said, and he led them past the shelves and to a door she swore hadn't been there previously.

"Wait," she said. "Before we go, could you help me find something? I'm looking for..." To tell the truth to a servant of Casvir's was one thing, but to an elf? "... elven monsters. Would you know where I could look?"

"Let's see . . ." Tazel immediately assumed the guise of a scholar, expertly darting between the shelves on his toes. His movements were smooth, his muscles held in perfect control, and Flowridia suspected there was more to his makeup than a mere hermit in the library. "Do you speak elven?"

She saw the word *burn* emblazoned in blood. Flowridia forced a smile, shoving aside images of desecrated altars. "I learned a few scattered words in my childhood, but nothing more."

"Then your options are limited." Tazel scanned the shelves with a scholar's eye, then withdrew a small, leather-bound book. "Any specific elven monster?"

He offered the book forward and the title, written in her native tongue, read: *Endless Night: Monsters of the Zauleen Providences.* "No," she lied. She accepted the book, ignoring how her blood ran cold.

"I've read that one. It's lacking. You might be better served finding a book on Solviran to Zauleen translations—plenty of those around."

"It might be a decent investment of my time," Flowridia said softly, enthralled at the book in her hands. "It's a language I plan to learn." To whisper words of love to Ayla in her native tongue seemed a beautiful thing, indeed. "You say you've read this one?"

Tazel beckoned for her to follow and led her through the shelves. "I have. I've lived long enough to meet a few monsters in my days; I wanted to see if their depictions were accurate."

"Were they?"

"Well enough." The man opened a door, holding it as she passed. "If you don't mind me commenting," Tazel said, scrutiny in his gaze, "you're awfully young to be a witch."

Inside, Flowridia saw more shelves, but in the center she saw an established campsite, complete with evidence of fire. A sleeping roll lay strewn beside it, along with a pile of well-worn books, various satchels, and more. "With due respect," Flowridia replied, feeling bold, "you're awfully elven to have a familiar."

To her relief, she saw Tazel crack a wide smile. "Well, Sol Kareena chooses who she will."

When he sat down upon a pile of books, Flowridia did the same across from him. From a satchel, Tazel withdrew a wrapped wheel of cheese and a variety of fruit.

Flowridia watched the daintiness with which he plated the food, prepared to decline any offer of meat when she recalled that most elves were vegetarian. So when he offered the plate of cheese, fruit, and nuts, she accepted with a gracious smile. "Thank you. May I ask where you find fresh food in a place like this?"

"I pay a messenger to deliver supplies once a week," Tazel said, plating his own food.

"How long have you been here?"

"Oh, gods . . ." She watched Tazel mentally calculate whatever series of numbers flowed through his head. "At least six years. I'm happier alone."

"You haven't run out of money in six years?"

Tazel glanced up from his plate, looked to the door, then finally met her eye. He snapped his fingers, and from his hand a single, silver coin flipped out and landed on the floor. "It's one of many strange talents I have, to summon silver at will. I'm always certain to keep a supply on hand, for when the golems shake me down."

She giggled and teased, "You could single-handedly destroy the economy with that." Grateful when he grinned, she added, "You could leave, then?"

He set the plate on his lap and began picking at it. "I could," Tazel said, his smile more grimace than not. "Truth be told, I'm hiding."

"Hiding?"

"If you can avoid golems, this is a surprisingly safe place to live."

Flowridia set the plate down, suddenly wary. "Am I in the presence of a fugitive?" she asked, as nonchalant as she could summon.

Tazel, however, merely chuckled. "Not quite. Elven celebrities are rarely known outside of their own culture. I'm one of the rare elves with an affinity for magic, which I think explains the important parts. But I've been more . . . disillusioned, you could say, in recent years. So I hide here, a thousand miles away from my homeland and a few key people in particular."

"You were a hero, then?"

"According to the titles they gave me, yes. But it's not a life I would have chosen for myself. All I ever wanted was to study my books." Tazel gestured to the variety of literature around them—*Biological Mechanics, Airships of the Elven Empire,* and many more, most detailing some affinity for invention. "I'm teaching myself everything I was never able to learn as a youth. Did you know the Iron Elves have invented mechanical prosthetics? Organs, even?"

Flowridia shook her head, unable to fathom the thought.

"Neither did I, until yesterday. Now, I'm learning to build a gear-driven lung." He breathed a sigh of absolute peace. "I'm happy here."

The little bird gave a faint tweet, and Tazel offered his familiar a bit of fruit. "Tell me about the world," he said, smiling at Ferseph. "What have I missed?"

Flowridia couldn't help but chuckle. "In the past six years? A decent amount."

They spoke pleasantly of politics, the state of kingdom affairs, the newly crowned queen of Staelash. "But if you're from Staelash, why are you here? Are you a student?"

"No." Flowridia set aside her half-empty plate. "I'm actually their diplomat."

"A high position, for a child of your age."

"I'm older than I look."

When Tazel finished his plate, he gestured to the book beside her. "Why elven monsters?"

"It's a long story. I . . ." She offered a shrug. "Truth be told, I met one. I wanted to know what's true and not."

"So there is one in particular?"

Caught in her lie, Flowridia blushed. She offered only a nod.

Tazel stood up, gingerly collecting his things. "There're a few more books out there that might have what you want. I'll be back."

When Tazel left, Demitri placed his head upon Flowridia's lap. Ana bounced beside him. *He's a loony.*

Flowridia frowned at her familiar.

But he isn't creepy.

Flowridia thumbed open her book to the table of contents, realizing The Endless Night was not among the alphabetized chapters. "Strange," she muttered, then realized she had drawn attention.

What's strange?

"Ayla's name isn't in here." However, near the top was a different name she most certainly recognized. Flowridia frowned as she flipped the pages to the appropriate chapter.

Bringer of War, it read, and so engrossed she was at the illustration, of Khastra as her transformed self, that she nearly shrieked when a voice said, "You've met the Bringer of War?"

"Yes, actually," Flowridia said, grateful to not have to lie. "She worked for Staelash."

"I'll admit, I don't know much of Solvira in this century. I've mostly studied their history as warmongers. Dragon Slayers. Witch Hunters. I've heard rumors their more recent monarchs have been more benevolent."

Flowridia had heard whispers of Solvira's sordid history, had heard her mother speak of witch hunts, but Empress Alauriel presented nothing but the very picture of kindness. "It's true," she whispered. "I've met the empress."

"With the Bringer of War, they managed to conquer their impressive empire. Not that they wouldn't have done well enough on their own, however. The Silver Fire is among the most powerful of known magics."

"I don't know much about it, to be perfectly honest."

"The Silver Fire? It's the capacity to absorb magical energy and release it in a pure and potent form—the Solviraes have weaponized it for destruction, but the Moon Goddess, Neoma, wielded it as a power of creation. She could create life."

Flowridia looked up at that, intrigued at the words. "That's incredible."

"Unprecedented magic and proof of Neoma's vast power," Tazel replied, and with it gave a solemn nod. "They say she was more powerful than Sol Kareena—and more ruthless by far. Though, I suppose they wouldn't teach much of that branch of history anymore, given Neoma died a thousand years ago."

"How did she die?"

Tazel's amusement shone in his smile. "They really don't teach that anymore, do they. She was killed by the God of Death at the end of the Solviran Civil War—who, in turn, was sealed beneath the earth by Neoma's power."

Recalling Casvir's words regarding the Civil War, Flowridia asked, "The God of Death?"

"I apologize—Neoma's daughter, Ilune, the Great Necromancer; she was colloquially known as the God of Death. The elves have long lives and longer memories. I was told firsthand accounts of the battle as a child. Scars of it still ravage the world, and apparently there are godly artifacts lost within the realm to this day."

Intrigued at the words, Flowridia nearly asked more, when a sentence at the bottom of the page stole her focus: *As a daughter of Ku'Shya, she remains a foe of Izthuni and his manifest form in the mortal realm (see: chapter 13: Scourge of the Sun Elves).*

"'Scourge of the Sun Elves?'" she said, distaste coating her tongue at the words. She began flipping to the chapter.

"Now, there's a legend," Tazel said, having settled across from her. "They use her Solviran title as the book's name, but the Scourge and The Endless Night are the same. The dwarven populace had their own name for her—*Gaping Maw.*"

"That's ghastly," Flowridia said, and within her stomach, dread welled.

"Since they seem to be using technical titles, I'm surprised they didn't use her true name."

"Ayla Darkleaf?"

Tazel frowned—not at the book, but at her. "Well learned, indeed, to know that name."

"I also met her," Flowridia said, assuming it couldn't be so damning to admit as much.

But Tazel's gasp said otherwise. Green eyes growing wide, he said, "By Sol Kareena's Light, she's back..." He placed a hand to his forehead, all color vanishing from his features.

"No, no. She's not. Ayla is dead." It burned her to say it, but Tazel finally breathed again.

Though he did remain stiff. "You're sure?"

"I watched her die," she said, hoping her fear masked the pain in the statement.

"And you've burned her? Scattered the ashes across the world?"

Flowridia shook her head.

"Then she might as well be sleeping."

When he moved to set aside the book, Flowridia shook her head. "Her body is in the possession of Casvir," she said, panicked. "He'll take care of it."

He slowly turned his head around to face Flowridia, gaze narrowing. "Imperator Casvir of Nox'Kartha, the most feared necromancer on the planet, has the body of Ayla Darkleaf?"

"He's the one who brought her back, five years ago. And I know what you must be thinking," she said, holding out a hand to calm him. "But he doesn't want her back."

Tazel remained tense. "And he'll properly dispose of her?"

Flowridia realized she couldn't summon the will to lie, so she settled on nodding. "But she was the Nox'Karthan diplomat," she added quickly. "She and I often met." Her breath hitched. "She was dear to me."

The fear in his eyes didn't fade, but any anger melted into sympathy. "You don't know anything about her, do you?"

Something about the question lacerated her wounded heart. It must have bled into her words. "I know much more than I think I wish to."

In gentle motions, Tazel stole the book from her grip. She let him, confused at the gesture. "Perhaps," he whispered, paternal in his tenderness, "it is best to let Ayla Darkleaf's history die with her. She was a friend to you, as you said. Don't tarnish your memories with this."

"She wasn't my–" Flowridia bit back her words, clenching her fists. "I've seen awful things. I want to understand."

Tazel, with care, returned the book to her lap, his eyes broken even as he smiled. "Flowridia, no one understood her. Not in a thousand years."

Limbs shaking, Flowridia opened the book to the ominous chapter and found her prize, that of Ayla's name in beautiful script. A pencil drawing, crosshatched and shadowed, showed a shadowy silhouette. Small and lithe, Flowridia knew that form, but a shudder filled her at the next drawing—elongated and monstrous, The Endless Night.

A clinical sort of writing met her view:

> *Among every race, there is the creature that causes the bump in the night. The Celestials speak of 'The Shadow,' and dwarves, 'The Gaping Maw.' Among human kingdoms, it is 'The Endless Night," but only the elves knew her true name: Ayla Darkleaf, Scourge of the Sun Elves.*
>
> *The details of her death remain unknown. But she rose as the first vampiric creature, then set up residence in the mountains of Kaas for nearly a thousand years, where she began her plague upon*

the Sun Elves. Known for her charm and genius, Darkleaf performed dark experimentation on stolen participants, often children, the remains of whom were commonly found without skin—

"Flowridia?"

Gasping, Flowridia looked up, realizing her eyes welled with tears.

"I did find other books on elven monsters," he said softly, "and a few translations. But are you all right?"

Her hands balled into fists, nails digging into her skin. "I won't pretend to know the legacy she left across the sea, but I know what I saw beneath the castle. And it was so utterly *sickening–*"

Her resolve cracked. Tears would come if she spoke another word of it. Flowridia stole Ana into her arms and held the book with the other as she stood up. "It wasn't the woman I knew."

Yet, wasn't it? This woman who had gleefully slaughtered the cavern of dwarves, had spared no innocents and decimated the Skalmites? Who had murdered an envoy from the Theocracy when they insulted her pride? Ayla had sworn to tear her apart; Flowridia had been spared because of her naïve, open heart. Ayla had been a woman of violence and fury, of genius and lust . . .

She heard Tazel say, "I'm sorry."

Still, her mind refused to process any of it, the damning knowledge swirling, never settling.

"I realize she was your friend."

"We weren't—!" Flowridia stopped as tears welled in her eyes. Bracing herself, she released a breath, then sniffed back the threatened sorrow. "Ayla and I weren't friends. We were never friends; we were. . ." Her grip on Ana tightened. Her softened in defeat. "I loved her. I apologize–"

"Flowridia," Tazel said softly, his interruption as gentle as the breeze at night, "sometimes the people who claim to love us most have their own motives. She wasn't capable of love."

But Ayla had loved. Ayla had been loved. Casvir said she had changed.

Unwilling to risk crying, Flowridia stepped toward the door, Demitri following beside her. She gripped the book, her fingers turning white.

"I'm sorry."

Flowridia stopped in the doorway. "It's a tender wound."

"Perhaps I'm wrong," he said, at which point Flowridia turned around. Tazel's apologetic gaze had not diminished, yet a certain wariness had come to join it. "Perhaps, instead, you are more than you seem."

Flowridia leaned against the doorframe. "I don't feel like much, lately." She smiled at him, tears flowing quietly. "Thank you for your help."

"It's rare to find pleasant company. Find me anytime." He gestured to the books on elven translations. "I'm always happy to help with study."

She forced a smile and left him alone, purging any deeper thoughts from her mind.

"Scourge of the *what now?*"

She sat in her new guest room, detached from the world beyond. Through her tears, Flowridia told Etolié the entire tale—of the labyrinth and all its horrors, of the research she'd found, even the strange elven man in the library. With Demitri curled around her, her face puffy and raw, she said, "It's all true, Etolié. Everything I saw. She had done it for a thousand years, and I don't know what to do."

"First of all, you should go learn Elven from Tazer."

"Tazel . . ?"

"Look, Flowers, not many elves are willing to teach outsiders authentic syntax. It might give you a way to keep your mind off everything."

"Etolié, that's not–" Her words caught in her throat, and behind her cries, she heard Etolié's gentle, *'Shh . . .'* from the mirror. "I love Ayla," she managed to say.

"And you're allowed to still love her, Flowers, even if the rest of us don't understand it." The Celestial watched with alert, bloodshot eyes behind the mirror. "I've never understood romance, but I've watched it enough to know it's complicated."

Flowridia simply continued sobbing.

"Listen, let me know if I'm stepping on toes, but you've been out camping with Tyrant Deathless for, what, a month? You need to give yourself time to mourn. This kind of information would rip open anyone's old wounds, but I'm not convinced yours ever healed at all."

Mourning precluded Ayla was never coming back. Insidious waves of doubt crept into Flowridia's broken heart. She forced a smile. "Am I allowed to call the kettle black?"

Etolié smiled with gaunt cheeks and tired eyes, no joy in the gesture. "You're the one having a breakdown, not me."

Flowridia wiped the tears from her eyes, sniffing as she said, "How are you doing?"

"I'm fine. I'm busy. If you want a subject change, I did some research on the Sha'Demoni situation."

"Please."

"The empress sent over some books, and I found a few things that might interest you." Etolié's face disappeared. Flowridia heard rustling paper. "Four arms and kinda spider-y, right?"

Recalling the demon, Flowridia said, "That's correct."

Etolié held a book up to the mirror. "Familiar?"

It was, and Flowridia's eyes widened as she took in the drawing of a four-armed demon woman with a spider's lower half, deathly thin with braided hair nearly to the floor. "That's her."

She heard Etolié laugh from behind the book. "Oh, Flowers, Flowers . . . You're so fucked."

"I beg your pardon?"

"Sorry, laughter is a well-documented stress response." Etolié's face reappeared, and Flowridia saw her nervously smile behind her fit of giggles. "She's known as 'The Coming Dawn.' No one knows much about her, only that she worked with a vampire hunter known as 'Dark Slayer' to bring about the end of The Endless Night some four hundred years ago or so. Technically, she's an elven hero."

So this was a deep history. Flowridia felt her blood run cold. The books didn't know much . . . but a certain half-demon in the castle had unparalleled knowledge.

"The Nox'Karthan library might know more," Flowridia said, though her breath caught in her throat at her own plot. "Etolié, I have to go."

"Flowers, tell Casvir. Tell him I'll send all my research because this is a *very real* threat to you and your well-being."

"Etolié, I really–"

"Better yet—I'll just pop over and deliver it myself."

"No, Etolié. I'll be fine."

"Will you? You were just crying your eyes out over your dead monster's murder spree."

Flowridia said nothing, merely looked away as she settled her thoughts. "We'll talk later," she finally whispered.

This time, Etolié let her go.

Khastra would know more than clinical history books. Perhaps she already knew of the war. Surely Casvir had said something. Perhaps this had all been settled without Flowridia's knowledge.

But she had to know.

In her search, Flowridia was told by a servant to seek the general in her private bath, and when she asked where that was, apparently Khastra had stolen and claimed it from Murishani. "Look in his domain."

The stairs to the library headed downward, but farther still, Murishani's domain also lay beneath the earth. Flowridia kept a hand on the wall, wary of labyrinths, but soon the stairs ended, and she was presented with a long hallway.

Lavish carpet cushioned her feet. Emblems of gold plated the sconces on the wall, subtle signs of finery otherwise unseen in the palace. Murishani's realm was beautiful, regal. Even the light shined brighter here.

Doors lined the hallway, but ahead lay an enormous archway, twenty feet tall at least. Beyond, all the light faded, lit only by scattered candelabras upon the walls.

Magic radiated from it, churning Flowridia's stomach. She held Ana in her arms, grateful the rambunctious critter had quieted down. Demitri, however, sniffed the air. *I don't like it here.*

"We just need to find Khastra," she said. Every step forward led to the ominous structure, but several doors lay to the sides. "Do you smell her?"

Demitri placed his nose to the ground. *I might, actually. There aren't so many dead things down here.*

Demitri led them to a door near the base of the staircases, well away from the ominous arch. *Here?*

Flowridia knocked, and to her surprise, it was answered.

A De'Sindai servant girl met her gaze—Flowridia's age at most, perhaps younger, but with her pink-hued skin and horns, Flowridia realized she had no actual way to gauge her age. "Can I help you, Lady Flowridia?"

The girl didn't seem nervous. Merely startled. "Do you know where I might find General Khastra?"

"She's in her bath. I will ask if she'll see you."

"I can wait–" The door shut.

Flowridia looked back to Demitri, smiling briefly until she stared again at the dark hallway. "Do you smell anything there?"

Whatever the spell is, it's masking my senses.

The door opened again, and the servant girl beckoned for them to follow.

The ground became stone. Flowridia set Ana down. Moist air enveloped her skin, the lights steadily dimmed, and the unmistakable scent of sage reached Flowridia's nose. Prickling memories of long ago brought the knowledge of plants and their properties; sage was a remedy for fear, to steady your heart and calm your breathing.

The girl led her around a turn. Flowridia saw her quarry.

Candles lit the room, casting eerie shadows across the damp walls, yet the ambience remained soothing. Centered was an enormous bronze tub, nearly as wide as Flowridia was tall. Khastra sat straight with her back to Flowridia, arms set on the curvature of the edge like a throne, the light reflecting the impressive muscles of her back and shoulders, cast in varying shades of blue and shining silver.

Two bars of metal ran parallel down her back, the skin around them red and raw. Her back had been broken. Flowridia realized that the torture she had seen was, perhaps, a drop in a bucket.

Two De'Sindai women stood behind her, plating her wet locks of hair into a single, thick braid. Flowridia had never realized how long it was; perhaps longer than she was tall. She noted that the two servants bore hair and braids in equally impressive styles and lengths, though neither stood taller than Flowridia.

Uncomfortable silence settled. In tentative steps, Flowridia approached, coming around the side. "Khastra?"

Khastra's glowing eyes spared her a glance. There was no shyness to her pose, but while Flowridia elected not to stare at her nakedness, any discomfort at the sight of her small breasts was far outweighed by the vicious scar between them. Great metallic pins clamped the two halves of her chest together, and nausea welled in Flowridia's stomach.

"Tiny one?"

"I was hoping I could speak to you," Flowridia said, noting that even seated, Khastra posed as though far taller than she.

The two women continued with their task of braiding the lengthy mane into a single rope. The girl who had led Flowridia inside stood respectfully apart, holding a towel in her arms.

Khastra finally said, "Go on."

Etolié had told her once to not be put off by Khastra's blunt airs, to simply speak her mind. "There is a war in Sha'Demoni," she began softly. "Did Casvir tell you?"

"He did."

"And did he tell you about my kidnapping."

"In passing."

"Your mother, Ku'Shya, has decreed my head as the price for your death."

"As is her right, according to Demoni law," Khastra replied, as though commenting on the dinner menu.

Flowridia steeled herself and asked, "What do you know about The Coming Dawn?"

Only now did Khastra fully face her. The half-demon raised an elegant eyebrow. "Is that who came to collect you?"

"Etolié found a drawing in a book. I'm very certain."

"Not many depictions of The Coming Dawn. She has rarely been seen outside of Sha'Demoni since the first death of The Endless Night; instead, she is now a lapdog to my mother."

Flowridia clung to every word. "You know her?"

"I know every member of Ku'Shya's court," Khastra said, but though Flowridia wished to melt onto the floor, the half-demon's words held no ire. "Be careful, tiny one. My mother was the first to mock Izthuni when he claimed a small elven girl to be his champion, but soon saw The Endless Night's growing power and sought to extinguish it. Ayla Darkleaf's death four hundred years ago brought fragile peace, but it seems my death has shattered it."

"If Ku'Shya knew you were here, would it stop the war?"

Khastra's concern faded into subtle indignation. "Doubtful. The insult stings worse than the crime. Which is why you should be *careful*. Ayla Darkleaf had many enemies, both of this world and the others. If not The Coming Dawn, someone else will come."

Flowridia recalled the labyrinth beneath the earth, perhaps adjacent to the realm she stood in now. Ayla was a woman of spite, and though Flowridia knew of her rivalry with Sora Fireborn and her lineage, she had never considered that there might be more.

"My presence in Nox'Kartha," Khastra continued, her tone pointed now, "will remain a secret until I deem it time."

Flowridia offered a quick nod.

"Are your questions answered, tiny one?"

She nodded again, though it was a lie. A thousand new ones welled in her mind, including the realization that Khastra would have known precisely who Ayla was even in Staelash, but her innately curious mind withered in the woman's domineering presence.

Khastra beckoned toward the small girl with her towel, then stood up. Flowridia looked away, demure at her nakedness, and accepted that this was her exit. "Thank you for your time," she muttered, and Flowridia saw herself out.

Once in the hallway, she finally spoke. "I feel like a fool, Demitri."

If it's any consolation, I think she thought you were a fool before, too. Nothing has changed—

His words ceased, and Flowridia stopped listening, because Ana suddenly darted toward the great archway.

"Ana!" she cried, but the little fox darted faster than she could keep up. "Ana, stop!"

The fox obeyed. Flowridia stepped beneath the arch to grab her, yet Ana continued to struggle. "What's gotten into you–"

"Lady Flowridia, whatever is the matter?"

Murishani's form appeared within the dark hallway, steadily approaching. When Flowridia stepped forward, the magical shield parted for her to enter. "Ana was misbehaving."

"Magical creatures are prone to behaving erratically under static, so to speak. There are some powerful spells here."

Flowridia glanced back toward the stairs, but saw nothing, as though the dark hallway stretched backward for miles. "Forgive me," she said softly, "but I should be going."

"Of course, Lady Flowridia,' Murishani said, offering his arm. "May I show you out?"

Murishani had been nothing but accommodating and friendly, yet something in her stomach screamed in revolt as she hesitantly looped her arm through his. "Lead on, I suppose."

He led her down the dark hallway, the candles casting shimmering lights across his opulent, gold-trimmed robes. Flowridia's free hand skimmed across Demitri's fur.

"I do hate to ask, but did you find what it was you sought?"

Flowridia nodded unwilling to elaborate.

"Goodness me," he replied, placing a hand on his heart. "A horrible place, Ayla Darkleaf's domain. An ingenious and dangerous mind, she had, but her application was unquestionably abhorrent." His hand patted hers. "Strange, what broken minds will do."

"What do you know?" Flowridia whispered, and his smile curdled her blood.

"Not much, though I tried to make nice with her. I brought her down here, but instead of reveling, she flayed her conquest alive."

Flowridia stiffened, swearing her heart skipped a beat. "What?"

"My domain is one of pleasures—of *every* variety, including the twisted sort Ayla requested. But you would know all about that, I'm sure," he said, his wink obscene and knowing and enough to make her gut squirm.

Perhaps her panicked confusion showed too obviously. "No? Lady Flowridia, I must ask then, what have you tried?" A pause, and his smile twisted into something coy. "What have you always wanted to try?"

Flowridia forced a smile, the inner voice labeled 'self-preservation' suddenly screaming at her to run. "Truthfully, I'd like to simply sleep through the night for once. Could you take me to my room?"

"I'd be a neglectful host without a tour–"

His words stopped; Flowridia squeaked at the grip on her shoulder. When she turned around and saw Khastra's severe gaze, she nearly fainted from relief.

"General, a surprise to see you–"

She pushed Murishani; he stumbled and let Flowridia go. Khastra placed her hand at Flowridia's back and led her away without a word.

She wore no armor, instead breeches and a shirt, yet still she remained imposing and grand. Her hair, shined and washed, travelled in a single braid down her back, nearly brushing her digitigrade knees. Flowridia said absolutely nothing, not until the scene returned to normal, the vision of the endless hallway rippling away. The archway became an ominous sight behind them.

"Thank you."

Khastra glanced down at her. "Stay away from him."

She continued escorting Flowridia up the stairs. "He's a tease, but he's only ever been polite–"

"You are a bigger idiot than Marielle, if you believe that."

Though shocked at the bluntness of Khastra's words, Flowridia realized the time for kindness had passed. "Why is he interested in me?"

Khastra stopped in the middle of the stairs. She grabbed Flowridia's shoulders, staring directly at her as she said, "I am not privy to his mind, but the reasons do not matter. Murishani is a manipulative and dangerous man. Next time, I may not be there to protect you."

Flowridia looked from Khastra's face to the floor. Already, the urge to second-guess her inner voice reared up, because Murishani had truthfully only ever presented the very image of kindness yet . . .

"You are nervous. What did he do to you?"

Flowridia's gaze shot back up. "It's only a hunch."

"Tell me."

Her posture fell. "I think he started the rumors about Casvir and I."

"Likely."

"He showed me other things, too. A-Around the castle. Secrets I shouldn't have seen."

Khastra didn't press, for which Flowridia was grateful. Instead, the half-demon released her shoulders. "Do not be alone with him." She continued escorting Flowridia up the stairs. "Murishani is the second-in-command of one of the largest empires in the world. Casvir is not a good man, but he is a man of honor. Murishani is everything the imperator lacks, and certainly not above slipping a knife through your back—or, more likely, convincing you to do it yourself."

Flowridia merely nodded, subdued beneath the reprimand. Neither said anything more until Khastra stopped at the crux of the second floor. "Tread lightly, tiny one. Nox'Kartha is not a place for the weak."

She left Flowridia alone.

Chapter 7

She spent the night in her ambassador's suite, plagued by tender dreams that burned her to think of in the daylight. She laid in a stasis in her bed until a knock at the door startled her.

Flowridia sat up, rubbing sleep from her eyes as Demitri spoke from where he lay beside her. *Smells gross. Must be Casvir.*

She couldn't help but chuckle at her rude boy. In her nightclothes, a bone-deep chill permeating her core, she stumbled from her bedside, gripping the doorframe for support when all the blood rushed to her head.

Casvir, imposing as always, stared down at her. "I apologize for the early hour. The grind of politics begins soon, but I wish to show you something. Will you come?"

She nodded.

"Put on clothing. We are going outside."

Within minutes, she had donned a high-necked piece of gaudy gold and pink. Not her favorite, but it suited her purposes. She and Demitri followed Casvir through the halls and down the stairs, his metallic steps unmistakable, and any servants they passed immediately ducked away or bowed. Flowridia preferred to not dwell on their thoughts. The rumors had travelled much too far for her comfort.

They exited through a door Flowridia did not recognize, but they immediately came upon a splendid sight.

The first hints of sunrise peeked beyond the horizon; within minutes, the sky would burst into brilliant shades of orange and blue. Despite the morning chill seeping down to her bones, she followed as Casvir led her to a copse of trees beyond.

She realized a path of stone wound between them, and through the array of greenery, thick bushes of flowers filled in the space. A colorful wonderland, fresh scents filling her nose as they stepped onto the path.

So engrossed she was, that Casvir's words startled her. "It is prudent to maintain a garden to entertain ambassadors, and so I invested money in gardeners many years ago. They cultivate the land, but none of them hold a candle to you."

Flowridia looked up from inspecting a particularly lush rose bush. "I have enthusiasm for gardening, I suppose–"

But her voice stopped when Casvir shook his head. "Never downplay your worth." He watched as she flitted about, following her lively steps as she inspected the floral masterpiece. Interspersed among the plant life were stone statues, benches, even a pagoda beyond. Funds had been invested here to make it a haven of idle entertainment. It seemed to never end. "If you need somewhere to clear your head, this place is open to you. Do with it as you wish; I trust in your talents."

Since returning to Nox'Kartha, Casvir's aura had been brusque at best. But here, alone, it felt like the woods again. "Thank you," she said, touched at the thoughtfulness. However, the sentiment was marred by a rising bitterness threatening to choke her. "You provide entertainment and havens to all in your servitude."

"Happy workers are productive."

"Does that mean you condoned Ayla's behaviors?" And Murishani's, and the torture onto Khastra's sentient body . . .

It was a cruel accusation, especially to one who had shown her nothing but thoughtfulness. "I built her labyrinth, yes. I told you that."

"And you gave your own citizens to be tortured and met to hellish fates?"

His response surprised her—never had he spoken so harshly. Not to her. "What I do for the greater good of my kingdom is not yours to denounce. Rest assured that those given to Ayla for experimentation were sentenced to die— the murderers, the rapists, those who harm children. The justice of my kingdom rewards the citizens who contribute but condemns those who break my laws."

Flowridia didn't say what she had seen of Khastra's fate—but the half-demon was no citizen, she realized. She recalled the priestess of Neoma who was slain to bring Ayla's return.

Casvir was a ruthless monarch, willing to burn the world for the betterment of his own. She would be a fool to forget that.

To her surprise, he withdrew the orb from his armor, the crackling beacon of power spiking against her senses at his touch. "In all my study, I feel nothing more or less of Ayla Darkleaf. Surprising, given the supposed power of this orb."

Though she felt like a fool, she withdrew the ear from her bodice and held it up to the orb, watching Casvir for a reaction.

"Perhaps it is, as I said, because she is something different than a ghost, in the possession of her own god. I cannot say." He looked beyond her, past her shoulder to the empty air. "But she continues to haunt you, in an entirely real way."

The words would have once drawn tears to her eyes, to know that Ayla cared still. Now, she felt only dread. "I hear her," she admitted, and to her surprise Casvir frowned. "At night. In dreams. The louder she speaks, the sicker I feel in the morning. The tighter she holds–" Realization struck her, a punch to her brutalized heart. ". . . the colder I feel."

"In sleep, our consciousnesses are far more susceptible to magical influence. Has she spoken anything of interest?"

"I think she tried to warn me of the demon."

Flowridia told him what Etolié had said of The Coming Dawn, passing it off as something she'd read for herself, and recalled from long ago the words echoing in her dreams the night before her abduction.

"Dawn . . . approaching."

She told him all. His gaze narrowed in disappointment. "You should have told me."

She merely swallowed her shame. "What does it mean, Casvir?"

"It means, with study, you may be able to speak to her in return."

Her heart might've once sang, but now, as she looked upon the shriveled, desiccated ear, it felt as cold as the labyrinth that had nearly swallowed her whole.

Her jaw set, stubbornly grit against the angry tears that might've risen—but not today. She had cried enough for Ayla Darkleaf.

Even if it wounded her beyond words to think.

"You maintain an impressive garden of your own in Staelash," Casvir said, startling her from her thoughts. "My connection to you was severed whenever you entered the premise. Was that on purpose?"

"In a way," Flowridia admitted. Her feet took idle steps forward, willing away the vitriolic thoughts in her head. "I wove wards of protection into the roots of the plants, preventing anyone who would try and harm me from entering. It also prevented eavesdropping, magical or otherwise. My mother taught me many things. Wards were a specialty of hers."

"Your wards are better."

He said it so definitively, so decisive. Surprised, Flowridia said, "What makes you say that?"

"The lingering connection I felt to your mother always persisted, even after the death of her familiar. You, however, I could not feel when you stepped behind your garden walls."

The statement welled a thousand questions and confirmed a few festering suspicions Flowridia had kept to herself. She turned back to face him, his cold aura odd among the sea of beauty. "So, you did know my mother?"

"She never knew me, but I certainly knew her. I granted her power hundreds of years ago. She was an intelligent woman, clever and capable, and with a mind for the macabre I wished to see flourish. Her remarkableness came from utter squalor; she was a woman with no title, no grand heritage, yet already renowned among her people as a medicine woman, working her way from poverty to fortune. So, I granted her what she always claimed to have—true magic—and watched to see how she would thrive."

He paused then, thoughtful as he studied Flowridia who watched with rapt attention. "I was a younger monarch then, seeking exceptional minds to fill vacancies in my kingdom. Had her familiar not been killed by the Solviran heir apparent, she might have been taken to live among mine." He watched her expectantly, and Flowridia realized he wished to verify if she knew this as well.

"Mother told me pieces of that tale."

"A pity she bargained to escape that marriage. Solviraes blood creates powerful children."

To speak so clinically of murder and rape chilled Flowridia's blood. She bit back her discomfort, hiding her expression by returning her attention to the path. Demitri, always attuned to her emotions, came up beside her and bumped her with his nose. "Then you're the same demon to whom she prayed–"

And to whom she sold her child.

Flowridia stopped. Casvir stepped up beside her. "Mother gave me to you," she whispered, pieces of her own history falling into place. "Aura appeared to me as a little girl because you had been watching." Flowridia frowned suddenly, furrowing her brow as she looked up to face him. "But why me? Mother had other children . . ."

But none of those other children were told a bedtime tale of their father, a paladin of Sol Kareena, sent by a demon in the woods.

"You know who my father is," Flowridia said suddenly. The very birds seemed to cease their morning song. Casvir, however, simply nodded. "You sent my father to Odessa. Why?"

He gestured to the pagoda beyond the path. She followed as he led her to a bench in the center. "I asked for a child," he said, not joining her when she sat. "Not any specific child. I sent a man I knew could sire a worthy heir for my power. Odessa may have been a failed investment, but that did not mean I could not salvage something from her squandered potential."

Flowridia's fingers went to idly stroke Demitri's fur. "But–" She cut off her words, realizing she danced dangerously on the line of disrespect.

She cringed when Casvir said, "Yes?"

"Nothing." Flowridia whispered, keeping her eyes to the ground. "You already told me you wish for me to stay in Nox'Kartha. That answers my question enough."

"Truthfully, my plans for you," Casvir said, his voice slow and thoughtful, "are still developing."

"I don't–" Flowridia bit her tongue, fearful to accuse the imperator of falsehood. Instead, she swallowed her words but flinched when Casvir spoke.

"Please, speak your mind," he said, sincere as far as she could discern.

Flowridia looked beyond the stone pillars, eyes caressing the garden life. "I don't believe that."

When at first he said nothing, Flowridia shut her eyes, unsure if she would be struck down where she sat or at least reprimanded.

His words surprised her, especially in so gentle a package. "It shows, at times, the abuse your mother inflicted upon you."

Flowridia's gaze shot up, her breath hitching slightly as she studied his thoughtful stare.

Casvir stared, his red eyes studying her every twitch. He sat at the bench across from her, and she didn't dare to look away. "Though I would reassure you that I mean you no ill will, you are wise to mistrust my words. Your trusting heart has been brutalized. The past is your greatest teacher."

The hand hidden in Demitri's fur clung to his soft coat, the poignant words piercing deep. Flowridia released a steadying breath.

"I do mean what I said, that my plans for you are still developing, but only because you are meant for greater things than I had anticipated."

Flowridia stared forward, curious to know more, but unsure if she were allowed to ask.

Casvir's stoicism cracked. He raised a single eyebrow, as if daring her to move. "Speak your mind."

"Who was my father?"

It was then that the sunrise burst through the scattered leaves, casting celestial flame onto the imperator's face, shadowing his conspiring smile. "Your father's name was Zanoram, and I met him on the road outside the Solviran Capitol. A prestigious paladin to Sol Kareena, yes, but far from home, weary of the road although he claimed to be travelling to see his family. I told him of a great evil within the Abyssal Swamp preying upon men and young women, and duty bound, he went. Odessa played her predictable part, and in the end, he lay dead, and she carried a child."

There was more, Flowridia knew, and she steeled herself to ask. "But who was he? 'Prestigious paladin' means nothing. There are many of those."

"His full title was Zanoram, Bearer of Light, hailed hero of the Theocracy of Sol Kareena, and the only son of Archbishop Xoran."

Flowridia's head swam, contemplating all the puzzle pieces that had suddenly been forced together. Chosen of Sol Kareena, claimed by the Goddess herself after a childish offering left at the altar, but for reasons deeper than she might have ever imagined.

"That birthright is yours to claim," Casvir said, voicing her final thought, "if you ever tire of the title 'Grand Diplomat.'"

The Theocracy of Sol Kareena was a monarchy, despite the title. Rights to rule were passed down through lineage, and female Archbishops were well-documented throughout their history. She would be the very first to claim a demon as a patron, instead of Sol Kareena.

"But I had not foreseen your potential for necromancy."

Pulled from her musing, Flowridia met his eye.

"Nor would I have ever thought you might tame a beast like Ayla Darkleaf. The Endless Night saved your life from the God of Order."

Flowridia recalled being cradled in the monster's embrace, Izthuni himself manifest upon the world, protecting her at Ayla's behest. It tore down the walls she had hastily constructed, the reminder of tenderness among monstrosity piercing her heart.

"Should you sign my contract and wish for your throne in the Theocracy, I will consider your terms fulfilled. But I do wonder if there is a destiny for you somewhere else."

The thought made her head reel. Flowridia released her breath, casting her stare to the stone ceiling, noting the abstract designs. "I have no idea what you mean by that."

"I mean nothing by it. I only mean that you continue to surprise me. I am content to merely watch fate unfold." Casvir spared a glance for the sun, silent a moment before he added, "My day must begin. But you are free to enjoy all the gifts my palace can offer."

"Thank you," she whispered, and she smiled as he left her, listening until his metallic steps disappeared down the stone path.

What are you thinking?

Flowridia contemplated Demitri's question, content to sit upon her stone bench and breathe the morning air. "I am thinking, that if I ever choose to reveal my heritage to the Theocracy royals, it would make for a rather awkward family reunion. I don't think my grandfather likes me much."

She chuckled at her own words, kissing Demitri when he rose to lick her face.

But a shadow followed Flowridia wherever she went.

She returned to the library and greeted Tazel like a friend. "I'm sorry if I was off-putting yesterday," she said sheepishly, unwilling to meet his gaze. "It's a difficult time for me."

His smile held the empathy of one who truly understood, full of sorrow and sincerity. "I was also once betrayed by someone I loved, who I was a fool to think loved me."

He said nothing more, but there was kindness in his words.

"I may not understand it," Flowridia said, her stare resting at his pile of books, unmoved from the day before, "but I want to know. I need to know everything."

With Tazel's assistance, she learned a tale of horror unbound.

Stoic throughout, she read of a thousand years of slaughter, entire villages gone in a night by The Endless Night. Some were clinical, but most were narrative accounts, written by the survivors of a genocide spanning generations of elves.

> *. . . remember fire blazing in the city square. "Stand in the light!" someone cried. "The Endless Night is weak in the light. We need only survive until dawn!"*
>
> *From the great shadows cast by the fire, the beast appeared. It stood taller than the buildings, and when it balanced on two legs and bellowed a roar—*

Flowridia remembered the deaths of the Skalmites, thousands in a bloodstained day and night, by the monster who grinned with a visage too horrifying to describe . . . and who had held her tenderly, who had stood between she and the God of Order and Sol Kareena both.

*. . . every inch of land lay covered in debris
and carnage, and already the scent of death and
stagnant blood began rising—*

*. . . caravans were abandoned. I remember
the desperate cries of horses—some left to die, and
others rearing up as their owners fought to unhitch
them from the wagons. I saw The Endless Night lift
one like a doll and ram it into the ground.*

*Then, the monster flinched. From the
torches' light, I saw a strange, arachnid beast, some
sort of demon crying out in the forbidden, demonic
tongue. She spoke wicked words, yet she was our
savior that night, luring the monster away as we
abandoned our wagons and ran—*

She read of the disappearances of children in the
night, the fates of those who came to find Ayla Darkleaf.

*. . . cannot say it all, lest my hand falter and
I stain this account with tears. But Karnilla, my
sweet sister, died a slow and agonizing death, taken
apart piece by piece while the woman was certain to
name every action, every severed part she held up
with her cursed instruments. At first I fought, and
then I sobbed, my heart shattered by her screams as
she cried my name.*

*When her cries finally stilled, I nearly
choked for relief—but then I saw it was a farce, for
the monster had merely removed her throat, yet still
she lived—*

*. . . she laughed all the while, chatting
pleasantly of the weather and her home as she
stitched the man together again, his face replaced
with another's—*

Thorough and gleeful, Casvir had said. Thorough and
gleeful in all she did.

And she read of later years, of corrupt and wicked
men who sought Ayla for political gain, to wield her as a
weapon.

. . . door was locked—not sure how she got in. Asked me what I was doing, asked if I was happy here, apologized for Master's behavior, said she didn't approve. She touched me on my neck and whispered that I was 'devastatingly beautiful.' Told her I had to be somewhere or be beaten more and ran—

. . . responsible for the slaughter of Baron Greatwhite and his family, leading the way for Lord Redwood to be elected Executor of the Highland Elves—

. . . overheard she and my husband in his bedroom. Mostly her. She's not quiet. I left that night to see my mother.

Later found out she slaughtered the entire household—Executor Wellrock and all—not a day later. It saved my life.

Perhaps she might've risen to her own power, save for her death by Fireborn hands. Tazel offered her a personal account, written by Yeshua Fireborn himself.

. . . and so it fell to The Coming Dawn to lure Ayla from her home in the mountains of Kaas— some old cohort of Mereen's who steps into shadows with the skill of The Endless Night herself. We were not told her name, only that she was of some importance in Sha'Demoni. I questioned the intelligence of siding with demons; Mereen said compromises must be made for the greater good. Raziel, my brother, agreed, and so the plan was set, despite my misgivings.

The demon, to her credit, delivered on her promise. I know not what she said or did, but in a cave far beneath the Mountains of Kaas, she lured the monster at dawn—

. . . in the great altercation, there came a moment whereupon the world faded, and it was she and I. She bared her fangs and leapt for my throat, but instinct decreed I would live that day—I smacked her with the blunt of my sword then bashed

her forehead with my shield. In her daze, The Coming Dawn grabbed her and flung her into the coffin.

My brother, Raziel, awaited to slam it, but in a final burst of vengeance, she grabbed his arm, shattering it as she dragged him inside. I ran to save him. Mereen slammed it shut.

I stared in shock at the screaming coffin— first bearing two voices but soon only one, the pitiful, furious, sobbing cry of the monster. I joined it.

A long and harrowing day. Flowridia shed not a single tear.

She stared at the blank pages, mind reeling to piece together the words with the puzzle of the woman she had loved.

The woman she still loved.

"Flowridia?" Tazel spoke gently, his words barely breaking through the muted fog surrounding her mind. "Are you all right?"

"I think I've read enough for today," she whispered, and she stood up, feeling as though her soul floated beside her own body, for she was a mere puppet on strings. "I appreciate your help, but I think I need to be alone now."

He gave no farewell but a nod.

Demitri and Ana followed, the former saying nothing as she climbed the stairs, heading not to her bedroom, but to Ayla's.

Flowridia, standing before the door, couldn't bring herself to enter.

Mom?

She shook her head at her familiar. Instead, she reached into her bodice and gripped the ear in her hand, the one forever placed beside her heart.

"Casvir said," she whispered, "that her death, in service of me, was as kind and poetic an end as she deserved.

That I was the only redeeming quality he ever saw in her." Her eyes shut, and this time she let her tears flow freely. "I don't know what I should do, Demitri."

You don't have to decide that now.

So wise, her sweet boy. Flowridia placed a hand upon his head. "I'm searching for answers I simply won't find. Crying into the void, as Casvir said."

Demitri licked her cheek. *We'll find them someday. Maybe you can ask her yourself, once you bring her back.*

Her limbs lost feeling at the statement, growing cold from the anxiety filling her. Bring Ayla back?

Scourge of the Sun Elves, who for a thousand years inflicted torture and death upon those surrounding her, with a body count of hundreds of thousands or more, and with no remorse. "I don't know what I want anymore." In measured motions, she removed the chain from around her neck. She held the ear in her open hands. "I don't even know if her love was sincere."

Yet her very soul rejected the notion. She saw the pain in Ayla's eyes at her apology, the desperation in her proclamation of love. For all her crimes, all her monstrous deeds. Flowridia remembered the night they danced, when Ayla had so lovingly led her across the floor, taught her to step, how to hold her skirt. How perfect, the love in her countenance. There had been no monster then, no fangs or death or talk of torture—only Ayla in her purest form, holding her close, changed by her love.

But ... had she been? That image of her secret chamber, of the victim on the slab bombarded her perfect scene. All that blood and those eyes—*those eyes.*

Soft tears streamed down Flowridia's face. "I never mourned her. For all my sorrow, I held to the hope of her return." Her hand clenched around the ear, trembling. "Perhaps that was my mistake."

A sob escaped her lips. The ear fell to the ground as she brought her hands up to cover her face. Ayla was gone, Ayla was gone ... and Ayla would stay gone.

Why did she feel so empty, still?

A final resting place, then.

Tearfully, she had knocked on Casvir's door, giving no explanation but requesting the body. He obeyed, and he did not ask. She was brought a plain, wooden coffin.

The box was light, its mistress small and shriveled, and so Flowridia carried it with ease down the labyrinth's halls. Demitri followed with Ana in tow, the former of which said nothing as he walked by her side.

She dared to return, yes. Aimless, she wandered, but there was only one destination. When the smell grew strong, Flowridia approached the archway without fear. "Prepare yourself, Demitri. But there is no danger here."

She entered the cathedral, braced for blasphemy and horror. Though it sickened her soul, she soaked in the details, marveled at the macabre creation. The statue of leather and flesh bore the Goddess' countenance, her jeweled tears shining. The mockery of stained glass held detailed scenes, ones Flowridia dared to approach and inspect. Visages of demons, of Izthuni and The Endless Night, a great, unblinking eye, and a spider-like monster bearing lengthy limbs, consuming elven flesh.

There was beauty in the horror, like Ayla herself. She had fought with the grace of a dancer on a stage, tearing her opponents to shreds in perfect sync. A wonder to watch, great and terrible both.

Demitri followed, soaking it in as she did. It wounded her to introduce this to his young mind, but he was hardly a child anymore. *I understand why you were scared.*

"I can take you back."

No, I want to be here for you. And for Lady Ayla.

Such a sweet boy.

Flowridia approached the altar, the box still in hand. The visage of the Goddess eternally wept, and Flowridia wondered why and how and all manner of impossible things, understanding she might never, save from the lips of the dead woman she held. Ayla had constructed a mockery of the Goddess, and in the end, the Goddess had slain her.

How a Goddess of benevolence could inspire such pure hatred from a monster should not have unsettled her so. Flowridia looked down to the altar between them. *Burn,* it read.

In its mirror, in a cathedral of divinity and light, she and Ayla had made love a final time upon this altar. Perhaps that's why it cut so deep.

She left it behind and instead went to the door to the back, prepared for the onslaught of terror. The smell sickened her, the corpse she had slain slowly emulsifying in the underground air. She looked around the display, recognizing its genius, though it wounded her so. This was Ayla's life; this was her legacy.

But not her love. Flowridia's foot brushed the discarded, translucent cloth she had dropped. With care, she placed the coffin on the ground and gathered the embroidered fabric in her arms. It bore the texture of silk, fine and soft, decorated with pastel thread. By chance, she saw the dress form from the corner of her eye, the unfinished gown, and realized they were the same. The white skirt, long and flowing, matched the fabric in her hands, and Flowridia recalled the leather book, *Flowridia Darkleaf* embossed in perfect script . . . and understood.

It should have frightened her, and it did, Ayla's presumptuous airs about romance both endearing and shocking. But in her broken state, Flowridia clung to the promise, the future stolen away, and knew assuredly that it had been true.

She touched the coffin, the one holding a monster too wicked for this world, the one who had wrought destruction and death, who left a legacy of horror too dark to contemplate. But when she opened the box, bracing herself for the eternal scream, she felt an outpouring of sorrow and love.

Flowridia set out the embroidered veil, folding it just so, and lifted the corpse into her arms, trembling as she placed it down. A funeral shroud it would be now, an ending instead of a beginning.

With finality, Flowridia placed the chained ear around the corpse's neck, letting the ear itself land gracefully onto Ayla's dead heart. She carefully folded the cloth to cover her love, the corpse visible beneath the translucent material.

Flowridia lifted the wrapped corpse and cradled Ayla in her arms. She cried, the suppressed feelings of the months welling up all at once. "I love you, Ayla," she managed between sobs.

"Please, never leave me."

She never would. "My heart is yours forever."

Demitri came and touched his nose to Ayla's forehead. *She always smelled so good.*

Flowridia laughed as she sobbed and brought a hand up to brush across Demitri's face. "She loved you too."

And so she cried for Ayla, for the life she lived, the legacy she wrought, and the love she'd lost. A semblance of peace filled Flowridia, to think, despite whatever pain had twisted Ayla's soul, that she had felt joy before her passing.

She had been loved.

When her cries stilled, Flowridia hummed a tune to send her off, the very same once sung at a funeral long ago, a song Ayla adored. She knew not the words, but this would be enough; it had to be.

She placed Ayla gently into the coffin, wrapped in a literal promise of love. The coffin itself she moved to the corner of the room, beneath a table, for there was nowhere else to put it save in the open.

But no. Ayla should be protected from horror in death. Even horror she herself had created.

As she passed through the laboratory, numb to the horrid displays, she happened a glance at a book, the very one she'd discarded—*Flowridia Darkleaf.*

Quite suddenly, it was pushed off the table by a force Flowridia knew not. She flinched as it fell to the floor, half-splayed, and narrowly bit back a shriek.

Her heart thumped to deafen her. A growl reached her ears; beside her, Demitri bristled, voice panicked. *This is haunted. We should go.*

But Flowridia remained a statue, some spell binding her to the ruined book on the floor. The spine had unraveled in the fall, splaying the pages like a fan.

Silence settled. When she finally breathed, the world turned again. Ignoring her familiar, she knelt down to repair it, finding it simple enough to reassemble. She held it in her arms as she stood up, idly opening up the cover—

And was shocked to find writing. Flowridia's breath hitched as she studied the words:

> *My heart sings when I think of you, Flowra.*
> *Forgive the impulsive use of my last name.*
> *Your name is such a joy to write, with all the*
> *flowing curves, each letter fading into the next. I*
> *often get carried away practicing it in my spare*
> *moments, etching it into my work, sometimes even*

humming it as I brush my hair. A pity, to have no surname to link it to. And so, I offer you mine.

You intoxicate me, my sweet summer blossom. To know you is to know pure joy, and though I remain unworthy to walk in your shadow, you dance with me in the sun. I am lifted in your presence. This feeling of love is so wondrous and new, and it wounds me that we must spend our days apart.

Someday, I hope to give you all you deserve. Someday, I shall steal you away, keep you by my side so all may see you belong to me and only me. Someday . . . Someday . . .

Until then, I cherish every moment in your presence. You are worth the wait.

I mean as I said, that it is a tragedy for you to stunt your nobility. Accept my name, and know I mean everything by it.

I love you. Be mine forever, darling.
-Ayla Darkleaf

Flowridia shut the book and clutched it to her chest, its contents more precious than gold. Yet, her nerves remained alight. There was no breeze to have unsettled the leather-bound book. She stared at the box on the floor, the impossible thought that perhaps this was more than a chance omen prickling at her nerves.

A goodbye from the void . . . or perhaps a plea to stay.

She approached the wall, and with Demitri in tow she revealed the passage to the stairs. With her eyes kept on the coffin, Flowridia stepped forward until the stairs stole it from her sights.

Flowridia began to fear the night, for there was no dark shadow to protect her from its inhabitants. Where there was once peace, she saw nightmares.

Visions of horror, of the God of Order approaching with his promise of an elemental death, of Ayla's screams as she shriveled and died. Even Mother returned to the forefront of her visions, her spirit invading the very laboratory Ayla had kept.

Sometimes she saw herself upon the slab.

The dreams were not from Ayla herself, she knew. Ayla's spirit lay beneath the earth.

And by every god—she felt so guilty to consider it.

"Your accent will get you thrown into prison, if your ears don't first."

Flowridia began bringing Tazel food, and in exchange she left a little more learned on elven syntax. A friendly face was rare in this place.

"Your grasp on the language is good," he said one day, each of them with a book in their hands, "which is impressive, given that Solviran Common holds roots in Celestière. But no matter what your disguise, your accent will give you away."

"Are you implying that I'll be hiding my identity?"

Tazel nodded. "Not many humans live in Zauleen, and even fewer are taken seriously. Elves are notoriously racist. I can certainly say I'm guilty of it in my past."

Flowridia shut the book, intrigued by his words. "But you've changed?"

"I saw the world and couldn't deny the truth—that everyone, no matter their shape, has the same soul."

Flowridia smiled at the sentiment. "Didn't you say you were an elven celebrity?"

"Given that I'm the rare elf granted a familiar, I suppose it was destiny." Tazel smiled kindly at Ferseph. "Sol Kareena saw fit to give me a destiny, and I did what I could with it, while I could."

Flowridia longed to ask what changed, but knew he'd never tell. However, the prickling hope of perhaps talking him into revealing it herself kept her speaking. "Tell me a story. What's something you've done?"

Tazel shook his head. "I'm much too embarrassed to talk about myself."

"I would genuinely love to hear. I don't know much about what would constitute an elven hero."

Tazel stood up and stole a book from the pile beside him, one bearing an elven title. He flicked through the contents and tapped a page before setting it down onto Flowridia's lap. The depiction was of an icy throne, upon which sat a woman with a wicked gaze. "Helfira: The Witch of the North," he said ceremoniously. "She plagued the Highland Elves for decades, sought to freeze them in an eternal winter."

Flowridia skimmed the page and realized Tazel's name was there. "You killed her."

Tazel nodded, though the imperceptible flicker of shame darkened his countenance. "I burned her alive, and then cursed her to linger as a spirit forced to protect the very people she sought to oppress. I was taught, as a child, that the greater good justified all means, but . . ." He shook his head. "The price was paid, but I retired shortly thereafter."

"And by 'retired,' you mean you came here."

"Gods, no," Tazel said, daring to laugh despite his fallen features. "Though I see why you'd guess that. Some curses require a price or spell component, some valuable, some rare. The price was 'blood of the dying.' My partner, at the time, slit her own throat so I could cast the spell."

Flowridia said, "I'm terribly sorry."

"It was years and years ago. Well before your birth. I was heartbroken, but not broken."

Not yet. The words weren't said, but Flowridia felt them nonetheless.

"In any case," Tazel continued, "I travelled and saw the world. I expected to see savages, but instead I realized the savages were my own kin. Especially regarding half-elves." He shook his head and sat himself back down, seated across from Flowridia.

Flowridia recalled the slurs, Ayla's hateful gaze, her crime within the cathedral. Apparently this was commonplace, and somehow it both wounded her and eased some crippling guilt to know it was not Ayla alone who held to this bigotry. "I met a half-elf who told me as much, once," she whispered, recalling the new high priestess. "Her name was Sora; she lives in Staelash, where racist sentiments can't stand to exist for long."

"A half-elf named Sora? Sora Fireborn, perhaps?"

Flowridia perked up. "Yes. She's the new high priestess of the city."

"Good for her," he said, a genuine smile twisting his lip. "She's my cousin, if you can believe it."

So he was Tazel *Fireborn,* of the same family lineage as Sora, which meant he, like all the other Fireborns, carried a blood feud that transcended generations against a particular not-quite-vampire.

All of this clicked together rapidly in Flowridia's head, forcibly tearing open the box containing sentiments regarding 'Ayla Darkleaf.' "You knew Ayla."

"I wouldn't call it that," Tazel said cautiously, his smile vanishing.

"Fireborns have carried a feud against Ayla Darkleaf for generations." She frowned, lip quivering. "And you purposefully neglected to mention that detail."

"I didn't want to hurt you."

Tears welled in her eyes, and all her focus shifted to preventing them passage. To think of Ayla, to think that this man had hated her so—

"I-I'm sorry," she stammered, wiping her eyes with her long sleeve. "I should go–"

"Did something happen?"

Flowridia shook her head. Demitri placed his head upon her knee in solidarity. "It takes time to accept that someone is truly gone," she said simply.

Whatever her acceptance, oh, she missed her.

When she looked up, she saw compassion in his scarred face, not the judgement she expected. "She was dear to you."

"She was wicked."

"And now she's dead," Tazel said with finality. "I don't think you've yet let her go."

Like clinging to water, Flowridia felt Ayla's memories slip through her fingers, faster the tighter she clutched.

"I met Ayla once."

Gasping, Flowridia looked up at him, any story of Ayla cherished indeed.

"My birth was called an omen, that I was blessed by Sol Kareena with the fate to slay the Scourge of the Sun Elves. I received a familiar when I was but days old. And so I was taught magic, yes, but also to dance, to fight, to be her equal and more in every way. She had demons, but I wielded pure sunlight.

"Ayla heard of this," Tazel continued, some distance fading his gaze. "I wasn't kept a secret, and I wonder, even now, if it was part of a plot I wasn't privy to. When I was younger than you, she attempted to take my life. I was still a child by elven standards and held no hope to defeat a thousand-year-old monster alone. It was then that Mereen orchestrated Ayla's great demise, commissioned my aid in creating a coffin with no shadows. You read the rest. I was spared my so-called destiny to slay Ayla Darkleaf and instead joined Mereen in her quest to purge the world of undeath."

"Who's Mereen?" Flowridia managed to ask, and swore she'd heard the name before.

"Mereen is my great-great grandmother. Across the sea, she's known as 'Dark Slayer' and made a name for herself killing vampires. She began the blood feud."

Etolié had mentioned the very title—a hunter once in cohorts with the demon hunting Flowridia. "She's ancient, then."

Tazel nodded. "Ancient, and immortal. Taught me everything I know." Hesitation steeled his tongue, but still he spoke. "Somewhere in the millennia, she lost her grasp on her soul. She's her own kind of plague." With a bitter laugh, he added, "We've come full-circle. I'm hiding in the library because she can't find me here. She wouldn't dare breach the palace walls of Nox'Kartha."

"You ran away?" Flowridia asked, her tears finally stemming.

"Aren't you doing the same?"

Here in Nox'Kartha, adventuring with Casvir, reality did seem far away. "If it's any relief to you," she whispered, "Ayla's body has been put to rest. The world will move on, even if I'm struggling—no sense in lying to you about that." She tried to laugh, but it barely served to mask her sob. But she withheld tears, and instead added, "There's so much I don't understand, but I don't believe anyone knew her. Not really. Not even me. Everything I read speaks of her undeath, but did no one truly know her in life? When she still held onto her soul? Or perhaps she never had one at all." She swallowed her emotions, yet her face still twisted in anguish. "My heart says she loved me, but I cannot reconcile it—this stranger of a woman, this . . . this *monster.*"

Tazel smiled, though it held no joy. "Excuse me a moment," he said softly, then he stepped toward his bag. He riffled through it a moment, then paused and heaved a great sigh before returning his attention to her. "I should not show you this. But there was someone who did know Ayla Darkleaf in life."

He returned and handed her a folded piece of parchment. "This was written to me six years ago. Consider it a chance to practice your elven."

It was all in elven. Beautiful script, immaculate in its artistry. Flowridia barely struggled at all.

> *My dearest Sunshine,*
>
> *I've contemplated our parting words a thousand times these past six months. I've been accused countless times of blind obsession, but to hear it from you, my protégé, hurt. Our family has hunted vampires for fifteen hundred years; it is a legacy I could not take more pride in. But you, my love, chosen of the Goddess herself, hold the greatest potential of us all. You know that.*
>
> *There is more to this tale I have never told you. I am in the unique position to have known The Endless Night, Ayla Darkleaf, personally, for I remember what she was in life. The circumstances of Ayla's death are shrouded in mystery, but I can account for the days before it.*
>
> *She was a strange little hermit, living in the woods. The citizens of Fallanar thought little of her, found her odd and unsociable, but otherwise innocuous. Never mind the missing children, who we scoured the village and the woods to find, and never mind my murdered husband or the constable. No one suspected she might be the culprit. No one thought to pay her any mind at all.*
>
> *Save one. One person met the monster and saw a soul within her.*
>
> *You know of my sister. Sarai stole and broke hearts wherever she went but never had hers stolen in return—not until she came to live with me to help in raising my son after my husband's death. She loved Ayla Darkleaf. She never had to say it, for it was in the way she spoke, the darling blush she gave at every tease, the songs she wrote to impress her, the days they'd disappear in the woods to waste time together. She loved Ayla Darkleaf, and though I*

loathe to admit it, Ayla Darkleaf loved her too. Sincerely and truly.

In death, she was a monster. In life she still murdered for pleasure. She had every opportunity for change, and perhaps nearly did so, for if there was ever a person kinder to her than my silly floozy of a sister, I have yet to meet them. But love is not redemptive, and even with the pure love my sister had, Ayla Darkleaf chose to become a nightmare. She turned me into the monster I am. And countless others. Countless other monsters walk this earth, damned because of Ayla Darkleaf's actions. To slay them is a mercy. When we have purged them from this world, to slay me will be a mercy too.

Ayla Darkleaf has a soul, as cold and wicked as it may be, and for that reason, it is a mercy to slay her.

My love, my Sunshine, I miss you.
-Mereen

A lifetime ago, Ayla had said she loved a minstrel.

Flowridia gently refolded the parchment along the lines. "You have a very odd relationship with your great-great-grandmother."

When Tazel laughed, she joined him, tears leaking out with each raucous sound. "Not a truth I typically admit," he said simply, sorrow in his smile.

Once the pained burst of joy had died, Flowridia whispered, "Ayla loved Sarai Fireborn. And Sarai wrote her a song to send her into the night."

Ayla had loved it so, though she had not rested.

"Thank you for sharing this," she continued, for though the words were cruel, the truths they spoke of wicked, it cleared the fog of a mystery Flowridia had not realized she sought answers for. "I . . ." She returned the letter, lip trembling as she smiled. "Can we study, please?"

"Offend me with your accent again," Tazel said kindly. "It brightens my day."

Like Ayla herself, Flowridia placed this knowledge and her feelings in a box, content to let it lie, though it screamed perpetually all through the days and nights.

Chapter 8

She did not see Casvir for two weeks. And so it surprised her, one evening, when he knocked on the door of her guest room. "I have found your orb," he said simply. "Can you be ready to leave at sunrise?"

Early morning light glittered along the horizon, and two horses awaited them in the courtyard of the palace. "Our journey will take us straight north," Casvir explained. "We will hit a mountain range by nightfall. I saw no use in taking a carriage for only that long."

"I don't mind riding," Flowridia said, approaching the skeletal beast. The dead eyes were glazed and fogged, yet she knew it must see something with how it followed her hand. She placed it gently on the horse's nose. "I think being outside will do me some good." She strapped her spear to the side of the saddle, feeling Casvir's eyes on her as she attempted to mount the horse herself. Bracing herself, she set one foot into the stirrup. With a heave of her small arms, she managed to lift her body and leg and successfully pull herself up.

Grinning, she steadied herself and patted the horse. But then she saw Ana staring up at her from the ground, bony tail wagging furiously.

"Casvir," Flowridia muttered, her victory short-lived, "would you mind handing Ana to me?"

Soon, Casvir directed his horse toward the gate, bidding Flowridia's to follow. She kept Ana in her pack, amused when the little creature peeked out and watched the world before her.

Demitri, she realized, would soon surpass her mount in height. "You're growing taller every day."

Demitri puffed himself up, adding an inch or so in height and bulk. *I plan on being bigger than Casvir.*

Flowridia spared a look for Casvir, enormous and imposing on his own skeletal beast, one much larger than her own. "I wish you luck, my dearest Demitri."

The streets of Nox'Kartha held some semblance of remembrance, and though Flowridia knew she couldn't navigate them on her own yet, she wondered if she would ever be able to travel the clean roads alone. She longed to explore, to understand this city of the dead, to report to Staelash that it truly was wondrous and grand.

Those they passed stopped and fell to one knee, not daring to stand again until they were well out of eyesight. Flowridia watched their eyes, how they shied away from Casvir. Yet some dared to follow her, staring with wonder and fear at the small girl who rode behind their king.

Upon reaching the outer gates of the city, the paths they took not unfamiliar, the iron bars lifted at Casvir's presence. The guards bowed, and the only sound aside from the muted, bustling city was the clopping of hooves upon the stone ground. Flowridia followed, but once they were beyond the great walls, she rode to his side, the sprawling fields opening to embrace them.

The sun touched her skin, and Flowridia smiled, basking in the warm air and gentle breeze. Elation filled her at her return to the outdoors, and she hummed a folk tune of youth, one she annoyed the orphanage matron with a lifetime ago.

She was surprised to hear the words recited back, though two octaves lower.

> *Bless the harvest, Goddess of Light*
> *Protect my family through the night*
> *And lead my legacy to be*
> *One to bring me close to thee—*

Casvir's voice stopped at Flowridia's laughter. "I didn't realize," she teased, "that a necromancer might sing a prayer to Sol Kareena."

"I can sing to whomever I wish."

And so passed their day. Within hours, they crossed a massive bridge expanding over an enormous river—the very same that would lead her to Staelash. By nightfall, they found themselves at the edge of a mountainous terrain, just as

Casvir had said. Grass tickled her feet as she stepped off her horse. Lights in the far distance drew their attention; the glow of the city they left behind illuminated the horizon.

Flowridia lifted Ana out of her travel bag while Casvir silently went to work setting up their camp. First the warming crystal, which he centered in the clearing, and then their bedrolls. He spoke suddenly, startling Flowridia. "How have you been sleeping?"

Before he could set it out, Flowridia took the plush roll from his hands. "Well enough," she said, letting it billow out before setting it down. The lie danced gracefully off her tongue, and she wondered what had provoked him to ask.

Demitri curled beside the bed, but Ana stole Flowridia's attention as she hopped through the grassy terrain, happy to be free at last.

Laughing, Flowridia chased after the frolicking creature. She dove to catch her, pulling the small fox into her chest and squeezing the bony form. The grass cushioned them as they fell, and when Flowridia rolled onto her back, Ana simply wagged her tail. Flowridia kissed her forehead.

But as soon as her grip loosened, Ana darted off again, brimming with pent-up energy. Flowridia rose to her feet and ran after her, chasing the lively fox but stopping just before scooping her up. Ana skipped left and right to avoid capture, and Flowridia indulged the sweet creature as they ran through the meadow.

The intricacies of her undead biology remained a mystery, but Flowridia set that aside for the chance to clear her head.

Night blanketed the sky when they finally returned to camp, and Ana was no less bouncy than when they'd started. Flowridia, winded from darting about the grassy terrain, settled against Demitri.

Ana continued hopping around camp, prancing in circles around the warming crystal. With light, tapping feet, she leapt onto Flowridia's lap, Demitri's tail, rolled in the dirt, and even dared to dart into Casvir's lap—who barely shot her a glance, and only lifted up his book to let her pass—before repeating her circuit. It wasn't until, as she stepped on his foot, Demitri released a vicious snarl that she finally froze.

Flowridia took the trembling creature into her arms and frowned at Demitri. "That was uncalled for."

She knows what she did. Now she'll stop.

Flowridia's fingers stroked Ana's bony form. She noticed the flicker of amusement on Casvir's face. "Impressive, how much personality your fox has retained," he said. "Skeletons are mindless and docile, more often than not."

Flowridia placed a kiss on Ana's skull. "Thank you. I don't know if I'd call it talent. Maybe just love."

"Love has no place in necromancy. She merely retains her soul."

Content to ignore Casvir's brutish sentiment, Flowridia coaxed the little fox to face her. "Is that true, Ana?" she cooed, childish in her tonality. "Is your soul stuffed into your skeleton?"

Ana's enormous eye sockets simply stared.

"She still holds use. She is perfectly compliant to your will, when you care to enact it."

Flowridia shook her head as she released Ana. The small creature curled up beside her, opposite Demitri. "I don't know if I have the heart for it," she admitted, and she thought of her mother and of Ayla, of Murishani and all the rest who had sought to manipulate her will. "I don't think I could control anyone; instead, I'm more often tricked into being controlled."

"You are gentle, but that is not a weakness in and of itself. Inspiring fear and respect in those you command, living or dead, does not mean to purge this trait. You will learn in time." He stood, suddenly. "Come," he said, and he offered a hand.

Flowridia accepted, though confused at the gesture. Once standing, Casvir took his hand back and led her away from the crystal, away from her sleeping familiar and into the dark meadow.

High above, millions of glittering stars swirled around her vision, their ancient light splattered like a dropped artist's palette.

"Life is fleeting, but death is permanent," Casvir said. "Controlling life means to wrestle consciousnesses until you pass or relinquish control, but you need only succeed once to conquer the dead, save only the most intelligent and willful. Perhaps the living have sought to destroy your will." Casvir stopped when the light was only a spark in the distance. "But your core is stronger than you know. We have discussed that life and death are mere opposites of the same coin of magic, correct?"

Flowridia nodded.

"Your garden was your greatest joy at home."

Again, she nodded. "I poured my heart and soul into caring for my plants."

"Sit down," Casvir said, and Flowridia obeyed, gracefully seating herself in the cold grass. It tickled her legs and feet. "Shut your eyes and meditate. Let your senses expand and touch upon all the life in this field."

Flowridia obeyed, finding this a trivial task. The grass sang the loudest, especially the strands she touched, but their roots expanded and led to more. She touched upon wildflowers, muted under the stars, and even felt the radiating life of insects and burrowing creatures. She felt their energy, the racing hearts of gophers causing her own to match tempo.

Casvir's voice wove into her ears. "Now, twist it. Look not for life, but for death."

Flowridia let her mind draw away from the frantic rodents and instead turn inward, letting that hollow feeling expand in her core. Emptiness seemed to seep from her fingers, yet rejuvenation came with it, an influx of life. She breathed deep, letting energy fill her body, pleasure flowing with it. A high she had craved, one she had not felt in weeks.

But Casvir's words reminded her to focus, to stay on task. Eyes still shut, Flowridia's senses expanded, touching not upon life, but on death.

She gasped, bombarded by stimulation. Beneath the earth were bones of every age, half-rotted corpses, the potential for great power in each dead thing. Even the wilted flowers radiated, the dried grass. All of it sang to her searching senses.

"Do you feel it?" she barely heard him say. Casvir himself radiated under this new search.

Flowridia offered a tenuous nod, clinging to this new sensation. Compliant, radiating with potential, and Flowridia dared to call them forth. Weakness seeped into her bones, her energy turned outward, but all around she felt the earth shake, the ground rustle. Each dead thing quivered and shook at her call, compelled to come forward, granted new life at her beckoning.

Flowridia opened her eyes and yelped. Where she sat, the grass had blackened and charred, the life utterly decimated at her touch. Before her, surrounding her, and still approaching, countless creatures, most only half formed.

The severed halves of rotted field mice, insect carapaces, rabbits, and more clawed their way towards her. Even predatory creatures, foxes and owls, shambled their rotting bodies closer.

Flowridia dared to glance at Casvir, surprised to see him looking pleased. "What do I do with them?"

"Anything you want," he replied. "They are yours."

Useless, was what they were, most of them only pieces of creatures. Rabbit feet and fox tails rolled toward her. "And if I don't want them?"

"Release them. Withdraw your influence."

Flowridia shut her eyes, skin crawling as undead *things* brushed against her skin and clothing. She felt a piece of herself within each. With force, she took it back.

When she opened her eyes, a small sea of carnage surrounded her, the fallen corpses now returned to static dead. But the earth as well—surrounding her was blight.

"Impressive," Casvir said, "though I would recommend avoiding drawing from life to grant death. Magical addiction is a real danger, and necromancers are especially susceptible."

"I didn't mean to do it," Flowridia said softly, her hand brushing against the blackened, dead grass.

"All the more reason to be careful."

When Casvir offered a hand to help her stand, she accepted, letting her touch linger a moment as she contemplated his cool skin, the lifelessness that sang when she'd let her senses caress it. Yet, her will had not touched his, not by miles, and though it confirmed her suspicions, it brought more questions with it. "Casvir," she asked as they walked back, "how can the dead be necromancers?"

"Accomplished necromancers often are undead, seeing their own self-mastery as the path to eternal life."

"So you did this to yourself?"

A pointed question, yes, but Flowridia was slowly accepting that Casvir was difficult to offend. "I did," he replied, "and it is something you, too, can learn. But you are not ready yet."

As they neared the campsite, Ana dashed toward them, perhaps bored of Demitri's silent company. Flowridia lifted the small skeleton into her arms and carried her. "If I may ask, why is Ana different than the creatures in the field?"

"You devoted your singular attention to raising Ana," he replied. "Those, you simply summoned as is. As we discussed, Ana had her soul returned to her, and her body morphed to match your intentions."

"I didn't tell her skin to desiccate."

"No, but was that your image of undeath? A skeleton?"

Truthfully, yes, or at least the most endearing image of it. A fox with rotting flesh was hardly an attractive option, though she would have loved it the same. Flowridia nodded.

"It morphed to match your intention, and thus your will."

The core of necromancy was utter domination of your spawn. It chilled her, to consider it, and realized why those who understood its nuances would choose their own path to undeath, rather than risk rebirth as someone's slave.

Casvir continued. "Khastra is an unprecedented experiment. Did she explain?"

"Enough of it, I think."

"Her grasp on undeath is tenuous, and in a very real way, she is half alive. Necromancy forced her soul back into her body and prevents rot, but she breathes and feels the effects of hunger, though she need not eat. Her will is mine, but like Ayla, to force it might break her mind."

Flowridia's heart sank at the mention of Ayla's name. She nodded, but realize she had stopped consciously listening, staring instead at the flickering crystal and the shadows it cast.

"Flowridia, are you well?"

Her gaze shot up. "I'm fine. She's a difficult topic."

No need to clarify which 'her' she referred to. Casvir seemed to understand. "You left her ear behind."

Flowridia nodded, the reminder enough to evoke a rise of emotion. "You can't feel her, can you," she whispered.

"No, I cannot."

The silence stretched long. Flowridia realized Casvir had done far more talking than she this evening. "You seem happier out of the castle," she dared to say.

"The challenges of ruling an empire are ones I revel in," he replied, withdrawing a book from his travel chest. "But I find my time on the road refreshing. It is a rare treat."

"Is it far, where we're going?"

"I do not quite know," Casvir said. "I feel the pull quite strongly, much more so than when I used you to navigate, but that may be because of my connection to the orb."

Flowridia, not quite ready to face her nightmares, gave a permissive glance to Casvir as she reached over to steal a book from his chest. He didn't stop her, and so she settled down with *The Bare Bones of Justice: The Morality of Necromancy,* until she felt her eyelids droop.

Sunrise broke along the horizon, but Flowridia had awoken long before. Tossing, turning, she eventually had to roll off Demitri for fear of disturbing him. She pulled Ana close to her chest and curled onto the bedroll, determined to feign sleep for a few more hours.

But when morning light met her eyes, she finally allowed the stubborn sting of failure drag her into wakefulness. Slowly sitting, still hugging Ana, Flowridia heard Casvir speak as she roused herself. "Did you sleep?"

"Not much," she admitted. Silence lapsed between them. The faint singing of birds combined with the insects of night made for an interesting ballad, and Flowridia found herself distracted by the chill breeze.

"You will need your strength today," Casvir finally said, setting his book aside. "There is much to teach you."

After last night, Flowridia expected as much. Still, he stood and stepped over the crystal with his clawed feet and offered a hand. She accepted, and Casvir's words surprised her. "Grab your spear."

She turned to Ana. "Wait here," she said firmly, and the little fox watched with an eerie tilt to her head. But her haunches stayed put, and Flowridia retrieved the crafted boar spear from the saddle of her horse.

Casvir had already gone, waiting perhaps a hundred feet away. Flowridia ran to meet him.

Swirling purple filled Casvir's hand. A spear, identical in size to Flowridia's, appeared in his hand. "Sometimes magic cannot protect you," he said, his voice stern, "and you have been gifted with a beautiful weapon." He matched her eyes, amusement in the curve of his lip. "Breathtaking."

Flowridia couldn't help but smile.

Casvir set his feet apart, one before the other, and held the spear forward. "Stand as I do," he said, smile fading.

"Feet apart; equal balance. Bend your knees—you must be light on your feet."

Apprehension filled Flowridia as she attempted to mimic his stance. Feet apart, left foot forward, she held the spear out, keeping eye contact with Casvir as he stepped closer.

His claw whipped forward. Flowridia was pushed to the ground.

"You have no balance," he said, expression blank. But he offered a hand to help her stand. "Try again."

Wary, Flowridia adjusted her stance, feet closer to her shoulders as she bounced lightly on her knees and toes. This time, when Casvir pushed her, she swayed, but she did not fall.

He nodded, approval in the gesture. "If you cannot keep a strong base, your opponents will dominate you at every turn. All your actions start at your feet." He pushed her again; Flowridia managed to keep her stance. "Better. You have the proper spirit."

Flowridia thrust her spear forward. "*Spear*-it?"

Casvir jabbed her stomach with the blunt base of his spear, but not hard enough to cause any harm. His amused quirk of a grin loomed above her. "Watch carefully." He held his summoned spear forward, a faint black and purple mist emanating. "Follow my stances."

She did. And she learned.

Within the hour, Flowridia's muscles ached and her breathing grew short. Sweat drenched her hair and clothing, but she kept pressing forward, repeating each move at Casvir's command, as unrefined as her motions were.

Hold stance, thrust, swing, and with that final step, Flowridia lost her footing. Casvir caught her arm, gently steadying her shaking form before speaking up. "I think you have learned all you can for today. Your stamina will increase with time." He released her, keeping watch over her labored breathing.

Across the field, Flowridia felt Demitri's hard gaze. She nodded to Casvir, using the spear to support her legs. "Will we do this again?"

"Every morning," Casvir said. His own weapon had faded from his hand. "And at night, I will guide your magic. Do you agree to this?"

Again, Flowridia nodded. "Thank you," she managed to say, though her words remained as shaky as her form.

"I have great faith in you, but also high expectations."

She managed a smile, exhausted as it was.

"Do you know any spells for cleanliness?"

Flowridia shook her head.

"You have an image to maintain," he replied, making great strides toward the saddlebags. He withdrew what appeared to be a small bean. "There is a saying, that those granted power have the obligation and responsibility to wield it. Your power dictates your status, and you must live up to that."

"So I'm not allowed to look like the dirty orphan I am?"

She teased, but he looked almost annoyed. "You are an adult woman and ought to appear more as one," he replied and he offered her the strange, greenish bean. "Attach this to your clothing. It will not clean you, but your garments will be maintained."

Flowridia obeyed, placing it on her shoulder, and marveled when all the dirt and sweat simply . . . fell off.

Casvir nodded in approval and went to pack their camp.

Demitri approached, his cold nose purposefully poking against her shoulder. *I think he said you look like a mess.*

"Good. It reflects my mind."

Demitri bumped her with his nose. *Stop ruining my jokes.*

She pushed aside his nose as she stepped past and knelt to roll up her bed. Within minutes, the entire camp was packed away, and Flowridia placed Ana into her pack before hoisting herself up onto her horse.

They spent the day in relative silence, riding as Casvir navigated.

Every morning, she fought, her muscles growing accustomed to the ache of physical activity, even if her reflexes were still pitiful. Each night, she studied, she learned, and she felt herself become more attuned to the dark power residing all around them.

The days grew colder, and one morning she awoke from dreams of a shrieking embrace only to realize her body truly was chilled. She sat up to find a canopy above them and a light blanket of snow all around.

Weather made no difference to Casvir. They sparred among the frost, though he did offer her a coat when they had finished, suited to her size and taste.

Late afternoon one day, they came upon a road, the clopping of hooves on frosty stone oddly grating to Flowridia's senses. "Aren't you worried about running into anyone?"

"This is the safest path through the mountains," Casvir replied, "and we are still in Nox'Karthan territory. What fear have I, as imperator, in greeting my people on the road?"

Flowridia accepted that.

No one crossed their path, and when evening fell they left the road and made camp just out of sight in a cropping of trees. Secluded, Flowridia felt far more comfortable by the enclosure of greenery.

The first blanket of snow melted, but the weather remained uncomfortably chilled.

She sat as near as she could to the warming crystal. Flowridia ate her dinner with Ana clawing at her leg, but also a small bastion of half-rotted squirrels circling her body. Demitri sat on his haunches, visibly wary of the display. But Flowridia offered a hand to one eerie servant, amused when the once-squirrel crawled into her hand. Not too horrifying; not with an understanding of anatomy to explain its rotted eye socket and matted fur. Flowridia knew she ought to be disturbed.

But what harm was there in offering kindness to a creature now passed?

"Have you always felt a connection to nature?"

Flowridia set the squirrel down, amused as it followed her hand when she brushed along the cool grass and fallen leaves. "I've always loved it."

"Your ability to force your influence upon simple minds is impressive," Casvir said. "Soon you will be ready to experiment with greater challenges."

"What do you mean?"

"Humanoid creatures have a stronger will than dead woodland critters."

Flowridia's hand stopped, and the squirrel caught up. It stared expectantly, its dead eyes oddly expressive. But she couldn't shake the image of the shambling dead outside of Mother's cottage, phosphorescent fungi slowly consuming them. "Perhaps," she said simply, knowing Casvir wouldn't take well to her apprehension. "In the meantime, I don't know what harm something small like this could do."

"By itself, very little." His stare grew more scrutinizing. "Come," he said, standing. He offered a hand, and she accepted. When Demitri and Ana followed, he stopped. "For his safety, Demitri may wish to remain here."

The small gathering of squirrels followed at her feet, and Ana bounced around them. Flowridia glanced apologetically at Demitri. "You know Casvir wouldn't say that if he didn't mean it."

I don't like leaving you alone. A faint growl echoed in his throat. *And certainly not with him.*

"What has he ever done to betray our trust?" she snapped. Flowridia left him.

Several steps away, Casvir spoke. "Living creatures do not tolerate me. Even intelligent ones, such as Demitri, distrust me."

Flowridia remembered Ayla sharing similar sentiments, though the so-called 'creatures of the night' had remained the exception. "A pity," she whispered, "that that's the price of undeath."

Were it the path she chose for herself, would she be content? Would Demitri hate her if she became like Casvir?

A question for another night. The last flickering of light disappeared behind the trees, the barest hints of stars coming to fill the void. "Have you ever tried to control the living?" Casvir asked.

Flowridia shook her head. "Only plants, and only as far as to coax them to grow."

"I suspect you have more talent than you realize. What I want you to do is expand the reaches of your control as far and as strong as you can. Feel the limits. Summon all you are able."

Flowridia sat on the ground, already well attuned to the small army of rodents following in her footsteps. But chattering night creatures surrounded them, and beneath her the dead practically vibrated at the touch of her senses. It had become so easy a thing, to let her focus drift outside herself. Her influence brushed across the creatures around her, gliding past some and grasping onto others.

"Bring them here."

Flowridia felt them all—the night creatures and dead alike. A slow, painstaking process, but she wormed her way into the minds of the weak-willed creatures around her. With each success, she felt the process speed, finding the ease at which she penetrated their minds steadying.

And as she focused, she touched upon the dead beneath her. The ground shook as claws unearthed themselves, as larger corpses joined the throng of vermin. Bears and wolves, the predators of this forest rose at her command, some living and others dead.

Her toes curled as tiny creatures skittered across her. Spiders crawled across her skin, utterly devoted to her command, rats, roaches—

"Hold your focus," Casvir's calm voice said. "It would not do you well to lose them now."

Flowridia released a breath. She opened her eyes, nearly gasping at the hundreds of creatures who had come at her summon. Alive and dead, they watched every movement. A small circle of emptiness surrounded both Casvir and Ana, but she felt the tension grow strong around them.

"Is this the limit of your power?"

Flowridia felt her concentration strain, but she knew this was not it. Her influence directed upward to the sky, touching upon owls and sleeping birds. She covered her hair as something whooshed beside her. Screeching bats threatened to entangle themselves, threatened to deafen her ears and break her concentration. Owls landed beside her, and other winged creatures dragged along the ground, their dead, rotted bodies unfit for flight.

Flowridia felt faint. So many consciousnesses, and the living still fought for control. Her head ached; sweat beaded from her pores.

"Truly impressive," she heard Casvir say, but then his words slurred, her vision growing dark. "To control both living and dead–"

The dead did not fight, but the living suddenly broke free.

They swarmed. Some ran away in fear; others turned on their counterparts, living and dead, and tore them apart.

Flowridia cried, "Stop!" but the living gave no response.

"Make them fight."

She obeyed.

The dead consumed everything, tearing through the living creatures like fire through paper. Trees and plants fell to their wrath, to Flowridia's wrath, she realized, but the carnage of blood and animal cries ripped through her soul, lacerating her heart. She shrieked, uncaring if her influence waned. She shut her eyes and covered her face.

Silence settled upon the clearing. Flowridia felt a clawed hand grab her arm and force her to stand. "There is no shame in failure, as long as you learn from your mistake." When Flowridia opened her eyes, the dark forest was stained with torn limbs and blood. The dead had fallen back as they should, now with their once-living counterparts to join them. "But to cower is to show fear. Pathetic displays are–"

Flowridia wrenched her arm away, furious at the tears welling in her eyes. "But I killed them, Casvir. They destroyed everything!"

"Death magic has a price. I do not think you have accepted that yet."

Flowridia brought her sleeve up to wipe her tears, furious at his words. Perhaps because she knew he was right.

"The living distrust the dead. Most are inclined to fight. In order to reach your full potential, you must learn to balance the costs."

"What use is there in reaching my full potential if I lose myself in the process?"

Tension rose between them. A dangerous undertone laced Casvir's quiet response. "I do not understand."

The smell of carnage slowly rose. Flowridia dared not step for fear of squishing her toes in gore. The silent screams of living creatures echoed through the night. "I hate this," she replied, her very soul sickened at the display before her. "I didn't choose my talents. If necromancy means only to destroy the world I love, perhaps I don't want it."

"Wasted potential is just that—a waste."

The words boiled her blood. Glaring, she tore her gaze away from the death to face Casvir instead. "You don't care for me at all. You're trying to mold me to your selfish whims."

"Your entire life has been an investment. I do not have failed investments."

"So I'm a project to you," she said, furious tears falling down her face. "A pawn. I never chose to be yours, Casvir!"

"No, you did not. But where would your life be without my gift to you? Your mind is keen, and your methods are clever, but without a familiar you are nothing more than a peasant girl with a penchant for gardening."

Flowridia tried to object, but her words died on her tongue as Casvir's own continued. "We rarely choose our own destinies, Flowridia. Instead, we grab opportunity, we work ourselves to the brink, and we embrace our potential. Otherwise, we stagnate." He stepped forward; Flowridia cowered. "You will not stagnate. Just as I have given you a destiny, I can take it away."

Flowridia cowered, crumpling under the harsh words and unquestionable threat. Mother had stunted herself forever, yes, but at least she had forged her own future.

"What do you want me to do?" she whimpered, and she hid her head in her arms, sheltered by the curtain of her hair.

"I want you to rise above your weaknesses and take your throne. Whatever throne that may be is your choice."

Flowridia heard footsteps through the crushed leaves.

When she finally lifted her head, Casvir had gone. Ana waited obediently beside her.

Flowridia summoned every ounce of courage she held and rose to her feet. With careful steps, she stepped through the bloodstained forest, sickened at the ruined plants and desecrated bodies.

Casvir had said she would soon be ready to raise humanoid creatures. Oh, the thought made her faint.

At camp, Casvir was nowhere in sight. But Demitri bounded toward her, his fur bristling at the evidence of her tears. *Say the word, and I'll bite his face off.*

"That's more dramatic than necessary." She embraced him, resting her head against his thick fur. "But if he comes back, tell him I'm asleep."

What happened?

She could feel Demitri's muscles stiffen. Hurt washed over her tired body. "I forgot what he was. And I realize now that I'm a fool."

Whatever words Demitri tried to soothe her with went unheard, her mind a virulent storm.

The night seemed endless as she tossed and turned, Ayla's grin lingering in her mind like the crescent moon. When she finally sat up, stars littered the sky, entire galaxies hers to witness. The celestial sight brought no comfort, however. And Casvir was nowhere to be seen.

Flowridia stood, frowning at the empty seat across from the warming crystal. But far into the field, a flash of purple met her gaze. Stepping beyond the line of trees, she saw the faint silhouette of Imperator Casvir against the brilliant moonlight. An enormous mace, conceived from dark matter, ripped across the skyline as he stepped, intricate and precise. She had seen him fight, yes, and to see him perform was a spectacle, but watching him practice, to see him repeat his steps over and over in sync, was nothing less than mesmerizing.

Flowridia drew closer, until she came near enough to see the glint of his black armor against the moon, the fine movements of his rippling musculature as he wielded his specialized weapon. Enormous and terrifying, yet Casvir moved with a grace betraying his stature. Not a dance, no; Ayla had danced, incapacitated her enemies with a refined elegance befitting her lithe form. Casvir crashed against his enemies like an ocean wave: smooth, unrelenting, and always emerging stronger than before.

But he stopped, luminous red eyes settling on her as she quietly watched. His weapon faded. "Trouble sleeping?"

"Don't pretend nothing happened." Her combative words drew a frown to his face. She withered, stepping back, as words tumbled from her lips. "Casvir, I'm grateful for everything you've done for me. I know our relationship is under contract, but I've come to care about you. I've come to trust you. And I've grown so much under your patronage." She bit her lip, unsure of how to articulate the uneasiness within her. Her vision fell to the dew-covered grass. "I think you're the only person who sees me for what I am and doesn't fear it. I accept that I'm a pawn to you. But I'm my own person, too. I have to do things my own way."

Casvir's gaze had never left her. Relentless, like all he did. "It was my mistake to expect you to be like Odessa. She was impulsive and dangerous, her methods questionable if not outright deplorable. But you are thoughtful, your methods balanced, your patience granting you a finesse I have never seen matched. For you to wield the coin of light and dark in tandem means to bring structure to pure chaos. Today you failed to balance them. Next time you will not, because you learn from your errors."

The words should not have been so touching, but Flowridia fought a smile.

"I chose you to be a pawn, yes," Casvir said, his words even and thoughtful. "But I have come to find joy in your company. You are my project, but you are also my pupil. I want you to succeed. The world has tried to break you, but I know you are better. I want you to be better."

Flowridia did smile this time. With her hands clasped demurely, she blinked away tears. She was surprised when he continued speaking.

"I would ask you a question, one I do not expect an answer for tonight: What *do* you want? You hold boundless potential, but why will you seek it?"

Flowridia looked to the ground, the question prickling in her head. Truly, she did not know anymore. With Ayla's death, she felt so lost, and with Ayla's crimes so horrendously revealed, she felt jaded.

"Think upon your answer. And once you know, pursue it relentlessly."

Flowridia shyly asked, "What is it that *you* want?"

"I wish to be a god, Flowridia," Casvir responded. "I will take up the mantle of the fallen God of Death, once I deem myself prepared to slay her in her underground tomb. Do you know why I founded Nox'Kartha?"

"Only that you and Murishani founded a haven for De'Sindai."

"The price of citizenship is to pledge to me as a god. They may pledge to others as well, but I gain that power all the same. I provide for what is mine, and my people are cared for."

Flowridia had suspected as much, yet there remained a lingering curiosity she dared to push. "But, why? No one is born with the aspiration for godhood at birth."

"You are correct." Utter stoicism steeled his features, despite the words trickling from his mouth. A gentle stream, never rushing, no, and never forced. Merely a delivery of facts. "I was born to nothing during the era of Solviran witch-burnings. My parents appeared as human as you, but that single drop of demon blood manifested acutely in my being. They ran from Solvira, only to be turned away from the Theocracy of Sol Kareena—and so my mother was burned at the stake for witchcraft, my father forced to leave her behind to save me. For five years we lived as nomads, until they caught us. They killed him and sought me next—but I had cried enough. In my calm, as the soldiers came to take me, the dead rose and slaughtered them all. Thereafter, they have followed wherever I have gone.

"I experienced the world as a pariah, threatened and spat upon by acolytes of so-called divinity. It merely fueled me. And when I saw the brutality inflicted upon my own people, I saw ... potential. The rest, the history books may tell you. That is why I have pursued this path; consider, now, why you would."

"I'll think about it," she promised.

"And understand, Flowridia, I do respect your talents," Casvir added, his voice as gentle as the night breeze. "Power requires sacrifice, but I do not wish to offend you. Give me time to rethink my lessons for you, and I can refine them more to your taste."

Casvir looked to the camp, to the faintly glowing crystal beyond. "You should sleep. The hour is late, and tomorrow we ride."

Flowridia stepped close to his side as he escorted her to the flickering light. His clawed hand settled at the small of her back.

Chapter 9

They met no travelers on the road. Instead, they came across a town. Snow fell in gentle, swirling wisps, settling onto the rooftops of the mountain village. Smoke from the chimneys bespoke warmth and comfort, and Flowridia saw evidence of people going about their day.

She stopped her horse and called out to Casvir. "Should we go around?"

"What use would that be?"

She glanced at Demitri, then to Ana peeking out from her bag. "We're hardly inconspicuous."

"Good," he said, and his horse continued forward.

Nervous, Flowridia said softly, "Stay close, Demitri."

People don't scare me.

Cottages appeared beside the road. The citizens they passed—all De'Sindai—looked perplexed, but when realization set in, they bowed and kept their heads down until they had disappeared.

The citizens in the city had done the same. Flowridia knew now that they pledged to him as a god, and it seemed he was a god to be respected.

'Wood's End,' read the frostbitten sign, and everywhere people scattered and bowed as they made their way along the dirt road. Large and well-populated, to call it a town was misleading; the quaint little city in the mountains seemed rather lively and rich. The sky displayed brilliant pinks and purples as the sun moved to set, and to Flowridia's surprise, Casvir stopped his horse in front of an inn.

"We will rest here for the night," he said, dismounting.

Flowridia slid down her horse, quickly whispering as she approached. "But, why?"

"Because it does my citizens well to remember who they serve," he replied, menace in his tone. "Let it be known that their king stayed in this very inn. It will help their business."

Flowridia unloaded her horse, unnerved at the wicked spark in Casvir's eye.

With one arm, Casvir carried what luggage he had before approaching the stable. Whatever conversation he had was short and precise. Two stable-hands suddenly emerged to lead the skeletal horses across the frosty ground.

Casvir had to duck as he stepped through the doorway of the large brick structure, and Flowridia followed at his heels, one hand kept firmly on Ana hidden in her bag. Inside, every patrons' eyes darted rapidly between Casvir and Demitri, unsure of who to fear more. Flowridia kept in Casvir's shadow, realizing a scant few looked at her with concern.

The young man at the desk, his skin a faint shade of purple and whose small horns pointed out from his black hair, seemed torn on whether to bow in silence or speak to his imperator. "I-Imperator Casvir," he stuttered, settling on both. "An honor. And a surprise."

"Your finest rooms for me and my companions," he stated, the brutal efficiency of his tone unnerving even to Flowridia.

"Of course. Our finest room with our largest bed for you and your . . ." He glanced nervously at Flowridia. "—your lady."

"Two rooms," Casvir said darkly. "I will not besmirch the honor of my ward."

"My-My apologies," the man said, eyes growing wide. "I did not mean to presume. Yes, two rooms, one for you, and one for–"

"Lady Flowridia of Staelash," Casvir interjected.

Flowridia feared the man's eyes would pop from his skull. "Of course." He bowed to her, stiff as he straightened. "I meant no insult."

"No insult taken," Flowridia said kindly.

The man nodded, anxious as his eyes fell upon Demitri. "And your wolf, your grace?"

"He stays with Lady Flowridia. But he can sleep on the floor."

A sudden snarl escaped Demitri's throat at the slight. The young man looked faint. "He will be cared for as any guest." He stepped forward, glancing rapidly between Casvir's bag and Flowridia's.

Casvir stepped aside, motioning to Flowridia. "Chivalry takes precedence," he said, voicing the poor gentleman's inner turmoil.

With a bow, the young man took Flowridia's bag, bedroll, and spear. "Follow me, please. Both of you." He made his way across the floor, maintaining distance between them and the patrons sitting down for dinner, and escorted them up the stairs. Between Casvir and Demitri's bulk, they had to go single file, the stairs creaking from the effort. Flowridia admired the polished wood; the inn was modest, yes, but held a quaint sort of richness she adored.

Two floors up, and the young De'Sindai led them to two adjacent rooms. "This one is for the lady," he said, opening the door. "Plenty of floor space for her animal companion."

Flowridia stepped inside, followed closely by Casvir, Demitri, and finally the harried gentleman, who carefully placed her belongings at the foot of her bed. Expansive yet cozy, the room held a comforting aura, and she realized she might benefit from a night inside, instead of shivering in the snow.

"The door in the corner leads to your personal bath," the man continued, and from his pocket he withdrew a key, which he handed to Flowridia. "And there are extra blankets in the chest if your, um . . ." He surveyed Demitri, his face growing pale. "Well, if your companion needs additional accommodations, don't be shy. If you need anything at all, there is a bell outside your door." He turned to Casvir, audibly gulping. "If you'll follow me, Imperator Casvir, I'll escort you to your room as well. After you're both settled, we can discuss options for your dinner."

"Thank you," Flowridia said sincerely, and after some rummaging in her bag, she withdrew a coin. She placed it into the anxious man's hand, noting how he softened.

Casvir followed the young man out. The door clicked shut, and Flowridia turned to Demitri. "This was unexpected."

I think Casvir enjoys intimidating the common folk.

"I don't think you're wrong." From her shoulder bag, she released Ana, who immediately began hopping around the bed. Flowridia giggled. "She's like a toy. I wind her up, and there she goes."

Demitri began sniffing around, investigating every corner and crack. *You should set wards around this room.*

Flowridia leisurely stripped from her travel clothes. "I'll do it from the bathtub. I'll relax better. Will you watch Ana for me?"

Demitri's gaze followed the tiny, bouncing skeleton. *Really?*

"Yes, really," she replied, frowning.

If you tell her to sit still, she'll listen.

"She's been cooped up all day. If she gets unbearable, I will, but give her a few minutes at least."

Fine.

Flowridia, dressed in only her underclothes, opened the washroom door. A small brass basin, perfect for someone of her stature, waited at the side of the room. It took some experimentation with the knobs, but she eventually figured out how to start the water gushing from the pipes.

It warmed at her touch. Flowridia quickly removed the rest of her clothing and stepped into the basin, humming contentedly as the water swirled around her body.

First, the wards. Flowridia sighed and let her senses expand, touching upon the water, the air, even the wood of the inn itself. She traced sigils into the bathwater. *Let there be safety, in both the light and the shadows.*

Content, she sealed the spell. As she settled in to relax, her thoughts drifted to the bath in Nox'Kartha, to Ayla's tub—which, in turn, caused her to frown. Determined to embrace the cheery light of the inn, instead of the memory of soft, magical ambience, she shut her eyes, soaking in the warm comfort.

A pity she had never visited before Ayla's death. What a scene they would have made, together under those crystals, their pleasured cries echoing against the stone décor—

Her eyes snapped open. Grabbing the soap, she scrubbed her dusty form with more force than necessary, hoping to wash away the uncomfortable warmth brewing within her.

Was this what acceptance felt like? To be able to reminisce upon Ayla with mere melancholy instead of tears? Perhaps.

Scratching at the door interrupted her. "Hello?"

Casvir is here. He wants to know if you're hungry.

"I'm hungry, yes. Would you tell him, please?"

A pause, and then Demitri's voice came again through the door. *You want me to talk to Casvir?*

"I see your point. Get him to the door; I'll tell him."

A few seconds passed, then came a knock at the door. "Lady Flowridia?"

"Don't come in. But I can be ready for dinner in a few minutes. Whatever they can offer, I will eat."

"I will deliver the message," came the reply.

Flowridia ran soap through her tangled hair.

When she finally emerged, one towel wrapped around her body and the other skillfully tied around her hair, she found Demitri lounging lazily on the plush bed, the frame sagging dangerously low under his weight. *Casvir left.*

Ana popped her head out from underneath the bed. Flowridia stooped low to pull the fox against her damp body and kiss her bony skull. "Stay under the bed," she said, and Ana immediately skittered back underneath. The towel dropped, and Flowridia changed into a cleaner dress. "That'll give you some peace while we eat."

Tell them to bring me something. I'm starving.

"I will." With a final, determined squeeze of the towel, she removed it from her hair and hung it up, along with the other. Though still damp, she wouldn't be going outside and so had no fear of her hair freezing to her head. After a quick kiss to Demitri's nose, she left, careful to shut the door before smoothly descending the stairs.

The main floor of the inn expanded in all directions around the stairs with the entryway before her. The dining hall stood behind. All around were tables and patrons filling the chairs around them—De'Sindai, but in all sizes and shapes. Some seemed merely inhuman, more like unto to Zorlaeus or their skittish attendant, while others were as enormous as Casvir, if not more.

She saw no sign of the imperator. A young De'Sindai woman with pointed ears approached her as she lingered at the foot of the stairs. Tall and willowy, she stood half a head taller than Flowridia, despite being hardly more than a child. "Lady Flowridia," she said, and she bowed politely. "If you'll follow me, we have a table ready for you and..." She glanced up the stairs, concern filling her face. "Will Imperator Casvir be joining you?"

Flowridia nodded. "I thought he would already be here."

At her beckoning, Flowridia followed the girl across the busy hall to an ornate table near the corner, away from the other patrons. Decorated with candles and a lavish tablecloth, Flowridia saw care had been devoted to make the space worthy of Casvir's presence.

Once she had sat, the girl lingered, glancing nervously around the inn as she whispered, "Lady Flowridia, is everything all right?"

Confused, Flowridia said, "I'm perfectly fine. Why?"

"If you need a diversion, we'll help you make your escape. My mother says she can have one of your horses waiting–"

"Stop, stop," Flowridia said, holding up a hand. "What are you talking about?"

The girl looked toward the stairs before answering. "Are you not a prisoner?"

"He and I are travel companions, for the time being. I signed a contract . . ." She trailed off, noting the relief filling the girl's countenance.

"Imperator Casvir is known for his business practices," the girl said. "He will do as you both agreed and nothing more." She smiled, though concern still bled through. "I'll bring you your dinner. Imperator Casvir said you had a strict diet."

When she turned to leave, Flowridia stopped her, placing a gentle hand on her wrist. "What is your name?"

"Atia, my Lady."

"Atia, what you tell me, I swear to keep secret, but . . ." Flowridia studied the girl, realizing her eyes were a vibrant shade of orange. Twelve at most, her demure body language brought to mind a younger version of herself. "You were willing to betray your king. Why?"

At the word 'betray,' Atia immediately flinched, eyes wide. Flowridia instinctively grabbed the girl's hands as they shook, smiling kindly. "I'll say nothing to Casvir. You have my word."

Atia nodded, but her stance remained stiff.

"You needn't be nervous around me, Atia," Flowridia said, praying she sounded sincere.

She released her hands, and the girl's posture finally relaxed. "Rumors have spread of your relationship with the imperator," she began, her hands settling to fidget with the auburn streaks of her hair. "Imperator Casvir demands respect from all his citizens, and while he's known to show some deference to foreigners, especially foreign nobility, well . . . as I said, rumors spread."

Flowridia's replied died in her throat when she saw the unmistakable form of Casvir as he appeared from the staircase. Smiling, she looked back to Atia. "Would you tell your cooks to bring some meat up to my bedroom for my wolf?"

"Of course," Atia said, understanding, and she disappeared behind a door in the corner.

A young man, the same young man who met them at the front, escorted Casvir to her table, bowing as he gestured. "Your dinner will be ready soon, your majesty."

Casvir sat to Flowridia's left, silent until the young man left. "I thought you would find me before you came downstairs."

"I thought you were already here." Looking around, the faces of the patrons perpetually glanced between Imperator Casvir and their own business. "I think you've made quite an impression."

"My people should fear me," Casvir said, though the nonchalance took away from the threat of the statement.

Atia reappeared, platters balanced on each arm. She offered a kind smile to Flowridia as she set down the predictable array of food—various cooked vegetables and fruit, along with fresh bread. And Casvir's, something fancy and smothered in gravy, which she placed with a polite nod. "Is there anything else I can bring out for you? Any drinks?"

"Water, please," Flowridia said. "If you don't mind."

"Of course," Atia said, and she skipped away, perhaps too at ease in the presence of her king.

Casvir watched her oddly as Atia left. "You grew up a peasant, Lady Flowridia, but you are not like the common folk. Not anymore. You have influence and power and a reputation that precedes you. You do not grovel for favors."

The soft bread filled her entire body with warmth. Once she swallowed, Flowridia said, "What do you mean?"

"Befriending those you rule over is a foolish endeavor. As much as you might try, you are nobility, and they are your subordinates." Casvir's red eyes studied the room, lingering on every face daring to match his. "And do not forget; this is not your kingdom. These people owe you nothing."

Atia's concern bespoke otherwise, but for Flowridia to mention her treasonous offer would no doubt ruin her and her family. She said nothing, instead returning her attention to her meal. "I've never seen you eat," she muttered, watching as Casvir picked up his fork.

"Ayla ate for show as well."

When the girl returned, she brought a pitcher and two cups. Condensation dripped from the polished wood—within, the water was surely cold. "Will you be staying with us for long, Lady Flowridia?"

"I'm not sure–"

"Our business," Casvir interjected, a threat in his tone, "is our own. Take care you do not forget your place, child."

Atia nodded and bowed, visibly trembling as she ran from their side.

"Casvir, I think you're being harsh–"

"Lady Flowridia," he said, the same threat readily apparent, "you will not reprimand me in front of my citizens. Understand?"

Flowridia nodded, shocked at the words.

"That girl is a child and warranted a warning before I disciplined her. You are not a child, and you know better."

Flowridia turned her face to her food, a fierce blush covering her cheeks as she picked at her food.

Casvir said nothing more. They ate in silence.

When her plate had emptied, Flowridia dared to whisper, "We're only staying one night, right?"

"I think we have made the impression we needed to."

Something in those words chilled Flowridia's blood. "I would rather not practice death magic in front of the living. Do you mind if I go to bed?"

"I do not," Casvir replied, and Flowridia slipped from her seat and went toward the stairs.

The silence meeting her as she passed by each table prickled against her already frayed nerves. Every eye followed as she disappeared behind the banister of the stairs.

The wooden steps creaked, even underneath her light form, and when she reached the second floor, a lithe, blue hand clutched her arm.

In the split moment before Flowridia lost her footing, dragged off by this interloper, she summoned her power. Purple smoke poured from the pores of her skin, immediately engulfing her in a cloud of death. She hit the ground and saw above her a familiar demon gasping at her damaged hand—The Coming Dawn. "Wait!" Flowridia said, but the demon spoke louder.

"Never alone. Should have stolen you at dinner."

Flowridia scooted herself back, energy quickly draining. There was no life to steal from to sustain her spell, save the demon herself who nimbly side-stepped her efforts to grab one of her arachnid legs. "You're The Coming Dawn."

The demon folded her arms, one pair atop the other. "You have done research. Now, if you would kindly extinguish death cloud–"

"Listen. I know you're here to appease Ku'Shya, but what if I said Khastra wasn't–"

Blood spurted. The demon suddenly cried out in agony as horrible welts bubbled and burst beneath her skin. Flowridia heard thundering footsteps.

The demon's skin turned black and slowly decayed. Casvir appeared, bursting onto the scene with his weapon swinging. The demon woman narrowly dodged. She fell into the shadow of a doorframe, vanishing from sight.

The cloud around Flowridia dissipated. Weakened but alive, she faced him. "What was that?"

"A spell you are not ready for."

She shut her eyes and released a stabilizing breath. "With due respect, I was trying to reason with her."

"I have sworn to keep you alive, per our contract. I will not put you at risk for a known enemy."

Flowridia merely stared at the shadow The Coming Dawn had vanished into, wondering if her words would have meant anything at all.

"She has been following us for some time," Casvir continued. "I had hoped coming here might draw her out. She will not die, but it will take time for her to lick her wounds. You shall be safe tonight."

Flowridia almost felt pity for the strange demon and her horrible screams.

"You handled yourself well."

"Thank you," Flowridia replied, surprised at the compliment.

"Be on alert tonight, in case there are others." Casvir continued ascending the stairs, and Flowridia followed close behind. "Demitri would detour anyone foolish enough to accost you, but stay aware of your surroundings."

An obvious solution presented itself, but Flowridia hesitated before voicing it. "Would it be safer for me to stay with you?"

Casvir stopped at the top of the staircase. "For your physical health, yes, but not for your reputation."

He continued toward his room, but once on level footing, Flowridia darted ahead. "What about my reputation?" she said, placing her hands on her hips. Her small physique blocked the door, but were Casvir determined he would have no trouble shoving past her. Atia's words ran through her head, though, as did the man's at the desk. "Really? All of Nox'Kartha thinks–"

"Yes." Casvir crossed his enormous arms in front of his chest. No anger in his stance, however. Instead . . . hesitation? "And forgive me, Lady Flowridia, but the idea is deeply troubling."

Flowridia nodded, his words confirming what she had suspected. Her arms fell to her side, her expression with it. "I'm sorry."

"Do not be," he said as he stepped around her. "Rest assured, though, while I do think highly of you, my intentions for you are innocent."

"As innocent as anyone grooming the heir to the Theocracy with dark, forbidden magic?" Flowridia replied, suppressing a grin as she fluttered her eyelashes.

A smile cracked Casvir's stoicism, as mischievous a glint as she had ever seen from him. "Precisely."

Flowridia grinned. "Goodnight, Casvir," she said, a strange relief settling into her lungs.

Casvir nodded politely. "Goodnight, Flowridia."

The door shut, and Flowridia returned to her own room. On the floor, Demitri snoozed contentedly on his side, an enormous, empty platter by his mouth. She stepped past him and knelt beside the bed, peering underneath. "Ana, you can come out."

The skeletal canine bolted into her arms, shooting up into her chest. Flowridia hugged her tight and kissed her skull. When she stood, she plopped Ana onto the bed before climbing in beside her and settling into the soft sheets.

As expected, sleep eluded her. Instead, her memories mocked her with images of horror.

Knocking pulled her from vain attempts at sleep.

Flowridia sat up, surprised to find it was still night, and saw Demitri sniffing at the door. "Who's out there?" she whispered.

I smell De'Sindai, I smell female . . . Demitri kept his nose to the ground. *I think she's young.*

Whoever the culprit, Flowridia doubted she was a threat. "Ana, stay," she commanded. Her bare feet touched the cold floor, and clad in her nightclothes, Flowridia cracked open the door.

She recognized Atia, who held a lantern up to light the dim hallway. "Lady Flowridia, I'm sorry to disturb you. I didn't want to ask in front of Imperator Casvir, but–"

Flowridia beckoned her inside, putting a finger in front of her lips. Once the door had shut, she whispered. "Casvir doesn't sleep. If you don't want to be overheard, it's better to be in here."

"My Lady, I know you're a diplomat, but rumors have spread among my people about your talents as a witch. Is it true you can heal?"

De'Sindai, of course, would have no quandary over whether one was a witch or a priestess. They were demon-descended themselves. "I can, yes."

The lantern flickered eerie light across Atia's face, but Flowridia still saw fear. "My mother was too afraid to ask, but I feel I can trust you. My sister is ill, and I fear she'll die if–"

Another knock, and then the door ripped open. Casvir stood in the doorframe. "I heard a disturbance." His glowing red eyes settled on Atia, who withered under the gaze. "I told you–"

"Casvir," Flowridia said, stepping in front of the cowering child. But she remembered his warning and tried again. "*Imperator* Casvir, she knocked on my door seeking help. And I've agreed to give it." She hadn't yet, but if it pacified the Tyrant of Nox'Kartha, she would lie.

"Go, then," he said, a threat in his tone. "I will follow."

Flowridia turned to Atia, as reassuring a smile as she could muster at her lips. "Take me to your sister," she said, and Atia led them downstairs—she, Casvir, and Demitri.

To the first floor and near the kitchen, but instead they were diverted to a doorway beyond. Perhaps this was where the family slept, Flowridia reasoned, and when Atia opened the door, it led to a small bedroom, one with a cot and a De'Sindai woman kneeling before it. The woman turned. "Atia, I could hear you coming from–" She stopped, eyes wide when she saw who accompanied the girl. Flowridia, yes, but Imperator Casvir stood behind, and the woman bowed in his presence.

Flowridia, however, stepped inside and went for the cot, where a small girl, no older than three, rested fitfully. Atia stood behind with the lantern.

Flowridia knelt beside the bed, daring to touch the woman's shoulder. She trembled, her breath catching. "Ma'am," she said softly, "I am Lady Flowridia of Staelash. Atia has entreated me to heal your daughter." The woman looked up, eyes still blown wide with fear. She matched Atia in physique, with auburn hair and gangly limbs. "Will you let me look at her?"

The woman managed a nod. Flowridia turned to the girl and touched her arm, letting her senses expand and read what the child's body craved. Her stomach was distended, bloated, yet no true sickness ravaged her young body.

With Ana, there had been no cause, simply corruption from the land. But here, she felt a disturbance from inside. Another entity existed within the small girl's body, an intruder poisoning her from within.

Flowridia gently moved the covers aside and coaxed her arms under the girl's form. A heavy weight with her limp, sleepy limbs, but the girl's eyes opened, delirium facing back. Cradled against her chest, Flowridia placed a hand on the girl's forehead and let a stream of healing magic flow through. The room glowed with soft, golden light, and the girl gasped, though not from pain. Strength filled her, but the sickness remained, and Flowridia hoped her silent words would be heard. *You have no place here,* she commanded the intruder. *Leave.*

The girl suddenly writhed, pained cries escaping her throat. Her mother moved to sit behind them, tears welling in her eyes, looking helpless at the sight of her trembling daughter. Flowridia stopped but let the healing magic still move freely through her. A new approach then, and she moved her hand from the girl's face to her stomach, keeping a tight hold on her small body. She braced herself, knowing what perfect precision she would need, realizing one misstep might kill the sickly girl.

Purple mist emanated from her fingers. A slight crackling of lightning, and then it vanished. The girl still breathed. She sobbed, but she breathed, and Flowridia felt relief.

A different spell passed her lips, and with her hand still on the girl's stomach, she beckoned undeath back into the parasitic intruder. The girl whimpered, pitiful as she clutched Flowridia's form. *You have no place here,* Flowridia silently commanded. *Leave.*

The girl began convulsing. Fear gripped Flowridia, but she maintained her healing, repeating her command over and over. *LEAVE.*

When the girl buckled over, Flowridia let her. Vomit and bile streamed onto the floor, and with it a rounded, tentacled creature. Moist and eerie, it twitched in the open air. Flowridia held the girl tight in her arms, away from the parasite, just as Atia came forward and smashed it under her shoe.

A grotesque, black stain might scar the floor forever after, but the life Flowridia had given it seeped away.

Exhaustion struck her, but she kept her spell. The little girl breathed easy; though fatigued, relief threatened to expel her own tears. The girl would live.

She smiled, letting her spell finally cease. When she stroked the hair from the young girl's face, damp from sweat and tears, color returned to her features. Flowridia placed a kiss on her brow, then looked up at her mother. "She will live," Flowridia said, and she offered the toddler forward.

The De'Sindai mother accepted, hugging the girl tight to her chest as she cried. "Thank you," she said. "Lady Flowridia, I am forever in your debt. Whatever we can do to repay you–"

"No, no" Flowridia said, shaking her head. "It's a duty I'm happy to–" She was cut off by Atia, who plopped beside her and hugged her tight. Flowridia returned the gesture, smiling at the soft revelry of 'thank you,' she heard from the girl's mouth.

"You're welcome," she whispered, savoring the loving embrace. Exhausted by her efforts, she felt sleep tugging at her eyelids. "For now, I need sleep. But if anything happens, don't hesitate to find me."

She left the joyous women, and once she'd shut the door, she remembered Casvir's looming presence. "You should return to bed," he said, though not unkindly. Odd amusement rested on his face, and Flowridia wondered until—

His clawed hand descended onto her head. Bracing herself, Flowridia stiffened as the hand ruffled her hair. "Excellent work," he said simply, and then he stepped away, heading alone toward the staircase.

Stunned, Flowridia glanced between the stairs and Demitri. "What was that?" she whispered.

I think you impressed him.

"He ruffled my hair."

I noticed.

"What does this mean?"

No idea. But you look like you might collapse.

Flowridia followed Demitri close as they ascended the staircase.

She fell back asleep in seconds.

The morning light peeked uncomfortably through the window, warming Flowridia's sleeping face. As consciousness floated down upon her, she realized she had actually slept through the night. Mother's cackling laughter echoed in her memory, but she shoved those thoughts aside, just as she shoved Ana off her chest.

She sat up, pulling the excitable creature into her arms, and turned to see Demitri watching her with one sleepy eye. *Look who slept.*

"Well enough," she mumbled, scrunching her nose at Demitri. "For once."

He stood and placed his nose against her cheek. *Good.*

Flowridia yawned as she rubbed her eyes, then noticed the tray of food by the door. "What's that?"

Breakfast. It's nearly noon.

Flowridia ripped aside the covers and jumped from her bed. "This is so embarrassing."

Casvir doesn't care. He came by to make sure you hadn't been kidnapped, but I think he's happy you slept.

"Still embarrassing." Ignoring the food, Flowridia stepped around and into the hallway. The next door was Casvir's, and she politely knocked. "Casvir? I'm sorry I kept you waiting."

She pushed the door open, revealing a room identical to her own. Casvir sat on the otherwise untouched bed, a book in his hand. "Did you sleep well?"

She nodded. "Are we going to stay another night?"

"I see no reason to."

"I can be packed in a few minutes."

"Find me when you're ready."

Flowridia ran back to her room, nearly tripping over the food placed by her door. She shoved her clothing into her bag, packed within a minute. "Demitri, are you ready to go?"

Demitri, to her surprise, plopped in front of the door. *I'll be ready as soon as the food is gone from that tray.*

Flowridia frowned but knew better than to argue. She set her supplies aside and sat on the ground to eat the room-temperature offering of fruit.

I think Casvir only did this to keep me locked inside.

"I doubt it was personal," she said between bites. But The Coming Dawn crossed her mind, as well as Casvir's plot to draw her out. "Or aimed toward you, at least."

Once she had eaten, Ana skittered around her feet and darted out when the door opened. She ran past Flowridia's feet, stumbling over her skirt and toward the precarious stairs.

"Stop!" Flowridia commanded, and the tiny skeleton froze in place. "Come here." Ana, on her unstable little feet, darted back to her and planted her bottom on the ground, wagging her tail as she watched Flowridia expectantly. "Good girl."

Casvir watched them, his befuddled expression humorous on his nightmarish figure. His own scarce supplies were tucked under his arm, and without comment he stole the bedroll and spear from Flowridia, leaving her with only her light bag.

"The horses should be waiting for us," he said before descending the stairs. Flowridia followed, with Ana at her ankles and Demitri close behind.

In the lobby, few patrons lingered, but those who did barely hid their curious glances. Knowing their suspicions caused a pit to expand in Flowridia's stomach, but she kept her eyes fixed solely ahead.

Winter's chill cut through her coat, the breeze icy. Their skeletal mounts waited outside, along with Atia who nervously held the reins of the undead monsters. At the sight of Casvir, the girl bowed low. Casvir took the reins without a word and quickly strapped their supplies to the saddles.

But Flowridia placed a hand on her shoulder and said, "How is your sister?"

"Leddie ate for the first time in days this morning. She's as happy as I've ever seen."

Flowridia smiled. "Good."

Atia nearly leapt into her arms, her gangly frame cushioned by a coat. "Thank you, Lady Flowridia."

"You're welcome."

"My mother wishes she had something to give you. She says you're always welcome here, though, and that you can stay for free."

When Flowridia pulled back, she slipped a few coins from her pouch and placed them into Atia's hands. "Give these to your mother," she whispered. "I hope to see you again someday."

Atia left with a smile and a wave.

She placed Ana in her bag, not wishing to push Casvir's patience more than necessary, though his stoicism suggested simply that. "You enjoy disregarding my command to stop befriending my populace," he muttered as he watched her mount her skeletal horse. No anger marred his tone, but curiosity. "Murishani does as well, and he is far more beloved than I." He mounted his horse; Flowridia wondered at his meaning.

All around, the town swarmed with life, despite the falling snow. The well-kept road held carriages, horses, and all sorts of walking travelers. Yelling in the distance drew her ear, and Flowridia could see the edge of a bustling market. Immediately surrounding them, like a strange bubble, those who passed slowed, paused, then bowed, some lingering on their knee for minutes, not moving until Casvir passed out of sight.

The market drew closer, and the sea of people parted to let them pass—a strange juxtaposition to what she had experienced in Staelash. There, the children danced at Marielle's side, the soldiers freely jested with their late general, and Etolié had been known to host parties devoted to Eionei's glory for the populace. Perhaps they simply inspired a different sort of respect.

Here in Nox'Kartha, no such comradery existed between the people and the ruling class. The people respected Casvir, but it was clear to Flowridia that respect and fear remained strongly intertwined.

The town faded away, the houses becoming more scattered until only mountainous terrain met her gaze. Despite the chill, the open air filled Flowridia with a brewing sense of joy and freedom, and she smiled at the sun basking on her face.

Casvir spoke to fill the quiet day. "To wield the powers of light and dark in tandem bespeaks an impressive amount of finesse. Your power will grow with time, but the ability to act with the care of threading a needle is nothing to dismiss."

Flowridia blushed. Their conversation drifted to talk of magic and its nuances.

Chapter 10

The terrain sloped downward for a time, the weather becoming warmer as they descended from the mountain. The trees grew dense as the days passed, the snow steadily disappearing, becoming nothing but patches before it vanished entirely.

Sparring with Casvir continued to be grueling work, but not nearly so difficult as verbally sparring with Demitri to get him to watch Ana.

Just tell her to sit.

"That's terrible parenting."

And, one night, after successfully raising an ensemble of birds and coercing them to fly, sleep evaded Flowridia's tired mind.

Stars glittered high above, dimmed by the full moon. Flowridia lay with her back against Demitri's sleeping form, Ana tucked under her arm.

What would Ayla have thought of her new odd companion? Perhaps an undead pet was what Ayla needed, a creature who would love her even in death. She recalled watching Ayla long ago, of her kneeling in the kitchen before a tiny Demitri, tentative in her actions, unused to affection.

Flowridia turned over, pain tightening in her chest at the mere thought of Ayla. Ayla was dead. Ayla would stay dead.

The stars glittered like fangs, and Flowridia shut her eyes, hating the blush she felt blossom across her cheeks.

"Accept my name, and know I mean everything by it . . ."
Flowridia awoke before dawn, the tender images of the night already fading from her memory. The tighter she clung to the gentle brushing of doll lips against her own, the silken, embroidered gown against her skin, the sweet whispers in the dark, the faster they vanished.

Like Ayla herself, whose face slowly became a shadow in her mind.

The vision came not from some ghost destined to haunt her but her own betraying mind. Exhaustion beat against her eyelids as she sat up. Immediately, her head fell into her hands, furious emotion spiking when tears brimmed in her eyes.

"Flowridia?"

Flowridia dared to face Casvir, watched as he set aside his book—*Great Composers of the Millennia*—then shook her head, hiding her face behind her thick, autumn locks. She clenched her hands, willing away tears.

Ayla was dead. Ayla would stay dead.

"Be mine forever, darling . . ."

Flowridia stood up, jostling Demitri and Ana, the crisp morning air cutting through the lost warmth of her bed. Too ashamed to cry to Casvir—not over this; not again; she'd cried a thousand times before—she managed to stammer, "I need to be alone," before a gasping sob stole her words. She ran into the woods.

Nighttime left lingering whispers. Among the cheery songs of birds were the hooting of owls and skittering insects. With each step, leaves crunched, and the light of morning slowly rose up behind her.

She fell to her knees with a furious cry, crushing a patch of fresh daisies. The gentle blossoms responded to her touch, the life within singing to her senses. She shook as she reached out to stroke those perfect petals. So soft, as perfect as the skin beneath her fingers—

Flowridia ripped them away, rage tearing from her throat as she crumpled the delicate petals between her hands. Another cry as she stood, stumbling back and nearly falling at the sudden rush of blood. A shuddering breath left her as she rested her hand against the bark of an ancient tree. Purple, swirling like mist, emanated from her hand unwittingly, and she watched in horror as the tree blackened and rotted beneath her fingers.

But the strength she drew was intoxicating. Staring at her hands, she set them back against the withered tree and absorbed every ounce of its life, reveling in the consumed energy. Her body ignited with pleasure; her head swam.

But she could not hold it. Flowridia screamed, energy ripping out of her as the forest crumbled and withered, life tearing away from all the trees and brush surrounding her. She felt pain as insects were crushed into dust, as birds perished, decaying under the purple fog covering her vision.

She sobbed, her soul sickened yet drunk off the exhilaration from the burst of energy. The forest, blackened and ruined, cried testament to the power of her rage, her sorrow, her loneliness . . .

As she knelt, her tears dripping onto the decayed ground, a cautious voice managed to weave its way into her mind. *Mom, let me help you.*

Startled, Flowridia looked up to see Demitri watching quietly from beyond the edge of the charred scenery. His gentle gaze held no judgement. *Will you let me come forward?*

She managed a nod and let her face fall back into her hands. Soon, she felt Demitri's enormous bulk pressing against her, and she wrapped her arms around him, sobbing into his fur. She managed three words: "I miss her."

And that's okay.

Her grip tightened. "I hate her."

That's okay, too.

Dangerous words left her throat. "I still love her."

This time, Demitri did not respond, but his body curled around her, engulfing her almost entirely in his fur. Encompassed by his form and freed from the words once threatening to drown her, Flowridia felt some peace return to her soul.

"What do I do, Demitri?" she said, but only after her tears dried.

That choice is yours. But I'll support you. And I don't think you have to decide anything yet.

Flowridia sniffed, pulling away from the tear-drenched patch of fur. "When did I raise you to become so wise?"

I think it's my job as a familiar.

All around Flowridia, the dead scenery spoke of her erratic crime. Guilt weighed upon her as she pulled from his embrace. "I don't understand what happened," she whispered. "Necromancy comes from nothingness. This was different, and that scares me."

I don't know either. But it's nothing we can't figure out together.

With one hand gripping his fur, she allowed him to lead her through the decaying patch of land and through the forest.

Back at camp, Ana immediately bounded towards her. She caught the little fox, bombarded by affection, and kissed her jaw before looking to Casvir. He stood at her return. "I have only one request for you: Do not wander off alone again."

Flowridia frowned as she pulled the creature into a tight embrace. "And why?"

His voice grew quiet. "Because we are being followed."

She stiffened. "She's still here?"

"Something different. I should have told you, but I did not wish to worry you. You have trouble sleeping as it is."

Flowridia stepped toward him, eyes narrowing. "Who?"

"A small party from the Theocracy of Sol Kareena. They would not dare approach when I am nearby, but I worry they could overwhelm you."

"But why?" she whispered, slowly looking out into the scenery around them. Trees covered the surrounding area, birdsong sang in her ears, but there was no sign of life beyond that.

"I suppose I do not know for certain. But I have no wish to find out."

Flowridia looked out into the woods, the beginnings of a terribly foolish plan blooming in her head. "We could orchestrate this." When Casvir said nothing, she continued. "You would watch the entire time but imagine if we give them the chance to strike. You and Demitri could leave me alone and let me wander for a while." She swallowed, her virulent emotions having barely abated. "With all the unanswerable questions in my life, let me have this, at least."

"No."

He matched the challenge in her gaze. "Why?"

"Your safety is written in your contract."

"You would be watching."

"No," Casvir repeated, darker than before. Flowridia bristled at the word, wondering a moment what was stopping her from simply running off herself.

The answer came from an unexpected voice in her head. *He's right.*

Flowridia turned her frown onto Demitri, who she easily faced eye to eye.

You don't owe the Theocracy your company—

"It isn't about owing anyone anything!" she cried, then immediately reeled herself back, biting back her own fury. "I simply want to understand."

"Grab your spear," Casvir said, ignoring her words. "We will discuss your plan tonight—*discuss*. And only if you impress me with your footwork."

With the incentive of finding answers, Flowridia realized she had never done so well—she even earned a ruffle to her sweat-laden hair.

All day, they rode in stark silence, and Flowridia wondered how Casvir could sense the other group's presence. But she kept her eyes peeled for any signs of life, beyond the birds and rodents scattering from Casvir's company.

When evening fell, Flowridia's annoyance had blown away like the breeze.

She ate her dinner as Ana playfully bounced around their small camp, flickering light illuminating her white bones. Flowridia's hand touched upon the dead creatures she had idly raised—two rabbits, both in various states of decay— and dared to breach the subject again.

With finesse.

"Is your history with the Theocracy a long one?"

Casvir looked up from his book. "You mean to ask why they hate us?"

Flowridia nodded.

"We stand at many moral odds. For a necromancer like myself to rule an entire country hardly endears us to them. We exploit the undead to do menial labor, and even if it allows my citizens the freedom to pursue their own endeavors, the Theocracy views necromancy as the ultimate evil use of magic. They would rather force their own to toil in the fields for generations than look for an alternative source of labor. Furthermore, my expansive trade empire values monetary gain above all, and they deem the cost of becoming a citizen absolute blasphemy. They do not look kindly upon so-called 'false gods.'"

"I suppose you employing the 'Scourge of the Sun Elves' didn't do much to endear you to them either," Flowridia said, bitterness in the words. She recalled Lord Ashwood, the confrontation at the ball wherein he insulted Ayla and earned he and his comrades a painful death. "In exchange for the orb the Archbishop carries, they asked for Ayla's ear."

"Fascinating. They value safety over power."

"Channeling holy light into the ear burned her," Flowridia said. "They would have given up a treasured artifact in exchange for her death." She felt her hand instinctively drift to the bony place between her breasts, just above her heart. "Would it have worked?"

"I cannot say. But the Theocracy of Sol Kareena could never have confronted her face to face, just as they could never destroy Nox'Kartha on the battlefield. So they turn to subterfuge, assassins, and trickery to try and fulfill their pursuits. Not a particularly righteous course, but I would never try and unravel their twisted morality."

Flowridia's hand gripped at the empty space, and she stared purposefully at the warming crystal. She nodded slowly, acknowledging his words, but refused to speak, unsure of the emotions swimming in her heart, threatening to pull her under, drown her.

What did it matter now? Ayla was dead. What use was there reminiscing on their attempt to kill her when their Goddess had succeeded for them?

She let her hand fall to her lap, the emotions settling into a swamp around her lonely heart. The world was better without Ayla.

"What troubles you?" Casvir asked.

"She was a monster only barely caged," she whispered, echoing the very sentiment she had been told long ago. "And I still struggle to accept that."

"Ayla always held her own agenda," he said, ignoring her remark. "Perhaps she might have grown docile given a few more years in my service, but I do not think she would have ever been domesticated. Not by me."

His choice of words unsettled her. The thought of Ayla kneeling before Casvir, content or not, always irked her, but to think of her purring happily by his side like a kitten? Even now, Ayla dead in her coffin, the thought made her blood boil.

Ayla would never willingly bow to anyone. Her stubborn hate defined her.

Yet, Ayla had once relinquished all her pride, pled for forgiveness she hadn't deserved. She had pledged her love with a vulnerability unmatched, a memory Flowridia cherished and adored.

"You said yourself I tamed a monster," Flowridia whispered, then she steeled her jaw. "Casvir, you speak often of my capabilities."

"I do, and I mean it."

Finesse and honesty could work in tandem. "The Theocracy has come to confront me."

"You do not know if it is you they wish to see."

"But who else could it be, Casvir? I can see this through; you know I can. I want to know what they could possibly want from me."

Casvir's severe gaze never relinquished, but Flowridia matched it, knowing he held the power to hold her captive should he choose to wield it. "Go, then."

Flowridia stood up, each motion stiffly maneuvered as she kept her focus on Casvir. "You mean it?"

"I find myself protective of you; perhaps it has clouded my judgement. Keep your wits sharp. I will be watching, but there is no telling what tricks they might conjure."

She knelt down and whispered to Ana. "Run. Toward the people if you know where they are. Don't stop until I say 'stop.'" Again, Ana bolted, and Flowridia ran after her.

The darkness dampened her vision, but Flowridia kept an easy eye on the stark white creature. "Ana, wait!" she cried, but Ana did not slow. Internally, she praised the little fox, wondering how one rewarded a skeleton for obedience. "Wait!"

Night creatures met her ears, and after several minutes, she slowed. "Stop!"

Ana froze. Flowridia sprinted to scoop her up. "Good girl," she cooed, winded from exertion. She cradled the fox like a child and glanced about, senses on high alert as she absorbed the unfamiliar territory. The warming crystal was well behind them, and she hoped Casvir watched.

She could find her way back. Hopefully. She had no doubt Casvir would let her wander all night if the Theocracy didn't show.

But being actually lost might be the best way to draw them out.

Flowridia took careful steps as she went toward where she thought her camp might be. A hooting owl stole her attention. She looked up, smiling at the golden eyes meeting her gaze. "Hello, friend." The owl simply stared.

The trees were not so thick as to obscure the stars, and Flowridia marveled as she watched the twinkling lights, how they glittered through the leaves. The moon waned but still reflected some light, a grin across the night sky. The stars flashed like fangs below the gentle curve of the celestial rock. Flowridia let her sights fall back to earth and instead plucked a wilting daisy from a bush. In practiced motions, she braided the stem into her hair, comforted by the familiar ritual.

Rustling leaves caused her to stiffen. Flowridia swung around. A small rabbit skittered into a bush.

She placed Ana onto the ground. "Stay," she instructed. Ana plopped her bony bottom down and watched, tail twitching as Flowridia approached the bush. "Hello, little one," she said softly. Her growing influence on the living coaxed her to try a spell. *Come forward. I mean you no harm.*

A furry bundle emerged from the leaves, its simple mind falling to her influence. Flowridia offered a gentle hand and let the rabbit sniff her fingers. When it rubbed its soft head against her skin, Flowridia smiled at the trusting creature. *You are an unexpected delight. Come join me.*

The rabbit settled beside her. Flowridia's fingers stroked its velvet fur. The breeze tickled the leaves and brushed at her hair, but a more concrete crunching stole her attention. She glanced back at Ana who twitched like a caged bird. Flowridia whispered to the rabbit. *Go home, sweet one. Danger approaches.*

The rabbit scampered away, and Flowridia stood. "Hello?" she called. "Is someone there?"

Fire suddenly lit, illuminating a face standing perhaps twenty feet away. A human woman smiled as she held a torch, her black hair plaited into a crown of gold. Another face stepped up beside her, and another, both human men, each with birds upon their shoulders and symbols of Sol Kareena engraved into their armor and robes. "Lady Flowridia," the woman said as she stepped forward, and her voice was familiar, as was the little bird perched on her arm, "perhaps you remember me. I'm High Priestess Lunestra of the Theocracy of Sol Kareena. You're safe now."

Given the recent revelation that this woman was her great-aunt, she hesitated in her reply, seeking familiarity in the woman's aged features. Flowridia resembled her mother in so many ways, but the warmth of her own skin bridged the gap between her parents, Lunestra's umber hue surely the same as her paladin nephew.

Flowridia smiled, and it was sincere. "I do remember you."

"We've been following, hoping for the chance to speak. Will you accompany us back to our camp?"

"I'd be honored," she said, and she prayed Demitri and Casvir watched. With meticulous movements, she bent over and picked Ana up into her arms, gauging their reactions closely. One of the priests couldn't quite hide his revulsion. His eyes widened, stance stiffening, but the other and High Priestess Lunestra appeared unconcerned. She stroked across Ana's spine. "Lead the way, please."

Lunestra gestured for her to follow, and the four stepped quickly through the trees. "An interesting companion you've found," she said, though no accusation could be heard in her voice.

"Ana ran off, disobedient little thing that she is." She prayed they didn't understand the intricacies of necromancy. "What do you wish to speak about?"

"Are you safe, Lady Flowridia?" Lunestra asked. "My companions and I would ask a favor of you, but if you are in danger, or if you are being coerced, or used, we can send you home."

Flowridia chose her response carefully. "I'm in no danger."

"Our spies have heard troubling rumors concerning you and Imperator Casvir."

If Staelash had heard as much, so too must have the Theocracy. She bit back a grimace and forced a lie. "I can't imagine what you mean, High Priestess."

A hand went to rest against the small of her back. "You sweet child," Lunestra said, leading her forward. In the distance, a campfire flickered. "You sweet, capable child, reassure me, please—has the imperator coerced you into anything untoward?"

"Gods, no," Flowridia said, quite sincerely. "Whatever his faults, he's a gentleman."

"You travel with him willingly, then?"

Flowridia spoke with care, recognizing the layered question. "We have a contract," she replied. "I aid him, and he aids me. Nothing more or less. And once the terms are complete, I am free to go home."

It would hardly be polite to press for details, but Flowridia could see Lunestra's internal debate.

The camp came into view. No other guards were present, but Flowridia didn't doubt that Lunestra and her priests were capable of defending themselves. All were armed, the priests quite openly, with swords at their belts, whereas the bird at Lunestra's shoulder bespoke her talents for magic. The aged High Priestess gestured to a log by the fire, and Flowridia sat with Ana cradled in her arms.

"When you worked for Staelash, you held something dear to you," Lunestra began, kindness still etched into her face.

Realization struck Flowridia, recalling their last meeting. "What sort of something?" she said, and then set Ana onto the log beside her. "Stay." She needed something to do with her hands; lying caused her to twitch. She pulled out the flower in her hair and idly braided it back into the thick locks.

Sitting beside her, Lunestra watched with open curiosity. "The ear of Ayla Darkleaf."

"I always held it close to my heart." Flowridia wondered if Casvir could hear her jest. She continued primping her hair. "For safety, I kept personal guard of it."

"That much was implied at our last meeting. Do you know where it is now?"

Her flower now secure, Flowridia's hands fell. "I don't see how that's important, given Ayla is dead."

"Forgive me," Lunestra said. "I mean no insult. Perhaps I should be more transparent; my kingdom seeks the body of Ayla Darkleaf, including the ear. We know it is in Nox'Kartha, and you can help us acquire it. Our kingdom would reward you. We would even be willing to trade for the orb."

So that was their bargain. Flowridia's hands threatened to clench into fists, so instead she lifted Ana back into her lap and distracted herself with her smooth touch. "You would have me steal Ayla's body?"

"For the sake of us all, yes."

"What use is a corpse to you?"

Lunestra watched with a motherly demeanor, but suspicion marred her gaze. "The corpses of monsters can be used for great evil. We seek to destroy her, once and for all. We would burn her, scatter the remains, and assure she's left to rest. She was dear to you, Lady Flowridia. The final gift you can give your friend is peace."

The implication, the hope of Ayla's return, reopened wounds Flowridia had never quite allowed to heal, but that paled to the sudden spike in fury at Lunestra's choice in words. "My what?"

"Your attachment to Ayla was made quite clear at our last meeting."

Flowridia forced a smile. "You would manipulate my apparent friendship for your own gain?"

"Lady Flowridia, this is for no one's gain—only the safety of the world. I understand that the bonds of friendship are complicated at times, but you mustn't let your feelings blind you toward what must be done."

Flowridia set her jaw, forcing her breath to steady. "The body has been put to rest," she said curtly, and her judgement knew she should stop there, say nothing more. But emotion forced her words. "Ayla Darkleaf was most assuredly *not* my friend, nor do I think she will ever truly be at peace because gods know I'm not either, but she's mine and mine alone. If I choose to burn her and scatter her ashes, then the honor is mine. That's what she was; she was *mine.*" She swallowed back tears. "And I was hers."

Lunestra listened, a kindness Flowridia knew she didn't deserve, then said, "I meant no offense. I didn't realize there was flirtation between–"

"By every god!" Flowridia said, exasperation in her wounded words. "Surely you were there. You must have seen it or heard the tale—The Endless Night betraying the God of Order when I protected *your* orb, and then as she rose to stand between me and your own benevolent Goddess. Ayla Darkleaf gave her life for me. That isn't flirtation. It isn't a crass fuck for the sake of diplomacy–"

"Lady Flowridia, do you know what she was?"

Scourge of the Sun Elves. A mad scientist who tortured and skinned her victims alive. An accomplished seamstress who created books and shoes and all forms of macabre art to play out the wickedness of her broken mind. Chosen of Izthuni, with whom she slaughtered entire populaces.

To ask why was to cry out into a void.

"She was a monster," Flowridia said, and for the first time, she accepted the poignant words, "who loved me with all her heart." She stood up, realizing their discussion was assuredly over. "If you continue to follow me, I cannot account for your safety. Casvir knows you're here."

Their eyes met, and the compassion in Lunestra's gaze threatened to shatter the resolve in Flowridia's bitter heart. She could go with her. Break the contract, or perhaps join her after. The body was hers to do with as she pleased, and though she had laid it to rest, she recalled Tazel's fear, and now Lunestra's, that someone would bring her back, whether or not it be by Casvir's hand. The Theocracy could scatter the ashes to the wind and guarantee it was done right.

But in the damning stretch of silence, a fundamental truth pierced her heart: Flowridia had not decided.

There, beyond the trees, were the glowing red eyes of Imperator Casvir watching her every move. Flowridia stepped out of their camp, Ana in tow, and disappeared into the forest.

Demitri stood near. She fell into the wolf's side, and with her free arm she hugged his neck and kissed his cold nose.

"Did you find what you were looking for?" Casvir asked, his rumbling voice soft.

Flowridia nodded.

"I will speak to you back at our camp."

He led them away, but Demitri bowed his neck down. *Get on.*

Flowridia stared at him oddly. "Me?"

Demitri's golden eyes stared up. *Get on, stupid.*

Touched despite the slight, Flowridia climbed onto his back, finding she could stay on quite comfortably if she gripped the fur on the nape of his neck.

He caught up to Casvir's enormous strides, more than capable of outpacing him.

At camp, Flowridia slid off Demitri's back but kept Ana to her heart, clinging to the offered comfort.

"As you requested," Casvir said, "I watched over your encounter with the Theocracy."

The statement lingered, and Flowridia looked away, keeping her focus on the warming crystal instead of the scrutinizing gaze of Casvir. "I'm a fool," she whispered.

"I was quite impressed by your diplomacy, actually. Everything was beautifully handled, until your tantrum at the end."

"Your words have been particularly biting lately." Flowridia sat beside the crystal, warming her chilled form.

Casvir sat beside her, near enough that their knees brushed as he settled. "People will say far worse to you. For her to imply that you and Ayla were merely friends was a misunderstanding; imagine if she had been trying to insult you."

"I can handle insults."

"But not for people to presume your virtue?"

She shook her head sharply. "I don't care what they say about my virtue. I know the truth, and that's enough for me. Let them say what rumors they will, that Lady Flowridia, Grand Diplomat of Staelash, spreads her legs for any man or monarch who might sign a treaty with her." She stared at the crystal, the display of flickering orange and yellow soothing to her frustrated thoughts. "But how dare they discount the woman I loved."

"News did not spread wide of your relationship with Ayla. Only your ruling council knew the extent of it."

Flowridia shook her head. "What they knew, they wish they could have made disappear."

Behind her, Demitri's warmth settled against her back, and Flowridia relaxed against him. She heard his voice in her head. *I know you loved her. And for all her oddities, I know she loved you too.*

"Thank you, Demitri," Flowridia whispered. Her blinking grew heavy.

Casvir looked between them, watching their interaction. "People fear what they do not understand. Ayla was a mystery, perhaps to all except you."

"I can't say I ever understood her. But I knew her heart." Tears welled in her eyes. "Like a fool, I trusted her. For all her wicked intentions, I loved her. I know I should have stayed away, but when she begged for my forgiveness, I gave it-" Flowridia bit her lip to ward away the threatened tears. But all the memories of joy and love, of Ayla's smile and laugh and gentle touch, came to her thoughts, and she heard her breath hitch. "I gave it because she had changed. You were right, Casvir—she was growing and changing her ways to be someone she thought was worthy of me. Perhaps she was still a monster, but I so dearly loved the woman she was becoming. I don't understand it, but I did something right by her."

"You did," came Casvir's gentle reply.

"I miss her so much," Flowridia said, tears steadily falling. "And I don't want the world to dismiss us. When they think of me, let them think of her. The world thinks I should be ashamed of her; I would keep her by my side forever and always if I could."

"Flowridia," Casvir said, "if it truly is your deepest desire, you know I will pour my resources into finding a way to bring her back."

Flowridia shook her head. "I can offer myself for her return, but I cannot sign her to you. She died to escape that fate. It has to be me who does it—alone." Her head fell into her hands as she squeezed her eyes shut. "But what wounds me the most is she still died a monster. She damned the world to the God of Order for the chance to live with me but betrayed him to save my life." She saw the scene behind her eyes, of The Endless Night cradling her before the great titan, recalled the cold touch and bitter scream. "The world is better without her."

"Are you?"

A quiet sob escaped her lips. With one hand, she tried in vain to wipe away the tears spilling down her face. "You said I was the one redeeming trait you ever knew in her," she said, calm despite her continued tears. "Whereas I think for me, she'll damn me to hell."

Casvir's clawed hand on her back startled her, but not as much as his words. "Then damn yourself to hell. Damn yourself, and have no regrets. Make certain every demon fears your name before you get there."

Flowridia stared at him, red-rimmed eyes wide.

"Whatever paths you choose, someone will hate you. Only be certain that someone is not you." A pause, and his expression softened. Never had she seen so genuine a gaze on the oft stoic imperator. "You are capable of greatness, Flowridia. I have seen it. Whatever you choose, you will have my support. If this is your greatest desire, be relentless. Be unyielding. You will find your power on the way."

Flowridia's gaze fell back to the crystal, her tears finally slowing. A bit of warmth seeped through the cracks of her bitter heart. A hint of a smile quirked at her lip. "Thank you, Casvir."

A comfortable silence settled between them. Casvir soon removed his hand. "The hour grows late. I would give you a lesson if you desire, but I understand if you are exhausted."

"I think a distraction would be better than to try and sleep."

Casvir stood and offered a hand. "Then, come."

She accepted.

Chapter 11

The forest grew dark, the air thick with trees and fog. Flowridia's horse struggled through the underbrush, its skeletal legs catching among the ferns and greenery. She kept Ana safe in her bag and cast her gaze back every minute to make certain Demitri still followed.

Beside her, Casvir seemed to have no trouble, but still his silhouette disappeared behind the mist, blinking in and out of sight like a candle.

Deeper, they rode. Spots of sunlight grew increasingly rare. Flowridia wondered what sort of creatures might follow them had Casvir not scared away all the living.

Evening came, and when Flowridia could barely see the horse's head from darkness and mist, Casvir proclaimed they would stop.

Flowridia glanced around at the trees and down to the brush below. "There's nowhere to camp. The plants are too thick."

"You will clear them."

Her bare feet touched wet earth, the cold mud and grass coating her like a moist bandage. She shuddered at the sensation. "With my spear?"

"With necromancy. Absorb their life."

Flowridia felt his scrutinizing gaze absorb every motion, every thought as she knelt on the ground and placed her hand onto the damp earth. Life pulsed, from fungal growths to roots and greenery, and her blood itched to steal it.

The impulse surprised her. Flowridia breathed out a steadying sigh, letting her thoughts clear, her mind focusing on the empty void. She felt energy flow within her and seep from her pores, watching in amazement when a purple mist rose from her skin. She blew out a breath, a visible cloud billowing out to choke the leaves beside her face.

Flowridia breathed deep. The cloud emanated; the surrounding life withered. She felt the energy cry out as it resisted her touch, but not for long. It seeped into her blood and bones, life threatening to burst from the seams. Oh, it was exhilarating, this absorption of energy.

"Flowridia, stop."

Flowridia opened her eyes, gasping when she realized what she'd done. The forest, once green and brown and damp, now stood charred, black. Energy still swirled in her hands, draining life from the air. The trees had withered, threatening to fall.

Death spread far and wide, far larger than they needed for camp. Flowridia brought her hand to cover her mouth.

"Impressive," Casvir said. "But to let pleasure dictate your actions is weakness. Greater spellcasters than you have fallen prey to pursuits of pleasure and addiction."

Stunned, Flowridia found she could form no words, though a blush did burn at her cheeks.

"Keep your indulgence in check."

Casvir said nothing more and instead began unloading the horses.

Later, she sat on her bedroll with Demitri behind her. Ana sniffed and batted at the heavy crystal warming their camp.

"Casvir," she whispered, and the De'Sindai king glanced up from his reading. "Do you know if we're close?"

"I sense that your orb may be in these woods. The black orb crackles, even as I sit here."

Very close, then. "Where are we?"

Instead of speaking, Casvir shut his book and withdrew a new one from the pile. *Maps of the New World*, it said, and he beckoned for her to sit beside him.

Her dress brushed against his armor, fabric singing against metal. His clawed finger tapped the spot labeled 'Nox'Kartha' before sliding it northwest. Over a mountain pass, over a small dot with the title 'Wood's End,' and past the borders of the tyrant's kingdom before settling on an outcropping of trees. "Verity Forest," Casvir said. "An ancient and unchartered place. Kingdoms have tried and failed to settle it; they say something haunts the mist. Tomorrow, we will spend time searching."

So the orb they sought was close indeed. She wondered if it reacted too.

Were it wielded, did the other sense their presence?

She slept peacefully.

Flowridia awoke to the singing of birds. The light barely broke through the line of trees, but when she sat up, she saw that the damage she had inflicted to the forest had nearly healed; only the immediate area of their camp showed signs of blight. Upon the ground sprouted new life—growing much more rapidly than it should have in its natural state.

"How did this happen?" she whispered, and when Demitri stirred, he looked about, as confused as she.

Casvir glanced up from his book. "My orb fostered a land of death; perhaps the orb here bears a different sort of influence."

They quickly cleared their camp and continued onward. He untied the horses and simply led them with his hands. "Should danger come, stand behind me. Your body is much more fragile than mine."

Demitri poked her with his nose. *Stand behind me too.*

Despite the affirmations, Flowridia felt a rise of apprehension in her stomach.

They trekked through the faint light of morning. She hugged Ana close to her body and kept a hand in Demitri's fur, letting him lead her forward as they followed Casvir.

"Where are we going?" she whispered.

"The orb speaks as we move this direction."

Flowridia heard rustling from beside them. She looked into the dark woods and saw nothing, yet leaves bent unnaturally. Dirt shifted.

She stopped, letting her hand untangle from Demitri's fur as she stared into the forest. Her mind cleared, and she focused her sight, an adage from Etolié whispering through her head: *"Illusions are only as real as you believe them to be."*

For half a moment, the shimmered outline of something large and reptilian stared back from the trees.

Flowridia gasped, aware of how Casvir and Demitri both stopped and stared, but she took a cautious step forward, the image becoming clear once again.

She saw the dragon sequestered in the woods, how it followed, how it shied as she reached forward. Her judgement said to run, yet as she took in the sight of those green scales laden with grass-like growths, of the plants springing forth from the dragon's body, how could she be afraid when flowers were woven into her own hair? The eyes meeting hers were intelligent, inquisitive, and when she offered a hand, it dipped a head down to meet it.

Embedded in its chest, amidst the foliage of plant-like growths, an orb shone, its color shifting in various shades of green.

Their bodies did not touch, but Flowridia felt warm air as the dragon sniffed. "Hello." She smiled gently. "Casvir," she continued, keeping her tone serene, "we have a shy friend following us. If you look closely, I think you'll see."

Casvir appeared beside her, and the dragon flinched, showing teeth when it saw the black orb in his hand. In his other, Casvir's mace appeared, and Flowridia immediately moved to stand between them. "No. No fighting."

"And how do you intend to steal this dragon's orb?" he said, his voice dangerous and calm. "Through flattery?"

"Let me try. Please," she said, and when he stepped back, she turned to the gargantuan creature standing before her. "He makes you nervous."

The dragon said nothing, merely stared as Casvir continued taking cautious steps backward.

"His intentions are good," Flowridia said kindly, and though she knew it was a lie, she prayed the dragon didn't. "And so are mine. My name is Flowridia, and I am the Grand Diplomat of Staelash. Do you have a name?"

The dragon faced her, stance still prepared to fight.

One snap of its jaws, and Flowridia would be dead. Demitri came up beside her, his presence inoffensive to the dragon. "Do you sense the other orbs?"

The dragon said nothing, but its stare appeared enraptured by her words.

"There is a man who seeks to steal them, and he'll use them to rip the worlds apart. My friends and I are trying to stop him, but to do that we have to collect them before he does."

The dragon sat back, revealing its chest and the orb protruding from it as it looked down from above the tree line. Flowridia recalled reading of dragons, hearing of their purpose, enlisted by the Old Gods to aid in balancing the world, and a question fell from her lips. "Are you the last of your kind?"

Perhaps it didn't know. What awareness would a dragon have toward others a thousand miles away?

"You were given a task, and you've performed it with honor," Flowridia continued. "For ten thousand years you've protected that orb." Maybe more, she thought, but she wouldn't make claims she couldn't verify. "We need it to save the worlds."

And then, clear as the breeze on the leaves, came a voice, soothing yet monstrous. The dragon's mouth moved, its tongue articulating in perfect Solviran Common. "In the time before the New Gods, I was granted a name. You may speak it. I am Valeuron."

"Valeuron," Flowridia whispered, sensing the innate majesty of it. "It's a beautiful name."

"I have felt the disturbances in the planes," the dragon said, his attention fixed to her alone. "Who is this monster that would steal what is mine?"

"Someone you know, I think. The God of Order, Soliel. He's come back."

"That is not a name I have heard spoken aloud since the Convergence," the dragon rumbled. "Yes, I knew him. He and his counterpart created us—myself, and my brothers and sisters. If he has fallen to madness, this bespeaks grave consequences."

"He's already shown he will resort to violence to get what he wants."

"And who are you, Flowridia, to stop an Old God? With the same trickery you used to desecrate my forest?"

The slight stung more than she expected, and she could have brushed it aside had she not understood the dragon's intention to insult her. "If it comes to it, yes. I value the greater good above my own name."

"We six were given the task," the dragon said, "to protect the orbs; to use them to preserve the careful balance of this world. I fear I am all that remains. Again I ask, Flowridia of no name, who are you to stop an Old God? Who are you to ask me to abandon my purpose of ten thousand years?"

Flowridia stared up into his gentle gaze, his words condemning, yet his eyes, a brilliant shade of jade, bore a softness to match his appearance. She did not doubt he could be fearsome, but here he was a creature of peace and tranquility, seeking only to preserve his home. "I am no one," she whispered, standing tall in her stance. "I rejected the name my mother gave me, and I never knew my father and have no wish to claim his legacy. The only name I might've claimed was lost with my lover's passing. So, I am merely Flowridia." She swallowed, summoning her bravery. "But perhaps that is enough. The mark I leave on this world is mine and mine alone."

With a fluidity his size should not have granted, the dragon reached forward with a single, clawed hand, moss and flower stems growing from between the scales. "Touch me, Flowridia of no name. We shall see each other." When she reached a hand out to meet him, the dragon did not shirk.

An energy radiated against her senses. Permissive, it waited for her to withdraw her defenses, then bore into the very core of her being.

For a breathless moment, she was a child—but not a child, no, a dragonling—cradled to the breast of a woman she instinctively loved. A voice spoke, feminine and comforting, alluring to Flowridia's very soul: *"My magnificent little Valeuron—yours is the destiny of Gods."*

All changed, and she was grown, offered an artifact of depthless power by a man Flowridia knew and feared. But here he was a friend, a father, a man whose kindness shone in his earth-speckled eyes, gentle despite his great stature. She stood in the throng of her brothers and sisters—five other dragons of majesty and splendor—who each bore the power of their orb and their duties. She stood beside one she knew well, one of bone and dark magic.

One by one, their lights extinguished.

Flowridia saw one who roared with the power of thunder, wielding lightning like a toy, fall to the sword and silver flame.

Such, too, was the fate of a great being of fire, drawn from its domain within the heart of a volcano, only to be consumed in silver light.

One's blood saturated the sea, strangled by the tentacles of some great monster.

And one fell to despair and loneliness, dying upon a throne of riches, its white orb held in an atrophied claw.

Flowridia knew the next. She saw the image of Casvir himself reigning terror and darkness upon a skeletal beast.

Then, a vision of a future not yet come to pass, of Valeuron erupting in flame, crying out as he burned alive.

The visions disappeared. Flowridia met Valeuron's gaze, the last of his kind, and she realized how lonely a life his must be.

His voice rumbled, its depth reflecting his age. "Child of Odessa; beloved of Ayla Darkleaf. I have seen your life; I know your death."

The dragon reared back. Flowridia cowered. Behind, Casvir's metallic steps approached.

With a single clawed hand, the dragon brought its nails up to the glowing spot between its scales. It released a pained roar, blood spurting as it plucked the orb from its chest. Then, shaking, its thunderous voice said, "My duty is fulfilled."

It returned to all fours with the orb in hand. Blood dripped onto the dark forest floor, but the dragon offered the orb forward.

A gaseous green radiated from the ancient artifact. Flowridia reached out to accept the gift, but a light from behind the dragon suddenly grew blinding.

The dragon clasped its claw around the orb and turned its serpentine head. When Flowridia peered behind, she saw the God of Order standing among the trees.

Dread clutched her gut. By the gods—how long had he been watching?

Two orbs shone in his hand, glowing bright in the presence of their companions. His armor glowed, the beauty of his ageless face framed by a magnificent halo. "Is this your loyalty, Valeuron? To hide from your creator, only to manifest to a powerless girl?"

"You're a fool to think her powerless." Valeuron's claws grasped the orb. "I have seen your legacy through her eyes, the fear you have inspired. The mantle of Godhood is no longer yours to bear."

From Soliel's hand formed a sword of flame. Flowridia glanced to the orb wielded in the dragon's hand, then back to Casvir. In his own clawed hand was his summoned mace, and the twitch of his smile bespoke his glee at the inevitable skirmish.

She dared not speak, lest she draw Soliel's attention.

"So it shall be violence between us," Valeuron said, sadness in his words. "For all your laws, you were always aimless without Her. What would the Great Mother say, to see you now?"

"She has her own crimes to answer for." Bitterness stained the words, the first deviation from calm she had seen from this fallen god. "We all must abide by our duties. I must undo the damage of The Convergence, and you must protect your orb. I understand."

Flowridia stepped back, her hand gripping Demitri's fur. Soliel tore his gaze from the dragon, drifting instead to she and Casvir. "You were difficult to hide from. I commend you for that." He withdrew a crystal shard glowing in shades of green; Flowridia recognized it as the same stone forming her bracelet. "And I thank you for leading me here. Leave your orb, and you shall live."

Flowridia heard a truly frightening sound—Casvir *laughed*. "I revel in the opportunity to steal yours."

"Very well, imperator. It will not be the first time I've slain you."

Valeuron's voice rumbled across the forest floor. "There is no honor in your so-called duty, Great Father." From his throat expelled a noxious, gaseous liquid, manifesting in a putrid flame. Sickly green stained the earth, sizzling and eating all it touched, the earth crying out as it poisoned the life within it. Soliel, too, gave a pained cry when the acidic spray touched his armor and skin. "With Her death, you have lost your soul."

Soliel glowed, and a shield of lightning danced across his armor. Fire erupted beneath the dragon's feet, burning foliage and scales and the soft skin beneath.

Flowridia screamed when the dragon cried out. Jaws against her shirt tossed her aside, and Demitri tackled her as another blast of fire might have consumed them.

From her wrist, she touched upon the crystal gifted from Etolié, willing a shield to protect them. Non-magic expanded to cover her and most of Demitri. At her feet, Ana cowered. Flowridia pulled the skeletal creature into her arms.

The earth rumbled. Skeletal hands and paws shot from the foliage and dirt, all rotted and putrid from the damp atmosphere. When the onslaught of death swarmed the God of Order, he swatted them aside with his burning blade. A thousand skittering undead would not be so easily thrown away, and though they burned, more rose in their stead.

The dragon rose to its feet, and Casvir shot out from beside it, summoned weapon in hand. In practiced motions, he charged forward, perfect precision in his swing. Distracted, Soliel grunted when Casvir's weapon clanged against his armor.

Clouds gathered high above, foretold by the thunder shaking the sky. Soliel's weapon met Casvir's, the resulting crash causing Flowridia to cower at Demitri's feet.

Flowridia attempted to rise. Teeth clamped against her shirt, stopping her from running forward. "Demitri—!"

Lightning struck, tearing through the trees, the dragon, and Casvir himself, who nearly matched the dragon's roar of pain. Fire burst from the ground, engulfing Casvir and the dragon both.

A burst of light—not of fire or lightning but pure and divine—illuminated Soliel's body from within, radiating out in an aura of purity. The halo at his head shone, testament of his divine blood. As he glowed, the undead ravaging his form screamed and burned. His flaming sword tore through Casvir's armor like paper.

One swipe; Casvir was cleaved in two, instantly cauterized by fire.

Flowridia screamed. She dropped Ana; Demitri released her. She ran into the fray, where the fire lay dying and Casvir lay in pieces. The maimed dragon fell, rolling on the ground to parch the flame. When the black orb rolled from the torn shreds of Casvir's armor, Soliel knelt to grab it.

All but ignored by the Old God, Flowridia stole it first. Immediately, she felt the crackling energy, the potential for mayhem threatening to burst from her soul. Power surged through her veins, like blissful fire through her blood. Her vision swam from the sudden influx of dark magic.

Soliel towered before her. "I know your death, Flowridia Darkleaf," he said, his sword held before him, lightning dancing from his form. The very vision she had seen before, on the fateful day of Ayla's death, the same that replayed in her nightmares. "Today is not that day." In his off hand, two orbs glowed. "But give me your orb, or I will be tempted to change your fate."

She did not cower. Like her own body, Flowridia felt the corpse of every dead thing, but knew they could do nothing to this resplendent God. In tandem with death, however, was life. An impossible plan formulated in her head.

The life around her suddenly cried out as she drained it into her very soul. She gasped at the power, the radiant energy—yet with the orb, she could filter it with ease, exempting Demitri and the dragon and every animal creature. The plants withered and died—

And were infused with death.

The plants she destroyed immediately saturated with energy, more pristine and perfect than in life. When alive, she could coax them to health, whisper sweet words to help them grow—here, they bent to her command.

The very earth betrayed Soliel, clinging to his legs, attempting to subdue him with vines and branches. Soliel cried out as he swung his sword, the plants severed by his flaming weapon and holy light, but still they burst from the earth, fell upon him in droves.

Flowridia stumbled backwards, shaken by her own power. Behind Soliel, the dragon loomed. Seared to the bone, a near skeletal face opened his mouth to roar. His beautiful form burned with the rest of his forest, destroyed in the onslaught of fire and lightning and death.

When Soliel might have escaped his prison of nature, Valeuron trapped him in a grasp of ruined scales and bone. He screamed as he held the radiant God, fire and lightning searing his body. He threw the God of Order to the ground, releasing another blast of acidic spray to coat him.

Flowridia ran toward the mutilated body of Casvir, gasping at the dark purple matter seeping from his lacerated torso. A clean cut—Casvir's legs rested only a few feet away; a blow that would have murdered a lesser man.

But Casvir, it seemed, was no mere man. When Flowridia knelt beside him, she nearly sobbed when he spoke. "I need my orb."

She held it out, remiss to be rid of it, she realized, but all that paled to the startled relief of knowing Casvir still lived. He took it into his hands, and all at once his bottom half reformed. Pure dark energy massed to create a shadowed body and legs.

Valeuron screamed and flailed, but his roar suddenly cut off. When Flowridia looked back, she saw that Soliel had removed the dragon's head.

Her heart clenched, gasping at the thought of the gentle beast, now gone. She had seen him fall—a death of flame.

Casvir, she realized, struggled to stand, his new legs shaking and struggling to stay corporeal. She offered a hand, but he batted it away. "You are too small," he said, but when Demitri appeared, Ana in his jaws, Casvir gripped the enormous wolf and allowed him to help him stand. His claw struck the air. Vertigo caused Flowridia's head to swim.

Casvir, with a hand gripping Demitri, knelt beside his severed lower half. He launched it into the portal.

From the dragon's corpse, Flowridia saw Soliel steal the third orb, fire and lightning now melding with a seeping, acidic gas.

A clawed hand grabbed hers. Calm even in the presence of defeat, Casvir marched her to the portal.

Flowridia caught Soliel's gaze, his fury matched only by her own hatred. The time would come later for mourning the loss of Valeuron.

The world shifted. Casvir's office appeared. The portal sealed shut.

Casvir collapsed, metal clanging against stone. Flowridia realized his summoned legs had vanished, leaving him a severed torso on the ground. She heard him groan.

Breathing frantic, Flowridia shook as she grabbed his burned hand. His armor contained his severed lower half, crumbled by the desk. "Casvir! Casvir, what can I do?"

"I am fine," he said, and his voice remained calm despite the fact he lay in two pieces. "I am thoroughly impressed at what you accomplished with the orb's power."

"Thank you," she said, but still she frantically inspected the burned line splitting his torso.

"I owe you an apology. I underestimated the orbs' power in conjunction with a God and nearly got you killed."

"Casvir, it's—"

"Our contract remains," he continued, ignoring her objections. "I will find you an orb. But it will have to wait."

"Of course," Flowridia said, heart still racing. "Casvir, will you recover?"

"Your concern for my well-being is endearing, but unnecessary. I am fine. My body will simply need time to repair itself."

"Casvir, you're missing your entire lower half."

"Not missing." He pointed at the twisted, broken armored legs and torso laying against the desk.

Flowridia stood and tugged at the severed lower body, jumping aside when the heavy armor clattered to the floor. Casvir watched with visible confusion as she tugged with all her strength at the mutilated lower half. "What are you doing?"

"If you aren't going to die, then let me try and speed up your healing."

Flowridia remembered words from long ago, of Thalmus saying holy magic wounded the dead. But perhaps the opposite might heal it.

With Demitri's help, they managed to set the lower body against Casvir's torso. But when she tried to take the orb from Casvir's hand, he stole it back. "Flowridia–"

"I have an idea. I swear to give it back."

To her surprise, he placed it into her hands.

Again, power threatened to overwhelm her craving body. But Flowridia placed her hands against the severed line of Casvir's body and armor and slipped her fingers in until she felt cold skin and muscle against her fingers. The living she touched practically begged to be healed, but Flowridia had to search, Casvir's body quite content, it seemed, to remain stagnant. She shut her eyes, letting her senses expand, and manually felt each strip of skin tingle, the torn muscles and bone relinquishing to her power.

Slow and bitter work, but fueled by the black orb, Flowridia managed to coax each severed vein and nerve together. Muscle repaired; skin sealed; Casvir's musculature was expansive, his bulk larger than anything she had ever healed, but with each passing second, another bit of skin repaired, layer by layer.

Only when she felt no more work could be done, and when what had once been a clean slice was nothing but a thin scar, did Flowridia remove her hand. Casvir sat up, his feet twitching as he tested the quality of her spell, and without looking up, she gave the orb to him.

Exhaustion, but not from her work, struck her then. Her face fell into her hands, tears welling in her eyes.

"Are you hurt?" she heard Casvir say.

Flowridia shook her head, relief flooding her in tandem with sorrow. Her tears were for Casvir, whom she'd thought was surely dead, and for Valeuron who had given his life for theirs, who would have willingly given her the orb had the God of Order not come to claim it.

So many questions remained unanswered. Valeuron had deemed her, she who came from nothing, whose love lay dead beneath the catacombs of the castle, who had slain her own mother and discarded her name, worthy. He had given his life for theirs, had seen her death as she had seen his and deemed it *not today—*

And Soliel had said the same, then called her a name known to no one but she and a book she kept treasured and secret.

"I don't understand what the dragon meant. I don't understand why it gave its life for us. I don't–" She bit off her words, unwilling to release her tears. Embarrassed, she cowered, knowing she had no right to cry when Casvir, too, had nearly died to save her. Her fists clenched, and she willed herself to calm.

She realized, then, what had been left behind. Ana thumped her tail beside her, but the horses, her belongings, her spear—all of that had been in the forest.

"You should rest," Casvir said, "but find me afterward. I would like to speak with you concerning your actions in the forest." Curiosity twisted his lip—not intrigue, no, but wonder. "Never have I seen necromancy used to manipulate nature's power. You continue to surprise me." With the desk for support, Casvir stood, ruined armor creaking as he did. He shook each leg, perhaps testing them, then gestured for her to follow, his stance proud even in the aftermath of defeat.

She followed her unconventional escort down the carpeted hallways. Though he aimed for her guest room, she stopped him when they passed the secret entrance to Ayla's bath. "I won't sleep if I smell like smoke and death."

When he left, she said to Demitri, "Do you want to join me in the tub?"

Wolves don't bathe in prissy tubs.

"Rude boy. Watch Ana instead." She looked down at the skeletal fox. "Follow Demitri wherever he goes."

You must hate me.
"I love you with all my heart."
Demitri left. Flowridia went to bathe.

Chapter 12

Alone, Flowridia's tears mingled with the bathwater. Valeuron's death had cleaved her heart in two.

First Ayla, and now Valeuron—both had given their lives for her, and the added weight brought guilt unparalleled. Ayla had loved her; Valeuron had barely known her yet died for her to live, had seen a glimpse of her life as she had seen his.

She wished so dearly to know what he had seen for her to be worthy of such kindness. Perhaps it might have alleviated her guilt, to understand *why*.

And so she mourned him, fearing she was alone to do so. Valeuron had been the last of his kind, no brothers and sisters to feel his loss. Soliel's betrayal toward a creature to whom he had been a father wounded her tender heart.

Though she knew Valeuron had once had a mother, for she'd felt that warmth herself, there was no Goddess of Chaos to mourn her son. She nearly hoped there would never be, if only to spare her the knowledge that all her beloved children were gone.

Cleaned of smoke and fire and dirt, Flowridia felt she might properly rest.

But when she was clean, she noticed the barest hints of a foreign smell wafting through the moist washroom— floral and sickeningly sanguine. Odd, but she paid it no mind as she wrapped herself in a fluffy towel. By the array of towels was a single robe; surely meant for Ayla, but with a train that must have dragged well behind her melodramatic, vampiric love.

The soft cloth served its purpose of protecting her modesty and keeping her warm. She sniffed her sleeves, disappointed to find it smelled merely of soap instead of memories. As she tied the fluffy robe around her waist, she spared a glance for the far wall.

Pressure suddenly clenched her chest when she saw what lay on the floor—Ayla's ear. She rushed to it and cupped it in her hands, the placement too meticulous to be accidental.

With the ear in the pocket of her robe, she drew a line across the wall and descended the stairs. What of her beloved's body?

There was no rhyme or reason to the maze. Perhaps from Sha'Demoni it held some semblance of pattern, but Flowridia simply prayed she found her destination. There was only one.

When the scent of death grew unbearable, she ran. Panicked breaths threatened to steal her consciousness, but she sprinted nonetheless, uncaring of the horror of the cathedral mockery or the putrid smell.

In the backroom, her worst fear lay manifest. Ayla's coffin was open, the makeshift funeral shroud strewn about the floor. Flowridia wailed as she fell to her knees before it. *"No, no, no!"* she cried and she clutched the cloth in her hands, desperately looking for something, some sign, some clue.

"There you are being."

Flowridia's blood boiled. She stood up slowly and turned around, unsurprised to see The Coming Dawn standing in the doorway, arachnid and deathly thin and far taller than Flowridia. "Breaking into castle is taking time, but so very worth it."

Flowridia glanced at the desiccated, rotted remains on the slab and stole a scalpel from beside it. She held it before her, level to the demon's chest. "Where is she?!"

The Coming Dawn stepped forward, uncaring of Flowridia's pitiful weapon, it seemed. "Where is who?"

Furious, Flowridia stole the ear from her pocket. "You left this for me to find, you sadistic bitch! *Where is she?!*"

"I am not knowing what you mean. But if you would kindly drop the weapon, I am stealing you now."

Flowridia shook her head. Fast as lightning, the demon slapped her hand; the scalpel clattered to the floor. The Coming Dawn grasped her with four arms—then shrieked when Flowridia suddenly crackled with undead energy. The demon cried, "Why are you always doing that?!"

Flowridia ran for the opposite wall; it parted at her touch. She ran up the stairs, keeping her pace even when the demon shifted out of the shadow at the top. "Small one, you are a nuisance–"

Maintaining her shield of dark matter, Flowridia barreled into The Coming Dawn, sending them both sprawling. The demon screamed and flung Flowridia toward the far wall.

Flowridia tumbled into the hallway, unsurprised when The Coming Dawn burst from a shadow, a little worse for wear. Her blue skin bore signs of blight, her meticulous braid slowly unraveling.

The pillars of sand shifted, surging toward the interloper. The Coming Dawn brought her hands to cover her face as she cowered.

Flowridia screamed, *"Khastra!"*

This stopped the demon in her tracks and the sand with it. "I beg pardon?"

Flowridia bolted away and toward the stairs on the third level. *"Khastra!"* she cried, throat tearing at the effort.

As Flowridia ran up the carpeted stairs, she ran right into the enormous bulk of the half-demon herself. "Tiny one, why are you–"

A sudden cry from below pulled their attentions. The Coming Dawn held all four hands to cover her mouth. "Khastra?!"

To Flowridia's surprise, Khastra's shock faded to . . . annoyance. "Hello, Kah'Sheen."

Flowridia suddenly hit the floor, pushed away by four spindly arms—arms now embracing Khastra. The demon, Kah'Sheen, clung to Khastra, her four eerie, glowing eyes filling with tears. She stood barely taller than Khastra, easily able to bury her face in the half-demon's shoulder.

Khastra gave a resigned sigh and half-heartedly wrapped her arms around the strange, naked demon. "Tiny one, this is my youngest sister, Kah'Sheen."

"You didn't bother to mention that sooner?"

Kah'Sheen suddenly looked up, fury on her tear-streaked face. "Why are you not dead?! They are telling us you are dead!"

"I am dead."

"Why are you not telling us?! Mother is distraught! She is eating the elves left and right; she is getting fat, Khastra!"

"It is not my fault Mother cannot control her appetite in times of stress."

Kah'Sheen clung with her bottom arms but proceeded to beat upon Khastra's chest and collar bones with her upper fists as she cried out; Khastra didn't budge. "You are being childish, Kah'Sheen."

Kah'Sheen's dramatics slowly drew a crowd. Servants peeked their heads out from rooms, skeletal guards looked uncertain of the threat, and pillars of black sand twitched . . . but seemed to have no purpose, for the intruder was no longer dangerous.

Metallic steps signified Casvir's approach.

In tandem with her smacking fists, Kah'Sheen cried, "I. Am. Not. Childish. *You–*" Her words went from stilted Common to rapid Demoni, a banter Khastra joined. Flowridia stepped away from the walls as shadows rose, summoned by the bickering duo, the forbidden language dangerous even uttered by squabbling sisters.

Khastra suddenly lurched, grimacing as she slumped against her sister. "Put me down," she said, and Flowridia's panicked heart jumped when she realized what was happening.

Confused, Kah'Sheen obeyed, and when Khastra fell to all fours, Flowridia dared to clutch her face in her hands. "Khastra, is it–"

"Yes," the half-demon snapped, then she turned to the inconsolable young demon trembling beside her, those four eyes still brimming with tears. "Kah'Sheen, it is not safe for you here."

Casvir ascended the stairs. Kah'Sheen disappeared into a shadow. Whether or not Casvir noticed could not be said; he looked straight to Khastra, then gestured to the servants flanking him. "Take her away."

"To the underground?" one said, but Casvir shook his head.

"Her life is more expensive than it is worth. She is done. Disassemble her. Keep her head; I want her mind."

Flowridia understood enough, her racing heart suddenly stopping. She met Khastra's gaze a moment, the half-demon's glowing eyes filled with uncharacteristic fear.

Flowridia released her. When servants came to grab Khastra, she cried, "Stop!"

They did, if only from confusion. Flowridia faced Casvir, brave in the face of his growing frown. "What are you doing?"

"Khastra is no longer an investment worth keeping."

"She is worth it!" When the servants moved to resume their path, Flowridia's body burst with dark energy. A cloud of black and deep purple seeped from her pores as she sat on Khastra's body in protest, residual fury from Ayla's disappearance fueling her courage. It filtered from her mouth as she spoke. "Let her move on if you won't keep her–"

Casvir lifted his arm, prepared to backhand her with his vicious claw. Flowridia flinched, bringing her arms up to protect her face. "You forget to whom you speak, Lady Flowridia. I will not be disrespected."

Shock stopped her words and magic both. His tension revealed his curtailed instinct to punish her for insolence. "Casvir–"

That same clawed hand gripped her arm and forcibly pulled her up, no gentleness in the gesture. She whimpered; her arm would surely bruise. "Pray you never make me remind you again."

Behind the menace of his rumbling words lay betrayal, of this man who only minutes ago praised her ingenuity. In the wilds, Casvir was a friend; here in Nox'Kartha, he was the brutal tyrant.

And she was a fool to forget that.

The servants all stared, but at Casvir's word they resumed helping Khastra to stand.

Casvir released her; Flowridia stumbled to keep balance, leaning against the wall for support. Her arm throbbed, and she fought to push back tears. "Then can we speak in private, please, imperator?"

"No."

Flowridia looked up to meet Casvir's severe gaze. "What if I can save her? I used the black orb to heal you–"

"It would only be temporary. If her heart has failed once, it will do so again."

"What about her original heart?"

"Ruined beyond repair and so discarded months ago."

"Casvir, there must be something–"

Casvir raised a hand; Flowridia cowered. "This is not a discussion."

He lowered it.

As he accompanied the party to lead Khastra away, Flowridia's mind frantically jumped to every little thing she knew of biology, of mother's teachings in her cottage, to

Flowridia's own understanding, Ayla's notes down below, Etolié's library—

And in Casvir's library, where a certain elf had an understanding of how to build mechanical lungs—

"Casvir!" She raced to him, noting his fury as he faced her. "Elven technology. Elven technology can save her!"

Casvir's gaze narrowed, but to her relief he said, "Explain."

"Elves have technology to create artificial body parts. There's an elf in your library who–"

"Find him. I will delay the procedure for ten minutes."

Flowridia ran.

Her own feet stumbled beneath her, and when she might've slipped down the staircase, lithe arms captured her and steadied her fall. "Small one," Kah'Sheen said, still carrying her as she ran, "I am seeing you save my sister. Let me help you."

Flowridia made no move to escape as Kah'Sheen slipped into Sha'Demoni. The world shifted into clouded shades of grey, fog-like in its density. Kah'Sheen danced down the halls with ease, apparently familiar with the castle as she wound her way through the corridors.

They reappeared outside the library. "Cannot phase through extra-dimensional realm," she said, and they ran through together, pushing past book golems and winding down complicated hallways.

But she knew the way, having come here more than once for lessons on elven syntax. Tazel looked genuinely shocked to see Flowridia and a half-demon suddenly barrel towards him. "Tazel, no time to explain, but the imperator needs you."

"I beg your–"

"My friend's afterlife will turn to hell. Bring every book you have on elven engineering and biological mechanics. You'll be paid. I'll make sure of it."

Tazel, however, looked near fainting at the sight of Kah'Sheen, who watched, in turn, with intrigue. "You're The Coming Dawn."

"And you are Fireborn. You are friend. You will come, yes?"

Tazel glanced between them. "I don't exactly have a choice, do I."

"You can fight, but you will lose," Kah'Sheen said.

Tazel gathered his books, handing a stack to Kah'Sheen and her many arms.

They ran.

Once they'd left the library, Kah'Sheen said, "Best I am not seen," and vanished. Tazel and Flowridia ran alone. They rounded the staircase leading up from the library—

And ran right into Murishani. The books scattered all about, some sliding down the staircase. The viceroy clutched her arms to steady her. "Lady Flowridia, exactly who I wanted to see."

"No time," Flowridia replied, tearing her arms away. She and Tazel knelt to pick up her dropped books.

"Come and find me later, won't you?" he said, crossing his arms over his lengthy, silk robe. "I overheard you have a bit of a conundrum."

"Later."

"An *eerie* problem, you might say."

Flowridia spared him a glance, catching his knowing eye, and for a moment considered dropping the entire quest and following the viceroy underground.

"Flowridia?"

Tazel pulled her from her trance. Wordlessly, she shoved past the viceroy. "Come alone," she heard, but nothing more.

She knew not how much time had passed, but Casvir remained, though the servants and Khastra had disappeared. "Impressive," he said simply, then looked to Tazel. "You are the engineer?"

Tazel paled at the imperator's stare. Frozen, he did not nod until Flowridia nudged him with her hip.

"Come with me," Casvir said, and he beckoned for Tazel to follow. "You alone."

Flowridia watched them step down the hall, though Tazel stumbled, perhaps to keep from fainting.

She trembled, the excitement of the moment quickly wearing off. Flowridia fell to her knees, head faint as she withdrew the ear from her pocket.

Kah'Sheen had not taken the body.

Murishani, she was very certain, had.

Flowridia went to her room, explaining quickly to Demitri the excitement of the past half hour as she changed from the robe into a dress.

You think that melodramatic ass has Ayla?

Flowridia couldn't even reprimand his language. "That's what my gut says. But I can't fathom why."

Khastra said to not trust him.

Flowridia didn't, she realized.

Should we find someone to go with us?

"Everyone worth asking is with Khastra." And Kah'Sheen had yet to be seen again.

Instead, she slipped the ear around her neck, comforted by the weight. Murishani had said to come alone, but Demitri hardly counted, nor did the mysterious haunt tied to the desiccated ear. They set off, though she bid Ana to stay put.

But she dared to stop for a trinket; she returned to Ayla's room, swallowing her emotions at the sight of the glowing memories, and from the vanity drawer she withdrew a jeweled knife.

Just in case.

Back down the staircase, past the library and farther still. When Flowridia stepped down into the familiar hall, her blood ran cold when she saw the arch and the ominous dark hallway.

Khastra would not be present to save her this time.

Darkness enveloped her and Demitri, punctuated with spots of light from the candles dotting the hall. Behind her, she was unsurprised to find the stairs had vanished, but when she focused and put her will behind it, she saw the illusion ripple and fade.

Flowridia stepped down the hallway, grateful to feel Demitri beside her. Her wolf stood as tall as she, her sweet boy all grown. "Murishani?" she dared to say aloud.

Speak of the devil, and he would come. Beside her, one of the closed doors suddenly creaked open.

No one stepped out, but a cloying, familiar perfume wafted out. Flowridia approached, the hairs on her neck standing on end as she peered within.

There lounged Murishani, spread out like a feline on his luxurious couch. The room was as dark as the hallway, but not lit by candles, no. Odd translucent orbs floated in shades of ice blue and white. The ghostly lights illuminated the couch and Murishani, along with the table and wine before him.

A door stood in the corner, and from beyond Flowridia heard the faintest whispers of moaning. Whether it were of pleasure or pain, she could not say, but it unsettled her resolve.

Murishani beckoned forward. "I had hoped you would come," he said, as sincere and friendly as she had ever heard. When Flowridia and Demitri stepped inside, the door shut behind them unbidden. "Come, have a drink. Do you drink?"

"Not in general, no," Flowridia admitted, and she stayed planted beside the door. The orbs slowly orbited the room, gently pulsing as though alive.

"I apologize, you innocent little dove. I should have known." Still, he drew a glass for himself and gave a slight sip. "Won't you come sit?"

"Where's Ayla?" Flowridia said, her hand surreptitiously gripping the doorknob.

It didn't budge. She'd suspected that.

Murishani could do many things, but outright kill her was not one of them. She hoped.

A smile leisurely spread across Murishani's face, one lacking any false graces or airs. Cruel mischief met her gaze, curdling her blood. "A weighty accusation. What use would I have for a corpse?"

"I don't know," she admitted. "And perhaps someone stole your perfume and spilled it in Ayla's bathroom. Perhaps my apparent *eerie* problems have nothing to do with the conveniently severed ear." Flowridia resisted the urge to touch her hand to her chest and pull comfort from the macabre trinket. "But there's no sense in me lying. You know every secret in this castle, and sometimes you make a few up for your amusement."

"Clever girl," he purred, and when he rolled into sitting, sensuality in every motion, Flowridia heard Demitri growl. "I see why he likes you. There's fire beneath that naïve little flower princess persona of yours."

Flowridia frowned. "Casvir and I–"

"Aren't fucking, I know." He waved off the words, shutting his eyes as he hummed. "And somehow that makes this all so much worse. It blows the mind, how dearly he cares for you."

Her bruised arm spoke of otherwise. "I don't think–"

"He *adores* you, and it's revolting. I have done all in my power to coerce Casvir with all manner of temptations for years, Flowridia. Flesh, wine, money—any indulgence you can think of, I have dangled before him. He craves power, yes, but not for any true purpose; only because he *can.* Sex, money, and power—those are the vices that drive this world. Every person falls prey to one of those. Even you, and your desperate need for Ayla Darkleaf's cunt."

Flowridia's hand moved from the doorknob to Demitri's fur, silently willing him to stop growling. To provoke the viceroy during his monologuing would not do well for her.

"Casvir's need for power has yet to cripple him, that patient bastard. In all my years knowing him, he has been aloof and unobtainable, utterly indomitable. He is *indifferent* to me at best, and I have devoted my life to his cause." His gaze narrowed, but instead of malice, Flowridia saw wonder. "But a few months in the woods together, and he garners the most innocent and precious of affections for you. You could ask for a corner of his kingdom, and he would grant it. You could ask for my job, and I'd be hung in the square to seal the deal."

"Viceroy–"

"Murishani, please," he said, 'tsk tsk-ing' her slight.

"Murishani, I'm sorry I disrupted your world. It wasn't my intention. It was kind of you to try and make nice at first–"

"Never mind," he said, shaking his head. "You're an absolute idiot."

Flowridia pursed her lips, biting back her tongue at the insult.

"I despise you, Flowridia." He said it so pleasantly, as though complimenting a decorated cake. "From your pouty lips to your dainty little ass, I hope you get burned at the stake and then eaten alive by sharks."

Juvenile, yet threatening all at once. "Give me the body, then," Flowridia said. "I'll be on my way as soon as I have the last orb. You'll never see me again."

"Flowridia, the body was never part of any agreement. You never signed Casvir's contract, and thank the gods for that. It means the body belongs to no one. I owe you nothing."

"Unless I tell Casvir," Flowridia replied, praying the threat held weight. Somehow, though her hair stood on end, she wasn't afraid. She had too much to lose. "He adores me, as you said. He'd force you to give it back."

Murishani quirked an eyebrow, and for the first time, she felt threatened. "Do you know what I do in this kingdom?"

"You're the viceroy. You make nice with foreign politicians and refuse to sign paperwork."

"I'm also the keeper of soul contracts." Murishani spared a glance to one of the beautiful orbs floating around them. When he beckoned, it slowly descended into his hand. "Should you have crossed Casvir in his contract, I would have intervened. My talents are utterly unparalleled, *unheard* of, save for those of the Solviraes bloodline. And even then, there's no finesse to them. They only destroy. Flowridia, I can touch souls."

Flowridia frowned, unsure of what to make of that.

Murishani cupped the orb and stroked it with his long, manicured fingers. "I can grasp them, stuff them into their bodies like a necromancer, or pull them out. I can even destroy them . . ." All at once, the orb in his hand glowed brighter than the sun, then dissipated. Murishani shone from within, silver smoke seeping from his nostrils as he breathed out. "And there are fewer threats as daunting as that. Utter oblivion. No afterlife. Nothing."

Murishani leaned over to the table and daintily removed the wine and glasses from atop it. "I can even touch the belligerent ones, ghosts cursed to linger on this plane. I can force invisible ones to manifest and grasp the ones with no anchor, who phase in and out of worlds. The only true safety for a soul is death, assuming a necromancer doesn't come to pluck you from the afterlife."

"I've heard enough," Flowridia said, gripping the doorknob again. Of course, it still didn't turn, but it gave her comfort, as irrational as it was. "Let me go. There is nothing to—"

Murishani lifted the top of the table, and there lay the body, eternally screaming as it met her gaze.

"What are you . . ."

Murishani placed a finger to his lips. He set the tabletop aside, then grasped the very air around the body—

And in his hand, he held a new orb. "Would you like to speak to her?" Murishani asked, no question to who 'her' referred to.

Flowridia simply stared, praying he lied for the truth was too terrifying to consider. She shook her head. "N-No. I won't owe you anything."

"Oh, no charge. My amusement is payoff enough. Although, I'll do something better; I'll place her soul back where it needs to be and seal it inside. Ayla Darkleaf would be back within seconds. A little crusty and over-baked, but you'd have the peace of her company while you wait for her body to be restored to its supple little self."

Flowridia's breath stopped. She swallowed the sudden rise of emotion because even the prospect, no matter how cruelly dangled, was the culmination of all her desperate dreams. "But, why?"

He smiled, tenderly stroking the luminous orb. "She cries for you, you know."

Flowridia glared. "Stop it."

"You were everything to her. She only maintains awareness beside her body; even now I hear her weep your name." His lip curled, any kindness twisting into cruelty. "'Oh, Flowra, Flowra!'" he said in mockery, "'How I miss your flowery head and delicious cunt—' I paraphrase, but you get the point."

"Murishani, shut up!"

"Careful," he cooed, bringing the light up to his face. His perfect countenance lay illuminated, wicked and lovely and all Flowridia hated. "Wouldn't want me to slip, would you? So delicate a thing, a soul."

Here was the true threat—not damage to her body, no, but utter dissolution of her dream, of her Ayla.

Ayla's soul—destroyed forever.

What gods could she ask to save her from this? "What do you want?" Flowridia asked, bracing for a demand she knew she couldn't give.

Murishani released the globe, letting it wander freely. It floated oh so slowly, joining the others in orbit. "Come to bed with me."

"W-What?" she sputtered, ignoring the snarl rising from Demitri's throat.

"Aside from you being an annoyingly pretty tartlet, what greater pleasure could I possibly have than to spoil Casvir's precious treasure? Above all else, I'm a man of pettiness. But believe me, Flowridia, I would absolutely make it worth your while." His wink filled her stomach with dread.

There was more to it. There had to be more. "You want a quick fuck, and you'll be appeased? You can't possibly be so desperate."

"I can wet my cock on anything I'd like, Flowridia. What I want is to revel in the consequences: your self-hatred, Ayla's inevitable tantrum, Casvir's delicious anger, etcetera, etcetera." He waved his hands, and Flowridia suddenly understood, a blow to her gut that lingered and caused her to sicken.

"You want Casvir to need you."

Murishani looked grossly unimpressed. "I believe we established that–"

"This isn't the first time you've tried to have your way with me." Flowridia clenched her fist, her whole body reeling at the thought. "I don't doubt you have a thousand and one bastard children, but Casvir wouldn't turn a blind eye if you had one with me. With our combined talents, it surely would be something special."

"Casvir would certainly think so, wouldn't he?"

Flowridia's fist trembled, her breath catching when she realized the danger here. She could not escape, lest he destroy Ayla's soul. Nor could she step forward; she would not play into his hands; her entire soul revolted.

But at the cost of Ayla's?

Flowridia's fist relaxed. She slipped her hands into her pockets, surreptitiously gripping the blessed knife sequestered within it.

She was very confident she couldn't be Etolié, who fucked men to kill them, nor her mother, who in every respect did the same. Instead, she took quiet steps forward, keeping her stare to the ground.

"Sweet Flowra–"

The use of Ayla's beloved pet name nearly pulled tears from her eyes.

"I'll be gentle and tender. It'll be making love in every respect–"

She stabbed her knife forward, aiming for his throat.

Murishani snatched her wrist. When she met his eye, his gaze spelled glee. "Clever girl–"

Demitri suddenly tackled him; familiars were so often overlooked. The enormous wolf dove for his face, snarling as he tore at Murishani's skin.

Flowridia ran for the door, banging on it with all her might. "Help!" she cried. "Casvir! *Someone!*"

Demitri suddenly howled, and when Murishani glowed in translucent light, he fought the grip. Flowridia recalled a time long ago, when Mother had pulled the very life from her familiar.

Her knife lay across the room. Flowridia dove for it.

Only for it to be plucked by a blue, lithe hand. Kah'Sheen emerged from a shadow. "Sorry, small one. Was too caught up in watching drama. I am rescuing you now." She threw the knife into the fray, where it hit its mark.

Murishani cried out, the knife protruding from his eye. Demitri stumbled over to them; Kah'Sheen grabbed him first. "One at a time," she said, and she and Demitri disappeared into the shadow.

Flowridia watched the writhing man, his hateful gaze searing when it met hers. "You won't sign yourself away to Casvir or to me. Do you truly think you're so special as to bring Ayla back by yourself? You don't know how."

"I'm willing to try," she replied, and with all the care in the world, she picked up the corpse and cradled it to her chest.

Kah'Sheen reappeared, grabbed Flowridia's wrist, and whisked them away.

They went straight to Casvir, the corpse still clutched in Flowridia's hands. And they told him everything, with Kah'Sheen even filling in details Flowridia forgot: *"He is saying he is hoping she is burned at stake and eaten by sharks—alive!"*

Casvir said very little for the exchange, merely listened and nodded as he sat at his desk, not even commenting on the apparent comradery between Flowridia and the demon who had once tried to kidnap her. When they concluded their story, he politely excused himself.

Flowridia wasn't sure quite what to expect next, only that she was left alone with a corpse and a half-demon with a vendetta against said corpse.

Which, of course, Kah'Sheen brought up the moment Casvir left. "If it is a consolation, viceroy is making unfounded threats."

Flowridia looked up at the nearly eight-foot-tall spider demon and said, "What do you mean?"

"Viceroy cannot destroy her soul. If to slay Ayla Darkleaf for good means to destroy her soul, it would be easy. We are trying that, a thousand years ago. Asked Solviraes to eat her soul. Did not work. Nothing works. She is always coming back." Kah'Sheen tilted her head curiously. "You are bringing Ayla Darkleaf back, yes?"

Flowridia took a step back, holding the corpse to her chest. "I'm very grateful you saved my life, but I'll try to kill you if you take her."

"Am not going to take her. Demoni law states intention is not crime. But as soon as you are succeeding, if Mother says to slay her, I will come."

Flowridia nodded, oddly relieved despite the delayed threat. "I understand."

"You are saving my sister's life. I am indebted to you for that much. So, I will not be taking you to Mother."

Flowridia frowned. "But your law says—"

"I plan to tell Mother the truth, as far as I am seeing. Khastra is alive and well in Nox'Kartha and she is faking her death to escape Staelash. And so, no crime. War is over!"

"You would lie to the Goddess of War?"

Kah'Sheen visibly cringed. "Yes," she squeaked, and she bit her lip with her pointed teeth. "It is what Khastra would have wanted. Tell her to write to Mother."

That precluded Khastra had lived; they had neglected to ask Casvir as much. Still, she was grateful. "I'll deliver the message." She managed to smile. "Thank you."

Kah'Sheen smiled, and it oddly wasn't terrifying—cute, even. "No, I am thanking you, small one. Khastra is dear to me."

Kah'Sheen left her, and Flowridia went straight to Ayla's bedroom.

She laid the corpse upon the couch. The shriveled, skeletal cheekbone sent a chill across her skin as her finger traced a line across the desiccated face, the blackened corpse's eternal scream still wrenching to her soul. With care, she took the chain from around the body's neck and clutched the ear in her hand.

Murishani always lied, yet there were bits of truth to be found—Ayla's soul truly lingered, as Casvir had said.

The weight of the day settled upon her. "Demitri," she said softly, keeping her gaze on the corpse of her love, "I'm going to sleep in here tonight. I . . . I need to be alone. Take Ana with you."

Demitri said nothing, though he did give a rather judgmental *huff*. With a quick command to Ana, the duo left her alone. Silence settled upon a room lit by globes and beautiful memories.

She stared at the corpse, forcing herself to gaze upon its gruesome visage. "It would be my most wicked act upon this earth, to raise someone like you from the dead." She set her jaw, the words unearthing from deep within her. "I still can't believe the magnitude of your atrocities—by *every god*, Ayla, so much of what you did was unspeakable."

The corpse said nothing, of course. It stared in eternal horror, face twisted in pain.

"And I know, if you were to come back, nothing would stop you from returning to what you once were. I would have nothing to bargain with, save my pleading soul, but true love means to accept someone for what they are—not to seek to change them."

She sat herself upon the bed and rested a hand against the corpse's cold cheek. "I also know you were changing into someone new. Someone different and better . . . Someone you thought was worthy of me." Flowridia leaned forward, ghosting her lips across the remains of where an ear once was. "The greatest injustice is that you were slain before the world could see who that someone would be."

She had awoken countless times in a cold embrace. She settled herself beside her lover's corpse, intention on her mind as she brought up a blanket to cover them. Though desiccated, the body was not fragile—she wrapped her arms around it and whispered, "The world will keep turning. Others will come to claim you, whether it be to control you or destroy you or use you against me." Her fingers caressed shriveled skin; tears welled in her eyes. "You were mine in life, and so it shall be in death. I swear to protect you, whether it be in preserving you until the day you rise again . . . or until I find a way to bring you true peace so you can rest."

She clutched Ayla tight, the words wounding her— surely they harmed Ayla as well. "But I have no direction, no idea how to bring you back. A blood ritual, yes, but to what end? Tell me what I must do."

In the tentative peace, Flowridia felt a shadow pass across her heart, a flicker of cold against her skin.

Exhaustion tugged at her eyelids. She fell asleep quickly.

And while resting in the arms of a loving embrace, soft and cold and full of new life, she heard a gentle whisper in her ear . . .
"Izthuni."

The next morning, Flowridia dressed in what she personally deemed as the finest of Ayla's gifted gowns. Embroidered silver stars covered a deep blue velvet sky, scattered at the bodice but thick and twinkling at the bottom. It swirled around her feet but bore enough weight to keep her warm in the winter chill.

Flowridia had only ever left the castle with Casvir, and only to traverse its beautiful streets and leave it behind. The idea of stepping out alone was daunting and exhilarating all at once.

Demitri watched her twirl in front of the vanity mirror. *You always look beautiful, mom.*

"Beautiful enough to say hello to a god?"

I'd say so.

So supportive, that familiar of hers.

A knock at the door disrupted her preening. Flowridia twisted the knob.

Demitri snarled. Flowridia grabbed a knife from the vanity and held it forward.

Murishani, with a few stitched cuts along his face and a bandage over his wounded eye, held his hands up in defense as he took a step back. "Oh, do relax. Casvir is right over there."

Flowridia dared to lean forward and peek down the hallway. Not twenty feet away, Casvir watched the exchange. His lip twitched at Flowridia's attention, revealing a flicker of amusement.

She kept her knife but relaxed her stance. "What do you want?"

"I came to apologize, Lady Flowridia of Staelash." He bowed low, his robes sweeping dramatically around him, his hair falling in sheets. "My behavior was abhorrent, and there is no excuse for it."

"That's one way to put it," she said, forcing a smile.

Murishani straightened up and grinned. "I came to tell you that, and to inform you that I am never to speak to you or acknowledge your presence ever again, nor come within ten feet of you without your express permission, extraneous circumstances notwithstanding. In addition, the body and soul of Ayla Darkleaf are never to be touched, or even thought about, and any and all, and I quote, 'silly loopholes,' will result in my head being removed from my body and thrown to the street sweepers."

He flashed his charming grin to Casvir. "Are we appeased, Cassie? Oh, wonderful." He returned his gaze to Flowridia. "It was an absolute delight knowing you, Lady Flowridia of Staelash."

With another bow, he swept away, leaving only his pride behind.

Casvir's metallic steps approached. "It is not his only punishment, but it is the one he least looked forward to."

Flowridia's arm bore hints of blue behind raw red. "You're a harsh teacher."

"It is how I have always inspired respect."

"Never touch me again." Her lip twitched, but she forced her emotions to steady. "Not in violence. I don't think I can forgive you a second time."

Casvir met her gaze, but Flowridia dared to match it, her quiet fury simmering. "Never disrespect me in public again."

She offered a hand forward. "You love contracts."

"Exceptions will be made in sparring and on the battlefield."

Flowridia couldn't help but scoff. "I don't plan on meeting you on the battlefield."

"I do not know your future, Flowridia. But your talents continue to surprise me." A genuine smile pulled on his thin lips, revealing an almost parental sort of pride. "I look forward to the day you are something to fear."

He shook her hand.

Casvir left her. Flowridia shut the door and returned to pinning her hair, but within minutes, another knock startled her. "Come in," she said, and was shocked to see Khastra step inside.

"Tiny one, may we speak?"

Flowridia nodded and pinned the last strand of her hair. She went to the couch and patted the space beside her, surprised at Khastra's contrite aura. As she did, the half-demon pulled down the collar of her shirt, revealing a smooth metal core where her heart should be. The skin around it burned raw and red, and when Flowridia listened, she could hear a faint ticking sound—Khastra's new sign of life.

"So far, it has worked well. I feel fantastic. And I have you to thank."

"I couldn't let them kill you," Flowridia whispered, smiling faintly at the seated half-demon, who still towered above her.

"I did not realize you knew the truth," Khastra continued, and she set her gaze on her hands instead, watching as they clenched and relaxed, clenched and relaxed . . . "And I would appreciate if you kept it a secret."

Flowridia nodded. "I don't know what Kah'Sheen knows, so I can't account for that, but I won't say anything." The arachnid half-demon had said a bit more than that, she recalled. "She's going to tell Ku'Shya that you're alive and well, and that you faked your death." At Khastra's amused smile, Flowridia realized this was, perhaps, standard behavior for dealing with her demon goddess of a mother. "Kah'Sheen also says to write your mother."

Khastra chuckled, and it was a sound Flowridia realized she missed. "I can do that."

"I wasn't aware you could simply write a letter to a goddess. It's rather endearing, actually."

Khastra continued laughing, genuine amusement in the gesture. Flowridia felt truly at ease in her presence for the very first time. "It is a tradition my second wife insisted upon, that I give my mother my attention."

The statement surprised her. "Your wife?"

"My second wife, yes. Far across the sea, when I lived in Zauleen. She insisted, if we adopted a child, that the child would know all of its family." Khastra's wistful expression faded. "We never had the opportunity. She was killed in the first civil war, when the elven lands split apart."

"I'm very sorry."

Khastra shook her head. "It was eight thousand years ago, tiny one. I do not live in the past."

"Forgive me," Flowridia said, mulling over how best to phrase what she hoped was not an offensive statement, "but I swear I've heard you mention your husbands."

"Yes, I have had husbands."

"And at least two wives?"

Khastra chuckled. "I have also had wives. I have loved many people in my long life, some of whom I was blessed to marry. Is this odd to you?"

Flowridia fell silent as she thought on the concept. She had never found a man she thought she could love with all her heart, but that was surely not the case for most women. How, then, was it odd for someone to love both? "Not when I think about it, no," she finally said.

Khastra kept her warm smile. "It is not a secret, though it has been a long time, I admit, since I have been with someone. Well before Staelash." She looked down at her hands, the skin turning white as she clenched her fists. "I did not come here to discuss pleasantries. I owe you an apology. I have been cold to you."

"No, no," Flowridia replied, daring to cover Khastra's fists with her hands. When the half-demon relaxed, Flowridia gripped them tight, marveling at the warmth of her undead skin. "I was hurt, yes, but then I saw what was being done to you. I thought it was your way of dealing with pain."

Khastra smiled, but there was no joy behind it. "I was cold to you about Staelash when you were homesick and heartbroken. I could have told you who Kah'Sheen was and stopped the threat on your life, but I was selfish and wishing to hide. I regret my treatment of you and would like to explain myself."

Flowridia waited with rapt attention, watching as the half-demon's glowing eyes softened.

"You have seen my life here and what it shall be. My legacy is one of battle and blood, and in Nox'Kartha, I will live again. In Staelash, I meant as I said—I had no love for it. I was bored and resigned. But against my own judgement, I sought to cast it aside without grieving what I had lost because . . ." She shut her eyes, her elegant features softening. ". . . I was hurting in ways I had not expected. And I am sincerely apologetic that you were a target of that. I wish to make amends, both to you and to them. Staelash should know I am here."

Flowridia kept her mirror always, as Etolié had implored. With care, she withdrew her hands from Khastra's and slipped it from her pocket. Khastra reached out to steal it, but Flowridia hesitated and gripped the trinket tight. "May I ask you something, first?"

Khastra watched, permissive in her stare.

"I hope it isn't overstepping my bounds to ask, but what about Staelash is hurting..." Flowridia trailed off, realizing, as she watched the subtle lines in Khastra's face, the signs of laughter etched around her eyes elegant and the only proof of her great age, that she already knew. Khastra had one joy in Staelash. Flowridia had seen the heartbreak on both ends, though De'Sindai and Celestial both had dealt with it in very different ways. "You and Etolié?"

Khastra shook her head. "Not in the way you think, tiny one. You know Etolié's proclivities toward attraction. She confided in me, long ago, her discomfort toward being pursued with romantic intention. Whatever my feelings toward her, my relationship with Etolié is my most treasured." Khastra's good humor faded by small and measured degrees. "In my bitterness toward Staelash, I elected to forget her as well. But I am a fool. I am her friend, and she is hurting."

"Is that why you stayed?" Flowridia recalled the words of their initial conversation in Nox'Kartha, the threats and discrepancies both. "By your own admittance, you told Emperor Malakh no to overseeing Staelash. But you stayed for over twenty years."

To her surprise, Khastra began chuckling. She sat back, a broad, wistful smile pulling at her lips. "I wish I had magic to cast illusions so I could better illustrate my story; alas, I do not. But believe me when I say for all my rage toward the emperor, there was someone else much angrier. I told Malakh no, and then Etolié burst into the throne room, already fuming, shouting obscenities at the *Emperor of Solvira*, in front of his pregnant wife, no less." Khastra's laugh was infectious, and Flowridia felt a smile tug at her own lips. "He was afraid she would try to make a claim for his throne, as a daughter of Staella, and could say nothing to her.

"In my long life, I had never fallen in love at first sight. Etolié changed that. She was beautiful, and she was furious, and when she left, resigned to her fate, I told him yes. Foolish, yes. But I was drawn to her passion and humor, and soon I began to know her heart. I loved her, and that never changed." Khastra held out a hand to take the mirror.

"Let me soften the blow," Flowridia said, clutching it tighter. "I'll talk to her first."

Khastra nodded. Flowridia tapped the mirror.

Within seconds, the silver glow faded, revealing Etolié's frazzled countenance. "It's been weeks, Flowers."

"Yes, and we left to go find the orb. I've been distracted."

Etolié perked up. "Does that mean what I hope it means?"

Flowridia shook her head. "No, but there's a more pressing issue we need to discuss." That particular conversation, the one where she explained that there was a *dragon* and that Soliel now had three orbs, promised to take hours. "I need you to sit down."

"Haven't sat down in days."

"Will you sit down, please? This might be difficult news to take."

The ice in Etolié's frown could have frozen the sun itself, but Flowridia saw the background shift enough to believe her when the Celestial said, "Lay it on me."

Unsure of how to open this, and not one to simply tear open a new wound, Flowridia said, "Ayla's been dead for months." Etolié's eyes widened, and she immediately regretted the opener. "And so has Khastra," she quickly added, grateful when Etolié's expression grew mild.

Mild, but then pained. "Yes. What about it?"

"Etolié . . ." Flowridia braced herself, casting aside all notions of tact. "Khastra is dead. But she's in Nox'Kartha."

Grief shifted rapidly to disbelief. A frown tugged at Etolié's now trembling lip. "Explain."

"She works for Imperator Casvir," Flowridia explained. "Casvir raised her after the funeral."

She dared to glance up at Khastra, the half-demon's face purposefully neutral. "She's the same as she was," Flowridia said, unsure of what she could say to placate both the Celestial behind the mirror and the former general whose hands tensed as they gripped the other. "Her mind is intact. She's still funny. Still kind. She's—"

"She's there, isn't she."

Flowridia looked back down to the silver, glowing mirror, realizing she had been staring at Khastra for the entire exchange. "Etolié—"

"Let me see her."

Flowridia didn't have to offer; Khastra reached over and plucked it from her hand.

In the split second before she spoke, Flowridia saw light fill the half-demon's glowing eyes and a smile that spoke of exhaustion, yes, and fear, but also depthless joy. "Hello, Etolié."

Sheer silence. And then: "You crystalline *bitch—*" And, oh, the obscenities Flowridia heard from the other end of the mirror—every variety of swear, some featuring Khastra and some, her mother. Flowridia blushed slightly at the non-implication of where Khastra could stick her hammer and watched as Khastra's glowing eyes widened with each ticking second of the Celestial's tirade.

Right as Flowridia was tempted to cover Demitri's ears, the Celestial finished with a question: *"Why didn't you tell me?!"*

"I thought this was the sort of news to deliver in person."

"Oh, *now* you decide to be tactful!"

Thus the rant continued, and Khastra sat stoic throughout. Flowridia pursed her lips, wishing she could disappear into the cracked stone beneath her feet and surprised that the woman who never lied had seamlessly spoken a falsehood.

From the mirror, Etolié's words cracked, the beginning of what Flowridia swore was a sob seeping through. But the mirror quite suddenly stopped glowing. Khastra and Flowridia were left in silence.

Khastra placed the mirror in Flowridia's hand, and then her face fell into her own. She did not quiver or seem to cry, but instead became as stone. Flowridia feared to touch her, knowing the slightest push might shatter her stiff composure.

When she slowly looked up, not at Flowridia, but to the door, she whispered, "Thank you, tiny one. Now I can move forward."

There was naught Flowridia could say, and so she let Khastra go, heartbroken for her defeated stance. This, the feared war leader, Bringer of War, general of the greatest armies the world had known—Khastra let the door fall gently shut behind her.

The silence rang loud. Flowridia tried to tap the mirror.

No one answered.

At the last minute, Flowridia wrapped herself up in a black woven shawl, stolen from Ayla's closet, and a pair of boots to match. For the best—when she stepped outside the great doors of the castle, gentle flakes of snow fluttered down to greet her.

Flowridia gazed down upon the city, grateful to find the path down the mountain was maintained enough to prevent frost from gathering. The shawl only slightly kept away the chill, like an embrace from its late owner, and Flowridia clung to the comfort.

The path was not long, the downward slope from the castle built into the side of the mountain an illusion of height. Flowridia breached the gate of the city proper and basked in the bustling energy.

The light dusting of snow barely had a chance to cover the roads; undead with their brooms and shovels worked to clear the area. Alone, Flowridia drew little attention and instead was able to watch the citizens bustle about. Mostly De'Sindai, yes, but a shocking number of half-giants also made up the populace, half-elves—any race commonly enslaved by humans and their Celestial counterparts.

Racial tensions were high in other parts of the world, but with the threat of the imperator's justice, everyone seemed to get along perfectly well. Flowridia passed a variety of shops, their roofs covered in a quaint blanket of snow.

Farther in, she saw a gushing fountain, clear and pristine despite the weather, with no frost at the sides. She watched as a small De'Sindai boy, his mother beside him, dipped his scraped hand within the waters. When he withdrew it, all damage had healed.

Curious, Flowridia stepped forward, letting her senses expand and touch upon the water. Healing magic, not unlike what she herself wielded, radiated from the enchanted waters.

She smiled at the notion and realized that while Casvir wielded his power with an iron fist, his populace flourished, his perfect semblance of justice undeniable. Happy citizens were prosperous, as he himself had said, but Flowridia's kind heart could see a place for herself here. The possibility remained; Casvir had offered employment.

She had not signed the contract, but she had also not said no.

Flowridia continued on her way, fascinated by the array of citizens and the life they lived. The white marbled buildings were rich, décor abundant in the way of statues and carved fountains.

One particular statue pulled her attention. Flowridia approached the gargantuan display of stone, marveling at how it captured the might of its mirror. At the entrance of the Theocracy of Sol Kareena was a great statue of the Goddess herself, but here stood Casvir, a god to his people, a hundred feet tall at least, a reminder to them of who they served.

Flowridia, admittedly, thought it needlessly pretentious, but also suspected it hadn't been his idea.

As she looked away, she noticed, standing on the other side of the statue, a familiar face. "Tazel?" she said, and she ran toward him, noting his utter confusion.

"Oh. Flowridia. Hello." He smiled, though it seemed unsettled. She noticed the pack on his back.

"I thought you accepted a job in the castle."

Tazel nodded. "The imperator paid me handsomely for my services, by which I mean he forgave half my debt to his library and said I could work the rest off over the next ten years. I accepted. I'd be a fool to actually stay, though. Kindly don't tell him you saw me. Once I've settled my affairs, I'll be sneaking out at nightfall."

Guilt clenched Flowridia's gut. "Let me talk to him. If I plead on your behalf, he might . . ."

The elven man shook his head, then gazed up at the statue once again. "I won't say I approve of necromancy, but I did save a woman in a terrible situation she could not have helped from a fate far worse. I remembered what it felt like to be a force for good." Tazel looked back to Flowridia, smiling faintly. "I do have to go. The world may need me soon. Flowridia . . ." His hesitation spoke volumes, and his regard for her, though he smiled, held regret. "You're young and full of all the potential in the world. Good luck."

He offered a hand, and when she reached to accept it, he pulled her into a hug she could not quite resist. He smelled of soap and freshly pressed clothing, and in her ear he whispered, "Your heart is good. Be careful of what you tie yourself to."

Tazel released her, and without another word went away. Flowridia watched him, unnerved by his statement.

She continued onward, grateful for the signs directing people to the various districts of the city. The religious district would hold what she wanted.

It was a lengthy walk, but not an unenjoyable one. The temple of Sol Kareena stood at the forefront, leading to an array of angelic gods. She resolved to visit Eionei's someday, to relay to Etolié whether or not it truly did put every party to shame.

Thoughts of Etolié darkened her mood. Flowridia worried, but there was naught to do about that yet.

Demonic temples were kept away from their angelic counterparts. Ku'Shya's domain was grandeur unmatched, bearing her sigils and guards to defend it. Flowridia passed it by, wary of further provoking the goddess' wrath, knowing her standing with the great demon was unsteady at best.

It was not difficult to find Izthuni.

The Temple of Izthuni lay in the shadow of an enormous wall, perhaps erected for the protection of his worshipers, or simply out of respect to the demon god's world. The architecture spiraled, a rounded building with pillars too thin to support the dark stone.

Casvir had said the god himself could appear within.

She approached the sole De'Sindai guard at the entrance, who looked rather surprised to see a small girl approach. "Are you lost, my lady?"

Flowridia shook her head. "This is precisely where I need to be."

The door itself was as rounded as the building, bearing circular seals and the sigil of The Shadow God. When the man touched the center, the seals began rotating, the flourished designs each spinning off in their own direction, leaving only blank stone—a stone that rolled away.

Flowridia saw nothing—merely darkness.

"Be careful, my lady," the De'Sindai said.

She entered the dark building.

When the door shut, Flowridia had never experienced such stifling darkness. Not even her hand before her face could be seen.

Something cold touched her back. She stiffened as a voice said, "And who are you, young one, to enter our temple?"

The sultry, feminine voice chuckled. A light came on before Flowridia's face, illuminating the pale, breathtaking features of the human woman standing before her. Not quite human—her red lips parted into a predator's smile, her white skin unnatural. Her hair was auburn, and her dress matched, split at the collar to reveal ample cleavage.

Flickering at the outskirts of light cast by the woman's lantern, which bore an odd and almost silver light, Flowridia saw other vampires come to watch.

"My name is Flowridia, and I'm the ward of Imperator Casvir," she said, praying her voice didn't waver. "My reasons to commune with your god are my own."

"Izthuni will eat you alive," the woman said, tongue flicking across her lips. "But only if I do not eat you first."

Perhaps it was meant to scare her, but Mother had spoken far too often of chopping her into stew. It seemed the threat had lost its potency. "Be that as it may," Flowridia said, perturbed at words, "I wish to see him."

"Imperator Casvir holds no sway over a god's domain." The woman leered closer, uncomfortably so, her nose sniffing Flowridia's ear as she paced. "Oh, you smell absolutely *decadent*."

By every god—she nearly rolled her eyes. Impatience filled her. "Do I?" Flowridia asked, exasperation in the words. "The Endless Night always said the same thing."

At the name, the woman stopped, the flickering lamp revealing a wary expression. "Ayla Darkleaf?"

"Yes, Ayla Darkleaf, my beloved," Flowridia said, smiling curtly. "How about we let your god decide if he'll see me?"

The figures surrounding them moved closer, until Flowridia could finally see features on the men and women standing behind her auburn interrogator. All were pale; even those with skin of a darker descent looked sickly, washed out. Yet their beauty was unparalleled, true predators capable of luring in any unwitting prey.

Upon their faces was fear, and in some, respect.

Except for one. "Beloved of Ayla Darkleaf? Truly?" the auburn-haired woman asked, and when Flowridia nodded, she laughed. "A bold claim, for mortal swine. But, please, lay yourself before Izthuni." She stepped aside, revealing a path guarded by more beautiful vampires. She offered the lamp. "Our god will gift us with your blood."

Flowridia gave a polite nod and accepted the gift, refusing to take a bite at her baited words. "Thank you," she said, and she stepped through the line of undead predators, purposefully staring at no one.

The shadows grew dense, and though the lamp kept Flowridia on her feet, the darkness seemed to slowly consume the light. She must have walked twice the length of the building, or more, yet there were no walls, no sign of an ending.

Alone, Flowridia stepped, her feet the only noise on the cold stone.

When the light had all but snuffed out, she heard a voice emanate from all around her. *Child of Odessa. You are beloved of Ayla, and that is why we will speak.*

Guttural and deep, the voice rumbled across invisible walls, shaking her to her core. The lamp extinguished.

Flowridia remembered from long ago the symbol of The Endless Night Ayla wrote in her own blood upon the wall of the Skalmite cave. She remembered the nightmarish creature who came and tore her to shreds. This demon knew her and remembered. Yet The Endless Night had still held some bastardized semblance of a humanoid form.

Skittering steps sounded before her. Despite the darkness, Flowridia could see, and she nearly dropped the lamp at what met her eyes. A spindly monster, one who towered at least four times her height on impossibly thin joints. Nothing human in that physique, or that stare—two spindly appendages supported his thin body, and the creature's balled joints rotated in impossible directions, his core spinning slowly, four arms spread wide from the center.

He suddenly fell forward, two of the arms catching him. Yet he moved with grace and perfect control, this Demon God of Shadow.

Now balanced on four legs, the face meeting hers held fangs jutting both above and below his rounded jaw. Within the depthless maw were rows upon rows of razor-sharp teeth.

He held no eyes yet clearly saw. Flowridia dared to bow, falling to one knee as she kept her eyes on the fangs. "You are Izthuni," she said, staring into the gaping maw of its mouth. She understood, now, the cultural names he had been granted.

A dangerous name to speak uninvited. Tell me your purpose.

Dark and all-consuming, his accent was reminiscent of the De'Sindai, though far more akin to Kah'Sheen who hailed from his realm. Flowridia straightened her stance, though she still cowered, faced by the God of Shadows. "I wish to bring back Ayla Darkleaf."

Laughter emanated, shaking Flowridia to the bone. The monster stood back up on his two spindly back legs, then arched the socket of what Flowridia could only guess was his back. In slow motions, he return to all fours, but upside down, if this deity were capable of being such, then lifted his front, all in purposeful, controlled motions. Leering now, his top half dangling like a hung corpse, Flowridia could recognize macabre beauty in his fluid motions—a dancer displaying acrobatics.

But Izthuni spoke, the depth of his tone rattling Flowridia's bones. *You do not know the price.*

"That's why I've come. Ayla is dead. And if anyone knows how to bring her back, it's you."

Bold of you, to make demands of me. Again, the god laughed, his gaping mouth dangling eerily from its slowly spinning core. *Ayla spoke of you with the delight of a smitten child, reserved and shy but with a joy to outshine all else. She waxed poetic of your kindness. Your gentle heart. She loved you with every fiber of her being, adored every piece of you.*

Despite her fear, Flowridia realized she was blushing, her smile beaming and demure. For she did not question Ayla's love, but to hear it spoken so beautifully by someone Ayla had respected—

Look at you, he said, almost affectionate in his tone. *As sweet as springtime, your heart and soul both.* The head leering above suddenly darted down. Flowridia gasped, those razor teeth and fangs mere inches away. *Tell me, Child of Odessa— would you destroy all of that to bring about her return?*

She stared into the abyss of his mouth, jaw trembling as she said, "I don't understand."

You have killed, but can you murder? Can you slay in cold blood? Izthuni's head slowly reeled back, returned to dangling high above her. *You lack conviction.*

"I can do it," she whispered, though in her heart, she knew she wasn't sure.

Izthuni laughed, and the sound chilled every nerve in her body. *If you insist. Prove yourself.*

One of those elongated claws reached into the shadowed terrain; from the air, he plucked a panicked figure—

Whom he promptly slammed into the ground. A woman coughed, and Flowridia realized she knew her auburn hair. This was the woman who had stopped her at the door. *This woman insulted you, Beloved of Ayla Darkleaf. Questioned your position. Spat upon your pride.* With those spindly claws, he lifted the dazed vampire up, dangling her not a foot away. *Kill her.*

"What?"

Kill her. Show me your devotion.

Horrified, Flowridia's stomach lurched as she met the woman's gaze, watched as her confusion vanished, replaced with fear. "She's helpless."

She is. Her name is Palace, and she kills mortals when she must, but never children. She has a lover named Lo, gone on an excursion to the Theocracy of Sol Kareena—and would he not be heartbroken, to find her dead upon his return?

The woman—Palace—struggled in Izthuni's grasp, though she hadn't a hope to escape. Flowridia's lip trembled. "Why would you–"

Humanize her? He laughed, and, oh, it rattled her very bones. Palace's eyes watered, meeting Flowridia's gaze with a silent plea for mercy. Izthuni said nothing more, merely held her closer to Flowridia.

She would be a fool to forget that Ayla was only one half of The Endless Night, for Izthuni, too, had slaughtered the Sun Elven populace, gleefully destroying entire cities in a night.

He and Ayla, together. Both monsters in their own right.

Flowridia looked down at her hands, letting a spark of blessed, healing light illuminate the scene. So simple, to hold the magic in her hand, easier to grasp than necromancy, even now.

She recalled Ayla's burned face, her scream when Flowridia had touched her.

Could she destroy her own soul?

She shut her eyes and grasped the image of Ayla in her mind, saw her sobbing at her feet at her apology, for Ayla had been willing to break her own heart rather than live a lie. She had admitted her vile intentions and begged Flowridia to cast her aside for guilt.

And what a remarkable thing it was; something so contrary to her nature, as Casvir had said. Ayla had loved her. Ayla had changed.

Flowridia would change as well. Damned she would be.

Flowridia opened her eyes and thrust forward her glowing hands—not to the woman's face, but to her chest. Palace screamed and writhed, but Izthuni held her. Even as Flowridia's illuminate hands slowly burned through her skin and bone, Izthuni held her fast, and only when Flowridia grasped her heart, tore it from the gaping hole, did she cease.

She fell as a corpse upon the floor, utterly still.

Gasping, Flowridia dropped the desiccated organ, watching in horror as it splattered on the ground. She stared at her hands, no blood coating them, but vile, watery ichor.

Ayla's existence is to spite Sol Kareena, Izthuni said, though Flowridia could not face him, *whose blood and very presence is capable of tearing her apart. Ayla requires the blood of life. Of creation. The blood of the moon.*

So it was as Casvir had done: bathed Ayla in the blood of the acolyte to the Moon Goddess to restore her body from stasis. "Priestesses of Neoma are all but extinct," she replied, hands trembling. By every god—Palace's screams still echoed in her mind. "Where can I find–"

There are none, Beloved of Ayla Darkleaf. Neoma's influence has waned with her death. There are only her descendants.

Shock stilled her actions; Flowridia slowly looked up, swearing that repugnant hole of a mouth stretched into a smile.

Only one line bears her blood. And that is the blood Ayla must bathe in to be restored.

Flowridia didn't dare to breathe; she feared her heart had stopped beating.

Ayla is my greatest creation. Izthuni pulled himself away, his entire body rotating back into the six-limbed being who stood on two. *Restore her, and you will have my favor.*

Flowridia could do little more than nod, her mind still processing the demon's words.

The lantern suddenly snuffed back to light. Izthuni disappeared. Flowridia stood alone with a corpse.

The lantern's light shone in an eerie silver light, reminiscent of the moon herself.

There was only one line.

And only one remained.

The lantern slipped from Flowridia's numb limbs, shattering into a thousand pieces. The light extinguished, enveloping her in darkness.

Only one, descended of the moon and stars both, the culmination of their celestial glory, the very power of creation coursing through her blood, yet with a heart as soft as gold, who had embraced Flowridia at the funeral and offered her nothing but love.

And, oh, how beautiful were her soft, silver eyes.

Epilogue

Within the week, outside the throne room, Flowridia heard a voice that caused her steps to stop and Demitri to frantically sniff the air.

". . . kind of you to meet with me, and I apologize for giving no notice . . ."

Though the door sat slightly ajar, Flowridia peeked through the crack between the hinges and the wall, breath catching when she saw a Celestial standing before the throne, luminous wings illuminate behind her, granting her a magnificent aura. Etolié spoke pretty words, her smile and stance every bit the monarch.

". . .wanted to personally give my congratulations and thanks regarding the embassy. The trade between our kingdoms has done wonders for the economy of Staelash, and the friendships fostered between our citizens bespeak a good future for us both."

Flowridia saw Casvir seated on his throne, but instead of the iron chair she saw a collected mass of giant bones, carefully assembled to create a sturdy seat.

"I would also like to present a gift, a proper thanks from Staelash." Etolié stepped forward, and Casvir stood to accept, his metallic steps echoing across the expansive room. He took what appeared to be a weapon of sorts, and when he withdrew the dagger from its scabbard, Flowridia saw that instead of metal, the blade shone a vibrant green. "The blade is carved from maldectine, utterly immune to any sort of magical barrier. Crafted by our late general before her untimely death."

"Very impressive," Casvir said, and judging by the intrigue in his words, and the way his clawed hand lovingly touched upon the pointed tip, Flowridia suspected he meant it. "I accept your thanks, Magister Etolié."

"I would ask, with your blessing of course, to stay a night or two in your city. Five days of riding takes its toll on any creature."

Even without sleep, Flowridia couldn't fathom the horse that could make the journey from Staelash to Nox'Kartha in five days.

"You will stay in the castle, as my guest," Casvir said, sliding the blade back into its scabbard. "Since Lady Flowridia has no doubt been listening this entire time, she will escort you to a guest suite on the second floor."

Flowridia couldn't say she was surprised. When she peeked from around the door, Casvir stared at her expectantly. Red eyes scrutinized her every move.

But though Flowridia beamed at Etolié, the Celestial kept her same half-drunken smile. "Flowers-Flowridia, wonderful to see you."

"Etolié, I—" She stopped herself from embracing Etolié, acutely aware of Casvir's presence. "Come with me. I'll show you around."

With a respectful nod to Casvir, Etolié followed, a dress of pure, molten gold swirling around her legs. Her silver hair, studded with gems, flowed mostly free, pinned enough to reveal her face. She looked stunning—and healthy, to Flowridia's relief, and the moment they entered the hall, away from Casvir's sight, Etolié pulled her into a tight hug.

A foreign gesture from the beloved magister, but Flowridia felt safe. Etolié's fingers dug into the fabric of her dress. "Tell me to steal you away," Etolié whispered, "and you're gone before Imperator First and Last can remove his dick from his self-righteous asshole."

Shocked at the insult, Flowridia shook her head. "I swear, Etolié, he's been good to me."

Etolié pulled back. The wings on her back vanished from existence, their radiant light fading. And with it, her façade of health flickered, her pristine, pointed face becoming gaunt and grey. But the illusion resumed, revealing only worry to mar her beauty. "I'm trusting you, Flowers." Then, she looked to Demitri, who waited alone in the hallway. Smiling, she pulled him into a hug as well. "And look at you, big boy! You're a good kid, protecting your Flowers."

She's so validating. I like her.

Etolié looked up at Flowridia, her fingers still in Demitri's fur. "Truthfully, I'm not here only to see you."

There could be only one other. "You hurt her."

"Bitch hurt me, too." Like her illusions, the façade of her fury flickered for just a moment; Flowridia saw immutable hurt. "But I have to see her for myself."

Khastra's whereabouts had been a mystery, ever since the fateful mirror conversation. Flowridia had left her alone. Her attempt to aid the half-demon had burned at the seams.

"I have a few guesses to where she might be," Flowridia said, and she gestured for Etolié to follow.

Etolié spoke of idle things, of home and of the people there. Flowridia loved to hear it, yet felt a distance between her and the tales, some ineffable chasm she knew not how to cross.

A query for another time. "I do have a question," she gently interrupted, too curious to let it go. "How in the realms did you ride here in five days?"

"Flying horse. Borrowed it from Eionei."

As one simply did.

Flowridia led her to the third floor and asked the skeletal guards at the door, "Is General Khastra in there?"

With a nod, one gestured for her to enter. Before Flowridia could stop her, Etolié ran inside.

Within, Flowridia saw a nightmarish scene, of the Bringer of War flexing her strength, battling an endless legion of death. They crawled up from the ground like macabre insects, moaning and screeching, but Khastra tore them apart, ignorant to their cries.

Etolié crossed the threshold, the boundary Flowridia had been warned away from. The moment her foot touched the dirt, the monster that was Khastra looked up as if struck. The undead disintegrated, crumbling to dust. A great *thud* cracked the shifting terrain when the hammer fell. Khastra came forward, subdued for her berserker form.

Flowridia remained in the doorway, watching as Etolié came to meet her, fearless in the face of the enormous demon. Khastra spoke a single word, and though it bore the stain of demon-tongue, Flowridia knew it well: *"Etolié."*

She had seen the wrath Etolié could muster, had heard her rage and rant from behind the safety of the magical mirror, but this was neither. Etolié's wide eyes softened, her breath hitching as she brought a hand up to cover her agape mouth. Flowridia watched her swallow her emotions, smile through her glistening eyes, and say, "It's been a while, ya big lug."

Khastra transformed from monster to woman, shrinking but keeping her gaze on Etolié all the while. Flowridia had never seen it, intrigued at the sight of Khastra's armor shifting back to accommodate her smaller size, of her claws disappearing, her posture straightening. Khastra beamed, genuine joy in her features. "It is wonderful to see you, Etolié."

Ever the diplomat, Etolié came forward slowly, but the moment Khastra's arms came around her, she clung to her armor with the same protective stance she'd held Flowridia, uncaring, it seemed, of the grime and ichor coating her body. Flowridia couldn't say she heard when Etolié broke in the ensuing silence, but when the Celestial finally pulled back, tears visibly welled in her eyes. Affectionately, she said, "You're shorter, you blunt-eared cunt."

Flowridia wasn't sure if she should balk at the slur, but Khastra beamed and replied, "In the surgery to repair my severed spine, they removed the shattered piece."

"That's what you get for letting Izthuni ram his claw up your ass." Etolié pulled one hand back to wipe tears from her eyes, adoration in her gaze. "Your mother would be so disappointed."

"Ku'Shya knows where she can stick my hammer." Flowridia watched Khastra's hands press at the base of where Etolié's ribs would be and saw sorrow flood her face. "I am sorry, Etolié. I have caused you pain, and I—"

"Stop," Etolié whispered, and Flowridia struggled to hear it. "None of that matters right now."

"Let us get you some food. I will bathe, and we will talk."

Etolié clung to Khastra once again. "Don't leave me alone."

Khastra stooped down, and with only a slight, surprised gasp from Etolié, lifted her up into her arms. In a proper embrace, the half-demon whispered something Flowridia couldn't hear, but suspected she wasn't meant to, realizing she was intruding on something private.

Khastra's lips brushed against Etolié's silver hair, tears welling in the half-demon's eyes when she planted a kiss among the array of star-lit locks.

Flowridia wasn't the help Khastra needed, and watching the duo reunite, she understood a truth too sacred to speak aloud, that Khastra held no loyalties save one—to the Celestial she loved with all her heart, enough to stay tethered to a place she loathed for twenty years with no expectation of reward. Khastra's joy came from Etolié's, and with Etolié's heart repaired, she could feel that joy again.

Flowridia backed away, leaving the pair alone.

At night, the great city of Nox'Kartha hardly blinked into restfulness. It bustled at every hour, Tazel realized, reminding him of home. Brilliant minds slept, yes, but elven inventors rarely slept at normal times, their genius manifesting at odd hours.

It was what set the Sun Elves apart—their worship of the Sun and her glory.

But Tazel stood not in front of any depiction of Sol Kareena, no, but of a long-dead deity.

In the religious district of Nox'Kartha, there was no temple to the late goddess Neoma, but Solviran immigrants had paid long ago for a memorial in her honor. Secluded from the main streets, a splendid garden encircled the stone path, one that ended in a fountain depicting a controversial, albeit beautiful image. Trees circled the stone alcove, and the fountain in the center burst with life-giving water, infused with magic far more potent than the rest of the miraculous healing springs.

A flower—a moonlily, he knew—formed the base, blossoming to reveal an amorous stone couple caught in a lover's tryst. Neoma, the Moon Goddess of Fertility and Life, took the lead, bearing a crown and falling robes, revealing most of her sensuous form. Her stone visage shone with passion and light, gazing adoringly at the woman in her arms.

She remained unnamed, but Tazel knew her—the fallen goddess, Staella, her cascading hair speckled with subtle, glittering stones. A tragic tale, Tazel knew. Neoma's death had shaken the worlds, even Sha'Demoni, for it had sparked a fear in all its inhabitants.

Gods were not invincible.

And no one knew where they went when they died. Or if they went anywhere at all.

The goddesses were not human, no, but man created gods in his image. Before the statue was a plaque bearing the name: *The Conception of Ilune.*

Tazel sat before it, one of the few places in the city not constantly brewing with social energy, calculating in his mind the craftsmanship of such an artistic feat. No magic; he would sense it. Pure engineering, those carved features, the detailed strands of hair and shining eyes, even the pores of their skin.

Perched on his head, Ferseph suddenly chirped nervously. Tazel instinctively wrapped his fingers around the hilt of his rapier.

A touch on his shoulder, lighter than the night breeze, pushed him to act.

Tazel whipped about, sword and all, a spell at his lips. Pure sunlight sparked at his fingers, waiting only his permission. Tazel had perfected the art of speed and finesse.

His rapier met a curved blade. Fire burst from his body, but the figure dodged—just as Tazel ducked beneath a sword intent on decapitating him. He kicked, and heard a feminine 'oomph,' and when he turned into an elbow waiting for his skull, he locked eyes with his attacker. "Mereen?"

Shock stole his focus. A swift punch to his chin cracked his jaw. Pressure slammed his chest, sending him toppling. His rapier clattered to the ground, just out of reach. Disoriented from pain, before Tazel could force a breath, a knee pressed against his back, keeping him on the ground.

He heard a voice that stole his will to fight. "Hello, Sunshine."

The pressure released. The steel-toed boot in front of him made no noise, as silent as the predator wearing it. Tazel spat blood when he sat up on his knees.

In six years, she hadn't changed. The ageless woman's skin reflected the moon's light, luminous and white, her hair hardly a shade darker. She pulled back her hood, each movement of her body, the purse of her lips, the gentle sway of her hips, familiar and daunting. She wore leather and weapons, displayed and hidden both, the very image of her title—*Dark Slayer.*

"I was surprised to receive your message," she said, her smile revealing perfect teeth, encircled by lips as red as the blood she craved. A silver knife at her hip glinted in the moonlight—as well as an elven weapon that chilled his blood, wood and silver and bullets capable of dispatching even the most powerful of sorcerers. "I thought you'd vanished forever this time."

A simple spell, to whisper words to someone he had known his entire life. He hadn't expected her to appear, though. "How did you find—"

"Sweetie, I've known." Her sardonic smile held ire. "And while I appreciate your consideration to my cause, I already knew of Ayla's rebirth. Imperator Casvir hardly kept her a secret, but while she was shackled by his chains, I could never come close enough to strike. Kind of Sol Kareena to slay her for me." Curiosity twisted her lip, intrigue stealing her poor mood. "You said you met a girl who knew her?"

Tazel remained kneeling before her, too shocked by her presence to stand. "It was how I found out about Ayla's return. Whatever our disagreements, I do still believe she's a plague on this world."

"Where is the body?"

Tazel shook his head. "I don't know. I think the girl might, but—"

Mereen's broad grin stole his words and chilled his blood. By Sol Kareena's Blessed Light, he had made a mistake. "Does she?"

"Mereen, she's no one—"

"You never could lie to me, Sunshine." She offered a hand; Tazel remembered then that he was still kneeling. She helped him to rise, her gloves well-broken in. *"No one* doesn't know the location of Ayla Darkleaf's body. Who is she?"

"Her name is Flowridia, but she's hardly more than a child. She's not important—"

A knife suddenly pierced beneath his chin, the tender skin splitting. He grabbed Mereen's hand, but she held the unholy strength of the dead—and the mesmerizing stare to keep him subdued. "Don't. Lie."

She removed the knife. Blood stained the tip, slowly dripping down the blade, and Mereen's breath hitched, her pupils expanding at the sight, her fangs growing long. Tazel recognized the agony of the gesture, to wipe the blood against her leather trousers and slip the blade away.

"She claimed to have been in love with Ayla," Tazel said softly. "But she was heartbroken. I showed her books on the Sun Elven Genocide at her request. She wanted to understand, and I truly don't believe she's a threat to us."

Mereen showed her back to him, a rare gesture of trust. She held loyalty to him still. "Tell me truly," she whispered, gazing at the amorous statue before them, "how sincere is her love?"

"Completely."

"And what of Ayla? She was known for playing with her food before devouring it."

"All I know is that Ayla died to save her life."

Mereen remained quiet for far longer than Tazel's nerves could stand. When she finally turned around, her sharp eyes had returned to a dark ocean blue, her mouth and lips as gentle as a kiss.

"Please, don't kill her," Tazel dared to say. "The girl is misguided, but she's practically a child. She's still innocent."

Mereen raised a single eyebrow, revealing a sadistic bit of amusement. "No one is innocent, Sunshine, but you know I only kill vampires. Not 'misguided' human children. If she wants me to kill her, she'll have to beg for it."

She smiled to match her wicked humor, and Tazel realized his great error.

"She knows more than she's telling, I assure you that. Perhaps I should pay her a visit."

Tazel grabbed her shoulder. "Don't you—"

She stepped into a full-body kick, her entire form spinning as her foot met his hand. In the same motion, she grabbed the fearsome weapon at her hip and held it aloft— Tazel stared down the barrel. "Click. Boom," she said simply. "Do not stand in my way."

She slipped her revolver back into its holster and took a step forward—far too close for comfort. Level in height, her full lips were but a breath away. "I miss you, my darling boy," she cooed, her eyes darting between his gaze and his mouth. "There aren't many left willing to follow me into the dark. Consider your loyalties."

She placed a peck on his lips, then smiled as she stepped away, leaving him utterly unstable.

"There's a war coming, Sunshine. Best prepare to fight."

Mereen disappeared.

End

All the alcohol in the world wouldn't drown Etolié's annoyance.

But who said she had to settle into the vat of her own complaints alone? Etolié, sipping at her summoned flask, sought the only person in the world with just as much bitterness and spite as she.

Khastra just hid it better.

Despite having access to the newly constructed manor, Khastra had set up a workshop of sorts in its own little building—or as little as a building meant to accommodate an eight-foot tall half-demon could be. Etolié had long ago deemed her the most interesting person in all the worlds, because who else would be shameless enough to have glowing, silver tattoos embedded into that blue, overly-muscled skin of hers? Horns and hooves and a tail completed the ensemble of the most interesting person in the world— one who was currently hunched over a bench.

Etolié often forgot that Khastra was just as much elf as she was demon, but her prowess for engineering always brought a stark reminder. Over one glowing eye, Khastra wore some sort of magnifier, and while Etolié couldn't say precisely what it was she molded with her tweezers and the glittering gemstones littering the table, it was certain to be perfect.

That over-polished weapon of hers lay forgotten on the ground. Ten thousand years of lugging that thing around—or however the fuck old Khastra was now—had surely contributed at least a little bit to her substantial bulk.

The half-demon in question didn't look up at her entrance, but she did mutter, "Good afternoon—"

And was promptly interrupted when Etolié all but collapsed against her back. With a dramatic groan, Etolié pressed her head against the cloth of Khastra's shirt, her silver hair splaying out as melodramatically as her antics. Though Khastra was seated, Etolié barely stood taller, because while her Celestial self was hardly short, this woman was fucking huge.

"This work takes precision, Etolié."

Again, Etolié groaned.

"What did Clarence do now?"

Khastra dared to invoke the name of the most boring man in the world, a gentleman Etolié would begrudgingly admit was her other favorite person, but by every god . . . "I don't know who stuffed a rod up his ass, but he's insufferable lately. I swear on Eionei's Asshole, I'm gonna take that ginger mop of his and—"

"Etolié, do not threaten violence against the king—"

Etolié lifted her head, petulant as she added, "I need sympathy, demon-spawn."

After two years, she certainly hoped Khastra was used to her constant verbal assaults, and given that the demon-spawn in question laughed as she set down her work, Etolié assumed all was well. "I do not disagree, but Emperor Malakh is breathing down his neck for the updated tax forms—"

"And mine, but I ignore it. Shit will get done when it's done." Etolié placed her head on Khastra's shoulder, letting her arms flop unceremoniously across Khastra's chest. Physical affection was weird and uncomfortable, but she found she rather liked it from people she adored—Khastra specifically. "We really should expand our council. Clarence is a competent numbers man, but you're probably right. He's overwhelmed." Her head tilted against Khastra's, pushing gently against the half-demon's pointed ear. "What are you working on?"

"A necklace." Khastra picked a single, miniscule gem, one that sparkled in brilliant shades of purple, then stole a lock of Etolié's silver hair to compare them. "Very pretty. It will be for you."

Every modicum of Etolié's pride melted into a puddle on the floor. "Oh, stop," she said, bringing her arms to rest around Khastra's neck. "You don't have to do that."

"Then I will not."

"You're a fucking tease, you over-sized goat."

Again, Khastra merely laughed.

Etolié pulled away, her pout returning. "Come on. I need a drink."

"You are always drinking, Etolié."

"I need a drinking partner, Khastra. Eionei's got some new brews strong enough to get someone like you wasted."

Khastra scoffed but moved to stand. Etolié slid off her, deliriously excited to watch Khastra fall to her own hubris.

You can find the rest of Etolié and the Whore on Patreon: https://www.patreon.com/sdsimper